THREE
DROWNED
GIRLS

BOOKS BY EMILY SHINER

EMILY SHINER

THREE DROWNED GIRLS

bookouture

Published by Bookouture in 2024

An imprint of Storyfire Ltd.
Carmelite House
50 Victoria Embankment
London EC4Y 0DZ

www.bookouture.com

ISBN: 978-1-83525-565-0
eBook ISBN: 978-1-83525-564-3

For Bruce
For your unending support, willingness to answer every police-related question I have, and for fifteen years.

PROLOGUE

MONDAY

The first gulp of water was ice-cold and made her throat feel like it was about to close up. She sputtered, pushing down on a slick rock with her hands as she tried her best to force her head up above the surface of the water. Water was over her head, her long dark hair floating out around her. She craned her neck back to look up, water burning her eyes, but all she saw was fragmented light, her own hair, someone standing over her.

She wasn't sure how long she'd been under the water or how much longer she could last. Each time she opened her mouth to scream, it rushed in, angry and bubbling, and she gulped it down without meaning to. She knew she needed to keep her mouth shut, but her lungs burned.

All she wanted was to breathe.

And her momma. She really, really wanted her momma.

Reality slipped away from her. She thought she was in the clouds, that the swirling white around her meant she was dead and maybe going to heaven, but then she remembered the white dress she had on. Her momma had been so happy with her wearing it, so happy for her to show it off, and she even let her wear it into the woods.

But her momma wasn't going to be happy when she found out she wore it in the water.

The thought of her momma, with long hair and big brown eyes that looked like hers, gave her some strength. She planted her bare feet against the bottom of the river. Small rocks cut into the soles of her feet, and thick mud squished out between her toes. Her muscles strained. Pain ripped through her legs. Each time she fought against taking a breath she felt like she was burning up inside.

"Momma!" The word left her lips in a scream as she pushed up, finally breaking through the surface of the water. Something strong that had been pressing into the top of her head slipped away. Her chest heaved, her lungs crying out, and she gulped down fresh air, her stomach twisting with river water, shivers wracking her body. She turned, reaching up with little fists to wipe the water away from her eyes, but where was her momma?

She gasped in air, filling her lungs, ignoring the churning in her stomach that always heralded her throwing up. She was going to be sick. Cramps shot up through her stomach, and she doubled over, wrapping her arms around her waist and groaning. A shiver ripped through her body, and she cried out again.

A hand on her head. She looked up, blinking into the sun, trying to see who was there, who had watched her almost drown, but her eyes were watery and blurry. Then the hand on her head pressed down harder, pushing her back down to her knees.

She fought, flailing her arms around her. She could hear water as it splashed up from the river. Then she was completely under the water. Everything was muted. She wanted to stand back up and find her momma, but her lungs cried out for air. She reached up, digging her nails into the hand pressed to the top of her head.

They weren't going to let her back up.

ONE

"This may very well have been the worst idea I've ever had." Freya Sinclair stood on the corner of Main Street and Fourth Avenue, watching small groups of tourists walk to the bakery and diner for coffee and breakfast.

She was home, but coming home like this didn't feel like a triumphant return. Instead, it felt like she was slinking into town, her tail tucked between her legs, her head down to avoid eye contact with anyone.

Across the street from her was the police department, which loomed over the antique store on one side of it and the bank on the other. It was huge, an imposing monolith meant to be the focal point of downtown and designed to make it easy for people to find it. It had been built first, with the rest of Main Street slowly radiating out from it like a spider's web. Even today, no matter where you were in the city, it was easy to get your bearings: just look for the tallest building.

Someone had planted bright orange and pink pansies in the flower boxes out front. Those, combined with the hanging ferns by the door, the colorful American flag, and the gray overcast sky, made the building look like something from a storybook.

Freya heaved a sigh and pulled her cell out of her back pocket—7:15 a.m. She still had a little time to kill before she was needed up on the fourth floor of the station. Turning away from the building, she glanced down the sidewalk, taking in the New Age crystal shop that had just popped up, the Tea-rific Tea Emporium, and Harold's Hiking.

New stoplights on Main Street—installed to help keep the flow of traffic moving smoothly and the crystal shop, Zen Crystals—were the only things that had changed in Fawn Lake. Everything else, from the towering mountains at the edge of Main Street to the old police cruisers parked in front of the department, were the same.

One thing that never changed was Parker's Bakery. Directly across from the police department, the bakery was busy all day long. All she had to do was go inside and she'd get to see Esther. She scowled and rubbed her hip. As soon as she realized what she was doing, she forced herself to stop, then turned back to Parker's.

Sure, her hip hurt. And everyone in town with access to the Internet, a paper, or a gossipy friend would know the truth of how she got injured. But that wasn't something she wanted to think about today.

Parker's Bakery was a beacon in the middle of the block. Warm light shone through the large front windows, and even though the wooden sign hanging above the door dripped rain from an earlier shower, it still looked welcoming. For a moment, she caught a glimpse of her reflection. Short, unruly curls. Brown eyes. A nose that looked just like her mother's, and lips like her dad. She couldn't deny her parents, not even with the scar across her forehead.

Especially not with the scar across her forehead.

A thick smell of sugar and vanilla hung in the air, and Freya inhaled it before planting her hand on the bakery door and pushing it open.

A wave of warmth from the oven washed over her, and she glanced around, taking in the small tables, the vase of flowers on each one, the shelf groaning with books in the back corner. Two teenagers occupied a far table, sitting so close together the girl was almost in the boy's lap. They whispered to each other but neither looked up when she walked in.

Closer to her, a table with three old men grew silent as the door swung closed behind her. Freya glanced at them, meeting the eyes of the first man. He had deep lines in his face and wore a ball cap low over his eyes. His red flannel jacket looked too big and was frayed around the collar. A flash of recognition crossed his face and he stood, planting his hands on the table and groaning as he did.

"Come on, boys. They let about anyone in here, it seems." He glanced at Freya as he spoke, then snatched his wallet from the table before shoving it deep in his back pocket. The other two men stood as well, although neither of them made eye contact with her.

Great. This is just what I was afraid of.

Coming home was always going to be hard. She knew that. Without thinking about what she was doing, her hand found her hip.

"Hurts, does it?" The man in red flannel paused before walking past her. He smelled this close to her, like old alcohol and body odor. "I guess it probably does. I guess some people might say you deserved it."

"Would you be one of those people?" Freya wracked her brain trying to think of the man's name. Greg? Gene? *George.* That was it.

George scoffed. He plucked a toothpick out of thin air and stuck it between his thick lips, rolling it from one side of his mouth to the other before answering. "I think that someone like you gets whatever they deserve. But then again, maybe you didn't get quite exactly what you deserve." He stared at her. "That's what I think."

A chill raced up Freya's spine, but she didn't step back from the man. "Good to know where you stand, George. It sure must be hard to breathe up there on your high horse."

He blinked at her and opened his mouth, but before he could say anything else, they were interrupted.

"Oh, Freya, I wondered when you were going to get in!" Thin arms wrapped around her as Esther stepped between her and George, effectively bumping the man closer to the door. "I've been looking for you this entire time and the moment I go to the back to take a batch of cookies out of the oven, you appear. How are you? Are you hungry? Let me get you something to eat."

"I'm not very hungry," Freya said, hugging the woman back. She was shorter than Freya remembered, almost like she'd shrunk a bit in the five years or so since she had been home. Still, Esther smelled just like she remembered, a mixture of floral perfume and cookies, and she hugged Freya tight, just the way she'd always loved.

"Well, I'm sure you have room to try a new recipe I've been working on. And coffee. No sugar, no cream, right? Or did that change?" Esther plucked at her sleeve, pulling her away from the door. "Don't let George get you down. He's mean as a kicked dog, that one, but he's not worth getting worried about."

Freya glanced over her shoulder as Esther guided her to a table. "He sure had an opinion about me being back home."

"Sure, well, everyone does. But most of us are thrilled." Esther scurried behind the counter and returned with a cup of coffee and a plate loaded with cookies. "Mint chocolate chip. I remember you always loved that combination."

"Still do." Freya took a cookie and nibbled off a piece. It was still warm, the chocolate chips melted and smooth, the mint taste a wonderful balance. "These are great, thank you. It's just... I hope I'm not causing problems for you coming back."

Esther didn't miss a beat. The older woman's blue eyes were still bright and sharp, and she flicked them over Freya before answering. "Darling, you need to understand something. Your parents—"

"I don't want to talk about my parents."

"Sure." Esther patted her hand. "I get that, I really do. But your parents are a sore subject here. After everything that happened, it's probably going to take a while for people to be comfortable with you around. You remind them of everything that happened."

Freya exhaled and shoved the rest of the cookie in her mouth instead of answering. She knew Esther was right, but that didn't mean she had to like it. "Okay. Then I'll just have to handle everything perfectly. Take care of business. Make them glad I'm home."

"That's the spirit. Now, do you want to take some cookies to the chief? He comes in here twice a week, without fail, and today's one of his days for baked goods. It might help make the day run as smoothly as possible."

"Sure, that sounds great." What Freya didn't tell Esther, though, was that if this interaction with George was any indication, it was going to take a lot more than fresh cookies to smooth over the fact that she was back in town. Fresh cookies might help, sure, but fresh cookies didn't change who she was related to.

Or the fact that her last name had been splashed all over national papers, bringing scrutiny to Fawn Lake in a way none of the residents ever expected.

TWO

"Freya Sinclair, back from the dead. Or, at least, that's the way this feels." Chief Callahan leaned back in his chair, his uniform stretching tight across his barrel chest. His cheeks were ruddy, his graying hair thin on top. It had only been five years since Freya had seen him, had sat in this exact chair across from him actually, but the man looked like he'd aged an entire lifetime.

The box of cookies Esther had pressed into her hands sat on the desk between the two of them, the lid still firmly in place. A box of her belongings sat on the floor by her feet, ready to be taken to her office.

"It's good to see you, Chief." She leaned forward, her hands tucked in her lap so he couldn't see them if they started to shake. "Thanks so much for offering me back my job."

"It's not the same job." Chief sat forward, matching her pose. It was a power move, one of the many he liked to use when he felt like he wasn't in complete control of a situation. "You'll be captain of detectives now, not a lieutenant. We restructured while you were gone. Got rid of some positions that were... superfluous. You'll answer directly to me, of course. Patrol Captain is Jacob Moore."

Freya nodded. "I remember him. He was always good on the road." Chief spoke like the restructuring was to be a surprise, but she knew it all. She'd set Google alerts for anything related to Fawn Lake, her last name, and the police department five years ago.

For the first year, her email pinged constantly through the day as various alerts rolled into her inbox. Recently, though, they'd tapered off, which was one of the reasons she felt comfortable moving back to Fawn Lake. It wasn't the only reason she was there, but if the emails were still coming fast and furious... well, she might not be sitting across the desk from Chief.

"There are some open cases I'm going to have you dive right into once we get you settled. Of course, there are always more rolling in from time to time, but things here have pretty much remained the same." He waved his hand through the air.

"The cases that are still open, will there be files in my office I can dig right into?"

"Files in your filing cabinet, yeah. Like I said, Freya, nothing here really changed. You have a new team, there are new people walking around downtown, visiting new stores, but it's the same old stuff, just a different day." He shifted his bulk in his chair, pinning her in place with a stare. "I was surprised when I got that email saying you wanted to come back home. How did you know about the open position?"

"I saw it on the Fawn Lake Police Department website," Freya told him, which wasn't a lie. What she didn't tell him was that she'd been watching the website obsessively, waiting for an opening to get back to North Carolina. Texas wasn't all it was cracked up to be, and Esther was here. Esther needed her.

"Well, then I'll just consider ourselves lucky." He paused, exhaling hard, like there was a bad smell in his nose he needed to get rid of. "Do you want me to issue a department-wide email that you're back?"

She froze. A chill danced up her spine when she thought about everyone's phones pinging at the same time with an email loaded down with her personal information. If she was being honest, that sounded terrible. "I'd rather you not. Word travels fast in a small town, and people will know I'm here before too long."

"Fair enough. I already told dispatch so they can keep you in the loop. You have the same call number as before, three-zero-one. My gift to you." Chief stood, his chair groaning in protest as he did. "HR dropped some paperwork on your desk for you to sign, so get that straightened out and you can start your morning. If I remember correctly, you're a bit of an early bird. That's what I told dispatch anyway, so they're expecting to be able to call you bright and early, starting this morning."

"Still am an early bird. I've never understood how some people can just lie in bed and let the day pass them by."

He stared at her, his gaze level, and Freya had the uncanny feeling he was reading her mind.

"Sometimes when we have trouble being alone with our thoughts then we just want to keep moving. I've seen it over and over with officers who have suffered some sort of trauma on the road, Freya. There's nothing wrong with getting a little sleep."

She didn't answer. Instead, she took a breath, held it, then slowly exhaled. "Am I in the same office as I was before?" Even to her ears her voice sounded tight.

"Sure are. I took the liberty of getting your duty belt and gear out. It's all on your desk ready for you, but you can have your radio now." He handed it across the desk to Freya, who took it and thumbed it on. "There's a Class A uniform hanging on the back of your office door in case you ever need it, but you're fine in what you're currently wearing for day-to-day work. You'll be in an unmarked Jeep just in case you go some-where you need four-wheel drive. Key for that is on your desk as well." He rubbed his chin as he thought. "What am I missing?"

"I think you covered everything, but if I have any questions, I'll pop down the hall and ask." She grabbed her box from the floor and was about to turn and escape his office when a thought hit her. "What about my team?"

"Candy Ellinger. Remember her? She was just a road officer when you were here before, but she's worked hard, gone to classes, and proven herself to be a great fit for upstairs."

"I only have one detective on my team? What if it hits the fan?"

"Then you pull Brad Williams from the road. He's a rookie, but he's tenacious. He has his eye on the empty office up here, and I know he'll do just about whatever you ask if it means he might have a shot at wearing a detective badge one day. There are people you can get help from, Freya; you just have to be willing to ask them."

"Not my forte." She inhaled. Held her breath. Exhaled.

Chief rapped his knuckles on his desk and gave her a stiff nod. "Better be on after it then. I'm glad you're back. Seriously. Our department missed you while you were gone."

"I had to go. You know that as well as I do."

"Sure, but—"

Whatever else he was going to say was cut off by the squawk from her radio.

"Central to three-zero-one."

The hair on the back of her neck prickled. She mashed the button on the side as she held it to her mouth. "Three-zero-one, go ahead."

"Three-zero-one, we just had a call about a body in the river. A young girl, caller estimates she's about five years old. Caller states they were fishing with their son, and they discovered the body. Before calling us, they pulled her from the water and performed lifesaving measures."

Chief stared at her. When she spoke, her voice was steady. "Central, is the caller still on the line?"

EMILY SHINER

12

"Negative. They said they'd stay with the body, but their son was traumatized, and they had to help him."

"Did they leave a callback number? A location?" While she spoke, she patted her front pocket for her keys before remembering Chief had said they were on her desk. "How am I going to find them?"

"I'll send it to your phone. EMS is en route."

It seemed too late for that, but sending EMS to any call with extended downtime was standard. "Ten-four, Central. Thank you." She turned to Chief. It had been years since she'd seen Candy Ellinger. The last time, the detective had been a sergeant on the road. "You said Candy is my new detective?"

He nodded.

"And she's as good upstairs as she was on the road?"

Another nod. "I said she was."

"Thank God." She hurried out the door, not even slowing down as her shoulder slammed into the doorframe. In the hall, she skidded to a stop.

Candy Ellinger stood in front of her, her radio in her hand. Her eyes were wide, her cheeks pink. Freya's only official detective had a short blonde pixie cut and wore small gold studs. She was dressed a lot like Freya, in khakis and a blue button-up shirt.

"I'm driving," Freya said, in way of greeting. "Let's go."

THREE

"What the hell is this?" Freya slammed on her brakes and guided the Jeep off the side of the road. Gravel spit out behind her until she came to a stop. "Did the circus come to town or something? This is crazy."

"We're late to the party, but I recognize the paramedics. Let's see what's going on," Candy said.

The two detectives slammed their doors behind them and walked towards the ambulance where a paramedic stood, his arms crossed, his mouth tight.

"I'm Captain Sinclair and this is Detective Ellinger," Freya told him, pointing to the badge on her hip. She'd only taken long enough to grab her gear from her office, then she and Candy had hit the road. All she knew was that a little girl's body had been found in the water, but then what was everyone doing out here, well out of the forest?

The man's eyes flicked over them. "Aiden Barrett." He nodded at Candy before speaking again. "The body is in the back of the truck." He pointed to the pickup parked next to the ambulance. Freya had seen it when they pulled up but hadn't paid it much attention.

"You moved the body? Why would you do that?" She frowned. "You know full well that you should have left her there, by the river."

"We didn't move her." The man closed his eyes for a moment, frustration emanating from every pore. "The guy who found her, with his son? They moved her."

"They pulled her from the river and performed CPR. That's what we were told," Candy corrected, stepping forward. "So why is there a body in the bed of that truck? I highly doubt you sanctioned that." She hitched a thumb over her shoulder, but before Aiden could answer, Freya spoke up.

"Who's in charge here?"

"I am." A woman about Freya's age waved them over. Her dark hair was pulled back in a low bun. "Briseyda Hernandez. Nice to meet you. I'm the lead paramedic." She shook their hands.

"Aiden over there told us there's a body in the back of this truck." Freya took a deep breath and forced herself to look around. In addition to the ambulance and truck, a third paramedic spoke to a man and younger boy. The two of them were about ten yards away. "Please don't tell me that guy," she said, pointing, "moved the body from the woods."

"Unfortunately, that's exactly what happened." Briseyda heaved a sigh. "He told me he didn't want to leave the little girl there by the river, so he put her in the bed of his truck."

"He thought he was doing the right thing," Candy said, and Briseyda nodded.

"Exactly right," she said.

Freya shook her head in frustration. "What about the little girl? Was she dead when you got here?"

"She was. I was going to body bag her, but I wanted to see you first." The paramedic gestured to the black body bag at her feet. "You okay if I do that now?"

"You can, but first... do you think there was any way she was alive before he put her in the truck?"

Briseyda frowned. "What are you asking me?"

Candy spoke up. "Do you think there's a chance the man killed the girl by moving her?"

"The ME will have the final say on that," Freya added when Briseyda didn't immediately respond, "but you're smart. I have a feeling you know more about cases you work than you let on." She took a step forward, closing the already small gap between the two of them and lowering her voice when she spoke again. "Do you think she was still alive when they pulled her out of the river? They said they performed lifesaving measures, but..." Her voice trailed off.

Already Briseyda was shaking her head. No hesitation. "Not a chance. Like you said, the ME will have the final say, but I don't think so. The skin, the lividity... I'd say she was gone for a long time before they found her."

"Okay. Thank you."

Freya and Candy walked over to the bed of the truck and looked in. The girl was smaller than Freya had expected. Slight frame, long dark hair that was stuck to her pale face. Her eyes were wide open, and it took her a moment to realize why.

Fish had chewed off her eyelids.

No marks around the neck. No bruising on the legs or arms. She wore a dress, which had probably originally been white but was now dirty gray. Freya's stomach turned as she lifted the camera that hung around her neck and snapped a series of photos, making sure to take in the girl's face, the lace on her dress, her long hair.

"It could be an accident. She lost her balance and fell in." Freya weighed her camera in her hand while she spoke.

Candy nodded. "Sure, but where's the report on a missing girl? If it was accidental, someone would be freaking out calling the police."

"Okay. Then that means we have to ask the next question: who would do this?" Freya asked, clicking her camera off. She glanced back at Candy.

Her detective's mouth was tight. "Someone sick. She's been in that water for a while. No way did she die this morning. It's some strange luck that she surfaced now, right when people were fishing there." She paused and glanced past Freya. "I want to meet the dad."

Freya nodded her agreement. "Come on—let's do that now. I can't wait to hear what his excuse is for moving a body from an active crime scene."

The women walked past the truck. Freya paused and grabbed her radio. "Central, this is three-zero-one. I need you to run a tag for me: YTV-9803. Send the registration information to my phone."

Her radio crackled to life. "Ten-four, three-zero-one."

"Just double-checking who the guy is?" Candy asked, walking quickly to keep up with Freya.

"Exactly." She pressed down on the call button again. "Central, are there any reports of missing girls? Has anything come in in the past week?"

"Negative."

"Okay, I want you to reach out to surrounding counties. Ask about a young girl, probably under seven. Girls like this don't just go missing. Someone knows she's gone and has to be looking for her."

"Ten-four, three-zero-one. I'll get on it."

Freya stalked away from the truck, taking huge steps that ate up the ground. "Who moves a body from a crime scene like that?"

"Someone who didn't go through Basic Law Enforcement Training. Someone who panicked in front of his son. Someone who thought he was doing the right thing in the heat of the moment." Candy held up her fingers, ticking off her answers.

Freya shook her head in frustration. They were almost to the man and his son, who were standing by a paramedic. "No, even people who don't go through BLET watch enough crime shows to understand they're not supposed to move bodies. It makes no sense, but I'm going to find out what was going through this guy's head."

"He panicked, like I said." Candy jerked her chin at the man. "I guarantee it. He's out here with his son, hoping to have a good time fishing, then this happens. He saw the girl, pulled her from the river, tried to save her to save his son from having to see his first dead body. Now we have to deal with a disturbed crime scene, but he did what he thought was best."

Freya looked at her. "You're probably right." Hand now outstretched, she approached the trio and first greeted the paramedic. "Captain Sinclair. Thanks for talking to these guys, but you're free to go."

The paramedic paused, then nodded, hurrying off. Freya waited until he was out of earshot before turning to the man.

He was younger, standing with his son pulled to him. One hand rested on the boy's shoulder, the other twitched at his side.

Nervous.

"I'm Captain Sinclair," she repeated. "And this is Detective Ellinger."

"John Reynolds." The man shook her hand. "And Jimmy."

Jimmy's chin jutted out a bit. He stared up at the two women with wide eyes. They were red-rimmed and his cheeks splotched. It was obvious he'd been crying. A lot.

"Well, Jimmy, why don't you go talk with Detective Ellinger? I bet the two of you can find some worms for the next time you go fishing."

Jimmy's face lit up at the same time Candy reached out to take his hand. Freya smiled at her and waited while the two of them walked off towards the edge of the woods, Jimmy chattering all the way.

Freya watched John. The man chewed his lower lip as his son walked off. He removed his ball cap and rubbed his forehead, wiping away a sheen of sweat even though it was still cool out. He was a bundle of nerves.

"Why don't you talk me through exactly what happened this morning?" Freya glanced over at where Candy and Jimmy were now lifting up some rocks to look for worms, then looked back to John.

"Jimmy loves fishing," the man said, clasping his hands together. "And I've been putting off bringing him out here because you have to come so early. He's four and going to public school next year, so I won't be able to keep him home on a nice day." He reached up, scratched the stubble on his chin, then reclasped his hands. "But he wore me down and we came out this morning. We'd been out here for a while when I saw something in the water."

He fell silent but Freya didn't speak. Best to let him grow a little uncomfortable and keep talking to fill the silence.

"Jimmy thought it was someone swimming, but I could tell right away it wasn't." She arched an eyebrow and the man continued. "She wasn't moving. Just... floating kinda."

"So you went into the river and pulled her out."

He gestured to his waders, which had shoulder straps like suspenders. "Jimmy was insistent I get her out, so I did. Then I did CPR, but she was already gone. I had to try something in front of my son."

It must have been terrible to realize what he was pulling out of the water was a body. How close had Jimmy been to the little girl? How much had he seen? The first time Freya had seen a dead body, the sight of it had stuck with her, visiting her every night when she closed her eyes. Was Jimmy going to deal with the same problem?

"It was pretty obvious she was dead, but I couldn't leave her there."

"You should have." Freya glanced at Candy and Jimmy. Still far enough away that the boy wouldn't hear the conversation. "You seem like a smart man. You don't know to never move a body?"

Silence. In her pocket, her phone vibrated, and she pulled it out to glance at it. Dispatch had texted, confirming that John Reynolds owned the truck parked behind her. She slipped it back in her pocket without responding.

"Jimmy was inconsolable. He kept saying that we couldn't leave her there, that it was the wrong thing to do, that she'd be cold there all by herself." He exhaled hard and rubbed his chin again. "I knew I shouldn't do it, but I didn't really have a choice, not if I was going to keep him from absolutely falling apart."

"So you, what, carried her out of the forest, put her in your truck bed for safe-keeping, then called nine-one-one?"

He was already nodding. "That's right."

"Do you remember exactly where you found her?"

This was key. Most average people would struggle to remember where exactly they were along a river when fishing. They just went out with their poles and bait to kill some time, not because they were obsessed with where the best fishing spots were. If John and Jimmy weren't hardcore fishermen, and it didn't sound like they were, there wasn't much of a chance they'd remember where they found the body.

"I've never fished here before," John began, and Freya silently swore, "but I had a pretty good feeling you'd ask something like that. I left a cup of bait on the shore as a marker so you could see exactly where we'd been."

She nodded. "Good. I need you to call someone to come stay with Jimmy."

"Right now? No, I need to get him home. He needs me."

"No, you need to call someone because you're taking me out there to where you found the body. A bait cup is good, John, but it isn't enough. Hurry up—the clock's ticking."

FOUR

Half an hour later, Freya and Candy followed John Reynolds into the woods. The trail they were on was wide and well maintained, which meant it was an official hiking trail, not one that had been created by hikers finding their own way through the woods.

Freya was right on his heels, wanting to make sure she didn't miss anything. Not that she thought he would hide any evidence—the man seemed too honest for that—but even honest people do stupid things sometimes.

Case in point: moving the body away from where he found it.

People tended to be smart until they were in a terrifying situation, then all bets were off. All she could do was hope he hadn't ruined any of their chances of finding the killer.

But water was a nightmare for evidence, so chances were good whatever had been there on her was already gone.

"How much farther, John?" Freya was in great shape, but they were hiking at a clip that would wear most people out and her hip was starting to burn. A camera swung from her neck.

Candy was right behind her, an empty evidence bag clutched in her hand. Just in case.

"Just around this bend." The man turned and pointed, then hurried on. Honestly, he probably wanted to be out of the woods as badly as she wanted to see the crime scene. Once he tripped over a root, but he caught himself and kept going.

And then they were there. John slowed down and cut off the path, walking over to the riverbank. He stopped at a small white Styrofoam cup, then bent down and picked it up to show her.

"Bait cup," he told her. "She was floating right there, and I waded in and pulled her out here." He gestured to the ground where drag marks were visible. The dirt where he stood was wet from him dripping.

So far, it all added up.

"About how far out was she?" Freya shielded her eyes with her hand and stared out at the sparkling water. Gorgeous, yes, but more dangerous than most people would ever know. The rivers here were unpredictable. Some of them ran over smooth flat rocks. Others had hidden deep spots in them, making them ideal for swimming but dangerous after a rainstorm.

"Ten feet or so. It wasn't difficult to get out there and bring her in. The worst part was seeing her face." He shivered. "I don't know who could do that to a child, Captain, but I hope you find them."

Freya didn't respond. She raised her camera and started snapping pictures. Unfortunately, her gut had been right: there wasn't much of anything out here to see. Thank goodness John had marked the location with a bait cup. This part of the river looked indistinguishable from about half a dozen other spots they'd passed.

"Why did you come fishing here?" She clicked off the camera and let it hang around her neck. "You're pretty far in. No offense, but you don't look like the kind of guy who's out here every single weekend. You're missing the fishing vest," she added, to soften the blow of her words.

"I am, aren't I?" John smiled ruefully and ran his hands down the plaid flannel he had on. "That's because I'm not a big fisher, you're right. But like I said, Jimmy loves it, so I'm doing my best. I let him pick the spot, and he was so busy chatting about Roblox that he just kept walking."

Freya shared a glance with Candy. It wasn't that she didn't trust the guy, it was just that his answers were perfect.

"Well, thank you again for calling nine-one-one and bringing us out here," Candy said. She produced a business card and pressed it into John's hand. "If you think of anything else, give us a call."

"Will do." The card disappeared into his pocket. He turned to go, then turned back. "I have one too. Just got them at work." Pride filled his voice and he fumbled with his wallet before handing a business card to Candy. "Do you think you'll find who did this?"

Freya looked at him. The man's hands were now gripped into fists. His jaw was tight. He was just a man who had dealt with something terrible and had been trying his best to hold it all together.

"It's my top priority," she told him. It didn't feel like it was enough to say that, but John nodded and turned, walking slowly down the path.

"Thoughts?" Candy asked as soon as he was out of earshot.

"Oh, I have a lot, but none of them revolve around John being our bad guy." Freya squatted down and looked out at the river. The water here was slower than upstream. Wherever the body had been put in the water, it must have washed downstream and then gotten caught in the doldrums.

"The little girl was in a white dress," Candy said, and Freya nodded.

"Not exactly hiking attire. Bare feet and a white dress?

Who brings a child out into the woods wearing something like that?"

"Well, her shoes could have fallen off in the water, but it almost looked like she was dressed up for a photoshoot. You know as well as I do that families love getting great shots in the woods. Or, barring that, it could be someone burying their child," Candy said. She stuffed the evidence bag into her pocket and rolled her shoulder to work out a cramp.

"You think someone's kid died and this is an unauthorized burial?" Freya couldn't keep the surprise out of her voice.

"I'm not saying that's my official position," Candy said. "But I like that a lot better than the thought that someone killed her and dumped her out here."

"Do you have that a lot in Fawn Lake? Unauthorized burials? I don't remember ever dealing with one when I was here before, but things change. It's expensive to have a funeral. Caskets alone can cost... thousands of dollars if you're not careful." She closed her eyes, thinking of the last time she'd offered to pay for someone's casket, then pushed the thought away.

"Not that I know of, but desperate people do desperate things."

"I'll agree with that," Freya said. "So we have a little girl who drowned and whoever knows panicked, too afraid to call us to let us know. Or someone was desperate enough to bury their dead daughter out here. And we have to consider it's possible someone killed her, either on purpose or by accident. No matter what happened, whoever we're looking for was at the end of their rope."

"Thoughts on how to find them?" Candy hurried after Freya. "This is my first murder. And it's not like there's a sign-in sheet for hiking, so that means it'll be tricky to find who was in the woods recently."

"No, there's not." Freya mulled it over while she walked.

"So we need to look for additional evidence. Find out if there are witnesses."

"So we're looking for anyone who might have been in the woods. Hikers disperse when they leave here, and some drive hours to spend time in our woods. Hunting them down would be tricky. But you know who else loves being outside?" Candy paused to step over a fallen log. "Hunters."

"Hunters." Freya nodded. "There are a lot of hunters around here with wildlife cameras up. If we're lucky, they might have caught something interesting. Don't some of them post clips of interesting animals they see on social media?"

"They do."

"It's a long shot. But the girl's body will go to the ME, and hopefully we'll get some answers soon from him. I want you on social media. Look for hunters who have posted trail-cam videos and reach out about footage they have that might be at all suspicious."

"They would have already reported it." Candy was breathing hard now, but Freya wasn't about to slow down.

"They're looking for footage of animals," Freya countered. "Not people. And what we would see as suspicious, they might not."

"So anything with a little girl wearing a white dress while hiking? Oh, and we'll need to look for any groups that enter the woods with a girl but don't have her with them when they leave."

"Exactly. Anything in that ball park." Freya blinked as they exited the thick woods. Her Jeep was the only one still parked on the side of the road and they hurried to it. "Think outside the box. Anything weird, I want to know about it."

"I'll also look for any recent deaths that match this little girl. If it is an unauthorized burial then we can wrap this up. The last thing I want is to discount that possibility."

"Good thinking. Thank you."

They climbed in, and the Jeep roared to life. Candy waited until they were on their way back to town before speaking.

"Talking to hunters is a good idea, Freya, but there's only one problem with it."

"Which is?"

A sigh. "They're not going to talk to us if they have illegal wildlife cameras up in the woods. The type of people to have those are generally preppers or poachers, and they don't take kindly to people poking about. You may not have dealt a lot with hunters or preppers before, but I have. They don't like people in their business."

Freya pressed down harder on the gas. "If they're posting videos from those trail cams, then they had to know we'd be coming for them eventually. They'll talk, especially if you mention they might otherwise be charged."

Candy didn't respond; she had her head down scribbling on her pad.

Freya kept driving. Nothing could stop her from working this case.

FIVE

"We have a lot of things to do, but one of the first is to check the schools," Freya said, drumming her fingers on the steering wheel. "I want to call the medical examiner right away, but I doubt they'll have any answers for us yet."

"It's still Lance Jones," Candy offered. "We had a rookie ask him one time why he stayed in Fawn Lake when a larger city would love to have someone as talented as him on their team."

Freya barked out a laugh. "I wager that went over like a lead balloon."

"You know it. Lance doesn't suffer fools."

"He never has, and that's why I like working with him. I'm glad to know he's still here, but he won't have any answers for me yet, so I'm going to give him some space before calling him. In the meantime, we need all hands on deck to find out who this little girl is."

They fell silent, then Freya pressed down on the gas. They were still almost twenty minutes away from the police department, and her hands were tied until they got there. Without being able to talk to Lance or someone who knew the little girl, all she could do was drive.

"Not exactly the welcome home you expected, huh?" Candy leaned her head against the window but turned to Freya while she waited for a response.

"Well, it's not like I expected a parade, although that would have been nice." She pressed down on the gas again. Ten miles over the speed limit wasn't ideal, but she didn't have time to drag her feet. "It's the time of year people start getting out, hiking to see waterfalls. You were right—visitors come from other states to hike our woods. That girl might not have even been from around here."

Candy inhaled sharply. "We can't rule out a waterfall accident. Like I thought earlier—a family photoshoot would explain the dress, and waterfalls are the perfect backdrop until someone falls. Everyone poses on the rocks at the bottom, in the spray, for a family shot and then someone slips. All it takes is stepping on a mossy rock and losing your balance."

Waterfall accidents happened more often than a lot of people realized. Tourists came for the gorgeous hikes and to take pictures of the waterfalls without realizing how many people died on them each year.

"The parents could be in shock," Freya said. "And you saw what the little girl was wearing. No locals in their right minds would let their daughter out in the woods wearing something like that. Now, a tourist, maybe parents looking for a nice picture of their daughter by the waterfall? That I could buy."

"I can reach out to the local hotels." Candy sat up straight. With a flourish, she pulled the notepad back out from her front pocket and clicked her pen before scribbling. "There are a few close to downtown that I'm sure will be overloaded with tourists. Nothing like a little knock and talk to see if they saw anyone with a little girl checking in."

"Good. Do that. There's always the chance they're staying in an Airbnb, but let's not worry about that right now. We're going to focus on things we can address, and Airbnbs are an entirely different ballgame than local hotels."

"Right. So you're going to wait to hear back from dispatch? Or are you going to swing by the elementary school and see if you can find anything out that way?"

Whatever Freya was going to say was cut off by the sound of her radio.

"Three-zero-one, this is dispatch."

Freya grabbed her radio and mashed the button without taking her eyes off the road. "Go ahead."

"None of the surrounding counties are reporting a missing girl."

"Thanks." Freya groaned and dropped her radio into the cupholder, then glanced at Candy. "You know what, forget waiting around to visit each hotel in person. Start calling them now, see if anyone remembers a family checking in with a young girl, brunette, under seven. If you get any hits, then I want you to swing by and pull security footage. This comes first, then reach out to the park rangers."

"You got it." Candy was already on her phone looking up the local hotels.

Freya glanced down at her speedometer. Everyone knew the police were supposed to set good examples for the rest of the residents. And sure, most people would probably say that the little girl was already dead, so pushing to almost twenty over the speed limit wasn't necessary.

But for some reason, she couldn't shake the feeling that she was waiting on the other shoe to drop. She was quiet the rest of the ride while Candy made phone calls. Each time her detective shook her head, got off the phone and sighed, then called another hotel, she felt the rubber band wrapped around her stomach tighten.

"Nothing from any hotels," Candy announced. "Most of the people who picked up sounded like burnouts working dead-end jobs, if I'm honest. I doubt they're paying any attention to a family with a young girl."

"Probably not." Freya gassed it through a yellow light then tapped the brakes once she turned on Main Street. Speeding through the backroads on the way to town was different than tearing down the busiest road in Fawn Lake.

"Drop me off and I'll hop on social media, reach out to some hunters. I doubt we'll get any real information immediately because it will probably take time for them to pull footage, if they even agree to it, but at least this way they can get started on it. Then I'll call park rangers, see if they have anything. I'm not holding my breath."

"Sounds good." She parked in front of the department and killed the engine.

The two women got out and Candy turned to her. "Are you heading to the school now?"

Freya closed her eyes. What she wanted to do was call Lance. But it was too early. Without doing that, however, she felt useless. "I am. What we need is a photo of her with her eyes blacked out. I can do that," she said. "The last thing we're going to do is pass around a photo of this dead girl with her eyelids chewed off at the elementary school. I'm calling that a final resort."

"Fair enough." Candy nodded, then glanced up at the building, obviously itching to start working.

"How about this?" she said. "You get in there and get to work. I'm going to call Lance, let him know I'm back and on the case, and see how long it's going to take him to get us some answers. I'll make sure he knows I don't expect any right away," she continued, cutting off Candy's warning. "But at least we're doing something. Then I'll upload these pictures to my computer and edit one that we can use to try to ID the girl."

"Deal." Candy rapped her knuckles on the hood. "I'll see

you up there," she called over her shoulder as she hurried into the PD.

"Yep." She was already pulling her phone from her pocket. She tapped speed dial number 7, the same way she used to call Lance when she lived here before. But before she could press the green call button, someone screamed.

Freya froze, then turned around.

There. At the end of the block but still in sight. Someone running, their black rain jacket flapping behind them, their arms pumping hard until she couldn't see the person any longer.

But who had screamed? She knew that voice, she knew—

"Esther..." Freya whispered. She swallowed the lump in her throat as her mind raced, trying to figure out what that meant for her or the woman who had raised her.

SIX

Shattered glass littered the sidewalk in front of Parker's. Huge jagged pieces remained in the bottom of the windows, looking more like broken teeth than anything else. Chunks of glass had been thrown five feet out from the bakery, covering most of the sidewalk in a thick glittering layer. It sparkled in the light from the bakery and crunched underfoot as Freya hurried towards the front door, her head on a swivel as she took in her surroundings.

Whoever she'd seen running down the sidewalk was long gone. They'd disappeared around the corner as she'd watched, and even though she knew there wasn't any way for her to hunt them down and find them now, she had to fight the urge to chase after them.

"Esther?" She pushed open the front door, ignoring the wide-eyed young couple in the back of the bakery. "Esther, are you okay?"

"Freya." The old woman had been standing by the broken front windows looking out at the sidewalk. Freya had missed her in her panic, but now she stepped forward, letting Esther fall into her arms. "I'm here. I'm okay. But why would someone do that?"

"I'm going to find out." She stepped back, running her hands up and down Esther's arms. *When did she become so frail?* "Did anyone get hurt? Did they say anything to you?"

"No." Esther shook her head, her white hair falling down from its bun. The way it curled around her face made the woman look even older than she was. "It was a man—I can tell you that much. I saw him out the corner of my eye while I was still behind the counter, but before I could turn to look at him, he broke out the windows."

"So he broke them from inside the bakery?" That matched up with the way the glass had been shattered all over the sidewalk, but why would anyone risk coming into the bakery to smash the windows? Why not just break them from the outside and then make a quick getaway?

"Yes. He was in here, then I heard the glass start breaking. I don't know what he used. I screamed; I couldn't help it."

"You're fine, right? You really didn't get hurt?"

"I'm not hurt." Esther took a shaky breath. "Just shook up." She rubbed her hands up and down her arms and refused to meet Freya's eye. "I just don't know why someone would do that."

"Because I'm here." The words were out of her mouth before she could stop them, and they hung in the air between the two women like a heavy accusation even though Esther hadn't done anything wrong. "It can't be coincidence that someone smashed your windows right after I get back in town." Agitated, she ran her hand through her hair, tucking a loose curl behind her ear.

"No, darling, don't think that." Esther frowned and gestured to the closest table. "Who knows why people do what they do. Drugs, maybe. Or maybe they got in a fight with their parents or spouse. You can't shoulder that blame."

"Right." She pulled out a chair and helped Esther into it before grabbing her radio. "Dispatch, this is three-zero-one. I need an officer across the street at Parker's. Someone smashed out the windows and ran."

"Ten-four. I'm sending someone now."

She snapped her radio back in place and hurried over to the windows. Outside, a group of tourists had stopped and were gawking. "Nothing to see here," she said, forcing a smile on her face. Inside though, she wanted to scream.

Moments later, a uniformed officer appeared. He nodded at Freya, then started talking to a young couple seated in the back of the bakery.

"Okay," she said, going back to Esther. "I'm going to see if this guy can handle things." Guilt ate at her. The longer she stood in the bakery, the longer it would take her to get in touch with Lance. But how could she turn her back on Esther right now?

She had to. For that little girl.

Steeling herself, she walked across the bakery to speak to the officer.

He glanced up at her as she approached.

"Ah, this is our Captain of Detectives. Captain Sinclair, I have Jenny Morgan and Brett Garren here. They were both in the bakery when the man came in and broke the windows." The officer had brown hair cut in a high and tight. His uniform was clean and perfectly ironed, his nametag shining.

Williams. So this was the officer Chief had told her was eager to get upstairs, eager to prove himself. He looked like the poster child for the police department. Impressive.

"Nice to meet you both," Freya said, shaking Jenny's and Brett's hands. "I'm sure you've gone over what happened with Officer Williams here, but why don't you walk me through it too? Start from the beginning."

The girl was silent, her face turned slightly away from her, but Brett spoke right up. "We were here just talking in the corner," he said, lifting one shoulder in a half-shrug. "Some guy in a black coat came in. He had a baseball bat and took out the windows. Just like hitting a homer. Crack." He mimed swinging a baseball bat.

Freya waited a moment after the boy stopped speaking. "Did he say anything? Was there anything about him that seemed familiar? Anything that really stood out to you? Besides the fact that he broke the windows?"

"No, nothing." He chewed on his thumbnail until the girl reached up and pulled his hand back down. "Sorry," he said to her, then turned back to Freya. "He was just a guy, you know? Just a guy."

"Just a guy." She closed her eyes and nodded. How many times had she mentioned to Esther that it would be a good idea to install security cameras? Cameras, even the fake kind you can buy on Amazon, tended to be great deterrents. Who knows, the guy may have still come in to break her windows, but they might have had an easier time finding him.

"Is there anything else you need from us?" Brett spoke up, pulling Freya from her thoughts. "I want to get Jenny home. She's a little freaked."

Freya looked at the girl. She'd seen a lot of trauma, a lot of pain, in her years wearing a badge. And while the girl had kept her mouth shut like she didn't want to draw any attention to herself, she didn't get the feeling she was *freaked*. Not about someone breaking the window anyway.

"Sure," she said, smiling at the boy. "Officer Williams has your information?"

"He does." Brett swung his arm around Jenny's shoulders. "Come on, babe. Let's get you home." He strolled past Freya, his eyes locked on the door. "We have better things to do than sit around in here and see what the cops do, right? My parents aren't going to be home for hours, so what do you say we head over to my house? See what we can get into. I'll have you back to school for afternoon classes, I promise."

Freya watched him go, then turned to the officer standing at her side. Williams had a small spiral notepad out, his barely legible writing scrawled across the top page.

"Freya Sinclair," she said, thrusting out her hand. "Although it sounds to me like you already knew that."

"Brad Williams. It's a pleasure to meet you, Captain. I've heard a lot about you." He glanced down at her hip, then back up at her face.

She winced. It was bad enough that everyone in town knew her history, but to be faced with it every single day, every single time she made eye contact with an officer? That was going to be hell.

"Put everything you've heard about me in the past." She straightened her shoulders, resisting the urge to rub her hip. "I'm here for a fresh start, and I don't want everyone looking over my shoulder for ghosts."

He leveled his gaze at her. When he swallowed, his Adam's apple bobbed, then he gave a nod. "You've got it. Clean slate. We all need that from time to time." He licked the tip of his finger, then flicked back a page in his notebook.

"Did you get anything out of Jenny? She sure didn't have a lot to say when I was standing here." She waited, tapping her foot. *Might as well trade one bad habit for another.*

"She didn't say much. Kept her mouth shut after she gave me her name. Brett's the talker in their relationship."

"I got that feeling." She paused. "Jenny Morgan," Freya mused, giving Brad a long look. "I don't know that name. Is the family new to the area?"

"I'm not sure. To be honest, I don't think I've ever seen her before. That being said, she looks like the type of person to fade into the background. Kinda a wallflower." He flipped his note-book shut and tucked it into his breast pocket, patting the flap to ensure the Velcro caught. "I can look into her though, if you'd like me to."

"I think that's a good idea. There was something about her that made me think she might know more than she was letting on. It could just be that she's in an unhealthy relationship. Maybe Brett's the kind of guy to talk over her all the time and that's why she was quiet, but I don't know. It's worth looking into, at any rate. And I need you to check with the stores in this block and see if their cameras caught anything."

Brad inhaled, then paused.

"What?"

"I hate to tell you this, Captain, but a lot of the cameras on the street are fake. Did you know that there are plastic ones you can buy from Amazon that look a lot like the real thing?"

Freya closed her eyes. "I do know that," she said, fighting back frustration. "Still, I want you to look, and I want you to let me know what you find by lunchtime."

"Sounds great," Brad said, but she was already turning away from him. Now that she had an officer on the case, she needed to make sure Esther was okay. Ten minutes. She'd give herself ten minutes to help Esther clean up, then she had to get in touch with Lance and the elementary school.

Whatever kind of easy first day she'd been hoping to have, this definitely wasn't it. Freya walked to the front door and flipped the sign to *Closed*, then turned to Esther.

"Do you feel up to making some coffee? You cook, I'll clean, and it will be just like old times."

The old woman smiled and stood up. "Coffee sounds perfect, my dear. The broom and dustpan are behind the counter. Let me get them for you."

Freya watched her go. *Moving back home was the right thing to do.* She could tell herself that until she was blue in the face, but this was quite a welcoming to come home to. Fawn Lake wasn't the sleepy town she had hoped it would be. It seemed like her hometown had some tricks up its sleeve for her.

Good thing she wasn't the same woman who'd fled town five years ago with her tail tucked between her legs.

SEVEN

Back in her office, Freya sat at her desk and put her head in her hands. She could feel a twinge of a headache starting right behind her eyes, and she grabbed for her purse and yanked out a painkiller, popping it dry.

It was one thing to come back home and start a job at her old department. There was sure to be enough stress and pressure from that alone, but then someone killed a little girl. And someone else was harassing Esther. And the thought that it might be because she came home?

No, don't think that. Groaning, she pressed her fingers into her temples. Hard.

Even though she knew Lance wasn't going to have an answer for her yet, she called him. The phone rang in her ear once, twice, then stopped.

"Freya Sinclair. My word, I never thought you'd be calling me again," Lance's voice boomed.

Even though her head was splitting, she couldn't help but smile. "Lance Jones. I guess I just missed you and had to come home."

A laugh. "Yeah, and are you still happy you came back, or

are you starting to regret it?" His words had always been as sharp as the scalpel he wielded during autopsies.

"My happiness might be tinged with a little regret, if I'm being honest. Tell me something good about the girl."

A heavy sigh. "Honestly, there's nothing much to tell right now, good or bad. I don't want to make any proclamations and then get held to them."

"You know me. I won't hold you to anything, I just need to know where I need to start looking for the parents."

A pause. "You don't have an ID?"

"Not yet, but we're working on it."

"Okay." He exhaled hard, and she could picture him running his hand through his hair. "Like I said, don't quote me. I haven't gotten to the meat of it yet, but she drowned. I haven't opened her up yet, but I expect to find water in her lungs. I'd say she's been in the water a day."

"I was thinking that she was drowned, not dumped," Freya agreed. "I didn't see any bruising or other injuries, nothing that would be consistent with her getting hurt and then put in the river. Do you think it was an accident?"

This time he laughed. "Now, now, Freya, you know as well as I do that's your cup of tea, not mine. I'll tell you the cause of death because that's what I'm good at; you figure out who killed her and why. That's why you wear the badge in this rela-tionship."

"Yeah, yeah, I know. How long do you think it will be before you can get me an answer?"

"Well, I bumped her up the waitlist for you, but I have to close someone else up. The family wants to pick up the body this afternoon and is causing a real stink about getting them cremated ASAP. As soon as I stitch him up, I'll work on your girl."

"Will you call me as soon as you know something?" She

found a pen on her desk and started tapping it. She was full of nervous energy but couldn't figure out a good outlet for it.

"Always." Another pause. "Listen, I understand why you left, I really do. I also understand why you're back. It's good to have you home."

"Thanks, Lance." She scratched the back of her neck with the pen then dropped it on her desk. "If I don't hear from you by quitting time today, I'm coming by."

"I expect nothing less. I'll be in touch."

She had barely hung up the phone and slipped it back into her pocket when a soft rap on the doorframe made her look up. "You free?" Candy peeked at her, only entering when the captain waved her in.

"Don't knock," Freya told her, gesturing for her to sit. "Unless I have Jesus himself sitting across my desk from me, I just want you to walk on in, okay? We're a team." She thought for a moment, then shook her head. "You know what, come in and meet Jesus if you see that we're chatting. Because if that happens, then things have gone really south."

"Noted."

"Tell me you have good news on the hunter front," Freya said.

"Like I warned you, they're a quiet bunch. I reached out to half a dozen I found posting animal videos on social media, but none of them have gotten back to me."

"They're terrified we're coming for them. It probably never once crossed their minds we'd want to team up with them."

"Exactly what I thought. As for the park rangers, there aren't any cameras, no logs of people going into the forest, nothing. They told me they'd keep an eye out, but there are shortages and cuts, so they're stretched a little thin." She shook her head in frustration. "Was that Lance?"

Freya nodded and tapped the pen. It was only when Candy raised her eyebrows and stared at it that she dropped it again, this time in her desk drawer so she wouldn't keep playing with it.

"Yep. He can't get started on the autopsy until he closes someone else up, but he did tell me he thinks she drowned."

Candy shivered. "That's a terrible way to go. It's my top fear when it comes to dying."

"It doesn't sound pleasant," Freya agreed. "And then someone broke the window at Esther's.

Candy's jaw dropped. "What?"

"Brad Williams is canvassing Main Street to see if anyone happened to catch our baseball star on camera." She felt her mouth turn down and took a shaky breath.

"Hey," Candy said, reaching across the desk to pat Freya's hand, "this isn't on you, okay?"

"It feels a little personal." She closed her eyes and took another deep breath. Anything to calm down, to stop the racing in her mind.

Candy inclined her head. "Sure, but that's all in the past, okay? And yes, small town, long memory, but trust me, the people who know you are happy you're home. You don't have to worry about that. I, for one, am glad to have you up here. Do you know how much testosterone there is in this department? Too much. I had to go out and adopt a female lab mix just to get some more estrogen back in my life."

Freya laughed in spite of herself.

There was a soft skittering noise, and Candy glanced past Freya and stilled. "What is that? In that tank?"

"Cinnamon." She didn't have to turn around to see what Candy was pointing at. "A tarantula."

"Why do you— You know what, I'm sure there's a story there, and I want to hear it, because the Freya Sinclair I knew before would have freaked out about a spider the size of my shoe sitting in her office, but not right now. Not until we get this case solved." She shivered. "But you have to tell me sometime."

A smile played on Freya's lips. "I will. And thanks. I'm glad you're on my team, Candy." The last time she'd seen the younger woman, the officer had been fresh-faced and eager but still a rookie. She'd grown up a lot more in the past five years than she would have expected.

"Me too."

"I'm going to get her photos uploaded and edited so we can use one of them to show around." Freya snapped open the camera's memory card door, but before she could pull it out, the sleek black phone on her desk rang.

"Or maybe not," she muttered, grabbing the receiver. "Fawn Lake Police Department; this is Captain Sinclair." She grabbed her pen back out of the drawer, clicking it a few times to prepare to write. Her desk wasn't completely covered with case files, but as she brushed them to the side, she realized she couldn't find a notepad.

"This is Mindy Stevens. I work at Fawn Lake Elementary." The woman speaking into her ear sounded breathless. Worried. Freya glanced up at Candy, who was still sitting across from her, and wiggled her pen in the air to ask for paper.

"Mindy, hi. What can I do for you today?" Freya spoke as she pushed back from the desk to allow Candy room to open another drawer. It was loaded with new legal pads, and she grabbed one and put it on the desk in front of Freya.

"I'm sorry, I didn't know exactly who I should call. Maybe I should have asked for an officer to come out, but I just needed to talk to someone." Her voice cracked, and Freya sat straight up, reaching out to grab Candy's arm to keep her from leaving the office.

"You just tell me what's going on, Mindy, okay? I'm going to put you on speaker so my detective can hear what you have to say." She pushed the speaker button on the phone, and when Mindy spoke again, her voice filled the office.

"I'm the school secretary at Fawn Lake Elementary," she

said, a hint of pride swelling in her voice. "The principal gave me the okay to give you a call. I wouldn't normally want to involve the police in school matters, but we have a student who has been missing for a few days from Mrs. Olson's class."

"Missing. You mean she's not showing up for school?" Freya made a note on the paper, her heart hammering wildly. "How long has she been out?" She willed Mindy to hurry and tell her what was really going on. Something about the reticence in her voice gave her pause.

"She's been out for over a week. I've called her parents, the principal has called her parents, even the school resource officer has tried to make contact with them. We just can't get in touch with them. I've worked at this school for twenty years and never had anything like this happen before."

Freya's plan had been to go straight to the elementary school, but talking to the parent of a missing girl? That had to come first.

She glanced up at Candy. The younger detective's eyes were wide.

"Okay, Mindy, I'm so glad you called. How about you give me the girl's name and the name of her parents, and I'll go out there to talk to them? Maybe they were confused about why you were calling. Maybe they got scared they were going to get in trouble. If she's sick and they had to keep her home, they won't want her to be punished for missing so many days."

"Thank you—that sounds great." Mindy sounded relieved. "Her name is Sophia Jernigan. She's six, an absolute doll of a little girl. Her parents are Veronica and Jackson. He's a lawyer, and she stays at home. Does a lot of volunteer work."

Freya's pen flew across the paper as she made notes. "And their address?"

Mindy gave it to her, and she jotted it down.

"Great, I really appreciate you calling about this. I'm going to head out there now with my detective, and we'll see if we can get this straightened out. Hopefully Sophia will be back at school tomorrow. Is there anything else you want to tell me?"

"No, that's it." Mindy sighed. "Thank you so much for taking care of this right away. I don't want to think about anything bad happening to that little girl. She's just so sweet. Have a great day, Captain."

Mindy hung up the phone, and Freya did the same before turning to look at Candy. Her detective had her slim arms crossed over her chest, a frown marring her face.

"You have thoughts," Freya said, ripping the piece of paper from the legal pad and folding it to slip it into her pocket. "Tell me what they are."

"No thoughts. Just concerns." Candy forced a smile.

Freya didn't return it. "You're thinking the same thing I am." Moving quickly, she ejected the photo card from her camera, slid it into her computer, then drummed her fingers on her desk while she waited for it to load. It only took a minute to edit a photo of the little girl by drawing a black bar across her eyes then email both copies to herself, then she gave Candy a nod. "Okay. Let's go."

Candy blinked. "You want me to come with you?"

"Yep, you're riding with me. Let's just hope there's some misunderstanding. Maybe she pulled Sophia out to homeschool her and forgot to turn in the papers. Maybe she was sick or on vacation." Whatever it was, they'd find Sophia.

Or maybe they already had.

EIGHT

Freya draped her wrist over the steering wheel, carefully taking the curves in the road as she drove to the Jernigan house. She recognized the name of the neighborhood but hadn't ever been there. River Stone residents kept to themselves for the most part. They were oil and everyone else in town who didn't live in the gated community was water. In general, the two didn't mix.

The small brick gatehouse at the neighborhood's entrance had been there for as long as she could remember. She pulled up next to it, rolled down her window, and waited for the attendant to lean out to talk to her. The day wasn't going to be sweltering, but she could already feel a line of sweat on her forehead. The weather could be tricky in early May, with the sun beating down on Main Street but the thick trees in the woods making the forests feel much cooler. She'd hoped for a nice calm start to her first day at the department, but clearly that hope hadn't been worth anything.

The sound of the gatehouse's window sliding open pulled her attention from the mansion in front of her, and she turned, putting a government-issued smile on her face before speaking. "Hi, I'm Captain Sinclair from—"

"Freya!" The man leaning out of the window cut her off. "Freya Sinclair! I heard you were coming back to Fawn Lake, but I didn't think I'd actually run into you for a while. Do you remember me? Sawyer Woods? From high school?"

"Sawyer?" She had to squint a little bit to recognize the scrawny kid who had sat behind her in biology when they were seniors. "Of course I remember you. It's good to see you."

He puffed up a bit. "Good to see you too. I was so excited when I heard you were coming back to town. Freya Sinclair. Wow. You sure have had an interesting few years, haven't you? I never saw you after everything went down."

As if on cue, her hip started to ache. She shifted position, doing her best to keep a polite smile on her face. Discussing her past was literally the last thing she wanted to do. "You never know what life is going to bring, do you? We just need to get buzzed in to see the Jernigans."

"The Jernigans, let me see." Popping his head back into the clubhouse, he grabbed a clipboard then leaned out the window as he looked at it. "I'm sorry, but I don't see where they put you down as an approved guest."

She frowned. Beside her, Candy shifted in the passenger seat. "They don't know we're coming, Sawyer. It's a surprise."

He grinned at her, then the smile slid off his face as he realized exactly what Freya must have meant. "Oh. I see. Right. Well, if you're here on official business, then I don't think I can stop you from going in there, can I?"

"Not really." Her tone was light. "So if you don't mind raising the bar, we'll be on our way. It was good to see you, Sawyer."

"You got it." He gave the two of them a stiff nod then slammed his finger into a button to let them through.

Freya gassed it, motoring past huge houses that loomed over them. Perfectly manicured lawns pressed up against the freshly paved road they were on. The mailboxes all had red flags up to let the mailman know they had outgoing mail. While some of the driveways had basketball hoops set up, none of the yards were littered with toys.

"Looks a little Stepford, don't you think?" Candy leaned forward, planting her hands on the dash as she looked out the windshield. "We're looking for number seventy-seven. Right there, on the left."

Freya nodded and pulled into a driveway that looked exactly like every other one in the neighborhood. The brick house in front of her had three stories. A silver Lexus sat in the driveway, and huge ferns hung from hooks on the porch. Even from inside her Jeep, she could see that the flowerbeds were all free from weeds, the mulch was fresh, the entire yard as green as a golf course.

"Seems like they have it together, doesn't it? Kind of odd nobody from the school can get in touch with them." She got out, slipping her keys in her pocket before adjusting her duty belt to try to keep it from rubbing. "Shall we?"

"Let's do it." Candy appeared at her side, craning her neck back to look up at the house. "Can you believe these places? They seriously look like something from a magazine. What did Mindy say the dad did?"

"He's a lawyer. This is lawyer money, Candy. Don't get it confused with police money." Freya chuckled to herself as they walked up the sidewalk and onto the porch. Overhead, three ceiling fans spun lazily, keeping the air moving. She pressed the doorbell and stepped back.

"Oh, believe me. My bank account keeps me from getting too big for my britches. I know the difference between lawyer and cop money. But seriously, this place is wild."

"But have you seen any signs of kids actually playing in the neighborhood?" She cut her eyes at her detective. "No toys. No bikes. No sidewalk chalk even. It's like the entire neighborhood *has* kids but wants to keep them hidden except for the basketball goals."

"Children should be seen and not heard," Candy said. "Isn't that what our parents used to say?"

The mention of parents sent a stab through Freya. She didn't have a response for Candy.

Luckily, her detective kept talking as if she didn't realize she'd stepped on Freya's toes. "Cross your fingers Sophia opens the door. I really hope this is all a misunderstanding."

"Me too." *Otherwise this is hitting a little close to home.*

She reached out to press the doorbell again when they heard someone calling from inside.

"I'm coming!" A man's voice, deep and laced with power.

One lock clicked. Then another. She heard a chain being drawn back, then the door finally swung open and Jackson Jernigan, clad in a custom black suit with an emerald tie tacked in place, stalked out. He glanced down at their hips and took in their duty belts, then dragged his eyes up to their faces before giving a sigh.

"Let me guess," he said. "This is about Sophia."

Freya stepped forward. "Mr. Jernigan, you're absolutely right. I'm Captain Sinclair and this is Detective Ellinger. We're here to talk to you about your daughter. Do you want to invite us in, or shall we have this conversation outside?"

Jackson paused, his eyes darting around the two women, looking at the houses across the street. As nice as the neighborhood was, the houses were still close enough together that any nosy neighbor would easily be able to soak up the drama from their front window.

"Of course you can come in," Jackson finally said, gesturing through the air to the open door behind him. "I do ask that you take off your shoes though. The cleaner doesn't come for two days, and I don't have time to sweep. Just mind the rug." He turned and strolled back into his house.

Freya gestured for Candy to follow, then carefully closed the front door behind her. A pair of heels sat by the front door next to a small pair of cleats. Before catching up with Jackson and Candy, she took her time in the hall, looking at the gallery wall of family photos. Most of them were older, shots of Jackson and—she presumed—Veronica. There were pictures of the two of them in school, then pictures of their wedding.

As she walked, the shots got more and more recent, until finally she found photos of Sophia. She was a pretty thing. Dark hair. Dark eyes.

The breath caught in Freya's throat, and she leaned forward to get a better look at the little girl.

"Captain Sinclair, I'm sorry, I don't have all day." Jackson's voice, full of authority, reached her from the other room. She took one last look at a photo of Sophia then hurried down the hall.

NINE

"You two are lucky because you caught me at just the right time," Jackson said, dropping down into an overstuffed leather sofa. On the side table next to him was a cup of coffee, and he grabbed it, took a sip, then put it back. "Please, feel free to sit in those chairs." He gestured at two leather recliners across from him before cutting his eyes at Freya and Candy's feet.

They hadn't taken their shoes off.

"Mr. Jernigan, we're here because we need to talk about Sophia. The school called us to let us know that she hadn't been in class for over a week. Where is she?" Freya wasn't going to dance around the question. She much preferred to cut right to the chase.

"Sophia? Oh, she's fine. You don't need to worry about her." The man turned and took another long sip of his coffee. "You just wanted to know where she is? I'm so sorry you drove all the way out here and I don't have anything else to tell you." He stood, giving them a firm nod.

"Please sit back down, Mr. Jernigan—we're not done. Sophia has been missing from school, and that's not something we're going to take lightly or ignore," Candy said. She glanced around the room they were in. No toys. Nothing made of plastic or in primary colors, for that matter. "We're going to need to talk to Sophia so we can confirm that everything is okay."

Jackson sat back down. He opened his mouth to speak, but before he could, Freya cut him off.

"Is Sophia here?"

Anger flashed in his eyes. "She's not. She's on a trip with her mother."

Freya nodded.

Beside her, Candy leaned forward, staring at the man. "Where did they go?"

He stiffened. "Does it matter? Why are you asking me these questions?"

"Because she was reported missing from school," Freya said, holding up one finger. "And nobody can get in touch with you." Another finger. "And you're not being forthcoming, are you?" A third finger.

"Honestly, this is ridiculous." Jackson scowled at the two of them. "Veronica took Sophia to visit her mother."

"And I guess you were just too busy to go with them?"

He barked out a laugh. "Busy, yes. But as you can see, I have some spare time." He spread his arms wide to encompass the room. "However, I'd rather chew off my own arm than spend one afternoon with that woman, so I stayed behind."

"Can you tell us why the two of you weren't answering calls from the school?"

"Because I have better things to do. Listen, I'm sorry Veronica wasn't picking up her phone, but that's not my problem. I have more important things to worry about than whether or not she told the school Sophia was going to be absent."

Candy spoke up. "When's the last time you spoke to your wife?"

Jackson stared at her. "This morning."

"And what about Sophia?" Candy's voice was tight. She leaned forward, staring at Jackson.

"Yesterday morning? The day before? I don't know. Like I said, Veronica is in charge of Sophia. Why are you asking me so many questions? This conversation is over."

"Nope, it's just getting started. I need Veronica's phone number."

He crossed his arms. "No."

Freya paused. She could fight him on it or get it another way. "Fine. I need you to take a look at this," Freya said. The tension in the room was tight. She tapped on her phone, pulling up the picture of the little girl from the river. The black bar across the girl's eyes hid her missing eyelids, but it was still clear the girl was dead.

Jackson sighed heavily and leaned forward, reaching for the phone, but Freya gripped it tight.

"This may be disturbing, Mr. Jernigan, so I'm sorry to have to show you this. But I'm going to need to you look at a photo and tell me if it's Sophia."

For the first time since they'd entered the house, he seemed subdued. Jackson drew another deep breath, then nodded. A frown furrowed his brow. "Do you think something happened to my little girl?"

"I'm not saying that," Freya told him. "But we are looking for the family of a little girl who was found drowned this morning. When the school called and reported Sophia missing, we knew we had to come talk to you."

Jackson spread his large hands on his knees. He looked down, then forced himself to look back up at Freya. All the bluster he'd had, all the power he commanded in a courtroom, was gone.

"Okay. Let me see it."

"It's graphic," she warned then handed over her phone.

Jackson took it from her carefully, like it was a bomb that

might go off. He stared at the photo, then shook his head. "This isn't my Sophia."

"Are you sure?" Candy leaned forward. "We need you to be really sure, Mr. Jernigan, especially since you haven't talked to or seen your daughter in a few days."

"You think I don't know my own daughter?" The fear was gone, and anger coursed through him. "This isn't Sophia." When neither Candy nor Freya responded, he handed back the phone and pulled his from his pocket. "Look. This is from last week. You can check the timestamp on it if you don't believe me."

Freya took the phone from him and angled it so Candy could see the photo as well. The same little girl she had seen in the hall pictures stood in the backyard, a croquet mallet in her hand, a triumphant grin on her face.

"Do you see? That's not my Sophia. I never would have let her cut all her hair off, but she got gum stuck in it up by her ear. The only option was a pixie cut. That girl," he said, pointing his finger at the other phone in Freya's hand, "has long hair."

She nodded and handed back his phone. "Thank you for showing us that, Mr. Jernigan. I'm so glad to know nothing's wrong with Sophia. We were worried." A pause. "Do you mind texting that photo to me? Just in case we need to reference what Sophia looks like?" She rattled off her phone number and watched as the man tapped on his phone. A moment later she felt hers vibrate.

"I told you she was fine." He stuffed his phone back in his pocket, anger making his movements jerky. "I don't know why you couldn't just listen to me."

"Because someone out there is missing their daughter," Freya said, standing. "And they haven't been forthcoming about it. So you don't get to be angry with us for doing our job when we're just trying to figure out who this little girl is."

Jackson nodded, momentarily mollified.

"Thank you for your time," Candy said. She reached out and touched Freya on the shoulder. "We'll see ourselves out." She stood, then bent down and picked something white up off the floor. "This Sophia's?"

"She loves hair ribbons. Or did, before she cut her hair." Jackson took it from Candy and stuffed it in his pocket. "It would be great if she'd stop leaving them all over the house."

The two detectives left him there on the sofa then hurried back through the house without saying another word. It was only when they were back in the Jeep and backing down the driveway that Candy turned to Freya.

"Are you thinking what I'm thinking? Because I'm thinking Jackson and Veronica have terrible communication skills, Jackson is an absent father because he's married to his job, and we caught him off guard with that photo?"

Freya chuckled. "Yep, pretty much sums it up to me." Her hands tightened on the wheel. The day was shaping up to be gorgeous, with a bright-blue sky and fluffy clouds since the rain had passed, but her mood was still dark.

"Great. Glad we're on the same page. I know you're going to the elementary school now. Let me text myself that photo."

Freya pulled her phone from her pocket without taking her eyes off the road. "Take this. My pin is one-three-six-nine. Text yourself the picture of the little girl with her eyes blacked out too. We're up for a long day of knock and talk, showing her picture around, and praying someone recognizes her. There's no way we're sitting still until we find out who she is."

Candy grabbed it from her and started tapping on the screen. "Exactly my thought. I know we didn't get anywhere with the hotels, but I'm sure I can make some traction with a photo."

"That's the plan. This photo is key." Freya took a hard left to make it through a red light."

"I figured. You think you'll make progress at the school?"

"I do. Teachers know everything." Freya nodded as she spoke, doing her best to drive the point home. "They might seem like they're not paying attention, but they know it all. Mindy, the school secretary? She knows Sophia is missing, and that's a start, but the teachers will know a lot more. Are there any other kids missing who just haven't been out of school long enough to trigger phone calls home or to the police? Is there anyone who might have a special interest in the kids?"

"Perfect. While you do that, I'll follow up with the hotels again. That takes precedence over reaching out to hunters on social media. I really think the hotels are more likely to give me an answer."

"You know how when you book a room you have to state the age of any children staying with you? Get in their systems."

"Without a warrant?"

Freya shrugged. "Get one if you need to. This is happening."

Candy was silent. The Jeep ate up the road, but it wasn't until they pulled into the parking lot at the police department and Freya unlocked the doors that she finally turned to Freya to speak.

"Good luck with the teachers."

Freya nodded. "Keep in touch. If you find anything, let me know ASAP."

Candy got out, and Freya gunned it, pulling out of the parking lot and heading towards the elementary school. She ate up the road quickly and parked, then hopped out and hurried to the front door.

Before she could pull it open, her phone rang.

"Brad, I'm just getting to the elementary school to interview Sophia's teacher," she said after she picked up. "What's going on?"

"I checked Main Street for working cameras—there aren't

any by the way—but as soon as I got back, dispatch got a call that I had to take."

"What was it?" She tapped the door handle and closed her eyes. Concern ate at her.

"Someone else called to report a missing girl." He sighed the words, already exhausted.

She froze. She could leave the school, head to the family right away. For a moment she considered it, then she shook her head. Ten minutes. That's all this would take. "Send me the info right now and I'll head out there as soon as I leave here." She paused, gathering her thoughts. "I want you to look up Veronica Jernigan on CJLeads. Call her and get verbal confirmation she has Sophia with her."

"Will do. I don't understand why parents wouldn't do everything in their power to protect their children."

She didn't answer. She couldn't. That was the one question she'd been asking herself her entire life.

TEN

Once inside the elementary school, Freya paused. The halls were decorated with so much bright artwork she imagined it must look like what people see when they tripped on acid. Paintings of dogs, pictures scrawled on construction paper, even clay figures set out to dry on bookcases lined the walls. The bright colors, combined with the peals of laughter coming from each classroom she passed, made her smile.

How could it not? The kids here were so happy, so vibrant, so alive. She slowed down as she reached room 105, the kindergarten classroom, and stood in the door a moment to observe.

A ring of children sat on the carpet, their faces turned up to a woman sitting in a rocking chair. The woman was older, with soft gray hair curled around her face. She held up a book, her voice soft enough as she read to make the children lean forward to listen but loud enough to keep their attention.

Another woman, this one younger, with a bright-red bob, cleaned a table close to where Freya stood. When Freya entered the room, the woman turned, a smile on her face. "Hi, I'm Mrs. Harris. Alma. Can I help you?" Her eyes drifted down from Freya's face and landed on her duty belt.

"I'm Captain Sinclair. I need to speak to Mrs. Olson."

"She's right there, reading." The woman pointed behind her. "Are you sure there isn't anything I can help you with?"

Freya shook her head. "No, I'm sorry. I really need to talk to her. I hate to interrupt, but—"

"Oh, I can take over reading." Alma gave her a smile before dropping her rag on the table and turning to walk across the room. She bent close to Mrs. Olson's ear, obviously whispering.

The older woman's eyes snapped up, and she stared at Freya, her mouth pressing into a firm line. She nodded, handed the book she was reading to Mrs. Harris, and stood, moving slowly at first before her joints warmed up. By the time she reached Freya, she had managed a small smile.

"Captain, am I to assume you're here about Sophia?" Her voice was gentle, kind. Exactly what you'd expect from a kindergarten teacher.

"Yes. Can we step into the hall?" Freya moved out of the way, gesturing for Mrs. Olson to lead the way, then followed her, closing the classroom door behind her. This wasn't a private location to talk, but at least they wouldn't have to contend with a bunch of eavesdropping kids.

"Is everything okay with Sophia? I've been so worried with her not coming to class." Mrs. Olson clasped her hands in front of her, staring at Freya expectantly.

"From what we've been told, she's on vacation. Sounds like Veronica just forgot to let the school know she would be taking Sophia out of class for an extended period of time."

The teacher shook her head. "So you came by just to tell me this? You're always welcome here, Captain, but you could have called. I hate that you had to make the drive just to tell me that." She paused. "It makes sense though, that she didn't let us know Sophia would be out of town. Doesn't surprise me honestly."

"What do you mean?"

"Oh, just that Mrs. Jernigan is the type of woman to act

before she thinks." Mrs. Olson leaned against the wall, knocking a piece of art with her shoulder. It depicted a little girl and a big brown dog. Without thinking, Freya reached up and adjusted the picture.

"How so? Do you have any examples?"

Mrs. Olson shook her head. "No, nothing specific I can think of. Sophia has always been a little mess though. Can't keep clean, always spilling things. You'd never think it, looking at her parents."

"She's messy? Are you sure we're talking about the same Sophia?" Freya frowned, her mind on the house they'd just visited and how perfect it was.

"Oh, yes. So messy." Mrs. Olson smiled like the thought of a messy kid was the best thing in the world. "But happy about it, not one of those kids who struggles with getting their hands sticky. Of course, I always do my best to clean her up before sending her home. Veronica has very... exacting standards, you see. She wants Sophia to be *just so* all the time." A pause, then her next words came out in a rush. "Not that I know her parents very well; they certainly don't volunteer in the class-room. They're more the kind to just spend money, not spend time."

That tracks. "Do you think there's friction between Sophia and her parents?"

"Friction?" Mrs. Olson paused, tilting her head a bit to look at Freya. "Do you have children?" When Freya shook her head, she continued. "There's always some friction between parents and their children, no matter what. It doesn't matter if the child is five or fifty-five, there will be some sort of friction between them. In fact, in all my years of teaching, I can't think of a single parent who didn't, at some point, become frustrated with their child."

"That's not what I asked." Freya smiled as sweetly as possi-ble. "And I think you know the difference of what I'm talking about." Time to change tactics. "What about other kids in your class? Any other girls been missing from school for a few days?"

"Kids are absent on and off all the time. There's always some virus going around."

"But nobody has been absent long enough for you to reach out to the police?"

She shook her head.

"Okay, do you recognize this little girl?" Freya pulled her phone from her pocket and tapped the screen to pull up the picture of the little girl from the river. Seeing it was sure to shock the older woman, but it had to be done.

She turned it around and offered to it Mrs. Olson, but the older woman wouldn't take it. Instead, she leaned forward to peer at it. "Oh, Lord, is she dead?" Her voice broke.

"Do you recognize her?" Freya held the phone out for a few more seconds then turned off the screen. "Is she in your class?"

Mrs. Olson shook her head. "No. I've never seen that girl before. I help with pickup duty every afternoon, so I know all the kids, not just my own, but not that one." The woman was pale under her rouge, and she closed her eyes, leaning her head back against the wall.

"I'm sorry to have to show you that. I know this is hard, but I just have one more question. Is there anyone you've noticed paying extra attention to the girls?"

Mrs. Olson opened her mouth but then snapped it shut. She shook her head, but the movement didn't have much conviction.

Freya pulled a notepad from her pocket and clicked her pen. "Mrs. Olson, I'm going to need you to tell me exactly who you're thinking about right now. Who was it that pays the girls in your class more attention than is necessary?"

"Am I going to get in trouble for talking to you?" Suddenly the teacher seemed both smaller and older. She appeared to shrink in on herself, like the weight of what she was carrying was too much for her to bear.

"Not at all. But if there is someone out there who hurt Sophia and you didn't give me the information before we found out the truth, I promise you, you will regret it." Freya tempered her words with a smile, but she meant them.

"John Frank," Mrs. Olson said, her voice barely a whisper. "He loves all the little kids here, but I've seen the way he watches the girls."

The hair on Freya's arms stood up. "Who is this man? How does he have access to the kids?"

"He's the janitor." Mrs. Olson covered her mouth like she'd be able to stop Freya from hearing the words. She glanced down the hall, leaning out past her to glance both right and left before looking back at the detective. "I know we shouldn't talk ill of people and I'm trying not to, but it's just not right, the way he looks at the little girls sometimes. I never let my girls go to the bathroom by themselves, just in case. I always make them go in pairs." She puffed up a little bit like she was proud of how she'd tried to take care of them.

"Did you ever talk to the principal about your concerns?" Before she finished her question, Mrs. Olson was already shaking her head. "Why not?"

"Oh, I couldn't. John's his brother."

Weight like a stone set heavy in Freya's stomach. She took a deep breath, fighting back the urge to scream. It seemed like there was a lot more going on at Fawn Lake Elementary than she or Candy had thought.

"Is John Frank here today? Or the principal? I'm going to need to talk to them."

"That I don't know. Well, hold on. My trash cans weren't emptied last night, which tells me John wasn't around, and I haven't seen him this morning. As for the principal, I think

Mindy did the morning announcements, so I don't know where he is."

Freya snapped her notepad shut and shoved it into her pocket. She was so angry she hadn't even made a mark on the paper. "Thank you, Mrs. Olson, for your time," she said, the words so routine they were seared into her mind. She pulled a card from her jacket pocket and offered it to the teacher. "Call me if you think of anything else. It doesn't matter how unimportant it may seem, okay? And have a great rest of your day."

With that, she spun away and stalked down the hall to the front office. If Mrs. Olson was right, and both the principal and janitor were out today, then she'd have to work hard to find them and question them. As much as she wanted to do that now, she had to follow up on the missing girl Brad had called about. Jackson Jernigan had made it clear nothing bad had happened to Sophia. But now Freya wasn't so sure.

Her phone buzzed in her pocket, a text from Brad.

Called Veronica, no response.

She swallowed hard.

Something terrible was going on at the elementary school.

ELEVEN

"What are you doing?" Chief's voice made Freya spin around.

"Getting my vest camera." She yanked a fresh battery from the charger and held it up to show Chief before clipping it to the front of her shirt and pressing the little button on top. "It wasn't fully charged when I left this morning, and I wanted to get a fresh battery before hitting the road again."

"What's going on?" He leaned against the doorframe. "Get me up to speed. What do you know?"

"Not too much right now. The girl in Clear Creek Forest? Candy's looking into unauthorized burials and following up on a few other options to try to ID her. Sophia Jernigan was reported missing from school, so Candy and I drove out there to talk to her parents. Jackson Jernigan swears the little girl we found isn't her, and she doesn't match the photos of our girl in the water. When Candy and I pulled up at the department, I got a call from Brad. Another girl has been reported missing. I just got back from the elementary school, and I'm headed back out, but first I had Brad call Veronica Jernigan. She's not picking up the phone." Freya glanced at her watch. "I've got to go talk to this other dad."

"You trust Jackson?"

She paused, staring at him. "Why? What are you thinking—that Jackson is covering for his wife?"

"Or that he doesn't know everything. What was your impression of him?"

Freya closed her eyes, conjuring up a vision of the living room. This wasn't something she had time for, but at least one thing about Fawn Lake hadn't changed while she was gone. Chief still loved knowing every minute detail of the cases she was working, even if he wasn't going to get out on the road himself.

"Spill, Freya." Chief tapped his watch. "I have a meeting with the city manager here in a minute about hiring. I'd like to actually have all of our cruisers and offices full, but getting money from them is like pulling teeth."

"The house was immaculate," she said, talking quickly. *Chief thought he had something important to do? What about me?* "Now, before you tell me that maybe they're just really clean people, when I say *immaculate*, I mean there wasn't anything out of place. No toys. No scribbled notes dropped on the floor. Nothing. It was like a showroom."

"Not every parent loves having a house that looks like a Fisher-Price factory. And that tracks with who Jackson Jernigan is. I hate to agree with him on that because I can't stand the man."

She shrugged. "Sure, I know that. Jackson wasn't worried, he didn't identify the body, and Candy and I have some leads to run down. Brad will keep trying to get in contact with Veronica, but there's not much else we can do there."

"Good." Chief turned to leave, then looked back at her. "I'm glad you're here. That you're the one handling this. Are you settling in okay?"

"Of course I am." The look she gave him said more than her words, and he sighed.

"I know it's probably hard being back here after everything that happened, that's all. I wanted to make sure you're okay. And that your head is in the game on this one."

"Why wouldn't it be?" Heat burned Freya's cheeks, and she stood up. There were few things worse than a man standing over you when having a serious conversation, and she hated feeling at a disadvantage.

"Because you tend to assume it's the parents—"

"I'm perfectly equipped to handle any case that lands on my desk," Freya cut him off, her voice sharp. "You don't need to worry about that, Chief. Just give me the space I need to do my job, and I'll put everything I have into finding this little girl."

"You're right." This time when Chief turned to leave, he didn't stop walking. His voice floated down the hall to her. "I can't think of a single person who would give more of themselves to make sure this case gets solved. Just make sure you're not too close to it."

She had no time to waste. Grabbing her keys from her desk, she turned to the door, but before she could leave, Brad stormed through it.

He walked with purpose, his brow furrowed, a notebook in his hand. Without preamble, he leaned against the wall and exhaled hard. "Captain—" he began, but she cut him off.

"Freya. Just call me Freya, Brad."

The officer nodded. He swallowed hard. "I tracked down Jenny, and I think she knows more than she's letting on. Of course, talking to her as a witness and interviewing her as a suspect are two completely different things."

"And let me guess, her parents didn't want you talking to her?"

"You got it. We'll have to come at it from another direction, but I really do think there's something there." Brad tapped the notebook he'd just put on her desk. "I made some notes in there, but I know you're busy with the missing girl I called you about. I'm more than happy to keep running with it."

She took a deep breath. Of course she wanted to be the one working Esther's case, but that wasn't an option right now. Brad was more than capable, and he'd take care of Esther. She had to trust that.

"As long as that's not going to pull you off the road for too long. I don't want to be the reason you get in trouble for not stopping cars, but I don't have time to worry about the broken window right now."

Brad barked out a laugh. "Are you kidding me? The last thing Chief wants is for us to stop cars unless we really don't have any other choice. Trust me, working on this case at least gives me something productive to do. Consider it mine."

"Then it's yours." She nudged the notebook closer to him. "Thanks for handling it. I didn't know you wanted to be upstairs so badly." She inched towards the door, gesturing for Brad to walk with her.

"I mean, being a detective is the dream, but I'm happy where I am. For now. I don't mind the weird shifts because it means I get time off during the week."

"Good attitude. Just stay on top of that case—figure out how to get to Jenny. I need to know why someone would target Esther." She groaned and rubbed her eyes. "As much as I'd love to stay and chat, I'm following up with that dad who called earlier."

"Okay. Just let me know what I can do." He headed off, waving his notebook at her above his head. "I'll let you know when I make some headway on this. And if I see Candy—"

"I'm going to call her now. Don't worry."

"She really looks up to you. She'll work her butt off to solve this case."

Great. The last thing she needed was for her detective to look up to her so much when she sometimes felt like she was barely holding it together. Pulling her phone from her pocket, she swiped it on, taking a moment to look at the home screen.

Her and Esther, back before everything happened, back when Freya was just a teenager and Esther had opened her home to her. She didn't have to do that, didn't have to let an unruly teenager with a sour attitude move in, but she had, and she was the only reason Freya was the woman she was today.

She'd just found Candy's contact and was ready to call her detective when the phone rang in her hand. "Candy? I was just calling you."

"Beat you to it. Hotels are still a bust. I can go farther out from Fawn Lake if you want. Keep searching."

"Hold that thought. I finished at the elementary school. Sophia's teacher doesn't recognize the little girl we found this morning, but she let it slip that the janitor's a little creepy. She doesn't trust him."

"Great. Just great." Candy exhaled hard. "We've got to look into this guy, so just let me know how you want us to handle that."

Freya stopped walking. Her mind worked overtime. "Brad took a call about another missing girl. We're going to follow up on her, then tackle the janitor together. Get back to the PD and you can ride with me." She hung up before her detective had a chance to answer, then pulled up the address.

It would take them fifteen minutes to get there. In the case of a missing child, every second counted.

TWELVE

"Turn here." Candy pointed up ahead, and Freya tapped the brakes before pulling into a gravel driveway. She killed the engine and glanced over at Candy.

"Second missing girl," Freya said. "What do you think the chances are that she's the girl from the woods this morning?"

"I hope she is." Candy frowned, then continued. "That sounds terrible, but you know what I mean."

"I got it. Nobody wants there to be a dead child, but we already have one. Let's not hope there's another missing girl right now." She paused. "Cases like this don't usually happen all at once."

"This is a new one for us. We've got credit-card fraud. A breaking and entering at Gayle's farm out on Highway Fifty-Four. A hit and run that I just wrapped up. Really, Freya, that's it. It's a small town and we have small-town crime. Or we did." Candy heaved a sigh. "Okay, you ready to do this?"

Freya's stomach growled, and she nodded. "Here, then straight to the janitor's. You can fill me in on what you've been doing on the way there."

Candy shook her head. "There's nothing to fill you in on.

Like I said, the hotels were a bust; nobody with a young girl has checked in recently. And as for any recent deaths? Nothing on any official record. I want it to be an accident, but I'm not so sure it is."

Freya groaned. "Great. Let's go."

The two women got out of the Jeep and walked up to the house. It was the second family home they'd been at in one day, but this one couldn't have been more different than the Jernigans'. Not only was there a tipped-over bicycle in the front yard, but an easel with a pad of paper on it was set up on the porch. While the Jernigan house looked like a child hadn't walked onto the property in years, this one was welcoming. Lived in.

"There's a moving pod," Candy said, pointing. "Right over there by the minivan."

"Good call. Looks like someone just moved in, but at least they seem to have gotten comfortable," Freya said. "That's definitely something we're going to talk about with Mr. Matthews."

The front door swung open before they reached the porch. A thin man in overalls walked out to greet them. He pulled a red bandana out of his breast pocket and ran it over his face, scrubbing it down his chin. A moment later it disappeared into the same pocket.

"Mr. Matthews?" Freya walked right up to greet him.

"Call me David." The man nodded at the two of them.

"David, hello. I'm Captain Sinclair. This is Detective Ellinger. Why don't you tell me what's going on? You've reported your daughter missing." She reached out; shook the man's hand.

"I'm glad you came." He wiped his hand across his forehead and sighed. "Maybe I'm overreacting, but I haven't talked to my Isa in a few days. I'm getting nervous about it."

"Okay, why don't you tell us what's going on with Isa? Start at the beginning."

"She's on vacation with her mom. They had some girls' trip

planned before Isa starts school." The man gestured to the pod sitting on the driveway. "We just moved in. Obviously. And Tina said she'd get Isa registered for school as soon as they returned from their trip. She's six and loves school, so she's been excited about that."

"What does she look like?" Freya asked.

He exhaled hard. "Gosh, she's cute. Looks a lot like her mom. Longer hair, but she always has it in a ponytail. She—" His voice broke, and he shook his head, scrubbing away tears. "I'm sorry, I'm doing my best."

"You're fine. When were they supposed to return?" Candy asked.

"Well, that's the thing." He sighed and shoved his hands in his pockets. "And that's why I'm feeling a little silly, if I'm being honest. They're not supposed to be back for two days."

"Then what makes you think something's wrong with Isa?" Freya asked. She glanced over at Candy, but her younger detective was turning away from the two of them, taking in the entire house, the yard, the pod. They'd only worked together as detectives for a few hours, but she already knew the younger woman wasn't going to miss a thing.

"I can't get in touch with them. It doesn't matter what time of day I call, Tina isn't picking up her phone. Sometimes it rings and goes to voicemail, but most of the time it doesn't even do that. Seems like they're somewhere without service." Mr. Matthews frowned. He glanced at Candy but then turned back to Freya.

"When did they leave?"

"Just three days ago. But for me to not hear from them..."

"You're saying that's not normal?"

"Isa's a daddy's girl." The man smiled for the first time. "I know every man says that about their daughter, but with Isa, it's true. We love spending time together, and it helped that her mom used to work full-time. I've always been the one picking

Isa up from soccer practice, that sort of thing. I'm the one who found her a team to be on, even before she started school here."

"So she's playing on a team now?" Candy asked, turning back to David. "It looks like you just moved in."

"Oh, the pod." David shook his head. "Yes, we just moved in, about a week ago. And then Tina swept Isa away without helping me unpack everything. It's been frustrating, to be honest, and not just for me. But I'll get through it. Tina wanted to take Isa on vacation before she started school, but Isa really loves soccer. Lives and breathes it, if I'm honest, so she begged to join a team before starting school. She did that, joined the team I found, but she's missing some practices and a game this weekend thanks to this trip."

"I didn't know you could do that. Join a team before you started at the school, I mean." Freya tapped her fingers on her thigh. A mom taking their daughter off for a vacation wasn't a crime, but David was really convinced that something was wrong. She wanted to see this through.

"Well, the coach at the elementary school said they don't normally do that, but a lot of their players moved on to middle school this year, so they were looking to round out the team. I was surprised, but Tina tends to get her way." A sad smile crossed his face but was gone a moment later.

"Mr. Matthews—"

"David. Please."

She nodded. Candy had wandered away from the two of them, and she wanted to keep his attention on her so her detective could poke around. "David. Right. I know this is a hard question to answer, but have you and Tina had any problems? Anything that makes you think she might have taken Isa without any intention of bringing her back?"

He was shaking his head before she finished the question. "No. Tina really wanted to move to Fawn Lake; it's just so beautiful here. And even though we've been here such a short time, she's already found a group of friends. I don't know how she squeezed in enough time to make friends when we just got here, but she hasn't started her new job yet, so that helps." He paused. "You know, she may have made them before we moved here. She mentioned she'd already been for coffee with some of the moms from Isa's team, that she was so happy Isa had new friends and she did too."

"What's her job?"

"She's a physician's assistant. Always wanted to work in medicine, and she is." There was a note of pride in his voice, but it disappeared a moment later, like he remembered he was upset with his wife.

"Why don't you call Tina now and we'll talk to her together? Tell her you really miss Isa and just want to say hi to her."

"You think we need to do that?" He nodded, more to himself than at her. "Okay, I think that's a good idea." A moment later, his phone was on speaker, the ringing loud enough to make Candy walk back over.

"We're calling Tina to see if she'll let David here talk to Isa," Freya told her, her voice lowered.

"Smart." Candy glanced up at David, who was staring at his phone with a mixture of hope and apprehension. "I didn't find anything out of the ordinary by the way. Nothing that feels suspicious. Everything's matching up with his story."

"Good. Thanks." Freya turned back to David. "Has she picked up at all since they left?"

David shook his head. "No, but—"

Tina's voicemail cut him off. Groaning, he tapped the red button to hang up.

"Does Isa have a phone? Maybe just one you use to track her in case she's not at the pickup location when you go to get her from practice?" Freya knew she was reaching now, but there had to be some way to not only put this man's mind at ease but also hers.

"No, she's always where she's supposed to be when I go to pick her up. The coach always sticks around with the kids, never makes them wait by themselves. He's great like that. Besides, Tina never liked the idea of her having electronics. She's much stricter about things like that than I am." He sounded defeated. His shoulders rolled forward like they were just too heavy for him to keep up.

"Do you know where they went on their trip?" She changed tactics. No reason to browbeat the man and make him feel terrible about things he could have done differently. That ship had sailed. What mattered now was finding Isa and making sure she was okay.

"I don't, not exactly. Some retreat, I think. At first it was just going to be Tina and Isa, then Tina mentioned some of her friends might come. That makes me a terrible father, doesn't it? Not knowing? I have no idea where they went; they were just so excited, and Tina swept her out of the house without giving me any information. I didn't think I'd have to worry about something happening to my girl. I'm an idiot." He slammed the heel of his hand into his forehead.

"Hey, no," Candy said, taking his arm and pulling it down. She patted the back of his hand. "You're not an idiot. You're stressed out because you love Isa more than anything and you need to make sure she's okay. Captain Sinclair and I need a photo of Isa and Tina. We're going to do everything we can to find the two of them." She pressed a card into his hand. "Here's my information so you can reach out if anything changes. Go get us that photo, okay?"

David nodded and walked back into the house, his back hunched. Freya waited until the screen door slammed shut behind him before turning to Candy.

"A missing girl," Candy said. "Maybe Isa's who we found in

the woods. She's new to town so it would explain why Mrs. Olson didn't recognize her."

"This is bad." Freya rolled her neck from one side to the other. "We've got to find her."

"Let's wait to see the photo before getting worked up," Candy said.

The sound of the screen door squeaking open made the two women pause and turn back to the house. When David reached the two of them, Candy took the photo and smiled at him.

Freya glanced at it, sighing in relief when she spotted the halo of blonde curls. The little girl looked nothing like the one found in the woods.

"We're going to do everything we can to make sure Isa is okay," Freya reassured him. "We'll be in touch."

They now had a missing girl in addition to a dead one. Time was ticking.

THIRTEEN

"Okay, tell me everything there is to know about this janitor," Candy said as Freya backed out of the Matthews' driveway and yanked the steering wheel hard. The map on the console adjusted, and Freya glanced at the directions before pressing down on the gas.

"Okay, this really bothered me. I talked to Sophia's teacher, Mrs. Olson, for a while. When I asked her if anyone had ever paid a lot of attention to the girls, she got a little shifty. I had to press her, but she told me the janitor had a wandering eye."

Candy sat straight up. "That's different."

"Definitely an angle I hadn't considered."

Candy nodded. "Earlier you said the teacher thought he was creepy, not that he had a wandering eye. That's worse. If he's involved... what? We think he kidnapped the girls? Maybe blackmailed the parents? Threatened them not to tell? That would keep them quiet."

"Could be he took the girls and threatened their mothers not to call the police, yeah. Generally speaking, mothers will do whatever it takes to protect their children." Freya rapped her knuckles on the steering wheel. "But get this. The janitor? He's the principal's brother. And neither one of them were at school today."

Candy arched an eyebrow and shifted in her seat. "That's enough to be concerning," she agreed. "I'm glad we're driving out there now. What was the guy's name?"

"John Frank," Freya said. "I don't remember anyone by that name from when I lived here before. The principal is Steven Frank."

"John Frank," Candy repeated then shook her head. "I don't know the guy. Doesn't really mean anything though. Just means he's been flying below the radar."

"It would make it too easy if you did know him."

"Let me call dispatch and see what they can dig up on him and his brother."

"Good idea. I want to know where these guys are right now and what kind of history they have. If he has priors and his brother hid them, then we're going to have to have a chat with him about why he would do that with little kids around."

"I'm on it."

While Candy radioed in to dispatch, Freya kept her eyes on the road. Her stomach was gnawing at itself, but the last thing she wanted to do was stop somewhere and get a bite to eat. No, it was better for the two of them to see this through. She'd only had her badge back a few hours and everything was falling apart —there wasn't any way she was going to take a break now.

Candy sighed, and Freya looked over at her. "Good news?"

"Get this. Looks like the janitor's real name is Aaron, not John. He just *goes* by John. Now, why do you think you'd change your name like that? Because I have a few thoughts."

"Easy. Because you have something to hide." Freya rolled her shoulders back. She tended to drive hunched over when she was stressed out about something, and today was no different.

"Exactly what I'm thinking." Candy lifted the radio to her mouth. "Central, run both the real name and the alias for me. I need you to look up all priors, any outstanding warrants, any tickets the man's had. If he's picked his nose in public, I want to know about it. Pretty much any dirt you can dig up on him. While you're at it, I need everything on Steven Frank as well."

"Ten-four, three-zero-two, I'll get on it, but it will take a little while to get back to you."

"I'll be waiting." Candy dropped her radio into her lap. "What's the play here, Freya? If we get lucky, the guy's home and we can deal with this now. But he wasn't at work, and neither was his brother. We can't assume he'll be waiting for us at home, but we can hope."

Freya stopped at a red light. According to the map, they had about five more minutes before they reached the janitor's house. It was smart to get on the same page, although Candy was right —it was entirely possible the man wouldn't even be there.

"We're just going to knock on his door and talk to him. See what's going on, ask him about the girls. I don't want to accuse him of anything or accidentally spook him, but if he's doing something he shouldn't be, we'll know it. I guarantee it."

Candy nodded. "Okay. And if he's not there?"

Freya didn't respond for a moment. A truck with blacked-out windows sped past them, but she barely noticed. "If he's not there, then we need to find him." The list of missing people they had to hunt down was growing. An itch at the back of her neck made her uncomfortable.

"And his brother too."

"Definitely his brother. We'll need to get dispatch to run his name too."

Candy sighed. "This doesn't look good."

"It doesn't. Call Mindy," Freya told her. "And make it snappy—we're almost there. I want to ask her something."

Candy took Freya's phone and called the elementary school. After two rings, the secretary's voice flowed through the car's speakers.

"Fawn Lake Elementary; this is Mindy. How can I help you?"

"Mindy, hi, this is Captain Sinclair. You were so helpful when we spoke before on the phone, and I hope you can help me again."

"Captain, of course." Mindy cleared her throat. The bubbly tone she'd used when she answered the phone had all but disappeared. "What can I do for you?"

"I didn't realize the principal and janitor were brothers," Freya said, slowing way down as she entered a neighborhood. "That must be wonderful for the two of them to get to work together all the time."

A slight pause. "They really enjoy it, yes. Although their paths don't cross very often on a normal day." Mindy forced a laugh.

"I imagine not. A principal and a janitor? But tell me, if I wanted to talk to one of them today, what's the best way for me to do that? Do I need to go through you?"

"Well, normally I'd tell you to make an appointment." Her voice was higher now. "And yes, I'd be the one to help you, although I have to say, nobody's ever wanted to make an appointment to speak to our janitor." Another laugh. "But you're out of luck today. The two of them are out."

"Oh, what a shame." Freya slowed next to a driveway but didn't pull in. Instead, she parked on the side of the road. "Where are they, do you know?" Before Mindy could respond, she chuckled. "That's a silly question, isn't it? Of course you know. I bet you know what goes on in that school better than anyone else."

"Well." Mindy's voice grew quiet. "I'll tell you, but this isn't common knowledge. Their mom has cancer, and it's not going well. Mr. Frank—Steven, our principal—told me they had to take off to go see her."

"That's terrible. Is she here in Fawn Lake? I hope she's close so they can see her as often as possible."

"That would be ideal, wouldn't it? But no, she's not. She lives in Bertmont, a little over an hour away."

"What a shame. Do you have either of their phone numbers?"

A pause. "I'm sorry, Captain, I can't just hand that information out all willy-nilly. I could lose my job."

Freya rolled her eyes. "Well, Mindy, I know how important you are over there, and I don't want to keep you any longer than I have. Thanks so much for your help!" She tapped the console screen to hang up before Mindy could respond.

"Cancer?" Candy asked.

Freya shrugged. "No reason not to believe her until we have no choice. Now, let's see if our janitor is home or if Mindy is right. I'd love to see his wandering eyes for myself."

The two of them got out of the Jeep and hurried up to the house. Candy rang the bell, and when there wasn't any response, Freya left the porch. She walked around the house, cupping her hands around her eyes to peer in the garage and any window she could find.

There was no movement.

"Nothing," she said when she reached Candy again. The two women stood on the driveway and stared at the house.

"I peeked in the dining-room window," Candy said, gesturing at the window at the far end of the porch. "There's a table there, but it's clear. No dishes like he picked up and left in a hurry. Maybe Mindy was right and he's in Bertmont."

"Wherever he is, he's not here." Freya kicked a rock. It skittered across the driveway and bounced into the grass. "Come on —we'll pick up some food on the way back to the office." Despite not wanting to take a break, it was well after lunch, pushing dinner, and if the two of them were going to be at all useful for the rest of the day, they needed to eat.

"Here's what I'm thinking for once we get back," Candy said as she and Freya walked to the Jeep and climbed in. "I'll send out a BOLO with the picture of Tina and Isa, see if we can't get some info on them. I'll also have time to dig into Steven Frank, see what his deal is."

"Love that, thanks," Freya said. The Jeep roared to life, and she pulled a U-turn.

"What's your next move?" Candy asked.

"I'm going to figure out what the delay is with dispatch getting us the information we need. And let Chief know what's going on because I'm sure he's about to flip out waiting on an update. Get back in touch with Lance. And I need to check in with Esther, make sure she's okay."

"I forgot about the vandalism!" Candy touched Freya on the arm. "What can I do to help with that?"

Freya shook her head, her jaw tight. Worry over Esther ate at her, a constant fear that she wasn't doing enough to help. She'd moved back home to be close to Esther, to help take care of her. Right now she wasn't doing any of that. No matter how much Esther needed her, she couldn't be there for her right now. "There's nothing we can do right now. We have one dead girl, two missing ones, missing mothers, and a possible principal/janitor predator duo that's left town. We have enough on our plates."

Guilt ate at Freya even though she knew she was making the right decision.

She wanted more time, but all she could do was hurry.

FOURTEEN

Freya could hardly believe it was just this morning that she'd been in Chief's office greeting him and getting ready for her first day as captain of detectives. Too much had happened in the few hours since she'd stood here, nervous that the town wouldn't let her forget her past and what her parents did.

And here she was again, back in Chief's office, ready to fill him in on everything.

It was no wonder her head throbbed.

She crumpled up the wrapper from her hamburger and tossed it in the trash before greeting the man sitting behind the desk. He wore a heavy scowl that only seemed to deepen when he saw her.

"You better have a good update for me." His voice rumbled a warning.

"Well, I have updates, but I don't know how good they are." Freya pulled out a chair across from him and perched on the edge of it so she could lean on his desk. "The dead girl? Nobody seems to know who she is. I'm going to reach out to Lance again, but he had someone to stitch up before he could get to her, so I'm not holding my breath."

"Surely he won't go home until we have answers."

Freya gave a half-shrug. The Lance she knew from five years ago would have stayed up half the night to get answers if that's what it took, but five years is a long time. People change a lot. She sure had.

"I'll find out when I talk to him. I already told you that while we were chasing our tails, Jackson Jernigan's daughter was reported missing. Well, not *missing*, exactly, but not at school, where she belongs. Then a different father called to report his daughter gone."

This made Chief raise an eyebrow. "Any ideas where she is?"

"With her mom apparently. But beyond that, your guess is as good as mine."

"You think they're connected."

Freya nodded. "It's too much of a coincidence, and I don't believe in those. One girl shows up dead, one is reported missing from the school, another dad reaches out worried for his daughter? I want to follow up with that and—"

"It's not related." Chief sounded so confident that Freya stopped talking, her train of thought gone.

After a moment, she shook her head to clear it. "I'm sorry, not related? What makes you say that?"

"There's no way something is happening to the girls in town. You're seeing ghosts where there aren't any because of your past."

Freya bristled. "That's a low blow... If you don't think I can do my job, then just tell me."

"I think you can do your job, but I don't want you running around town trying to make connections where there aren't any. Need I remind you that you left, Freya? You don't know how things operate in Fawn Lake anymore, but let me tell you: we don't have little girls go missing all at once. And what's the link between them?"

"Really? Is that what you think? Did you know the principal of Fawn Lake Elementary hired his brother to be the janitor and the way he watches the little girls makes the teachers there uncomfortable?" Chief's eyebrows flew up and Freya nodded. "Yeah, that's right—Candy just got confirmation on that. How convenient that the two of them weren't at school today and we can't get in touch with the janitor. I'm going to dig up his number in The Last One, find him somehow, because you can't tell me the odds aren't good he has something to do with all of this. What do you think about that?"

The Last One, or TLO, made it easy to not only look up a person's address and phone number but also their known associates. It was invaluable.

Chief opened his mouth. He closed it. When he tilted his head to the side like he was sizing her up, Freya leaned even closer to him. If there was one thing she'd learned in her career in law enforcement, it was to not let men in power intimidate her.

"How do you know all of that?" he asked.

The question shouldn't have surprised her, but it did.

"Good old-fashioned policing. Which, by the way, I'm going to get back to. Unless you want more of an update about what I'm doing that is." She stood, planting her hands on his desk and staring at him. "No? Okay, then I have some calls to make." She turned to leave his office, but he spoke, stopping her in her tracks.

"Have you been looking into the vandalism at Parker's?"

She turned back. Shook her head. "Williams has been handling it; I couldn't walk away from the girls. Why?"

"Just asking. I know Esther's important to you. But I appreciate you putting your time and effort where it really matters."

"You're welcome." She had to swallow around a lump in her throat. Even though she knew what she was doing was right, it was hard to feel like she'd turned her back on Esther. That wasn't what was going on. The girls needed her more, and she knew that.

"That's all." Chief turned to his computer, dismissing Freya. "I expect another update tomorrow. Every day, in fact, until you get this handled."

"I'm handling it." Freya spun on her heel and marched into her office. In the back of a desk drawer, she found some Tylenol and popped two pills dry before calling Lance.

"Freya, my favorite captain of detectives, how did you know I was about to call you?" he asked, picking up on the first ring. "Honestly, I'm surprised you're not knocking down my door right now."

"I had to fill Chief in on how the case was going, so I thought I'd call from the comfort of my office." She leaned back in her chair, ignoring the groan it made. "Talk to me. Tell me everything about the girl. I know you know something by now."

"Well, yes." He paused, and she held her breath. "But it's not much. She drowned, which is what we thought. I scraped under her nails, hoping for a skin sample, but either it was an accident and she didn't have anyone to fight back against or the water washed it away. Nothing there."

"Tell me you have more than just that." She closed her eyes, trying to take deep breaths.

The case wasn't going anywhere. And without more evidence from Lance, an ID, or—God forbid—another body, she was at a dead end.

"She's young. I'd say around five or six. No other bruising or injuries, so if she did fight back, it wasn't very hard. I still can't rule out that someone drowned her, but there is a possibility it was accidental."

"If it were accidental, then I'd think we'd have some upset parents on our hands," Freya mused.

"I agree. That's part of the reason that makes me think someone hurt this little girl."

"You have anything else for me? I'm desperate, Lance, and you're the best in the business."

He barked out a laugh. "Flattery will get you everywhere with me—you know that. But even as the best in the business, I don't have anything else for you. I'm sorry. I did take X-rays of her teeth so you can use that for identification."

Freya sighed. "I appreciate that. Without a set to compare them to, I'm still at a standstill."

"I know. I just wanted to have that available for you when you were ready for that step. It's unfortunate there isn't a national database to compare the teeth to."

"Yeah, and I can't ask every dentist office in the surrounding area to compare the teeth to every young female patient they have." Freya sighed again, running her hand through her hair. "But it's fine. I'll do everything I can to find her family so she can get the burial she deserves. Thanks for the update."

"Anytime. Let me know if you have any other questions. And swing by to say hi sometime, will you? Fawn Lake is lucky to have you back."

"Talk to you later," she mumbled, then hung up. Having someone, especially a person she admired as much as she did Lance, tell her it was good for her to be back was nice, but it still hurt. Everything about being back in Fawn Lake felt painful, like the edges were too sharp.

"Okay," she muttered, pushing up from her desk. "To dispatch. I need to figure out why they haven't gotten me any information on John Frank yet. And then I'll call Esther." She glanced at her watch.

It was quitting time for almost everyone else in Fawn Lake, but with one dead girl and no good leads, Freya didn't think she'd be in bed anytime soon. She had work to do.

FIFTEEN

It was hot, and that brought people to the water. More people meant more eyes; more eyes meant someone might see what was happening. The leader shifted position, their toes sinking into the mud at the edge of the water. It lapped up against their skin, and they shivered even though the sun was hot on their back.

They'd had to walk much deeper into the forest to find privacy than they had in the past. For a moment, they'd been afraid nobody would be able to find them, but they shouldn't have worried.

When people are committed, things get done.

When people are committed, they'll do whatever is asked of them.

When people are committed, everyone benefits.

This river was old. As old as the mountains it cut through. It twisted and wound its way around rocks and trees, forming eddies and small pools, sometimes slowing enough to look like glass, other times splashing and dancing over exposed rocks.

It was quiet here.

It was perfect.

The little girl approached, her hair tied in braids, her white dress swishing around her skinny little legs.

It was time.

SIXTEEN

TUESDAY

The next morning dawned bright and early, the last fingers of fog retreating as the sun rose over the horizon, the clear-blue sky promising a hot day with relentless sun. Freya parked in front of the police department, nosing in between two marked cars, then slammed her door hard, disturbing the silence around her.

Frustration coursed through her. What had started out as a simple, although terrible, case of a dead girl had ballooned. If she wasn't careful, it was going to spiral even more out of control. She knew as soon as she walked through those doors of the police department that she wasn't going to have a moment of rest. And after last night, where she barely slept for thinking about the day and the cases, she needed coffee. Good coffee. Not police-issue swill.

She turned away from the police department and hurried across the street to Parker's. The residents of Fawn Lake had rallied around Esther since the vandalism and the place was full, the front door swinging open and slamming shut regularly as Freya walked up. She took in the plywood covering the broken windows then held the door for an old man who shuffled out with a sack of baked goods clutched to his chest before ducking inside.

"Coffee?" Esther asked when Freya reached the counter. "And let me guess: a bear claw."

"You better believe it." Freya dug in her pocket for her debit card, hurrying so she could get to the office as quickly as possible, but Esther waved it away.

"Your money is no good here, my dear. Besides, the grapevine is talking, and it sounds like you have your hands full." Even though the woman was older, she moved confidently. Her white hair had led many people in the past to think she'd be frail and slow, but Esther nimbly packed a box full of donuts, placing the largest bear claw on top, then passed the box and a cup of hot coffee to Freya. "Take care of your team, darling, and they'll take care of you."

Esther's hand trembled as Freya reached for the coffee. Freya frowned, taking the cup from her. *Best not to bring it up in front of so many people.*

She'd bring it up later, alone. When she had more time.

"Oh yeah? Is that why you have such a huge team here working with you?" Freya winked and Esther huffed. "You know, hiring some people to help you out really isn't a bad idea. You could rest."

"I hate rest." Esther flapped her hand at Freya to make her move out of the way.

"You could work on more recipe development," Freya called, stepping out of the way of the crowd. It pushed forward, everyone wanting to start their day with something fresh and delicious. That or they were all a bunch of looky-loos, there just to see where a crime had been committed.

Whatever the case, she had work to do. Worry over the girls ate at her, and she hurried back across the street and up to her office, stopping only at Candy's office to ask the detective to meet with her.

"I brought donuts," Freya said, flipping open the box and putting it on her desk. "But take that bear claw and I'll fight you. Have you heard from Brad?"

"I'm here." The rookie appeared in the door, his cheeks red. "I saw you come across the street and wanted to catch up."

"Great." Freya tossed a box of tissues on her desk to use in lieu of napkins. "Dig in. I want to know everything. It's boots-on-the-ground day, you two." She grabbed the bear claw from the top of the box and took a bite. Yep, sugar was just what she needed to start the day. It was then she noticed the Manila folder sitting on the corner of her desk. "What's this? Either of you know?"

Both Candy and Brad shook their heads. Freya picked it up, fingered the edge, then opened it. A single piece of paper was nestled inside, and she grabbed it, dropping the folder to her desk.

"Oh, it's from dispatch, finally getting back to us about the janitor and principal. Last night they told me they were covered up with calls and having trouble finding the information we wanted. They must have left it here sometime overnight."

"What did they find?" Candy leaned forward, the donut in her hand forgotten.

"Who's that?" Brad asked at the same time.

"Janitor and principal at the elementary school," Candy explained while Freya read. "According to Sophia's teacher, Mrs. Olson, the janitor, good old John, is a bit of a creeper and likes looking at little kids. Apparently, John isn't his birth name, which makes him worthy of being counted a suspect in my book. Oh, and he was hired by his brother, the principal."

"Great." Brad exhaled. "So you think the janitor might be good for this. But the girl in the woods didn't go to the school, right?" He pulled out a chair across from Freya. "What does the report say?"

"The school didn't ID her as a missing child, you're right, but I'm not letting John slip through my fingers. It's a small town, so there are plenty of opportunities for someone like him to run into young girls. Looks like he switched from using the name Aaron about three years ago when he moved here from Alabama. And the reason he moved here?" Freya glanced up at Candy and Brad, her eyebrows raised. "Any guesses?"

"Misconduct with a child?" Candy offered. "No way would he change his name and move away from somewhere to become an elementary school janitor unless he didn't have a choice."

"Too many traffic tickets?" Brad shrugged when Freya frowned. "I'm just being optimistic. Do I think the guy fled the state and changed his name to avoid traffic tickets? No, but it's better than the alternative."

"Indecent liberties with a minor," Freya said, snapping her fingers and pointing at Candy. "Got time served after spending eighteen months in jail." She exhaled hard and dropped the folder to her desk. "We need to handle this."

"Let me get this straight." Candy cleared her throat. "This guy, Aaron, got arrested in Alabama for being inappropriate with a minor, moved here and changed his name, then his brilliant brother hired him at the elementary school?"

"You nailed it. We're not talking MENSA candidates here," Freya agreed. "We need to find these guys. Are we sure they're visiting their mother?"

"I'm not convinced. I did look up tax records for Bertmont and I think I found her. Tons of Franks there though. I need to make sure I have the right one, but I had to get some rest." Candy sounded apologetic. "I did look into Steven, John's brother. He's clean as a whistle, at least on paper."

"That's the same thing dispatch said in this information," Freya said. "We're going to dig into him though. The timing on all of this is just so weird. I feel like it's all falling apart since I got back, and yet you two told me things hadn't been that crazy before."

"Crazy, sure," Brad said, "but not like this. This is above and beyond, especially for a small town like Fawn Lake."

"Here's the plan," Freya said. "Candy, I want you to narrow down some addresses for us to check so we can find Mama Frank. Her two sons deserve to be locked up for running this little scheme. We didn't get any hits on Tina or Isa Matthews yet, but the BOLO is still active."

"You got it. I also put out a BOLO on John and Steven's cars. No hits yet, but hopefully that will pan out."

Freya nodded, pleased. "Good thinking. Brad, are you needed on the road?"

The rookie shook his head. "No, the team is full, and I talked to my lieutenant, Shayla Dalton. She said I'm fine to help you out. The last thing she wants is to get on your bad side, if I'm being honest." He started to laugh, then caught the expression on Freya's face and stopped. "Not that she's scared of you. Well, she may be a little bit scared of you."

"Fair enough. I want you to reach out to Tina again, see if you can make contact with Isa." She took another bite of the bear claw. "I would normally just chalk it up to domestic issues with the wives not communicating with the husbands, but I don't want to jump to conclusions here. Best to be thorough."

"Don't tell me you trust Jackson," Candy said. "Because I don't. Call it my smarmy lawyer instinct."

Freya laughed and Candy continued.

"I'm serious. He may be telling the truth about where Sophia is, but that doesn't mean I trust one word out of his mouth otherwise."

Freya nodded. "Do I trust him? No. Not at all. But I think you're right—I don't think he's lying about his wife taking Sophia on a trip. It's not a bad idea to follow up on that though. Make sure everything's above board. I'd love to know where they are and when they're coming back. I'm sure the school would too."

"Oh, before we do that, there was a reason I came up here, and it wasn't just because I could smell the donuts from downstairs. I took a really interesting walk-in report about twenty minutes ago." Brad took a huge bite of a donut and groaned. "Kenneth Harmond. Said he hasn't seen his neighbor's daughter in a while, but he hasn't been able to catch the mom out on her own to ask her about where she might be."

Freya paused, her bear claw halfway to her mouth, and looked at Candy. The younger detective looked ill and leaned forward, touching Brad on the arm to get his attention. "Please tell me this Kenneth guy lives in River Stone or down the street from the Matthews family and we're talking about the same girl."

Brad shook his head, and Freya felt her stomach sink. "Wish it were so, but no. He lives a bit farther out of town on a little dirt road, he said. If you're okay with it, I'd like to follow up on the call and visit the family he's reporting. I'll do that, then talk to him again if need be."

"Of course. I want to come with you though. You can reach out to Tina afterwards." Freya put down her food. It had turned to a rock in her stomach, and she suddenly felt ill. "Please don't tell me this is going to become an epidemic of missing girls."

The three fell silent. Down the hall, a phone rang, but none of them moved.

"Well, thinking and wishing isn't going to get things done." Freya shoved the last of the bear claw in her mouth and forced herself to swallow, despite her discomfort. Who knew when they'd have time to stop for lunch? "Candy, run the rest of these down to dispatch, okay? And, Brad, on the way to this house, I want all the information on the break-in at Parker's yesterday."

Brad nodded and wiped his mouth with a tissue before tossing it in the trash. "Okay, let's go. You drive, and I'll bring my notes." He pulled a small notebook from his pocket. "See you later, Candy."

As much as Freya wished she could sit in an office and work through the evidence, that wasn't an option. It would take time, and she didn't have that right now. Not when they had another missing girl on their hands.

SEVENTEEN

Brad waited while Freya got out of the Jeep. Her jaw worked and her eyes flicked around the house in front of them, soaking in all the details. She drank up the house while he watched her, making sure she didn't miss anything.

"You coming?" Freya turned back to him. She was halfway up the walk to the small house. It had a distinctive lean to it, like it was tired of sagging under the pressure of the roof. Still, even though it looked old and in disrepair, the front walk was lined with flowers. A fern hung in the oak tree they parked next to, and there were bright-blue planters on the porch loaded with marigolds.

Someone loved this house, even if they didn't have the money to keep it looking its best.

"Coming, yep." Brad caught up with her. Birds serenaded the two of them as they walked up the uneven brick path. Once on the front porch, Freya knocked on the door, then stepped back, letting Brad take the lead.

"Doesn't look like anyone's home," Freya remarked after a moment. She walked along the creaking porch and pressed her hands up against the front window. Even from where he stood,

Brad could tell how dirty the glass was. Freya cupped her eyes and leaned forward, peering into the house. "Nothing. No movement. No lights. You sure this is the right address?"

Brad yanked a slip of paper from his pocket and glanced at it, stepping back to compare what he'd written down to the house number hanging by the door. "Yeah, six-nineteen Deep Gap Road. This is it, but it looks like we're out of luck. We'll have to come back later and try to catch someone home. We can always ask patrol to pop around throughout the day to see if they can find someone here."

"Not a bad idea. I'll reach out to Captain Moore and see if he's okay with sparing some of his people for this. I know it's not what patrol needs to be doing, but something's going on here, and we might need all hands on deck."

Freya and Brad turned to walk back to the car. The sun beat down on them, the heat already oppressive. Neither of them spoke as they made their way down the rickety wooden steps, both of them focused more on making sure they didn't fall through the wood than anything else.

"Wait." She held up one hand and shifted her weight; the wood underneath screeched in response. "Do you hear that?"

Brad held his breath, focusing to try to pick up what Freya had heard. "Birds," he whispered. "No, wait. Whistling."

"Whistling." She nodded; her cheeks flushed. "Around back —let's go." She motioned him forward, and they cut around the right side of the house, the two of them moving quickly. The grass here was sparse, lanky in some places and practically dead in others. Brown patches of dirt dotted the side yard.

The backyard housed the garden. It was pretty clear the homeowner spent a lot of time outside working in the dirt. The ground was tilled, prepared. At the end of each row were home-made painted wooden signs declaring what was going to be growing where, but nothing was coming up. Strange, especially with the warm weather and gardens all over town boasting green seedlings.

Snap peas. Bush beans. Corn. Zucchini. Pumpkins.

To the right side of the garden were the flowers. Some early bloomers, like daffodils, added a splash of color, while other plants were just budding out. A few of them had been planted recently, the shovel used to relocate them lying in the grass by the edge of the garden.

Two plastic lawn chairs were set out in the yard, both facing the garden behind the house. One was empty, but someone sat in the other.

"Is that the mom?" Brad kept his voice quiet. The person sitting in the chair had long brown hair. Their legs were out in front of them, crossed at the ankles. It took a moment for Freya to respond.

"They have on headphones. I can't imagine mom here would have a lot of spare time to sit around and just listen to music, not when there are so many other things that need to be taken care of. Let's go find out."

Nerves tickled the backs of their necks as the two of them walked up to the person sitting in the chair. As they drew closer, the whistling got louder, and he relaxed as the person's profile came into view.

Not a woman, and certainly not old enough to be the parent of the house. The teenage boy sitting in the chair looked like he'd only shaved a handful of days in his life. A fresh cut on his chin still looked angry and red.

"Excuse me." Freya planted her feet in front of the boy and spoke. "Can you take your headphones off?"

The boy's eyes flew open. She mimicked removing headphones and he followed suit, his eyes wide.

"Hi." The smile she gave him was disarming. "I'm Captain Sinclair, and this is Officer Williams. Do you live here?"

The boy nodded. He glanced back and forth between Freya and Brad, his fingers twisting the headphone cord.

"Great." Another smile from Freya. "We're looking for your mom. Is she around?"

"My mom?" The boy shook his head. "She's not home."

"Okay then. What's your name?" She glanced around, then grabbed the empty lawn chair and pulled it in front of the boy, turning it so she could face him. She sat down and crossed her legs, leaning forward like they were two good friends just catching up over a beer. Only a foot of space separated the two of them.

"I'm Zach. Zach Brown. Why are you looking for my mom?" Nerves made his voice break.

Freya ignored the question. "It's nice to meet you, Zach. Can you tell me when your mom might be home?"

When he shook his head, she tried a different tactic. "Okay, that's fine. Who else lives here with you? Your dad? Any siblings?"

The boy flushed. He'd been calmly twisting the cord to his headphones, but now the movements were jerky. He yanked it hard, wrapping it so tightly around his fingers that it looked like he was going to cut off circulation.

"Yeah, my little sister. *Half*-sister."

"You don't sound pleased about her." Freya glanced up at Brad.

"Tell us about that." Brad stepped forward, closing in on the boy a little just in case, although the kid didn't look like much of a runner. The black T-shirt he had on was for some band Brad had never heard of, and his dark jeans were too baggy to let him get a quick getaway. Even his sneakers were black; dirty old Converse that had seen better days.

"Well, yeah. Sisters are annoying." Zach gave a nod like he had found himself on more solid ground and was pleased about it.

"What's your sister's name?" Freya asked. "I have a sister too. She's younger and was always a pain growing up. Man, I wished time and time again she'd move away, maybe with my dad, maybe with a neighbor. Just go... somewhere. You know?"

Brad watched her, his eyes narrowed. She was lying. Her entire private life had been splashed across front pages; articles had dissected how everything in her past had gone wrong.

She was an only child.

But Zach didn't know that. He leaned forward, his eyes lighting up. "She's the worst. Liz always wants to be in my room, always wants to interrupt me when I'm playing with my friends. But she hangs out with her dad a lot, so that means she's not always here."

"Hey, sounds like her dad being involved means you get some alone time. Lucky you. Seriously. I would have given my right arm to be left alone when I was younger." She paused, then spoke again when he didn't respond. "Hey, how old are you, anyway?"

"Fourteen." He cleared his throat. "She's six."

"Wow, that's a big age difference. No wonder you're so glad to get some alone time." Freya tapped her chin, giving off the impression she was really thinking something through. "Do you know where she is?"

Zach's shrugged. "Spending time with her dad."

"Sounds fun for her, but hard to get left behind," Brad offered.

"Yeah, but it's fine. I'm used to it. *Her* dad comes by all the time to take her camping or to his place." The boy's voice was laced with tears, and he stood, his knees almost knocking into Freya's. "Anyway, I better get inside. I'm not really supposed to talk to people."

Quick as a wink, Freya pulled a business card from her pocket and pressed it into the boy's hand. "We don't want to get you in trouble, but why don't you ask your mom to call us when she gets home? I'd love to talk to her."

"Yeah, sure." The boy turned towards the house, casting a worried glance over his shoulder at Brad.

"Hey," Brad called, unable to help himself, "do you and your sister like school? Get good grades?"

A pause. "We're homeschooled." The boy turned towards the house and hurried inside. The door slammed and locked.

"Why'd you ask about school?" Freya asked as the two of them walked back to her Jeep.

"She wasn't reported missing like Sophia was. Maybe it wasn't within their timeframe to report, but I thought maybe something else was going on. And I was right." Brad shrugged, then adjusted his duty belt. No matter how the officers placed their keepers, the entire thing pressed down on their hips all day long. It was uncomfortable at best and painful at worst.

"Homeschool kids." She stopped, one hand flat on the hood of her Jeep as she looked at him. Behind the house, the screen door slammed. Probably Zach going back outside now that they were leaving. "Good call, Brad. Homeschool kids aren't accounted for the way kids in public school are. If one goes missing, it would most likely be up to the parents to report it."

Or a concerned neighbor, in this case.

"You know what? Let's go pay that neighbor of theirs a visit." She pointed to the house next door. "What do you say? Hop in—we'll take the car in case we need to scoot."

They'd barely backed out of the driveway when her phone rang. Without looking at who was calling, she stabbed the screen, answering the call on speaker. "This is Captain Sinclair."

"You sound so official answering the phone like that." Esther's voice filled the Jeep, and Freya and Brad grinned at each other. "Listen, darling, I know you're busy, but why don't you come to dinner tonight? I'd love to have you over, see how you're settling in. We haven't shared a meal since you got back."

"I'd love that, but I don't know that I can. This case I'm working on... it's rough." Freya hadn't buckled in, and the Jeep dinged warnings at her.

"I'd love to see you."

Freya groaned, scrubbing her hand down her face. "Five thirty sound okay? I'm not staying long, Esther, I'm sorry. I just can't."

"Perfect. And Freya?"

"Esther." A smile played on Freya's lips.

"Thanks for making some time, even if it's not very long. I miss you." She hung up before Freya could answer.

"She's slick, isn't she?" Brad asked.

"So slick." Kenneth Harmond's driveway was right down the road, and Freya slowed down to pull in. "You'd think she'd been the one to raise me from when I was a baby. I swear, out of all the people in the entire world I've met, that woman knows me better than any of them. I don't know how I got so lucky to have her, but I'm not going to turn down dinner with her. I'll just have to take my case files along with me."

"Doesn't hurt that she can cook," Brad offered.

Freya nodded, but there was a look on her face that said, *Or that she'll take my mind off things.*

EIGHTEEN

"Mr. Harmond?" Freya walked up to the man washing his car in the driveway, her hand outstretched. "I'm Captain Sinclair, and this is Officer Williams."

The man turned to greet her. He wiped his hand on his pants, then his handshake was firm. "Pleasure, Captain."

"We spoke on the phone when you called to report your neighbor's daughter missing." Brad shook the man's hand. "Thanks for calling us and letting us know that you had a concern. If more people did that, then we could better look out for the community."

"It seemed like the right thing to do." Kenneth Harmond straightened up, pressing his hand into his lower back as he did. He let out a soft groan, then gestured to a ring of chairs around a fire pit. "Why don't we sit? I love nothing more than how clean my car looks after I've washed it, but I think I might be getting a little old to do it myself."

"It's a gorgeous car," Freya said as she and Brad followed him to the chairs. "What is it, a cherry red seventy-one?"

"Nineteen seventy, but close. Mercedes Benz 280SL. It's been my pride and joy for the past twenty years. I bought it off my old boss when he had a heart attack." He ran a hand through his white hair. "Got it for a song actually. I think he was worried his wife would sell it to someone who wasn't going to appreciate it like I do."

"You can tell how you take care of it." Freya sat silent for a moment, then gestured at the house next door. "Why don't you tell us about your neighbors?"

Mr. Harmond sighed and glanced over at the house. From where the three of them were sitting in the front yard, they couldn't see the backyard, but it wouldn't have been surprising if Zach was back out there listening to music now that they'd left him alone. What else did a homeschooled teenager have to do when his mother wasn't around?

"Well, it's a mother and her two kids," he said, speaking slowly. Each word was carefully chosen, like he was giving them great weight. "I don't see the mother very often, but the little girl is always playing outside. Or she was anyway."

"How long ago did you say it was since you've seen her?" Brad was jiggling his foot. He caught himself and planted it firmly on the ground.

"Oh, what did I tell you? A few days. Not quite a week. It was strange enough to make me feel like I needed to reach out and let someone know. She's always around, hiding in bushes, catching butterflies. Once I found her up on my porch because she'd picked me some flowers and was leaving them there for me."

"She sounds like a sweet kid," Freya said. When the man nodded and smiled, she continued. "Tell me about the mom. We met the son but haven't had the opportunity to meet her."

"Linda," the man told her. "That's her name. She's always coming and going, more going than coming recently. And drags that little girl along with her. The past month or so they were going all the time, the two of them."

"Dad isn't in the picture?"

He snorted. "Not that I've seen. There have been a few evenings with men over there visiting, if you know what I mean." Now it was his turn to wait for Freya and Brad to nod their understanding. "But no man around regularly, nope. The little girl, Liz, she told me she sees her dad pretty regularly, that Linda will drop her off with him somewhere and then she gets to go camping or hiking with him. She'll be gone a day or so, sure, but I don't think she's ever been gone this long."

"Any idea when you last saw Linda?" Freya kept glancing at the house next door. "Or what kind of car does she drive, do you know?"

"An old beater pickup. White, although it's covered with mud half the time like she's been out four-wheeling. And she usually comes home late, so if you come back tonight, you might have a better chance catching her." He rolled his shoulders back and stared at Freya. "You don't think I'm just an old man jumping at shadows, do you?"

"Not at all. Trust me, we'd rather someone call and report a concern than let it get out of hand." Freya pulled a card from her pocket and passed it to him. She watched as he turned it over in his hand then tucked it into his pocket. "You'll let us know if you think of anything else, won't you?"

"Sure will. I hope nothing's wrong." He hesitated, his eyes jerking to Brad. "You'll find out though, won't you?"

"I plan on it." She stood and shook his hand, then before Brad could walk to the car, she marched across the yard to the house next door. "Zach!" she called loudly, strolling right around the side of the house.

And there he was, just like she's imagined. Sitting back in the same seat, the same headphones clamped on his head. Freya walked up to him and plucked them off his head.

"Hey!" Zach wheeled around in his seat, his face contorted with anger. His cheeks blazed red, and he glared at Freya. "What did you do that for?"

"Where does your mom work, Zach?" She held the headphones up, out of his reach as he stretched to grab them. "Easy question, easy answer."

He kept glaring at her but didn't stand up. Instead, he dropped his hand back into his lap. "This isn't legal."

She shrugged. "Just answer the question."

Silence grew between the two of them for a minute before he shook his head, admitting defeat. "Fine. She works at the gas station on Old Mountain Road. You happy?"

"Thrilled." Freya handed him his headphones and hurried back to her Jeep, only pausing long enough to throw Mr. Harmond a wave. As soon as she and Brad were buckled in, she started the vehicle and tore towards town.

"Think she'll talk to you?" Brad waited until they were on a main road, halfway to the gas station, to speak. He reached up with his right hand, holding on to the safety bar as Freya gassed it around a curve.

"Only one way to find out." Her words were clipped, and the Jeep jolted to a stop when she slammed on the brakes, parking right in front of the gas station. Without waiting for Brad, she leaped out and hurried in.

A man stood in the snack aisle, clearly choosing between two kinds of chips. Freya glanced at him and walked up to the counter. Behind it stood a woman, her graying hair scraped into a thin ponytail. She had short pink nails, small daisy earrings, and wore a thin cardigan.

"Linda Brown?" Freya asked, glancing down at the woman's nametag for assurance.

"Yeah, in the flesh. You need me to start a pump for you?"

"Nope, just wanted to talk to you about Liz." Freya tapped the badge on her duty belt, then waited for the woman to glance at it and back up at her. "Someone reached out to the police to check up on her welfare."

"On Liz's?" The woman appeared shocked. She took a

small step back and glanced past Freya. "And it took two of you to come check up on her?"

When Brad appeared at her side, Freya stepped over to make room for him at the counter. "We take the possibility of missing children very seriously. I'm sure you can appreciate that."

"Of course I can—how awful." Linda gave her head a little shake. "But it's no surprise someone said Liz is missing. She's been with her dad for a week or so. He and I are separated, but I still want her to have him in her life. Little girls need their fathers, don't you agree?"

"Definitely." Freya's mind raced. "Do you have a recent picture of her so we can see what she looks like?"

Linda laughed. "Oh honey, I have more pictures than you'd have time to see, I can pretty much guarantee it. Just hang on." Like magic, her phone appeared in her hand. She tapped and swiped and then turned the screen around for Freya and Brad to see. "She got her daddy's hair, and I'm grateful for that. Isn't she a cutie?"

Freya stared at the little girl on the screen. She was pale, with bright cheeks and a smattering of freckles across her nose. Even though her hair was braided in pigtails, wisps of it fell around her face.

"Mind if I take a picture?" Freya asked as she angled her phone over Linda's. A moment later, the girl's image was on her screen, and she tucked her phone away. "Her dad is a redhead too?" she asked, and Linda nodded.

"Redhead and over six feet tall. His hair was the first thing I noticed about him, but he has the temper to match. So does my Liz, but I adore her. She's sporty, just like him."

Freya frowned. "But you homeschool, right? What kind of sports can homeschool kids get involved in around here?"

Linda tucked the phone back into her pocket. "Oh, which-ever ones they want. All the public schools are desperate for athletes, so even homeschool kids can get in on the action. She's been taking part in every sport she can at the elementary school for a year now. Loves getting out there and sweating. Me? Not so much."

"We'd love to talk to him," Freya said. "Do you have a phone number or address?"

"An address, ha! The man lives in a camper and moves it around as he sees fit, so I never know where he is. And he doesn't have a phone. Doesn't believe in them."

"I'm sorry, he doesn't believe in phones?" Freya didn't try to hide the judgement in her voice. "How do you two coordinate picking up and dropping off Liz?"

"Facebook Messenger. He swings by the library to use their computers. Here, I'll give you his name, although good luck getting in touch with him. He has his account locked down tight and doesn't always respond to message requests." She ripped off a piece of receipt paper, scrawled a name on it, and pressed it into Freya's hand. A pause. "He's a great guy, James is, but not much for being on the grid, if you know what I mean."

Behind them, the man with the chips had made his choice. He cleared his throat, and Brad glanced over his shoulder at him. "Well, we don't want to keep you when you're busy," he said. "Thanks so much for talking to us."

"Anytime, anytime. I appreciate all you do." Linda threw them a smile. "Y'all have a good day. Come back sometime."

The door jingled closed behind them.

"You're thinking something," Brad said as they made their way to the Jeep.

"Yeah," Freya admitted. She waited until they were inside and she'd backed out of the parking space to speak. "Linda seems lovely."

"But? There's always a but. Even I know that much."

Freya smiled. "To let your daughter go off for days or a week at a time with a guy who doesn't believe in phones? You can't tell me that doesn't rub you wrong on some level." She paused, tapping her fingers on the steering wheel. "Let's look this guy up. You have Facebook, right?"

Brad shot her a look. "You don't?"

"No reason to. Here." She handed Brad the receipt paper. "Find him."

Brad pulled his phone from his pocket but then stopped. "You're kidding," he said, waving the paper at her.

"What?" They were on Main Street, eating up the road to the police department. "I thought your generation was good at electronics."

"First of all, you're not that much older than me. Secondly, I'm better than good, but it has nothing to do with that. It's the guy's name. James Smith."

Freya groaned. "You've got to be kidding me. That has to be the most common last name."

"Agreed. We didn't get lucky on this one."

"Do you think it could be fake? James Smith? I feel like I'm grasping for straws, but come on." She rubbed her temples.

Brad tapped on his phone. "Could be. Maybe he changed it to hide. Didn't she say he wasn't much for being on the grid. What does that mean?"

Freya slammed her open palm onto the steering wheel. Frustration coursed through her. "It means he's going to be a complete pain to find, and while we look for him, we need to find something that ties all these girls together. There's a link, I know it."

NINETEEN

Freya smoothed down the top she had on. It was wrinkled, like most everything else she'd yet to unpack in her home, but at least it was something nicer than she'd normally wear to work. A mixture of guilt and frustration ripped through her when she thought about the suitcases and boxes she needed to unpack. They lined the halls of her home like dead-eyed sentries.

They gave her the creeps, to be honest, but she'd been thrown right into work and hadn't really had time to worry about unpacking and making the house a home. Sure, she was lucky to have someplace to come back to, but her childhood home wasn't exactly filled with cozy memories.

Pressing her finger against the doorbell, she peered in through the screen door. Now, Esther's house? That was where the good memories were. Freya didn't have to close her eyes to picture the many meals she'd had there, the way the woman did her hair the one time she went to homecoming, how the kitchen smelled when she was baking.

A shuffling from inside caught her attention. Esther was dressed in khakis and a button-up shirt, her usual uniform when not donning an apron. She peered out at Freya, then swung open the screen door.

"Since when did you start ringing the doorbell?" The older woman pulled Freya into a hug. "I won't stand for it. It makes me feel like the tax man is at the front door."

Freya laughed. "Noted. Now, what in the world smells so good? It's like I just traveled to Italy or something."

"Lasagna," Esther said, leading the way down the hall. "With extra ricotta and garlic, just the way you like it. I was at the farmer's market last weekend and picked up some roasted garlic. That stuff could kill vampires from two towns over. Get in here and set the table for me, would you? I have the dishes out already. And what is that in your hand? A file?"

Freya winced. "It's just this case I have; I can't really walk away from it. I have to work on it, but I didn't want to miss dinner." Guilt pricked at her. What she didn't tell Esther—what she couldn't—was that part of the reason she felt like she had to come to dinner was to make sure she was okay after the break-in. She hadn't been around much to check on her, not when she was running down leads in the case.

But she also couldn't turn her back on the case. Not now.

Esther sighed and rubbed her hands up and down Freya's arms. "You're a good woman, darling, but you're going to burn out if you're not careful."

"Yeah, well, there's something to be said about going down in a blaze of glory."

"I disagree. But we can talk about that later. For now, take care of the table. Dinner's almost ready."

"Four plates?" Freya picked up the stack of chipped, mismatched china and eyeballed Esther. The woman was now busying herself looking in the oven. "Four plates, Esther? Is this a two-course meal and I just don't know about it?"

Esther ignored her, pulling the lasagna out of the oven and putting it on the stove with a thunk. Shutting the door, she heaved a sigh, then finally turned to face Freya. "I invited company."

"Company?" Freya's voice felt tight. With the way she felt eyes on her no matter where she went in town, she wasn't entirely sure she wanted to see anyone tonight. "Isn't dinner together our thing? Who in the world would you want to invite? Besides," she said, her voice dropping, "I'm not sure I'm really up to seeing anyone. Honestly, I'm not sure anyone is up to seeing me."

"It'll be fine. They're lovely," Esther said. "They even helped me—" But whatever the people Esther invited to dinner had helped with was cut off by the doorbell.

Esther's cheeks were pink, and her eyes shone as she flapped a hot pad at Freya. "Go get it. Shoo."

"I'm not a cat you can shoo," Freya said, but she walked down the hall to the front door anyway. Butterflies danced in her stomach as she reached the screen door, but the front porch light was off, and she couldn't see who was standing there. Taking a deep breath, she pulled the door open.

"Hi!" A small girl, only reaching up to Freya's hip, with long blonde curls, darted past her. "Bye!"

"Hi?" Freya turned, watching as the girl ran into the kitchen, then looked back at the door. "Oh, there's the parent. Good. I thought maybe Esther was just inviting the neighborhood kids over."

"I'm Paul Meyers, and that's Marla. She loves Esther." The man had thick brown hair that needed a trim, dark eyes, and broad shoulders. He smiled at Freya, the expression on his face apologetic, then stepped into the house.

"I'm Freya." She thrust out her hand, needing to put something between her and the stranger. "How do you know Esther?"

"We live two doors down and helped her repair her back fence after a bad storm two weeks ago. Well, I did the manual labor and Marla drank lemonade while she and Esther watched. We were quite a team."

Ahh, it makes sense now. "This must be your thank-you dinner."

"You nailed it. She's a great lady. And when she invited us for dinner, she said she had someone for us to meet, so I guess that's you." He smiled at her.

He hasn't read the papers. It was pretty clear by the way he was looking at her, not like she had a second head but curiously, like he wanted to get to know her. Freya felt herself relax a little and closed the door behind him before leading him to the kitchen. "Your wife couldn't join us?"

"That would be a sight." Paul chuckled and Freya stopped, turning to look at him. "I'm sorry, gallows humor. My wife died three years ago. It's just the two of us, and I know I shouldn't make jokes, but that's how I deal with terrible things that happen. A lot of people don't get it."

"No, they don't." She gave him a nod, then gestured to the stack of plates she hadn't put on the table. "Do you mind setting the table? I'll help Esther with the food. Looks like Marla is ready to eat." She pointed to where the little girl was already sitting in a seat, downing a glass of water with lemon slices floating in it.

As Paul walked over to the table to set it, Freya hurried over to the counter where Esther was mixing up a salad in a large green bowl. "What is this?" she asked, taking Esther by the arm. "Please tell me you're not trying to set me up on a blind date."

"I'm trying to help you meet people." Esther turned and smiled at her, patting her on the shoulder. "It's okay for you to have friends, you know. Especially ones who aren't officers, who don't live that life, and who can give you a break from that pressure and stress."

"So the friend you decided to introduce me to just happens to be a single dad down the road?"

Esther winked. "Lucky, isn't it? Now, darling, carry the lasagna to the table for me. I'm hungry, and this smells too good to wait."

Freya didn't have any other choice. Even though what she really wanted to do was turn tail and run for it, there wasn't any way she was going to leave Esther. She plunked the lasagna down in the middle of the table next to the salad and garlic bread and sat across from Marla, who was studiously staring at the lasagna while kicking her feet under the table.

"Thanks for having us over," Paul said, holding out first his and then Marla's plate for Freya to serve them. "This is always a treat, Esther."

"Esther's a great cook," Freya said, giving him a smile. "But tell me about you two. You're not from Fawn Lake, are you?"

"No, we moved here last year. I needed a change of pace, and Marla loves being outside. It works out perfectly because we've been spending as much time hiking and swimming as possible."

"Nice that you can take time off during the day to do that." Esther smiled to herself, pleased.

"What do you do that you can walk away from work when you want?" Freya took a bite of lasagna. It was hot, but the cheese was nice and gooey, and Esther had been right: the roasted garlic was amazing.

"I work in online security," Paul explained. "As long as things are running smoothly, I'm not really needed. It's ideal for keeping an eye on the kiddo during the summer." He reached over and ruffled Marla's hair. "Freya, Esther tells me you're a detective."

"I am." Freya nodded. "Yeah. Just moved back home, and I'm back at the first department I ever worked at."

"Why did you leave? If you don't mind me asking."

She paused, a forkful of lasagna halfway to her mouth. "It... I just—"

"Freya had an opportunity in another state and couldn't turn it down," Esther offered. "We were sad to see her go, but it was the right move at the time. And now she's back."

"Right." Freya cleared her throat. "Anyway, Marla, tell me all about you. What do you like to do?"

"Everything." Marla had a piece of lettuce stuck between her teeth. It was darling. "When Daddy isn't working, we do everything. Hiking. Swimming. Board games. Oh, I just learned how to fish but I won't hook the worm." She wrinkled her nose. "Too squirmy."

"Valid concern." Freya took another bite of her lasagna. "Do you like to read?"

Marla nodded. "Yep."

"Marla's a cool kid," Paul added. "I know I'm biased, but it's true."

"Daaaad." Marla rolled her eyes, and Freya couldn't help but laugh. As soon as the sound bubbled out of her, guilt flooded her veins, and she quickly glanced towards the kitchen where she'd left the file. How could she sit at the table and have such a good time when she should be working the case?

But maybe she could do both. The little girl sitting across from her was the perfect way for Freya to work the case even while she was enjoying herself.

"Hey, Marla, do you go to school at Fawn Lake Elementary?" Freya tried to keep her voice even.

"Yep."

"Do you ever notice that some of the girls skip a lot of school?" Freya stabbed another bite of lasagna to keep from staring at the little girl.

"Yep." Marla was much more intent on her dinner than looking up at Freya, but that was fine. "But Dad says I have to be at school." She shoved her lower lip out.

"Well, school's kinda like your job right now, you know?

When you get older you'll have a different job, but right now this is yours."

Marla sighed. "But they get to go spend time with their moms." She looked at her dad. "I said my dad could come, and they said no, it's only for girls."

"You know how kids can be," Paul said. He lowered his voice. "Anytime someone's different they... they can turn on that person."

"It's terrible. Have you had the opportunity to speak to any of the moms about it? Maybe they don't know your situation."

"Nah, I'd rather Marla not hang out with mean girls. Anyway, we've run into some of them before while hiking and they're not super friendly, so the girls are definitely taking after their moms."

"Nice people."

"That's what I thought." He paused. "I don't know, I'm just doing my best. Keeping her safe."

"That's really all you can do." Freya didn't realize how sad her voice sounded until she caught Paul staring at her.

"You say that like something's going on." Paul's voice was soft, his eyes were dark with concern.

"I have a case," she said, choosing her words carefully.

"Let me guess, the case is something you probably don't want to talk about?" Paul shot her a small smile. "Maybe one to do with the girl found in the woods yesterday?"

"Pretty much."

"You know I hate it when you bring work home." Esther clucked, then pushed back from the table. "I'm getting more salad dressing. How anyone can eat rabbit food without it drenched in the stuff, I don't know."

"How about this?" Paul said after Esther left the dining room. "If you give me your number, I'd be thrilled to let you know if Marla expresses concern about a friend from school."

Freya paused. "That's a sneaky, roundabout way to get my number so you can call me later."

He held up his hands. "I'm not saying I wouldn't love to get to know you better, but I'm not that clever. Trust me."

When Freya leaned forward to hand him her business card, he smiled and pocketed it before handing her one of his.

"I'd love to tell you more—" Freya began, but a loud thunk and yell from the kitchen cut her off.

TWENTY

WEDNESDAY

"So Esther fell pretty hard, huh?" Candy pushed a Styrofoam cup of coffee across Freya's desk towards her. "Is she okay?"

"She'll be fine." Freya sighed and took a long sip, closing her eyes as she imagined the caffeine pumping through her veins. "She caught her foot on a chair leg and just... tipped." She flicked her hand through the air to demonstrate. "Her knees are bruised up, but she'll be fine. It was upsetting, and Marla was pretty worried about her."

"Marla?"

"The neighbor's kid. Esther invited her and her dad Paul over for dinner as a gotcha for me to meet someone."

"You don't sound too mad about it though. That's good."

"He's nice, but even if he were a jerk, Marla's a really sweet kid just doing her best to fit in at school with a single dad as her parent. Paul said she likes anything where she can run around outside."

"He didn't have any worries about the school? No rumors about anyone in particular, like the janitor?"

"The janitor is an issue," Freya admitted. "I don't care if he flew to Europe, we need to find him and figure out how we're going to get him back here. The principal too. Brothers stick together and all that, but it's one thing to have your brother's back and another entirely to look the other direction when your brother breaks the rules and preys on kids." She paused. "We haven't gotten a hit on their BOLOs, so please tell me you found an address for their mom."

Candy grimaced and Freya sighed. "Seriously, Candy, I need that address yesterday. Whatever else you're working on, put it to the side. The janitor hurt those kids, or he didn't, but either way, he needs to answer for working at the school with his history."

"I'm sorry." Candy blinked hard, her cheeks bright. "You're right. I dropped the ball, but I'll handle it. I promise you. It's been difficult to get that information, but that's no excuse. I've also been looking James Smith up on Facebook, but he's a ghost. There are so many of them to sort through, it's proving impossible to find him." She paused, then nodded. "I'll shelve that for now and get on the address."

"Good. This can't wait." Freya stood to stretch. Reaching as high over her head as she could, she leaned to the left, then to the right. Her muscles ached and tugged, but it felt good.

"Does your hip hurt?" Candy had stood up and was walking around Freya's desk. She paused, leaning forward and touching her own hip. "I can't imagine it doesn't, but it's been years."

"It hurts," Freya admitted. Uncomfortable, she dropped her hands back by her sides. "But I don't want people to know that."

"I won't say a word." Candy paused, chewing her lower lip. "If you need me, let me know. Otherwise you won't see me for a while."

"Good. Order delivery if you get hungry. I don't want you thinking about anything until you get me her address." Freya opened her laptop and pressed her finger to the biometrics key to unlock it. The Fawn Lake Police Department must have gotten a nice grant to pay for the updated equipment. "I'm going to look up other elementary schools in the area. It's entirely possible the little girl in the river didn't go to school here and is from another county."

Candy nodded. "Sounds good." She left, and Freya searched for local elementary schools, calling the closest to Fawn Lake.

Half an hour later, she'd spoken to seven elementary schools, ranging from ten miles away to close to a hundred and gotten nowhere. According to the school secretaries, all the girls at their schools were accounted for. Either they were in class, or the staff knew where they were. The one time a secretary had hesitated, she had forged ahead, describing the little girl from the river.

But nobody knew who she was.

She sighed and closed her computer. Her head hurt from stress, and her mouth felt dry. Sitting in her office trying to find the girls wasn't working. She had to get out, had to knock on doors.

Time was ticking. And they still hadn't heard anything about Tina and Isa Matthews.

Even though Candy said she would find Mrs. Frank's address, it was taking too long. She hated to look over her shoulder, but she was going to do just that. But before she could get out from around her desk, an officer appeared at her door.

He was holding something in his hand, the shiny plastic of an evidence bag catching her attention.

TWENTY-ONE

"Captain Sinclair? I have something that I thought you would want to see." The officer was blond. Older than Freya had thought at first, with pocked cheeks. He hunched forward a bit, pulled down by the weight of his vest, and held the package out to her.

She hurried around her desk, dragging her fingers across its surface as she did. "Thank you," she said, reaching for the bag. "Where did you get this?"

"Someone from the elementary school just brought it by. Mrs. Olson, I think? She found it in her classroom and thought that we might want it here."

"She's Sophia's teacher," Freya said. The plastic evidence bag crinkled as she took it from the officer. "Did you talk to her, or did someone else take custody of this from her?"

"I spoke to her. I was on the first floor when she came in wanting to talk to someone. Unfortunately, she didn't have this wrapped up when she came in, so her fingerprints are all over it, but I figured it was still important to wrap it up, so we didn't contaminate it anymore."

"Good thinking. What did she say about it? Tell me exactly." She turned the bag over in her hands, looking at the picture inside from all angles. She hoped there would be something written on the back, something that would clue her in to where the picture was taken, but the back was blank.

"It was under the cubbies the kids use for putting their stuff in every morning. Sounds like there was a spill and they had to move the cubbies so the floor could be mopped. This photo was under there."

"That explains why it's a little water damaged." Freya set the photo on her desk and tried to smooth it out. "She didn't say anything else?"

"Just that she thought it was odd because that's not how Sophia liked to dress. The kids had to bring in photos of themselves for a class project, but she never saw this one. Said she thought you might want to see it after your discussion the other day."

In the photo the little girl was wearing a floaty white dress. Her hair was pulled back from her face in braids, and she had on a full face of makeup. She squinted into the sun from where she stood in the water, about five feet out from the shore of a lake. Ripples in the water indicated that there were other people there with her, out of view of the camera.

"I wish there were a way to tell when this was taken." She rolled her head from side to side. "Thank you for bringing it right up to me, Officer."

"Sure. Anytime." He paused, still standing awkwardly in the door. "Is there anything else I can do for you?"

She shook her head but didn't look up from the photo. "Nope. If you don't know where this was taken, then we're done here. I appreciate it though. Have a good one."

"You too." The officer turned, his duty boots thunking on the floor as he left her alone.

Freya frowned, torn between waiting to check in with

Candy and leaving. Waiting was tempting, but what she needed to do was find out where this photo was taken.

Grabbing her keys, she picked up the photo and headed downstairs. There was only one place she knew where someone could take one look at this photo and tell her exactly what lake Sophia had been at when it was taken.

Five minutes later, she walked into the front door of the Fawn Lake Visitor Center. It was busy, with tourists checking out the pamphlets of various local attractions and the racks of home-made crafts and canned foods they could buy. Ignoring the pack of hikers standing by the door checking a map, she walked over to the help desk.

"Hi there," the woman said. "What can I do for you today?" She looked to be about Freya's age, with dark hair hanging around her face, but when Freya glanced over the counter and saw that the woman had on hiking boots, she relaxed. She'd know where this lake was, Freya was sure of it.

"I need to know where this picture was taken," Freya said, putting Sophia's photo down on the counter. "Can you tell me the lake? I know we have a ton of them here and it might be tricky, but I figured you guys would be the ones to know."

"I'm not the person to ask," the woman said with a sorry shake of her head, "because I just moved here and don't know the area well enough yet, but let me grab Tim. He's the one you want. In fact, he just started leading hiking tours." She waited for Freya to respond.

"Thanks. If you could get Tim, that would be ideal."

"Sure." The woman smiled again and disappeared through a small door into a back room.

Freya drummed her fingers on the counter and turned to take in the action behind her while she waited. The visitor's center boasted a small gift shop filled with locally made pottery, postcards, and jelly. She watched a young woman examine a coffee mug while she waited.

"This is Lake Everett," a voice said behind her, causing Freya to whip back around. "You can tell because of the curve of the shoreline, and there's this little bit of an old stone wall right here just visible." He tapped the photo where it still sat on the counter. "There used to be a homestead here on the property, probably, oh... a hundred years ago or so. Most of it has fallen down, but there's just enough left that you can use it to identify what you're looking at."

"You make it sound like a no-brainer," Freya said, trying to stay calm. "Are you sure about that? Do you have any doubts about it being Lake Everett?"

"I wouldn't want to swear on it in court because I don't like lawyers," Tim told her, throwing her a toothy grin. "But look," he said, tapping the photo again. "Right there is the stone wall. If you hiked out there you'd be able to see it still standing. It would be easy to determine exactly where on the lake this photo was taken, if you wanted to."

"That doesn't matter as much as just knowing what lake it is, so thank you." Freya took the photo, folding the plastic evidence bag around it and sliding it into her pocket. "I really appreciate your help with this. The last thing I wanted to do was wander around in the woods for days trying to figure it out on my own."

"Definitely not a good idea, but I'm happy to take you out there if you want." Tim produced a brochure from under the counter. "It's my new hiking tour company I just started, but for you, I'd be more than happy to waive the fee."

Freya was already shaking her head. The last thing she wanted was to get involved with some guy who thought that she was relationship material, and this felt more like boyfriend pitch than a sales pitch. "I really appreciate your help today, but I don't need to get out there." She paused, thinking. "Have you hiked out there very often? Maybe taken people on tours to the lake?"

"Sometimes." His grin was lazy, and he leaned on the counter to get closer to her. "It's pretty, Lake Everett, but a lot of time families are looking for waterfalls. Dads want to show off for their kids, feel macho climbing the rocks around our waterfalls. It's dangerous, but they like it, so we end up elsewhere in the woods. The lake is too chill for a lot of dads." He laughed.

"What about groups of people but not families?"

"Groups? Sure, groups like to go there too. It's a pretty easy hike, so I don't recommend it for teens because they'll get bored, but it's great for younger kids."

"Tim, this was so helpful." For the first time all day, she felt a flash of hope. "I'm going to get out of your hair."

"Did something happen out there?" Tim's eyes flicked to the photo again and he tapped the counter, lowering his voice as he did. "You know, trauma tourism is a very real thing. If it's presented correctly, it could bring in a load of visitors to the area. Why is that photo in an evidence bag?"

"Tim. What was your last name?"

"Johnson."

"Tim Johnson. You never saw this picture, okay? I hope the best for your new hiking company, but I don't want you to breathe a word about this to anyone."

Tim nodded, flushing. "Okay. I hope you can take care of whatever happened out there."

"I will, but please don't turn this into fodder for trauma tourism."

"I won't."

"Good. Thank you again for your help." She forced a smile then swept from the welcome center, desperate to get outside and into some fresh air.

Trauma tourism. The thought of it made her angry. Letting the door slam shut behind her, she turned back to the police department, already yanking her keys from her pocket. Maybe he was right, and this was Lake Everett. He sure sounded confident anyway.

But Freya refused to leave things up to chance. She had to know for sure if that was where Sophia was standing.

"I'll just drive out there myself," she muttered, pulling her keys from her pocket as she hurried down the sidewalk. "I'll make sure this is really Lake Everett and then..." Her voice trailed off.

Then what? She still wasn't any closer to finding Sophia. Plenty of kids went to the lakes to swim, especially as the weather got warmer. One strange picture of Sophia in a dress at the lake didn't mean anything... except the dead body they'd found had been in the river. Rivers and lakes weren't the same, but something ate at her. She needed to learn more about Sophia. About Liz. Isa.

There was something tying them all together.

And she needed to find the Frank brothers.

Her phone binged.

She pulled it from her pocket and checked her text.

I found their mom.

Throwing her shoulders back, she called Candy as she walked to her Jeep. "Hey, give me the address. I'm driving there now."

TWENTY-TWO

An hour and a half later, Freya pulled up to a small blue house perched high on a hill. She'd relied on her GPS to find the location, and she tapped the built-in screen in her Jeep to shut up the cheery little voice telling her that she'd arrived at her destination.

Two cars sat in the parking lot, one an old Cadillac with a dent in the back bumper, the other a little Corolla. She eyeballed them, trying to decide if either one of those were the type of car an elementary school principal or janitor would drive.

Could be. How much money did those positions make anyway? Probably not a lot, but used cars were cheap, especially if you didn't mind driving around with a dent in the bumper.

It was worth the call to dispatch to run the plates. A moment later, her answer came back.

"Three-zero-one, the Cadillac comes back to Bethany Frank, the Corolla to Steven Frank."

That was the answer she needed.

She got out and hurried up to the front porch. The air was thick and muggy, and she felt like she was swimming. Her curls stuck to the nape of her neck, and she wished for a breeze before reaching up and lifting them off her skin. For a moment, she felt some relief, but as soon as she let go of her hair, it rested back on her neck and the oppressive feeling returned. If only she had a hair tie to corral it. She rolled her shoulders back, adjusting the fit of her belt on her hips, then finally climbed the four steps to the porch.

The porch itself was neat but old. The painted wood was chipped and sagged a bit in the middle, but there was a small wicker bistro set that looked newer. For a moment, Freya stood on the porch, drinking in the sound of birds calling, and tried to picture what she was going to find in the house.

What kind of woman could raise two sons that ended up like the Frank brothers? She wasn't entirely sure, but she wanted to find out. She grabbed her phone and sent Candy a text to let her know she'd arrived, then she pressed the doorbell and stepped back.

It took longer than she liked for her to finally hear footsteps. A moment later, the door swung open, groaning on its hinges as it did.

"Can I help you?" An older woman leaned forward, peering through the crack between the door and the doorframe. "Is something wrong?"

"Mrs. Frank?" Freya pulled out her wallet and flipped it open, so her badge was visible, then lifted it up for the woman to see. "My name is Captain Sinclair. I'm with the Fawn Lake Police Department, and I'm here looking for your sons."

"Fawn Lake?" She seemed to draw herself up a few inches. "That's well over an hour away. What in the world would bring you here to my front door?" She squinted, looking at the badge, then up at Freya's face like she was trying to reconcile the two of them.

"I'm here to talk to your sons. Are they around? We've been looking for them."

The shift was so subtle that Freya almost missed it. A younger, greener detective probably would have, but she saw the way the woman's muscles all seemed to tighten, how she gripped the edge of the door a little harder, how her entire body seemed to brace against it like she was doing everything in her power to keep Freya out on the porch.

"Why are you looking for my boys?"

"Because there's a missing girl and I want to talk to them about her. I'm especially interested in speaking with Aaron." She purposefully used John's birth name to try to throw his mother for a loop.

"They're not here. You need to leave." Her voice had darkened. There was a bite to it now.

"Steven's car is here, ma'am," Freya said, daring to show a bit of her hand. "Now you can tell them that I'm here to talk to them and that I'm not going to leave until I do, or I can drive back to Fawn Lake and come back with an arrest warrant for Aaron that will ensure he doesn't have a choice but to talk to me. What do you prefer?"

It was a stand-off. The woman blinked once at Freya, then spat on the porch between them. Shocked, Freya watched the thick glob land on the wood, then looked up at the woman.

"I'd do anything to protect my boys, and the sooner you realize that, the better off the two of us will be. Now, Captain, I suggest you head on out of here. You're not welcome here without a warrant, and you're more than welcome to go get one, but I can promise you my boys won't be hanging around here when you return."

She slammed the door. Freya took a step back as the shock of what just happened rolled over her. She could bang on the door and cause a scene. Try to get the Frank brothers to come out and talk to her.

But causing a scene was the last thing she needed to do. She didn't have proof John was even there, and she didn't have an arrest warrant in hand. Hell, even if she did, she wasn't in her jurisdiction, and someone else would have to serve it for her.

"Gonna hide behind your mom, huh?" Freya yanked her phone out of her pocket and called Candy on the way to her Jeep.

"That was fast." Candy sounded more chipper than Freya felt. "Please tell me they both confessed, one to kidnapping and the other to aiding and abetting, and you're on your way to go rescue our missing girls."

"How about I met their mother, and she wouldn't let me in to talk to them? When I told her I'd come back with an arrest warrant, she basically laughed me off her porch and told me they wouldn't be home by the time I got back." Freya backed down the driveway and pulled out onto the road, pressing down hard on the gas.

"Lovely woman. Can't imagine why the police want to talk to her sons. Want me to get started on the warrant?"

"That would be great."

"Consider it done. And I'll loop the local cops in to serve it for us, so you don't have to drive back out there."

"Wonderful. I'm not bringing it back here so Mrs. Frank can spit at me again."

Candy gasped. "She didn't."

"Oh, she did." Freya merged onto the interstate, pressing down harder on the gas. It had been a shot in the dark to drive all the way out here to try to handle things with the Frank brothers, and she hated that it had taken up most of the afternoon. "But that's fine. Joke's on her. We can still get a search warrant and get into John's house."

"Good call—if you can get a magistrate to give you one. Let me guess, you're stuck in the car, and I'm your warrant girl?"

Freya grinned as she passed a minivan. "You're reading my mind! By the time I get back, you should have that done, then we'll get in his home. If he's hiding anything, we'll find it."

"You got it."

She squeezed the steering wheel. "We have to be thorough. Anyone who even looked at those girls is a suspect. Someone murdered a little girl, and we've got more missing. I don't trust anyone."

"Freya, you don't have to—"

"Let me finish, Candy. Focusing on the wrong suspect in the past blew up in my face. You know it did, I know it did, geez, everyone in the entire county knows it did. I was lucky to walk away with a bullet in the hip and my career still salvageable. I'm not sure what's going on, but I'm not going to ignore the fact that John Frank is a creeper who shouldn't be anywhere near kids. Best-case scenario? He's innocent of any wrongdoing since he moved to Fawn Lake. But I'm still going to nail him and his shady brother to the wall for this little stunt."

"Fair enough. For what it's worth though, nobody in your position would have made a different decision. You shouldn't beat yourself up about it."

"A different decision would mean that three more people would still be alive. That's something I have to live with for the rest of my life. I'm not going to let John Frank keep me up at night the way my other decisions do. Just get that warrant. I can't wait to get into his home."

"You got it. Drive safe."

Freya hung up. Jeeps were noisy at high speeds, and the thrumming sound her vehicle made as she ate up the interstate was calming. She pressed down harder on the gas.

What she said to Candy wasn't a ploy for attention or for sympathy; it was just her being honest. She'd screwed up once before and people died. She'd got shot. She'd almost lost everything.

That wasn't going to happen again.

TWENTY-THREE

Freya got lucky on Main Street. There weren't often parking spots directly in front of Parker's, but there was one today. She pulled into it and parked, sitting for a moment in her vehicle to admire the new glass windows.

The glass people worked fast, much faster than she would have thought possible. The replacement windows were so new there weren't any smudges or fingerprints, but that would soon change. There weren't very many little kids who could resist pressing their faces up against the glass when Esther was baking chocolate chip cookies.

Getting out, she sniffed the air. Even with the ovens off for a few hours by now, the air still smelled delicious. It was no wonder Esther didn't want to close up shop anytime soon—everyone in Fawn Lake knew and loved her. Even people on diets would stop by just to smell the air and soak in the scent of her fresh sourdough.

Esther opened the door for her before Freya could even reach for the handle. "Freya, my darling. You look hungry. Have you had breakfast?"

"Breakfast?" Freya asked, following Esther to the counter.

"Esther, the afternoon is flying by. I'm here because I didn't have a chance to eat lunch, and I'm going to count this as a slightly early dinner."

"Early dinner, of course," Esther repeated, nodding. "That's what I meant to say. So no lunch for you yet? Let me make you something."

Freya watched as Esther cut a fresh bagel and piled it high with cheese, turkey, and vegetables. Esther seemed fine right now while making the sandwich, but Freya frowned. A sense of unease washed over her. Sure, it was easy to mix up words and get confused, but what if Esther was confused because of her fall? What if she was more rattled after it than she had let on?

"There you go, darling." Esther put it on a plate and grabbed a bag of chips to balance on the side. Moving faster now, she picked up a paper cup and handed it to Freya. "Help yourself to something to drink. Probably skip the caffeine though, just in case. You don't want to have trouble falling asleep tonight."

"Thanks," Freya told her, pulling her wallet from her pocket. "This looks amazing. I honestly didn't realize exactly how hungry I was until I smelled what you'd been baking."

"Tsk. Your money isn't good here. I told you that." Esther flapped her hand until Freya put her wallet back where it came from. "Now, I'd love to sit and chat, but I have to start cleaning up and prepping for tomorrow's bakes. Are you going to be okay by yourself?"

"I'm eating on the run," Freya said but then paused.

Esther saw the look on her face and hurried around the counter, pulling her into a hug. "Are you okay, darling? Really okay?" she murmured, rubbing Freya's back as she spoke. "I worry about you, not because you're out there dealing with bad guys, but because I don't know if you're fully healed."

Freya paused before speaking. "I thought this would be easier," she admitted. "Coming home. I know everyone hates my parents for what they did, and there are a lot of people who hate me for not stopping them earlier, but still, I thought I could come home and feel good about it."

"You didn't know." Esther pulled back, her hands cupping Freya's cheeks. "You didn't know, and I didn't know. The entire town didn't know! Your parents were sneaky, Freya. How was anyone supposed to know they were killers? They hid it so well. They never slipped up, not until the end. And then you were the one to catch them."

Freya wiped the back of her hand across her eyes. She hated crying, and especially hated the fact that her parents still had enough power over her to make her cry.

"I know that. I just... If I had been more aware of what was going on in the basement, I could have said something. Or done something."

"You were a teenager. A kid. You didn't have the power to do anything. And then, when you were older, when you got a badge of your own, you hunted them down. They tried to run and hide, but you caught them. Remember that."

"I wish the rest of the town would remember that," Freya said, a dark laugh bubbling out of her.

"They will. They'll see how amazing you are, darling. You took a bullet for the town," Esther said. "Remember that. You put your life on the line to stop them."

Freya nodded. She sucked in a shaky breath and hugged Esther. Anything she could have said died in her throat, so instead she kissed the woman on the cheek and turned away.

She hit the door at a brisk pace, hurried up to the fourth floor of the police department, then into Candy's office, only pausing long enough to put her food on the detective's desk before speaking.

"Tell me you got the warrants. Please—I could really use

some good news." Freya was beginning to feel desperate, which was never a good feeling. She took a sip of her Sprite—no caffeine here—and waited for Candy to answer her.

"I did my best." Candy sighed, leaning back and stretching her arms over her head. "Insufficient evidence to get a search warrant. The magistrate wanted to know exactly what we were going to be looking for."

Freya stabbed her straw into her cup. "Who was it?"

"The magistrate? McMurray. You know she can be a stickler. I don't think I've ever seen her bend the rules, not even when it was time sensitive."

"And you explained that he's got a record? That he didn't register as a sex offender, and we think he might have something to do with the missing girl?"

"Oh, I told her. She wasn't interested. Said that she'd be more than happy to sign the search warrant in the middle of the night while she was in bed with George Clooney if we came back with more evidence. But she did give me an arrest warrant for him since he failed to register as a sex offender and then was working at the elementary school."

"That's something, I guess. Can you take care of that? Send it to the local cops and have them swing by Mrs. Frank's house. She told me the boys wouldn't be home when I came back around, but I doubt she's counting on me calling in local reinforcements."

"There are few people in the world cops love arresting more than pedophiles." Candy grinned at her. "And I already sent it over to the Bertmont police. Hopefully he'll be in custody before nightfall."

"That'll be fast work," Freya remarked.

"Like I said. Pedophiles. Cops don't want them out on the street. I can guarantee you, as soon as I sent this over there, that whole department started buzzing. John Frank better hope he can hide, or that whoever comes out to arrest him is gentle."

"Let's hope he doesn't run or he's just going to drag this out. Thanks for handling it." Freya threw her trash away.

"What are you going to do now?" Candy asked. "Do you have a plan of action?"

"I'm going to speak to Mindy again." Freya gave a little nod. "Really push on her about telling me about any other kids who haven't shown up for class in the past two weeks. Isa and Liz don't go there, but she might have more information. She might be able to link them together for me. The school is supposed to wait a certain number of days before they contact police, but if I impress upon her we have a problem and that I'm worried, I think she might give me the information I want. If not, sounds like I'll need to wait for the magistrate shift change to get a warrant if McMurray is in a mood. I wish homeschoolers had to report to someone so we could keep better track of them. How else are we supposed to know if a child is in trouble?" She rubbed her temples, trying to relieve the pressure she felt growing there.

"I don't know." A pause. "While you do that, I'll handle Steven Frank's arrest warrant, see if we can get a two-for-one deal on having them sent back to Fawn Lake. McMurray was going to take a late lunch break, so I prioritized John's arrest warrant. She'll be back soon, and I'll be waiting for her. And I'll get back over to John's house. Sniff around, try to find anything that looks out of place, anything that will ensure she signs the search warrant for me."

"I don't care what you find as long as it gets us a warrant to get in there. Just... do your best to make it happen. I'm going back to look for Liz Brown again."

"You got it." Candy turned away from her and pulled her keys from her pocket. "I need to speak to the patrol lieutenant on shift."

Freya sank back into the chair. For just a minute, she allowed herself the luxury of closing her eyes. Everything fell away—the pressure of the case, the fear that she was barking up the wrong tree, the worry over Esther. For just a moment, it felt like everything was back to normal and she was in control.

But then she opened her eyes and stood up, grabbing her car keys.

It was getting late. But nothing was going to stop her from finding the missing girls.

TWENTY-FOUR

Mindy exhaled hard, the sound of her frustration coming through loud and clear in Freya's Jeep.

"I know you're not technically supposed to report kids until they've been missing for more time than this," Freya began, but Mindy cut her off.

"You're right, we're not. And if Principal Frank were here, he'd never let me talk to you about this. But he's not here, and I don't know how to get in touch with him. Do you know how frustrating it is to try to run a school when the principal has gone AWOL? I'm just the secretary. I didn't sign up for this."

"I can only imagine the pressure you're under." Frustration ate at her. She needed information from Mindy, but the woman was, right now, only interested in getting a few things off her chest.

Freya slowed to a stop at a red light, drumming her fingers on her steering wheel as she waited for Mindy to continue.

"It's so much pressure," Mindy moaned. "I almost didn't even pick up the phone when you were calling. Everyone else is gone, the day is over, and I'm here trying to figure out the password to the principal's computer. Pretty sure that's hacking."

She paused. "I'm also pretty sure I shouldn't have said anything to you about that."

"I didn't hear a thing. I'm not calling to get on to you about trying to do your job, Mindy. I'm calling because I need to know if there are any other students who have had a number of unexplained absences."

"Right. You know, I was almost ready to walk out the door when you called." She paused, as if she were waiting for Freya to apologize. When Freya didn't, she continued. "Luckily, I can see that information without having to get into his account. Each morning, all the teachers fill out an online form, and it compiles into a master form so I can easily click through and get the information I need. Give me just a minute. Let me think about it."

Before Freya could respond, there was a soft *boop*, then classical hold music filled her car.

"Great." Freya gassed it through the green light, grateful she'd called instead of swinging by the elementary school unannounced. If she'd missed Mindy, then this would have all been put off until the morning.

And there just wasn't time to wait.

"Okay, this is weird." Mindy's voice was so loud that Freya jumped.

"What's weird?"

"We have a number of students who have been out for a few days, and they all began their absences on the same day."

Freya's grip on the steering wheel slipped. She took a deep breath, trying to clear her head as she worked through what Mindy was saying. "Can you give me their names? And ages? And I need information on their parents too. Where they live. Where I can find them."

A pause, then a heavy sigh. When Mindy spoke again, her words were slow, careful. "Captain, I want to help you, I do, but I don't want to lose my job. You have to understand that this is all I have. I called you about Sophia because she'd been gone so many days that I was legally responsible for getting the police involved. But what if I give you this information and then I get in trouble? I'm not legally required to give you their names yet. When Principal Frank gets back—"

"I don't think you need to worry about that. Listen, Mindy, the information you've given me so far is invaluable, but I need more. I need to know who these little girls are."

Silence. It lasted so long that Freya got worried they'd been disconnected. When Mindy did speak again, there was a tremble in her voice.

"How did you know they were all little girls that were missing?"

"Lucky guess." She inhaled. Held the breath. Exhaled. "Mindy, what do I need to do or say to ensure that you'll give me this information? These girls might be in danger, and I know you don't want that. Your job is important, and I get that, but don't they deserve to be safe? Sometimes doing the right thing can be scary. I get that. I don't want you to feel pressured, but I need those names. We don't need to wait for you to get permission, right? You can make this decision on your own."

"Yeah, no pressure there." The woman choked out a laugh. "Let me... You know what? Let me sleep on it, okay? I'll get back to you in the morning. I'll know by then what I think I should do. I'm sorry, Captain. I really am. But I don't know what to do, and I don't want to do the wrong thing. Please don't be mad at me, I just... I don't know what to do." She hung up before Freya could respond.

"No!" Freya slammed her palm down on her dash, the sting in her hand helping her focus. "Does she want a warrant too? I'll just get a stack of them and hand them out like candy." Groaning, she closed her eyes and rubbed her temples. "I don't know where to take this case right now."

She halted at a stop sign, thinking through her options.

After finding Mrs. Frank's address, Candy had gone back to looking for Liz's dad on Facebook but still hadn't been able to pick him out of all the other anonymous James Smiths.

It was time to swing back by and talk to Linda.

When Freya pulled up to the house, the first thing she noticed was that it looked even emptier than before. She turned off her Jeep and hurried up to the front porch. "Mrs. Brown! I need you to come out and talk to me. This is Captain Sinclair from the Fawn Lake Police Department!" The pounding from her fist echoed around her.

No response.

Stepping back from the door, she looked at the windows, but the curtains didn't move. If there was someone in the house, they were being perfectly quiet, making sure she couldn't tell they were there. Inspired, she walked over to the window and cupped her hands around her eyes to peer inside.

It was difficult to see past the curtains, but Freya let her eyes adjust. A sagging sofa sat opposite the window she stared into, the coffee table in front of it loaded with plants. Some of them were ones she recognized—an African violet, some type of fern —but others she'd never seen before.

There were also glass bottles and jars on the table. A few of them were empty, but most were full. Freya squinted, trying to make out what was in them.

Spices? Herbs?

To the right of the sofa was a stack of books, but no matter how hard she tried, Freya couldn't read the titles on the spines. More glass jars sat by the stack. The bookcase on the other side of the sofa was groaning with books and knickknacks. She could make out some crystals, a few more plants, more bottles.

A battered rug, a stack of CDs in jewel cases. But that was it.

Nobody was there, no lights were on, there wasn't even a TV left blaring to make people think someone was inside. It was a ghost house, and Freya stepped back from the window, anger making it difficult for her to think straight.

Something terrible was happening to the little girls in Fawn Lake. There had to be something that tied them all together. Some public school kids, one in homeschool, one that had just moved to the area. There was a link. She knew it.

What could it be that tied all the girls together? She ran a hand through her curls as she thought, then scuffed her toe into the ground. There was a small rock there and she kicked it, watching as it bounced off.

Like a ball.

Like a *soccer* ball.

Her heart started beating faster. Isa played soccer. She yanked her phone from her pocket and checked the photo she'd taken of Liz. The little girl was in a jersey, a grin on her face, standing in front of a soccer goal. And hadn't she seen a small pair of cleats by the door when she entered the Jernigan home? She had. She was sure of it.

Someone was coaching that soccer team. She had to find out who it was.

She glanced at her watch. How long ago had she hung up with Mindy?

There was a very good chance she was still at the school. Freya had to find out.

TWENTY-FIVE

Fawn Lake Elementary's front door wasn't locked even though most of the lights in the building were off. Freya jerked it open and walked in, the desire to find Mindy driving her forward.

Her shoes squeaked on the freshly mopped tile as she made her way to the front office. The air smelled like antiseptic, and she rubbed her nose. Dark classroom windows stared at her as she passed them. Schools felt strange without kids running through them. Haunted. Liminal.

The front desk was empty, but there was a little bell to ring for service, and she tapped it. Leaning forward over the desk, she looked at the doors behind it, trying to tell if any of them were open. Three were closed but one at the end was open with a light on. She drummed her fingers on the desk, then rang the bell again.

"I'm coming! Hold your horses, nothing—can be that big of a deal. The day is done, and I just want to go home." A woman's voice came from the final room with the open door, and a moment later she walked out. *Mindy.* As soon as the woman was just a few feet away, Freya could easily see her nametag.

"Mindy," she said, smiling at the woman as she approached.

"I'm Captain Sinclair. Rather than trying to come to an agreement on the phone, I figured it would be a much better idea for me to come see you in person."

Mindy froze. She had on black dress pants and a gray cardigan, and her fingers found the bottom edge of it. Her red reading glasses were propped on top of her head, blonde hair with dark roots pulled into a messy bun.

"Captain," she finally said, swallowing hard like it was difficult for her to speak. "What a surprise. I wish you'd told me you were going to be coming. How did you get in?"

"Front door was still unlocked." Freya shrugged. "Don't worry, Mindy, this isn't an inconvenience for me. I was in the area and thought I'd just swing by and get the information on those students who haven't been in school."

"Of course." A long exhale and she reached out, resting a hand on the desk between them. "You just have to understand that our students have a right to privacy. And as I explained to you, I can't lose my job." She choked on the words.

"I understand, and I don't want you to lose your job, but this is bigger than both of those things. Mandatory reporting doesn't only extend to when students have missed a certain number of days, does it?" No response. "Fine. Do you know why the principal and his brother have both disappeared?"

Mindy shook her head. "Like I told you, they're visiting their mother. Her cancer took a turn for the worse."

"Funny, I went and saw her and she was feeling good enough to spit on the porch between the two of us." When Mindy didn't say anything, Freya continued. "Do people know that you're in on the secret that there's a pedophile working at the elementary school? Or is that something you thought you were going to be able to keep hidden?"

"Keep your voice down." Mindy looked past her, her eyes darting left to right. "Do you not realize that I'm the only person here running the show? Why do you feel like you can come in here and ruin everything?"

"Oh, I'm not the one protecting him. And I'm not the one refusing to work with the police." Freya grinned. Mindy was on thin ice and they both knew it.

"Everything alright, Mindy?" A man's voice from behind Freya made both her and Mindy turn to look. The owner of the voice was younger, with a nice beard, and a whistle hanging from his hand. He twirled it as he waited for a response.

"Jerry, hi. Yep, everything is fine." Mindy forced a chuckle. "Nothing to see here."

"Just that it's not very often the police stop by the elementary school." He caught his whistle and shoved it in his pocket. "Hey, I know who you are." He pointed at Freya. "You're that cop who got shot and left town. I'm shocked you came back."

"We were just going to talk in that office back there," Freya said, jerking a thumb over her shoulder. "Have a nice day." Without waiting for Mindy to respond, she went around the desk and took the woman by the arm, leading her away from the PE teacher. "Hey, who coaches the soccer team?"

Mindy tripped, but Freya had a tight grip on her arm. "That would be John Frank."

Freya's heart sank. "Of course he does. Is there a second in command in case he goes missing and can't make a practice?"

Mindy shook her head. "I've helped out once or twice, but I'm not great at it. You definitely don't want me on your team."

Freya didn't laugh, and she didn't slow down until they were both in the last room and Mindy had closed the door.

A circular table sat in the middle of the room with plush chairs tucked in around it. In one corner was a vending machine full of snacks, and next to it, on another table, sat a stainless steel espresso machine. It was surrounded by mugs and to-go cups, pump bottles of syrups, and canisters of ground espresso. The whole room smelled like a fancy coffee shop.

"Nice teacher's lounge," Freya said. "Did our taxes pay for that fancy espresso machine?"

Mindy shot her a glare. "Okay, you wanted to talk to me. Talk."

"We have some missing girls as well as one dead one," Freya said. "Something terrible is going on, and you're not playing ball. Now, you give me names and photographs of any girl who hasn't been at school in a few days and I'll walk out of here, no harm, no foul. If you don't though, I'll get a warrant. How are people in town going to feel when they realize you were hindering an investigation? Your principal fled and you're the one left here for everyone to direct their anger at. Don't cross me on this, Mindy."

Mindy swallowed. Her fingers found the edge of her cardigan again, and she twisted it hard, stretching the fabric out as she thought. "I could get in trouble if I help you."

"You're already in more trouble than you realize. Trust me, you want a friend in this."

"And you're going to be that friend?" Mindy stopped yanking on her cardigan and looked Freya right in the eyes.

"Right now I'm not your friend," Freya told her. "But if you work with me, I won't be your enemy. That's as good as you're going to get, but the offer is off the table in..." She looked at her watch. "Five minutes. I'm sure you have a nice printer here that can handle spitting out all the information I need without any problem."

Mindy sighed. She leaned forward, planting her hand on the table between the two of them. "You need to come back with a warrant."

"I can do that." Freya stared at her, looking for any cracks, any weakness. Mindy squinted, her mouth pursed. She'd obviously found her hill and was willing to die on it. "Should I bring a news crew too, or do you want that to come later?"

Mindy stared at her, but Freya didn't blink. It was only

when Freya sighed and pulled her phone from her pocket that the other woman nodded. Her mouth was a straight line, and her cheeks were bright red.

"You need to leave. You're not welcome here, and you're trespassing. You can't just... you can't just walk into a school like you did. It's illegal." Mindy clenched both hands into fists.

Freya ignored her; pressed call. "Hey, Candy. I need you to get another warrant—this one for records from the elementary school. I need information on every girl who's been absent for the past month, how many days they've been absent, and contact information for their parents. Oh, and photos of them. Explain to McMurray that we have reason to believe the girls are in clear and present danger." She listened for a moment, then nodded. "Great, thanks." She hung up and slid her phone back into her pocket. "Lead the way, Mindy, and I'll be out of your hair. Oh, and who's been cleaning this place with John Frank running away from his problems? Smells like a hospital, and I could probably eat off the floor."

"I did it." Mindy straightened up. "Someone had to step up, had to take care of things. It wasn't Steven's fault his brother messed up."

Freya stared at her. "You knew something and you didn't say something. That's why you step up to help the soccer team when John's not available, isn't it? Don't want anyone knowing just how close he gets to the kids, do you?" Mindy didn't respond. "I'm going to find these girls, Mindy. And then I'm coming for anyone who let them down." She took in the woman's pleading eyes, her red cheeks. "There isn't ever a good reason for you to overlook someone hurting little kids."

Just as Freya turned to leave, the other woman spoke. "Please." She grabbed Freya's arm. "Please, you don't understand."

"Explain it."

A heavy sigh. Mindy closed her eyes and took a deep breath, then gave her head a shake. "I love him."

"Who, John?"

"No, his brother. Steven. I found out about John's past when he applied for the job, but Steven asked me to overlook it. Told me his brother was different, had changed, wasn't like that anymore. I love him, and I did what he asked."

"Does he love you?" When Mindy didn't respond, Freya continued. "Steven. Does he love you, or has he been stringing you along so you'd do what he needed you to?"

Mindy opened her mouth but then snapped it shut. She gave her head a little shake. "I'm sorry," she said, her voice small. "I did what I thought I needed to because I thought he loved me."

"Look at this." Freya pulled her phone back out and swiped to find the unedited picture of the dead little girl. She enlarged the photo, making sure Mindy would be able to see all the grotesque details.

Her missing eyelids. Her blue lips. The way her skin had taken on a gray hue.

Then she turned the phone for Mindy to see. The woman gasped, her hand on her chest. She shook her head but didn't look away from the screen.

"That's what I'm trying to avoid. That right there. This is what happens when people fail kids. They die terrible, awful deaths." A pause, while Mindy wiped a tear from her eyes. "Is this what you want?"

"I'm sorry." The woman took a shuddering breath. "I didn't... I wouldn't hurt them."

"You better hope that none of the girls from your school turn up like this. If you refuse to give me their information and they die, I'll come knocking."

Mindy nodded, suddenly cowed. "You're getting a warrant for their information?"

"I am. I'll be back. For all the information on the little girls and to talk to you. You better think about how much more you're willing to do for a man who doesn't love you, who's willing to ask you to put kids in danger for him. Decide if you want to be that person. I can't force you to give me information on the girls now, but when I get back, you won't have a choice." Freya clicked off her phone's screen and slipped it into her pocket. "This is your last chance to help me out. Do you want to make things easy?"

Mindy shook her head. Her eyes were squeezed tight, and she'd balled her hands into fists.

"Fine. I'll be back."

Mindy nodded at that, the movement small.

Anger rushed through Freya, and she turned and hurried out of the school, already dialing Candy, who picked up on the first ring.

"The girls all played soccer," Freya said, hopping into her Jeep. "And guess who coached them?"

Candy sighed. "John Frank."

"The one and only," she confirmed. "Any hits on the BOLO on his vehicle?"

"Not yet. The Bertmont cops are hunting him down though. They'll find him, Freya."

Freya didn't respond. She couldn't. Instead, she stabbed at her phone then started her Jeep, gassing it as she tore out of the elementary school parking lot.

There was only one thing for her to do while she was at a dead end. It was the same thing she'd done in high school when she was overwhelmed, when her parents had abandoned her and she'd moved in with Esther. It was the same thing she'd done after she'd made such a huge mistake arresting the wrong people for a heinous crime.

Her tires threw gravel as she yanked the wheel and turned around in the parking lot. This time, instead of heading back to the office to beat her head against the wall, she drove towards the forest.

"Into the woods I go," she muttered to herself, pressing down harder on the gas. Her Jeep ate up the road, and she gripped the steering wheel tight, keeping her eyes locked ahead of her.

There weren't any clues in town to help her figure out what was going on with the missing girls. But the forest? That was where this all started. That's where she had to go.

TWENTY-SIX

It was the right thing to do, to take care of problems, to make the world a better place.

But that woman detective wouldn't keep her nose out of things. She was walking through the woods now, her pace slow and measured, like she wasn't in a race against time, like she didn't need to hurry up if she was going to stop what was already in motion.

The leader watched her. Watched Freya as she tucked an errant curl behind her ear. Watched her as she stepped over a root, careful not to catch her toe so she didn't fall forward.

They watched. And waited. And thought about what to do next.

TWENTY-SEVEN

The woods here were a special kind, thick and overgrown, with tall trees spreading their branches wide above the ground, creating a canopy that seemed to constantly drip water. The first time Freya had heard the forest here was a temperate rainforest, she'd laughed, but it made sense now.

She'd had to consult a map to get her bearings to head to Lake Everett, but now her feet remembered the way. Pine needles cushioned the sound of her footsteps. From time to time, she had to step up over a root, but she moved on autopilot, working her way deeper into the woods.

In half a mile, she'd reach a clearing where the lake was. Although Freya wasn't entirely sure what she wanted to do once she reached it, she knew she needed to see it. Needed to see where the photo of Sophia had been taken, where the little girl had stood in the water.

And then? Once she was sure there weren't any ghosts lingering around the lake? She'd disappear back into the woods.

Something terrible was going on in her town. She had to stop it.

Birds fluttered and sang overhead, and the smell of honeysuckle sweetened the air. Bright, glossy leaves of poison ivy grew wide as the vines worked their ways up the trees, covering them in a green blanket. On the ground, ferns grew, unfurling slowly, a soft green carpet. The sky overhead was already growing dark, thick clouds bunching and gathering off to the west. It was too early for night to fall, but she'd seen something earlier in the day about a bad storm moving in.

But she ignored most of it. She was on a mission. Completely focused.

After a while, the woods opened up ahead of her, and she stepped out into a clearing. A brisk wind blew across the surface of Lake Everett, bringing with it a chill that made her wrap her arms around herself. Even though the sun beat down on her, it was always cooler in the woods and by a lake.

The lake itself wasn't the biggest in the forest, but it was deep, and large enough for stand-up paddleboarding. Someone was out in the middle of the lake, their bright-orange paddleboard catching her eye. She ignored them and walked around the edge of the lake, constantly scanning for the remains of the rock wall.

When she saw it, she stopped, her hands clenching into fists. Right here was where that picture of Sophia was taken. The little girl had been a few feet out in the water, eyes locked on the person standing on shore. She turned in a slow circle like she expected to see someone there with her.

It had to just be her imagination. The woods have eyes, everyone knows that, but those eyes aren't always human. Birds, squirrels, even deer could all be watching her from the safety of the woods, standing far enough back in the shadows that she couldn't see them.

It still felt like something was watching her.

Something. Or *someone*.

Freya turned back to the lake. "Nothing to see here," she muttered. "What, did you think you'd find ghosts? Some evidence that something terrible happened here?" She gave her head a shake to clear it, then looped around the lake. She'd make it back to the gravel lot where she left her Jeep, but there was no rush. She planned to go the long way around, to walk next to the river.

Since walking into the forest, she still felt eyes on her. Goosebumps broke out all over her arms, and she resisted the urge to look around her. It was chilly. A storm was coming. There wasn't any reason to assume someone was actually watching her.

What would they want with her?

She scoffed, the sound loud in the silence. The path she was on was narrow from disuse. Plants encroached on both sides, vying for more room to grow. She brushed through ferns and poison ivy but didn't slow down. Up ahead of her, the path would reach the river. She'd walk along it for a mile or so, then finally be back at her Jeep.

Nothing to worry about.

At first, the sound of the water was too faint to hear, but with each step she took, it grew louder. Pretty soon, she could hear it crashing over river rocks and gurgling through brush. A few minutes later, she was standing at the edge, looking down at the river. The dirt under her shoes fell away to the water, cascading five or six feet before disappearing into the river, but farther downstream that changed. There were plenty of places along the river where the water lapped right up against the ground, making it an ideal spot for animals to come drink.

She walked to one of those spots, taking in the different types of prints. She immediately recognized raccoon tracks, which looked like baby's hands. Deer prints and something too large to be a coyote were also there.

Walking faster now, she kept one eye on the path ahead of her and one on the river. The closer she got to the gravel lot where she parked, the better defined the path was. Now the plants were beaten back a bit more and she didn't have to pay as much attention to where she was stepping.

The path and river turned to the left, and Freya looked down at the water. She was drawn to it, to the way it reflected the little bit of fading sunshine that worked its way through the thick trees and made it sparkle, to the way the water foamed white when it eddied against a rock.

Then something caught her eye. Something pink, down in the mud by the water. Wet fabric in a pile made her freeze. Her right hand drifted down to grab her gun, but she didn't pull it.

It was too small to be an elementary school girl. Much too small.

But could it be a baby?

TWENTY-EIGHT

Freya slipped in the mud, falling down and sliding the rest of the way to the water. Her heart pounded and her head hurt as she picked her way over some fallen branches to get closer to the thing on the ground.

Pink fabric. Lace. She leaned closer. It had been here a while, mud splashed up on it, what looked like hair spreading out like a spiderweb in the muck.

Her breath caught in her throat. Turning, she broke a stick off the branch behind her and lifted the fabric. The thought that it could be a baby, that someone had brought a baby out here and then left it, that she could be the one to find a dead—

It was a doll. The head lolled back, one eye springing open. The other was glued shut with mud, a smear of it across the porcelain cheek, one hand cracked like someone had stepped on it.

"Thank God," Freya murmured, pulling her phone from her pocket to snap a few pictures. She managed to get some from all angles, then checked again to see if she had service. The thought was laughable, and she wasn't surprised to find that she didn't have any bars. "At least it's just a doll. A stupid doll. But who would bring it out here?"

She opened the voice recorder app on her phone. "The doll is about three feet from the water's edge. Given its current condition and how muddy it is, it appears like it's been here for a while." She stood, looking around her. "There aren't any other signs of someone being in the woods. It's entirely possible it was dropped here by a family who was out hiking, but given the missing girls we're dealing with, I'm worried it might be connected to them."

She pressed the red button to end the recording but didn't put her phone away. What she should do is get back up on the trail and return to the department. It wouldn't be a bad idea to have a team come out here and sweep the woods in case there was a clue here that she was missing.

But it would take her a long time to hike back to her Jeep and even longer to make it into town. By then, night would have crept even closer, the storm would be inching towards the forest, and any clues that might still be left behind would be well on their way to being lost. Torn, she looked up at the path. She could run. She could push herself, but what if she returned too late?

Resolute now, she turned her attention back to the river. She would walk along its bank here for a bit, then scramble back up to the trail when the undergrowth got too thick. It wasn't ideal, but it was better than nothing. If she had a plastic bag in her pocket, she'd pick up the doll, but taking the pictures like she did would have to be enough for a while.

At least until she got back out here.

Having given up on the idea of leaving, Freya picked her way carefully along the riverbank, looking not only on the side she was walking on but across the river as well. The water was low but would swell later, and she didn't want to miss anything.

In some areas, large rocks stuck up out of the water, their tops covered with moss.

She looked away from them, walked a few paces, then swept her gaze across the river.

Once, a plastic Coke bottle bobbed by, and she fished it out, slipping it into her pocket to throw away later.

Five minutes later, she was being eaten alive. She slapped mosquitoes that landed on her forehead and swore as one bit the back of her neck. Just a few more feet and she'd climb up the incline to the trail. It would be harder to keep an eye on the river from there, but it would be easier going.

"Almost there," she whispered to herself, stopping by a fallen tree to rest. The rough bark bit into her hand, but she gripped it tight, leaning against it to take some of the weight off her hip. Another mosquito whined in her ear, and she jerked her head to the side as she slapped it.

Something caught her eye. Leaning forward, she squinted.

There, in the river. Up against a mess of sticks that had snarled on a rock. It was a dark spot, right under an old oak tree, and the dancing water made it hard for her to tell what she was looking at. If she'd been up on the trail, there's no way she would have been able to see something there in the water.

Letting go of the tree, she stumbled forward, barely paying attention to the cold water as it flowed in her boots. It immediately soaked her socks and began to wick up her pants. Freya didn't look down as she snagged her toe on a flat river rock. Wheeling her arms, she stepped forward, catching her balance on a boulder.

But she never took her eyes off what was in the water.

As she drew closer, she saw gossamer threads spread out from the shadow. They were pale, and long, thin lines of thread that reflected the light and almost seemed to glow.

She reached for them but yanked her hand back at the last minute. They swirled in the water, tangled in the current, some of them wrapping around a piece of wood sticking up from the bottom of the river.

Her shirt was tucked into her pants and water seeped up it, the fabric clinging to her skin. She shivered but couldn't tear her eyes away from what was caught up in the river. The water bubbled around it, foaming a bit in the hair.

Because that's what they were, the long strands in the water. As much as she didn't want to admit it to herself, didn't want to see what the threads were.

Hair. And clothes. And there, sticking up from the water like a twisted branch, white and gnarled, a hand.

It was small. With painted-pink nails.

TWENTY-NINE

A fine mist had started. The air was heavy and humid. Small drops of water started breaking through the mist as the storm crept up. A howl of wind cut through the woods, making the trees sway with it, their branches rubbing together in an unholy symphony. It had been an hour since Freya found the body in the water and now the scene crawled with cops and paramedics.

"Quite the find," a voice to her left said. Freya whipped around to see who was talking to her but then relaxed. Lance Jones towered over her and pushed his glasses up on his nose while waiting for her to respond.

Built like a brick house, Lance had bright-red hair that led to some people in town calling him The Leprechaun. But never to his face.

"If I'd gotten back up on the main trail, I don't think I would have seen her."

He shook his head. "Probably not. And then she might have gotten dislodged from the sticks and swept downstream with this upcoming storm. I'm going to have her taken right to the morgue so I can get to work tonight." He paused, glancing out into the water where the men were slowly extracting the body from the river. "Is she your missing girl?"

"Which one are you talking about? Sophia? No, her hair doesn't match. Isa has blonde hair, but this girl doesn't look like her, and Liz is a redhead, so it's not her." Anger and fear laced her words, and she shook her head. "But there are other girls I'm worried about, and the school wouldn't give me information on them, so I'm not entirely sure what I'm looking for." Frustration rushed through her at the memory of how Mindy had waffled, and at how unwilling she'd been to be helpful until she returned with a warrant. She was scared for her job, but why couldn't she be scared for the girls? "This has spiraled out of control."

"You'll get it back under control." Lance sounded sure of himself.

Freya turned to Candy. "Any word on the warrant for the elementary school?"

"Magistrate is reviewing it. Knowing McMurray, you probably won't get it until the morning and can show up bright and early to talk to Mindy." Candy gave Freya a firm nod.

"Good. Thank you."

"You'll need to hurry," Candy said. "Not because I know you really want more pressure on you to solve this case, but summer break is coming up in a couple weeks. As soon as the kids are out of school, then families will disappear all across the country for vacation. If there are more little girls missing, it'll be almost impossible to tell for sure until they get back in the fall for school and they don't have their kids with them."

"Wonderful." Ignoring the pit growing in her stomach, Freya turned back to Lance. "How long do you need with the body before I can get some answers?"

"You know as well as I do that answers take time, and if she's like the first girl you found, there may not be any evidence to speak of." He glanced at her, then took her by the elbow to pull her out of the way. The men carrying the girl's body walked past them to a waiting body bag.

The thick black plastic opened like a maw, and Freya watched as they carefully laid her in it and then zipped up the bag.

She was young. Too young to be left out here in the woods without her family. Freya was terrible with ages but thought she looked about the same age as Marla. Dressed in a white dress, with a white hair ribbon still holding back some of her hair, it would be easy to pretend the little girl was sleeping.

Freya wanted to pretend the girl was on her way to a party, dressed like that. The wet dress clung to her body, showing how skinny she was, how her knees jutted out. The contrast of the dress with the dark woods, the tangles of briars, and the thick carpet of dead leaves made her head spin.

Overhead, trees stretched towards the sky. Looking up at them allowed her to see their limbs, how they twisted and grasped for the light, how the leaves spread a canopy over them, thick enough to block out the last of the dim sunlight but not thick enough to act as an umbrella.

Large raindrops pattered against the black plastic, but the girl was protected now.

"And you know as well as I do that little girls don't just go missing. They don't end up in the river all alone, washed up, dead, without someone worrying about them. At least, that's how it's supposed to go. Why don't we have anyone frantically calling to let us know that something happened to their daughter?"

Lance shook his head, then lightly touched Freya on the shoulder. "Finding out the answer to that is your problem. I'll get you all the information I can on this little girl, okay? But you need to give me some time to take care of it. Come see me in the morning." He nodded at Candy as a goodbye, then left the two women there, following the black body bag as it was carried down the trail.

"How are you holding up?" Candy spoke first but only after the body bag had disappeared. The two detectives were alone now, the photographs taken, the baby doll she'd found bagged as evidence. What had happened here in the forest was a mystery, and it was up to them to determine what it was.

"Terrible." Freya rubbed her eyes with the back of her hand and pulled her phone out of her pocket to flip through the pictures of the missing girls. "I keep looking at these, but this girl is not one of them. What the hell is going on around here? Why now? Why these little girls? None of this makes any sense."

Candy grabbed Freya. "You know better than anyone that crimes like this don't make sense. Killers don't make sense. But I'm more worried about you, okay? Stumbling on that by yourself? I don't know that I could have handled it very well. It's one thing to see a dead body when someone overdosed or got shot, or something like that, but a little kid? Kids never do anything to deserve dying like that. They just want to be loved."

"You don't have to tell me that." Freya forced a smile. "Seriously, though, I'm fine. I need to pop a Tylenol for my hip and crash. I'll get the warrant in the morning and talk to Mindy ASAP. Lance won't have anything for me tonight. Anyway, he told me to come by in the morning. I'll visit Mindy first to give him a little extra time so he doesn't feel pressured and get grumpy."

Candy laughed. The sound felt wrong in the stillness of the forest. "I think a little grumpy might be his default, honestly. But he's really good at his job. You know as well as I do that he'll get this taken care of in no time flat."

"I do." Freya turned and made her way up the bank to the trail. "And you know what that means, don't you?"

"What?" Candy puffed a little as she appeared at Freya's side.

"That we need to get our butts in gear. He's on top of this. We have to be too."

"But we are. It's not our fault that every single time we turn around, we've reached a dead end. Nobody could have predicted something like this happening."

A fat raindrop hit Freya on the top of the head. The two women were silent as they hiked along the path. When they reached their vehicles and made it back into cell service, their phones both pinged.

"Good news or bad news?" Freya said as they both pulled out their phones. It was raining harder now, but they stood at the edge of the woods, thick pine branches offering some protection.

"Ooh, the Bertmont police served our warrant. Looks like John and Steven are headed to jail." Candy's cheeks were bright with excitement.

"Go. Now." Freya took in her detective, her dirty boots, her wrinkled clothing. They both needed a good night's sleep, but if the two men posted bail and got out tonight, they'd be in the wind. "Don't let them get away without talking to them."

"On it. First I'll call over there to let the Bertmont police know I'm on my way so they can drag their feet a little, make sure the two of them are still there when I get there. I'll talk to them both, then handle their extraditions, get them moved to Fawn Lake. Don't worry—the two of them aren't going anywhere." Candy shoved her phone into her pocket. "I'll grab a room there tonight, if you think that's okay."

"More than okay. You handle them, Candy. I'll handle Lance and Mindy." Her eyes burned from exhaustion.

"We've got this." Candy threw Freya a wave and headed towards her car.

"We do." Freya's Jeep lights flashed when she pushed the

unlock button. The lights were bright in the gloom. "Drive safe. We're going to show everyone in Fawn Lake what happens when people turn their back on kids in need."

Candy kicked a stick out of the way. "Which is?"

"The kids die. And I come for the person who refused to help them out."

THIRTY

THURSDAY

Freshly printed information on a dozen girls in the kindergarten class sat on Freya's passenger seat, along with a list of all the girls on the Fawn Lake Elementary School soccer team. She'd been at the elementary school since 6 a.m. waiting for Mindy to arrive, had served her with the warrant, and gotten what she needed. She'd barely flipped through them before hopping back in her Jeep to see Lance.

The Fawn Lake hospital was a ten-minute drive from the elementary school, but she could make it in seven if she was really pushing it. After parking close to the back of the lot, she checked her phone for any messages from Candy or Chief, then hustled inside, the sun just barely lighting up the sky to the east.

Automatic doors hissed open, and she paused for a moment, blinking in the fluorescent lights, before reorienting herself. It was her first visit to the hospital since arriving back in town. The nurses at the front desk glanced at her when she walked in, but she didn't stop to chat. Instead of heading towards the main elevators that would take her to patient rooms, she veered off to the right and hurried down a staircase to the morgue.

Most of the patients and their families walking by this door had no idea what was behind it. When Lance Jones had been hired as the ME, a sign had been placed over the door proudly announcing his location. He'd taken it down the next day, thrown it out with the hazardous waste, and the hospital didn't replace it.

Soft classical music reached her ears as she entered the morgue door at the bottom of the stairs. She stopped long enough to don a paper gown and tuck her curls under a cap, then quickly snapped on rubber gloves and walked over to where Lance was standing by an examination table, wearing a matching white robe, a clipboard held in his hand.

"I wondered how fast you'd get here." Lance smiled, the corners of his eyes crinkling. "I had a pretty good feeling you wouldn't be dragging your feet this morning."

"I knew seven thirty wouldn't be too early for you, and I would have been here earlier, but I had to stop by the elementary school first. Please tell me you have something."

"Oh, I have things, alright, but none of them are good." He swept the white sheet off the body on the mortuary table. It was the first time Freya had gotten a really good look at the girl she'd found in the river, and the sight of her made her stomach drop.

"How old do you think she is?" She didn't realize she was moving until she was standing across from Lance.

The ME flipped a page on his clipboard. "Five to seven. It's really hard to tell, especially since she's bloated from being in the water. The cold water does help to preserve her body, but it makes some things more difficult. I was able to get fingerprints, but that took a while."

"She fits the age range of the girls I'm looking for," she murmured. "What else?"

"She's been in the water a few days unfortunately. I found water in her lungs consistent with drowning, just like the first girl you brought me. She wasn't assaulted," Lance said, "so that's a relief. I'll know more in the future though. Remember that. Things can still crop up later. And I took X-rays of her teeth of course."

"Great. Thank you. And thank goodness she wasn't assaulted, although that seems a small mercy at this point. So what we have is she's young, she drowned, and all this happened a few days ago?"

"That's what I have for you. I'm going to perform an autopsy to make sure I'm not missing anything, but my part is mostly done. It's up to you to figure out who she is."

"Yeah, I'm working on that." She yanked the papers Mindy had given her at the elementary school out of her back pocket. "Take a look at these with me, will you? I know her features are distorted from being in the river, but we might be able to make a positive ID."

"What do you have?" Lance put down the clipboard and moved around the body to stand next to her.

"I had the elementary school print off the information they had on girls who hadn't shown up to class for a few days. This is them." She flipped through the pictures, holding each one up next to the girl on the table.

None of them matched.

"This is all of them?"

"Well, all of the girls go to the elementary school," Freya said, then stopped herself. "No, that's not right. One little girl is homeschooled." She pulled her phone from her pocket. "I got her photo from mom."

"Good, because there isn't a lot of government oversight in North Carolina, so I don't think you'd be able to easily get a picture of her without mom cooperating." Lance frowned and tugged the sheet back up over the girl's body.

"What do you mean by that?"

"My sister homeschools her kids out by the beach. North Carolina is pretty lax about requirements the parents have to complete in order to homeschool. As far as I know, there aren't

going to be official records beyond that of the homeschool exist-
ing, attendance, and test scores. You could reach out to the
North Carolina Department of Non-Public Education for more
information. They'd be the ones to ask. It's great for parents
who are super involved and aren't afraid to buckle down and get
stuff done, but not so great for kids when their parents don't
care. Those are the kids that slip through the cracks."

"Like Liz." Freya groaned and tucked the papers and phone
back in her pocket. "So unless I can get the homeschooler information directly from the department, I'm out of luck on that
one." Her mind raced. Could the first girl be homeschooled? It
would explain why the school didn't have records of her.

"You're in a rough spot, for sure." Lance crossed his arms
and leveled his gaze at her. "But besides that, my old friend,
how are you? How's Fawn Lake been treating you?"

"You mean besides missing girls, two dead bodies in the
river, someone breaking Esther's window the day I got back, and
Esther falling?" She ticked off the items on her fingers then
shrugged. "So good to be back."

"Are you in your old home? I can't remember if you sold it."

"No, I kept it." She rolled her head. There was so much
tension in her neck she could use a massage but could only
imagine the optics on that one if she took time away from the
case to decompress. The town would have her head. "I didn't
want to deal with listing it and having people wanting to see it
just so they could see where it all went down, you know? The
last thing I wanted was for it to turn into a destination for looky-
loos."

"That's probably smart. If you need help going through
everything or taking stuff to the dump, just let me know. I have a
truck." Lance grinned at her, and her stomach flipped.

Perhaps years ago there could have been something
between the two of them, but not anymore. Not when she was
busy picking up the broken pieces of her life and trying to slot

them all back together. Not when she barely felt like she had her head above water.

"Maybe I'll just burn it down," she joked. "I won't file an insurance claim and pretend it's arson, so it's not like I'd get in trouble, right? I always joked that I'd rather burn it down than go through all the boxes in the basement and attic, and that still holds true."

"I'll bring the marshmallows," Lance responded, throwing her a grin. He clicked his pen and held up his clipboard for her to see. "Anyway, I'm back to it. I'll call you if I find anything you need to know about."

Freya nodded. Suddenly the smell of the morgue was getting to her. She wanted nothing more than to get out of there, to suck down some fresh air, to get away from Lance's watchful eye. Everyone in Fawn Lake knew some of what happened to her, but not very many people knew all the details.

Lance did. Esther. Chief. Candy.

But even though they all knew the truth, that didn't mean she wanted to talk about it. She fled the morgue and the hospital, deciding as she drove away what her next step was going to be.

It was going to be big. And if it didn't drive out the killer, she wasn't sure what would.

THIRTY-ONE

Sophia Jernigan. Isa Matthews. Liz Brown.

Those were the names Freya already knew, and she skimmed right past them as she read through the rest of the list.

Four more names. Four more girls who hadn't been in school. Of course, they hadn't been absent long enough to require a phone call to the police for a welfare check, but a warrant got around that pesky little detail. Just the thought that there might be other girls out there being hurt, away from their families, that there might be something wrong with them, made her heart ache.

Madeleine Travis.

Steffie Rhodes.

Amber VanHorne.

Lena Reid.

In addition to their names and photos, Freya had addresses and contact information for their parents. It would be so much faster to call the families and check in on them one right after the other, but she knew what would happen if she did that and spooked a parent. They'd be in the wind, their kid in tow. She had to get a move on.

Brad picked up on the first ring. "Freya. What can I do for you?"

"I have four names of little girls who are missing from school," she said. "And I'm going to text you information on two of them. The sooner we can get out there and meet the parents and figure out what's going on, the sooner we can keep the girls in Fawn Lake safe. You busy or are you in?"

"Oh, I'm in. Send them to me and I'll head out now."

"Perfect. Hey, make sure to ask if Madeleine's still on the soccer team, okay?"

A pause. "You got it."

She hung up without saying goodbye and snapped photos of the information for the first two girls, Madeleine and Steffie. After watching her phone to ensure the pictures went through, she plugged Amber's address into her GPS and pulled out of the parking lot.

The town of Fawn Lake wasn't huge, but her destination was twenty minutes away, taking mostly backroads, and she rolled down the window as she drove. Just when she was about to curse her GPS for getting her lost, she pulled up to a small single wide trailer. It balanced precariously on cinderblocks, the entire thing leaning to the side just a bit. The gentle tilt made it look like it could come crashing down in a strong wind.

Freya parked and walked up to the trailer. She carefully stepped up the three cinderblock steps, then rapped on the door before turning and standing in the yard to wait.

One minute passed before the door swung open. A thin woman wearing a pair of leggings and an oversized T-shirt stepped out. Her hair was in a high bun, her face free of makeup. She had deep circles under her eyes and rubbed her face before finally speaking.

"Hi. Can I help you?" She sounded exhausted.

"I'm Captain Sinclair from the Fawn Lake Police Department," Freya said, stepping closer to offer her hand. "Are you Amber VanHorne's guardian?"

"I'm her mom. Tiffany. What can I do for you? Is something wrong?"

"No, I'm following up on some girls who haven't been in school in a while, and Amber's name is on that list. I just need to talk to her, make sure she's okay, then I'll be on my way."

The woman stared at her. "I don't think that's the best idea, Captain."

Freya felt the hair on the back of her neck stand up. She forced a smile. "It's really not an option." That wasn't exactly the truth. Tiffany could easily refuse to let her inside, then she would have to come back with a warrant. Without Tiffany inviting her in to see Amber, she was stuck.

"Listen." Tiffany walked down the steps, closing the door behind her. "I don't know why this is an issue. Her doctor promised me they'd contact the school, let them know she was going to be out for a while."

Freya frowned. "They obviously didn't do that. Tell me what's going on."

Tiffany sighed, crossed her arms. "She's been sick for a week. Mono. You ever had it?" When Freya shook her head, Tiffany continued. "It's a nightmare, Captain. She feels terrible, has no energy. I'm obviously not working while I take care of her, but I can't even get a good night's sleep, I'm so worried about her. I just sit by her bed listening to make sure she's okay."

That explained why Tiffany looked so tired.

"I'm sorry she's so sick, and I hate to push it, but I just have to see her. I'd like to talk to her, if possible, but at the least, I need to see her."

Tiffany nodded. Sighed. "If that's what it will take for you to leave, I'll do it. No offense, Captain, but I don't want to spend all day standing out here talking to you."

"None taken. Lead the way and I'll get out of your hair, okay?" Freya waited for Tiffany to open the door, then followed her into the trailer.

From the outside, it looked like it was falling in. Inside, however, the trailer was cute. A red gingham tablecloth covered the table. There was a vase of wildflowers on the kitchen counter next to an open box of saltines and some ginger ale.

"She's not really throwing up," Tiffany said, following Freya's gaze. "But she doesn't have an appetite. She's lost so much weight, and her doctor told me this was just how the virus worked, that I needed to keep on top of getting some food in her. She wants crackers, so she gets crackers." She shrugged. "I promise you, she normally eats better than this."

"I'm not here to judge what you're feeding her," Freya promised. She followed Tiffany down the hall to a small room at the end of the trailer. The door was cracked, the light inside turned off.

Tiffany walked in first, scooting around a bed to click on a small lamp. "Hey, Amber," she said, pulling some of the blankets down to speak to her daughter. "You have a visitor. Can you sit up? Say hi?"

The girl grumbled at her mother, and Freya couldn't help but smile. She pulled Amber's photo from her pocket and glanced at it. A moment later, the girl sat up, her hair disheveled, her eyes half-closed, a beauty mark visible on her right cheek.

"Say hi, Amber," Tiffany coaxed.

"Hi," the girl said.

"Hey, Amber," Freya said. Relief rushed through her. She'd been afraid, as much as she hated to admit it, that the girl wouldn't be there, wouldn't be safe. Amber was really sick, that much was obvious, but she was alive, and that was the important thing. Her beauty mark perfectly matched the one on the girl in the photo. "I'm so sorry you're so sick. I bet your mom is taking good care of you."

Amber groaned. "I'm just so tired."

"We're going to let you sleep," Tiffany said, helping her daughter lie back down. She pulled the blankets up around her shoulders before fluffing her blanket. When she clicked off the lamp, Freya turned away from the bed.

"Happy, Captain?" Tiffany sighed and leaned against the wall. "She's fine. Well, sicker than I've ever seen her, but fine."

"I'm sorry I had to make you wake her up," Freya said. "I hope she feels better soon and that you can get some rest."

"Rest will be good." She managed a small smile. "I don't think I was this exhausted when she was born. It's insane."

"I'll get out of your hair," Freya said, walking down the hall through the living room and kitchen. "Just one more thing. Has Amber ever talked about playing soccer at school?"

Tiffany paused, leaning against the wall while she thought. "She talked about it once," she said, speaking slowly, "but loves the flute more. Besides, some of the soccer moms are kind of cliquey." Another pause. "I just want Amber to have fun. She's a kid. But some of the moms demand perfection in every way. They're just... not my type."

"Understandable. Thanks again for letting me bother you."

"Not a bother," Tiffany said. "Well, a bit of one, if I'm honest, but I get why you came by. I'm more frustrated with the doctor's office for not letting the school know Amber's been sick."

They said goodbye and Freya hurried to her car to text Brad.

Amber's sick with mono, but she's safe.

She was just plugging Lena's address into her GPS when Brad responded.

Glad to hear it. Just left Madeleine's house. She's not home. I bet she's still on the team—there was a soccer ball in her yard.

THIRTY-TWO

Freya pulled into Lena's driveway on two wheels. She threw the Jeep into park without stopping all the way, making the vehicle lurch, then ran to the front door.

"Mr. and Mrs. Reid!" she yelled while pounding on the door. The doorbell looked broken, the plastic button cracked, but she mashed it anyway. "Hello? This is Captain Sinclair from the Fawn Lake Police Department!"

Slow footsteps made her step back from the door. Her heart slammed out a dance in her chest, and she gasped for air.

Lena had to be here. She had to be okay.

"What's the fire?" The man who opened the door moved slowly. He was bent, his back tight and painful, and he turned his face to look at her. "Is there a problem?"

"Mr. Reid?" Freya held out her hand. "I'm Captain Sinclair, looking for Lena Reid and her parents."

The man frowned. "I'm sorry, young lady, but there isn't anyone here by that name. I'm Roger Hargrave."

Her heart sank, and she pulled her paper with Lena's address from her pocket. "Isn't this thirty-two Sugar Maple Way?"

He nodded. "Sure is. My wife and I bought the place a month ago."

"From the Reids?"

"I don't remember their name, but my wife would. She's sleeping right now." He peered at Freya. "She hasn't been well." A pause. "Do you need me to get her up?"

"No, I don't want to wake her. But let me ask you one thing —do you remember the family you bought the house from having a daughter?"

"Oh, sure did. Cute little thing. Is that who you were calling for? Lisa?"

"Lena," Freya corrected.

"Lisa. Lena. My memory isn't as great as it used to be unfortunately. But yes, there was a little girl here."

She pulled out the paper with the pictures of the little girls. "Do you recognize her in one of these photos?"

"That one." The man stabbed his finger on Lena's face. "Cute as a button, she was. We ended up making her bedroom into an office. Great natural light. Her mom told me Lena liked to sit by the windows and watch the birds. When she wasn't kicking a soccer ball around, that is."

Her heart sank. The list Mindy had given her had Lena on the soccer team, but Freya had hoped it was a mistake. "Thank you for your help." She was thinking fast. "Hey, do you know if they left a forwarding address for any additional mail got missed in forwarding?

"Not with us, but maybe with the realtor? We both used Sadie Owens. You know who I'm talking about? Her office is right downtown."

"I know exactly who you're talking about," Freya told him. "Thank you so much for your help; I'll get out of your hair now." She threw him a wave and hurried to her Jeep, calling Brad before she backed down the driveway.

"The school has the wrong address for Lena," she said when

he picked up. "But I'm going to swing by the realtor and see if she has a forwarding address. Please tell me Steffie was at home when you got there."

"She wasn't there, and neither was mom. The neighbor I spoke to told me the mom, Kirsty White, asked her to get the mail for a week or so. She actually gave me mom's number and I FaceTimed her. Steffie's just fine—they're in Tennessee for a few days for a wedding. She plays soccer but twisted her ankle a week or so ago. Mom was pretty confused why I was asking."

"At least that's some good news. Freya pulled out of the neighborhood. "So we have two more girls we can't account for?" The light turned red, and she sped through it.

"What do you want me to do now?"

She could hear him start his car, and she waited for the noise to die down. "It's time to dig into the soccer team. I need to know everything there is to know about it. Who runs it when John Frank is out of town, if the other kids on the team are okay. I want to know everything."

"You've got it."

"Reach out to a mom whose kid we've already confirmed is on that team, like maybe Steffie's mom if you think she'll talk to you again. As soon as I get the Reids' address from the realtor, I'm passing it on to you."

"You have a plan."

"I do." She didn't want to think about the plan and how angry Chief would be. She turned onto Main Street and parked right in front of Sadie Owens' office. "And I know this is a lot, but I want you to reach out to the North Carolina Department of Non-Public Education. Lance mentioned something about them, so see if they'll give us information on girls registered to homeschool in Fawn Lake. We need those names, Brad." A pause, while she exhaled. "Okay. I'll be in touch."

The real estate office looked like something out of a magazine. It catered not just to locals looking to move but anyone who thought Fawn Lake sounded like the perfect place to raise a family. Cushy sofas and thick rugs greeted her. When the woman at the front desk waved for her to sit and kept talking on the phone, Freya ignored the direction and leaned on her desk.

The woman frowned, her cheeks pinking as she glanced at Freya.

"You know what? Something's come up. I'll have to call you back." She hung up the phone, straightened some papers on her desk, then looked at Freya. "Can I help you?"

"I need to speak with Sadie Owens."

The woman perked up. "I'm Sadie. Are you looking to buy a house?"

"Looking for information actually." Freya flashed her badge. "I'm Freya Sinclair from the Fawn Lake Police Department. The Reid family moved from thirty-two Sugar Maple Way, and I just need to get their new address."

Sadie was already shaking her head. "I'm sorry, I can't just hand that out."

"Sure you can." Freya smiled. "What if I told you the daughter is missing? Would that inspire you to help?"

Her jaw dropped open, but she still shook her head. "I'm serious, that's not something I can just hand out." A pause. "But I can tell you this—they didn't leave a forwarding address with me."

"Really?"

"I'm serious," Sadie said. "If they had, I wouldn't give it to you, but they didn't. So we're both in the clear."

"Wonderful." Freya drummed on the desk. "That's just great. Thanks." She hurried outside to her Jeep, taking time to move it to the police department. Sadie seemed like the type of person to happily throw a fit over a vehicle taking up a parking spot in front of her business.

On her way into the office, Freya called Candy for an

update on the Frank brothers. While the phone rang, she spritzed some water into Cinnamon's tank, then made a plan.

Candy didn't pick up. The missing girls were piling up. There was one thing to do to help move the investigation along, as much as she hated to do it.

She had no choice.

THIRTY-THREE

"I'd like to thank you all for coming this morning on such short notice. I'm sure you all have a lot to do today, and I know it's hot, so I'll try to be brief." Freya cleared her throat. She was dressed in her Class A uniform, with shiny black shoes and brass buttons up her navy-blue jacket. Wearing it always made her feel like she was going to star in a circus, but Chief wouldn't let anyone have a press conference without dressing up to the nines, no matter how hastily put together it had been.

"I called you all here because there's been a number of children going missing in Fawn Lake." She paused, letting that sink in. The names of the little girls who hadn't been at school in a few days were on a list in her pocket. She and Brad had spent a few hours that morning trying to find the Travis and Reid families but to no avail.

"I'm afraid I can't release names at this time, as we haven't been able to get in touch with all of the families." She felt her face burn as someone with a TV camera stepped closer. She recognized the logo on the side and knew she'd be the number one news story that evening. "But we are asking for help from the community so we can make sure we find these missing girls and bring them all back home, safe and sound."

"What do you want us to do?" The question came from a mousy woman up front. She gripped her reporter's microphone like it was a lifeline and held it out to Freya.

Freya gritted her teeth. "The Fawn Lake Police Department needs your help. If you have neighbors or friends with kids, check in on them. Make sure they're okay. If you have any concerns at all, say, maybe you haven't seen a neighbor's child in a few days, reach out to us. We have officers and detectives working every lead that comes into the department."

She exhaled. Her fingers hurt from gripping the sides of the podium. When she looked up, she caught sight of Chief. He hadn't been in his office when she went to run her plan by him and now he stared at her, the furrows in his brow so deep they looked painful.

"Are you going to say anything about the dead body you found in the river yesterday?" It was the same woman, the corners of her mouth curling into a smile.

Freya gaped at her, then pulled herself together. *How did she know about that?*

"I can assure you that we're working overtime to find out what happened in Clear Creek Forest," Freya said. "As of right now, we have no reason to believe anyone else is in danger, although we always recommend that you're careful and aware of your surroundings when hiking, camping, or swimming. Our department offers pamphlets with information that you can use to ensure you're as safe as possible when in the woods."

"There was another body in the river? When were you going to tell us about this?" A young man, his goatee barely coming in, held up another microphone. He looked worried.

"We can't disclose any additional details without first notifying the family," Freya said, digging her nails into the wood of the podium. "I can assure you, however, that when we have information, we will pass it on."

Someone in the back of the room raised their hand, but she ignored them. "Thank you so much for your time. If you have any information, please contact our department and someone will help you. Have a good rest of your day."

She was fleeing. What was worse, everyone there knew she was fleeing. Their eyes on her felt like accusations as she turned and walked out of the room. It was only after closing the door behind her that she exhaled, sagging against it and closing her eyes.

"There's nothing quite like a press release to bring the crazies out of the woodwork, is there?" Chief's voice interrupted the one moment of calm she'd had all day.

Freya didn't open her eyes when she responded. "You know it. And I know what I'm probably in for now. Everyone will be jumping at shadows. But you know what else? There's also nothing like a press release to get more information and maybe even get the bad guy to mess up."

Chief sighed. Freya heard him lean against the wall next to her. "We could have come up with a better way to handle this if we'd worked together, Sinclair. I wish you'd asked."

"I did ask. Each time I leaned into your empty office and asked your empty desk if you thought it was a good idea, you never responded." A smile played on her lips but quickly disappeared. "That was exhausting. And I want to know who in our department thought it was an okay idea to tell that reporter about the body I found last night. But you know what? My press release is already on the news. People are seeing it. They're questioning the last time they saw the little girls in their lives. Someone is going to come clean on this. Trust me."

"You sound confident."

She kept her eyes closed and took a deep breath. "I'm confident because my team and I are out there working hard to find whoever's hurting these girls. Now that the community knows something's going on, they can keep an eye out too. Getting everyone on the same page is the best option for us right now."

He chuckled. "Well, you certainly know how to get people's attention."

"Thanks." Freya opened her eyes. "I learned from the best. In fact—" The ring of her phone cut her off. "Hang on, maybe this press conference is going to have worked even faster than I thought it would. You owe us all dinner if this call helps us figure out what's going on."

Chief scoffed. "Deal."

She tapped the screen. "Captain Sinclair—how can I help you?" The voice in her ear made her pause, and she looked over at Chief, raising her eyebrows. "Hi, yes, I'm available." She paused again. "Of course I can head over there—just send me the address and I'll go now."

A moment later, she hung up the phone. She tucked it into her pocket and pulled out her keys.

"Who was that?"

She blinked, still trying to wrap her mind around the conversation she'd just had. "That was dispatch. They had a call from Lara Richards, a nanny. She saw the press conference and wants to talk to me."

THIRTY-FOUR

The list of missing girls in Freya's pocket felt like a rock that could weigh her down at any time. She'd gone over it so many times that she had all the names memorized. She could have picked each of the girls out of a crowd at a moment's notice. She was fully prepared for running into them, their parents, or their friends, and yet she still carried their information in her pocket.

Just in case. Just in case her memory failed her or there was a specific detail she wanted to recall. Just in case it took her longer than it should to remember something about one of the girls, or in case she saw a doppelgänger.

Officers were spread out across Fawn Lake, canvassing neighborhoods looking for the missing girls. Brad was in charge of it. He'd divvied up the names of the girls on the soccer team and had officers going door to door. Having an entire team of officers working to find the little girls gave her time to hunt for the killer.

Reaching into her pocket, she fingered the edge of the list of missing girls, then pressed her thumb against the doorbell one more time. The problem with apartment complexes is that it was impossible to tell whose car belonged to who. Lara said she'd be home, so where was she?

"Lara Richards, this is Captain Sinclair. I need to talk to you!" Freya pounded on the closed door with the side of her fist.

"I'm coming!" The voice was faint at first, and Freya had to resist the urge to press her ear up against the door to confirm she hadn't imagined it. "Give me a moment!"

Freya stepped back. A minute later, the door was unlocked, then swung open. In front of her stood a young woman with her hair up in a towel. She had on a hoodie and sweatpants and carried a mug of something steaming.

"I was just getting out of the shower," she said, gesturing behind her into the apartment. "I couldn't get here any faster, not with clothes on, at least. I'm sorry! I thought when I called that you'd be busy and I'd have some time to get clean before you came."

"Not a problem. I'm sorry for almost knocking down your door." Freya smiled to try to put the woman at ease. "I really appreciate you reaching out to me."

"Not a problem. Want to sit?" She gestured at two wrought-iron chairs on the porch.

Only after the two of them were settled did Lara roll her shoulders back and give Freya a nod. "I called about Jessa. Maybe it's nothing; maybe I'm just overreacting."

"I doubt it. It's the people who don't worry about whether or not they're overreacting who are." Freya smiled at her. "Talk to me. There's no judgement here."

"I was Jessa's nanny for three years." She laughed. "I think I use that word loosely."

"Nanny?"

"Yeah. Jennifer Peters, Jessa's mom, didn't want her in public school, so I went from hanging out with a preschooler to acting as her full-time tutor. I know a lot of people wouldn't want the job, but Jessa and I had a blast. She's such a funny kid with a great sense of humor. You know how everyone hates dad jokes because they're so hokey? Jessa loves them! I don't know how she makes stupid jokes actually funny, but she does. And she loves *Star Wars*. I tease her all the time that she's a huge nerd, but I am too, so that's probably why we get along so well."

Freya waited, watching Lara. She looked really young to be a nanny. Then again, some wealthy families paid a small fortune to ensure their kids grew up with a parental figure who wasn't going to leave them. It was entirely possible the Peters family paid out the nose to have Lara nanny their daughter, intending she'd grow up with Jessa.

"Can you tell me why you left the job?"

"Oh, I didn't leave it. Are you kidding? Sure, Jennifer's difficult at best, but the money was great. They sent Jessa to boarding school." Lara shrugged and shoved her free hand into her hoodie pocket.

"But you called me after seeing the press release, so you obviously have some concerns."

Lara took a long sip of her coffee before speaking. "You know, I've met a lot of moms, and they all want things as perfect as possible, right?"

Freya nodded, but it was clear the woman wasn't really talking to her.

"But Jennifer was on an entirely different level. She's a photographer and is absolutely obsessed with perfection. Her shots aren't those artsy ones that you see in magazines. They're posed and perfect and not a single hair is out of place. Everything's... perfect. Shiny. Not a smudge to be seen."

"I bet it was difficult to live up to her standards."

"You better believe it. Poor Jessa just wanted someone to play with her and not fuss when she got dirty, but Jennifer... man, she was a piece of work."

"And the dad?"

"Winston? Oh, just as uptight. He does something with

numbers. Banking maybe? But... international. Don't think for a moment that he's the guy at the bank setting up your account or depositing your check. He's big-time, that guy is. Wanted me to iron his shirts once when I was watching Jessa, so I did, but apparently I did it wrong and he lost it."

"Was he ever violent with Jessa?"

She scoffed. "No, because that would have meant he had to notice that she existed. He was not an involved parent, believe me. Neither of them were, but he was in his own world." A pause. "Maybe that's not entirely fair. Jennifer loved Jessa; I know she did. Or she loved the *idea* of Jessa. She doted but from afar, if that makes sense."

"Did Jessa and Jennifer get along?" Freya felt a sinking feeling in her stomach, and she was pretty sure she already knew the answer to her question.

"Oh, sure when Jessa was good. And not too loud. And didn't act out. And didn't talk back." Lara began counting things off on her fingers. "And when she didn't make a mess, or refuse to finish her meal, or snort when she laughed." She sighed and shoved her hand back into her hoodie pocket. "I swear, sometimes I felt that little girl only got to be a little girl around me. The pressure on her to be perfect? Insane. I would have cracked."

"So when's the last time you saw her?" *Alive.*

Lara blew out a puff of air. "Let's see. Jennifer texted me to let me know that I was no longer needed about a week ago. It was out of the blue really. You know how rich people can be, so capricious. She'd been talking about boarding school for the past month or so after she started hanging out with this new friend. I wish I could tell you her name, but I forgot it. Anyway, she wasn't what I'd consider Jennifer's type. They were definitely a strange fit."

"And you haven't heard from the Peters family since then?"

"Nope." She popped the *P*. "And I really don't care if I do.

So rude honestly. I knew Jennifer and I weren't ever going to be friends, you know? I'm the hired help. But the women she chose as her friends? Definitely not my type anyway. So I got a job working downtown at Harold's. I love being outside and hiking, so I thought it would be kinda fun to help people find the gear they need." She shrugged. "It's not the same as spending all day in the woods, but at least I won't have to deal with a harpy like Jennifer Peters."

"I need to talk to Jennifer. Where do you think I could find her?"

"Like I said, she's not out in the world taking exploratory shots. She has a studio on the outskirts of town. I can't guarantee she'd be there, but that's where I'd look." Lara gave Freya a soft smile. "Do you think Jessa will be okay? Growing up in a house like that. It has to be a ton of pressure on a little kid."

"I have no idea, but I really appreciate you talking to me. Good luck at Harold's. I might see you in there sometime."

"Hey, yeah, I'll look for you. Have a good one." Lara wiggled her fingers at Freya then ducked back into her apartment. Freya listened as she closed and then locked the door before turning and hurrying to her Jeep.

Once inside, with the AC running, she tapped on her phone to wake it up and googled Jennifer Peters and her photography studio, then sent Brad a text to meet her there. He responded immediately confirming. A quick text to Candy asking for an update on the Frank brothers remained unanswered, but she wasn't worried.

Candy was good. She'd handle whatever the Frank brothers threw at her.

All she needed was one break in the case.

And this might be it.

THIRTY-FIVE

Brad pulled into the parking lot of Caught in Time, Jennifer's photography studio, right behind Freya, but she was already waiting for him at the business's front door by the time he got out of his car.

"Ready?" She wiped her brow. The day was hot, the sun beating down on them relentlessly.

"You better believe it. I'm sweating like a—"

"Stop there. What do you say we find out what Mrs. Peters has to say about suddenly deciding to send her daughter to boarding school? There's something here—I can feel it."

"Great. Then I'll check in with the officers canvassing neighborhoods looking for the girls on the soccer team. So far, so good. The four girls we checked up on this morning are the only ones missing from school. Everyone else on the team was there today."

"Good work. Just keep me updated when you get more information." Freya didn't wait for Brad to respond. She had to move.

Stepping inside the studio was like getting hit in the face with an arctic blast. The AC was cranked so high goosebumps broke out on Freya's arms before the door had closed behind the two of them. She rubbed her arms and glanced around her.

The place was immaculate. Immediately in front of them was a sleek black desk, free from any fingerprints. A computer sat open on the desk with a planner next to it, but nothing else was on its surface. Behind it, a high table with a huge vase of red roses drew the eye.

Freya looked around, taking in the black leather sofas, the oval coffee table made of the same slick black material as the desk, and the three doors set throughout the room.

"Door number one, two, or three?" she asked Brad. Without waiting for a response, she walked to the first and knocked, then tried the handle. "Ooh, locked. I wonder what secrets are back there."

"The only secrets are my client portfolios." The voice coming from behind her dripped with ice. "Is there something you need? I'm happy to find a time for you to come back sometime this week."

"That won't be necessary." Freya turned and extended her hand. "Jennifer Peters? I'm Captain Sinclair."

The woman's blue eyes flicked up and down Freya, taking in her duty belt, the way her pants were wrinkled, and the fact that her shoes were scuffed. Even without saying a word, it was clear the woman had passed judgement on her and found her wanting.

"Are you sure you don't need an appointment? I have a stylist I can set you up with before you come for your photoshoot." The woman flicked her slim wrist through the air, her silver bangles jangling. She had a severe black bob cut right to her chin and bright-red lips.

"Officer Williams and I wanted to come talk to you about Jessa."

"Jessa? What's going on? Did something happen?" When

Jennifer Peters frowned, her forehead remained smooth and flawless.

Good Botox.

"There seems to be a rash of missing girls in Fawn Lake," Freya said. Over Jennifer's shoulder, she watched as Brad walked to the desk and looked down at the open appointment book. "Jessa is one of them, in fact. I just finished talking with Lara about her."

"You did what?" Jennifer's jaw dropped. "Why in the world did you feel the need to talk to Lara?"

"It's a long story. Seemed like you and your husband were really happy with Lara as a nanny/teacher until you decided to send Jessa to boarding school. Let's talk about that. Why the change of heart?"

"We let Lara go because she's irresponsible and never met our standards," she sniffed in response. "My husband and I have a certain way we like things done, and Lara just couldn't do what we want. Jessa deserved better. I want her to be perfect. To be clean, not a filthy little thing." She exhaled hard. "We figured there was a better option out there. Jessa deserved better, so we looked for better."

"That's unfortunate."

A long silence. It was long enough that Brad looked up and made eye contact with Freya.

"Not really. We're sending Jessa to boarding school because it's a better fit for her since her father and I both work so much and she's an only child. We value our careers and wanted to ensure Jessa would get the education she deserves. It's hard for that to happen in a town like Fawn Lake. I'm sure you know that first-hand."

Freya ignored the slight. "What boarding school did you send her to?"

"Does it matter?"

"It does when nobody seems to have any idea where she is."

"St. Mary's Preparatory School for Girls. It's the best. I wasn't going to send her somewhere subpar."

"Oh, I haven't heard of that one."

"Do you make it a habit to keep up to date on the names of girls' boarding schools? That's an odd hobby, I must say." Jennifer laughed, then crossed her slim arms, her silver bangles jingling.

"I do when a girl is reported missing." Ignoring the way the woman stared at her, Freya pulled her phone from her pocket. "Let me just look that up."

"It's prestigious. And new." The woman smiled. "In Connecticut."

"Well, I'll be. There is a St. Mary's in Connecticut. Shall we call them, just to check in on Jessa? What do you think?"

"I think that it seems a little extreme to do that when Jessa is happy at school. She's not in danger, Captain, and she's certainly not missing. I know exactly where she is."

"We definitely don't want to be in your way, Mrs. Peters. Do you happen to have a photo of Jessa? I'd love to see what she looks like."

Mrs. Peters smiled and shook her head. "Of my daughter? Of course I do—just hang on."

She turned away, walking behind the desk before pulling out a huge photo album. "I love digital photos because they take up so much less room, but some clients appreciate being able to touch photos, to really see my work up close." She opened the photo album and spun it around to face Freya. "These are all of Jessa."

Jennifer wasn't kidding. Freya flipped through the album quickly, taking in the shots of the girl. In most of them, she was posed in the studio, but there were some more candid shots towards the end.

Jennifer spoke up before Freya could ask about them. "I don't love candid shots, but Winston does, so I snapped some for him. Those are from when Jessa ran track, oh, two years ago? She stopped when she realized running in circles wasn't any fun. She loved going to see her friends play sports before she went to boarding school. She didn't mind watching them play; she'd even make signs with their names to cheer them on."

Freya pulled her phone from her pocket and took a picture of one of Jessa's photos before closing the album and pushing it back towards Jennifer. "Thank for showing me those. They're great shots."

Jennifer flushed. "I pride myself on doing the best possible work I can," she said, walking out from behind her desk to talk to Freya.

"You can tell." Freya glanced at Brad, who was watching their conversation with interest. "We'll get out of your hair, but quick question before we go: Lara mentioned that you'd made some good mom friends."

"Is that a crime?" A perfect eyebrow arched up.

"Not at all. From what I've heard, motherhood is difficult and practically impossible on your own. Anyone I know?"

"I doubt it." Once again, her eyes flicked up and down Freya's outfit.

"Oh, you'd be surprised. I know so many people."

Jennifer shook her head. "I highly doubt you know Hannah Weber. Linda Brown. Or Sharon Ring."

A chill raced up Freya's spine. "Linda?"

"That's right." Jennifer's smile spread. "She's amazing. So supportive—has such a willing ear to listen."

"I'm glad you have such great friends." Freya paused. "You have a good day. I'm sure I'll come back and chat with you some more."

"I will. You may see yourself out, Captain." She turned around, frowning at Brad when she noticed him still behind her desk.

"Great," Freya said, walking to the front door. "You have a good day."

She waited until the door shut behind them before turning to Brad. "Linda Brown and Jennifer Peters have nothing in common with each other. The fact that they're friends?" She shook her head. "I don't buy that for a minute. We need to find these moms."

THIRTY-SIX

Zach was sitting on his front porch when Freya and Brad pulled up. He raised a hand in greeting, then scowled when he recognized her Jeep. No matter, it hadn't ever bothered her when people weren't happy to see her. The most important thing was that she got the information she needed to find Linda and figure out what the connection between her and Jennifer really was.

"Hey, Zach!" Freya called out to him as she and Brad walked towards the front porch. The teenager had already stood up and opened the front door to the house, but he paused when she called out. "I just need to talk to you for one minute, okay! Don't go inside."

"What do you want?" He turned, a deep furrow between his brows. "Why do you keep showing up? Like we told you, Liz is with her dad."

Freya shrugged. "I'm not looking for Liz this time. Is your mom home?"

"She went to work." Zach crossed his arms. "Why?"

"No reason." She wiggled her fingers at him, then she and Brad hurried back to her Jeep. "We're going there now, but if you see her first, let us know," she called out to him from her Jeep.

"Linda works a lot for someone who's supposed to be home-schooling her kids," Brad remarked as Freya tore across town.

"You're telling me. And from what I've seen, Zach doesn't seem like the type of kid to go out of his way to learn on his own."

They pulled up at the gas station. "This place is slammed," Freya said, scanning the parking lot as she got out of the Jeep.

"Check out the tour bus. That's where some of these people are coming from." He pointed at the long tour bus parked off to the side of the gas station. *Family Friendly Tours* was written on the side. The driver leaned against the door smoking a cigarette. He looked bored with the whole thing.

They hurried to the gas station, walking past the crowd of adults standing outside smoking. Freya waved their smoke away and held the door for Brad before walking in behind him.

The gas station was hopping. It was mostly older adults, but there were some younger ones who looked freshly out of college. They were all loading up on snacks, their arms full of chips, candy, and sodas. A line for the bathroom stretched halfway around the gas station, with at least two women crossing their legs and doing a little dance as they waited.

"Looks like the circus came to town," she said, her voice dry. "What a day to try to come talk to Linda. Do you see her?"

Brad was taller than Freya and turned, taking in all of the gas station. It smelled in there, hot and like body odor, and he wrinkled his nose. "There's a man behind the counter, but I don't see her. Zach said she went to work. Would he lie?"

"I'd wager he's a teenage boy more interested in listening to music than what's going on with his family." Freya pushed through the crowd. The floor felt sticky, and she wiped away some sweat beading at her hairline. It was brutally hot in the gas station and that, combined with the stress she felt pushing her to find Linda, made her feel sick.

"He is the poster child for disaffected teens." Brad was looking in the other direction.

Frustration surged through Freya. She pushed past the line of people waiting at the counter and leaned one elbow on it. The man working the register barely glanced at her. "Hey, there's a possibility she's in the back. But if she's not here, he might not have known where she was and just wanted us out of his hair so he said the first thing he could think of. She's..."

"Flighty," Brad finished as Freya cleared her throat to get the clerk's attention.

The man stared at her. Shook his head. "You'll need to go to the back of the line and wait your turn like everyone else, sweetheart."

There was a loud click when Freya yanked her badge from her belt. She slid it across the counter and waited for the clerk to look at it. "Captain Sinclair with the Fawn Lake Police Department," she said, tapping its surface. "I'm looking for Linda Brown. I was told she was here."

"You were told wrong." The clerk turned his full attention on her. "She's not on the schedule for the rest of the week."

Freya frowned. "I need her phone number."

He paused, glanced at the crowd of people behind her, then shrugged. "You know what? I don't get paid enough to tell you no, and if it gets you out of my hair, I'm fine with it. Give me a moment." With that, he turned and lumbered away, exiting through a door behind him. Just a minute later, he returned and handed a yellow sticky note to Freya. "There you go. Is that all you needed?"

"Almost." She slipped the sticky note into her pocket, well aware the man she'd cut in front of was now standing next to her trying his best to be involved in their conversation. "You ever meet Liz? She come by here often with her mom?"

He wrinkled his nose. Shook his head. "I've seen the boy."

"Zach."

"Yeah, Zach. He's come with Linda before on her day off but the girl? No." He frowned, and Freya waited. "You know what? I have seen the girl, but she didn't come in. Waited in the car. I asked Linda about it, and she said it was always dirty in here."

Freya glanced down at the counter. It was covered with smudges and a smear of something that looked like peanut butter.

She *hoped* it was peanut butter.

As much as she hated to admit it, she agreed with Linda on that.

"I appreciate your help," she told him. "Good luck with... this." She waved her hand to encompass the zoo parade behind her. By now, more people were in the line and not milling around.

"Sure—you're welcome." The clerk motioned for the man next to Freya to hand him his purchase. "Next!"

Freya and Brad pushed their way back out of the gas station, well aware of the interested stares that followed them. Once outside, she leaned against her Jeep and dialed Linda's number.

"Anything?" Brad stretched, then rolled his neck.

"It's ringing." She tapped her foot, fear eating at the back of her neck. "Still ringing. Aaand her voicemail box is full. Of course." She stabbed at her phone's screen to hang up, then drummed her fingers on the side of her phone. Her head hurt, and she open her Jeep then dug around in the console to find some painkillers. After swallowing two dry, she turned back to Brad. "You never found the father, did you?" She'd put Brad back on it after Candy had left for Bertmont.

He held up his hands. "Kept coming up empty, sorry."

"Not your fault. A man like that, he obviously wants to hide. There are more people out there who don't trust the government than you realize."

"Preppers. As for dead ends, the homeschool people you wanted me to reach out to? So much red tape with bureaucracy. They pretty much laughed at me when I told them I wanted information on homeschoolers in the area. But don't worry," he said, seeing the look on Freya's face, "I hit them with a warrant. They said it would have to be reviewed by their lawyers, so they're definitely dragging their feet." Brad hopped in the passenger seat. "What's the plan now, boss?"

"I want you looking into St. Mary's Preparatory School. We need to know if Jessa is really there."

"You got it. Mom gave off some strange vibes, didn't she?"

She didn't have time to answer before her phone rang. "Candy," she said, already buckling up. "What's going on? Do you have an update for me?"

"Merry Christmas, Captain. John and Steven Frank just arrived. I have them in separate interview rooms. Care to join me?"

THIRTY-SEVEN

Before entering the interrogation room where John Frank sat by himself, Freya watched him through the window. The man shifted constantly, rocking back and forth on his chair. He would catch himself, stop, then shift more. It was like something inside him was on the move, something keeping him from being able to fully relax.

She, on the other hand, felt great. This could be the break she needed in the case. These two men, one in the room in front of her, the other in the room behind her, could end this. If they were involved in what happened to the little girls, she'd soon know about it.

Candy touched her on the shoulder. "Do you want to be a part of Steven's interview? I want to get this going, but I'm happy to wait on you if you want."

"Go for it. I'm fine with you handling things with him. He knows what he did wrong, and I have a pretty good feeling he'll be the easy nut to crack. John, on the other hand..." Freya let her voice trail off as she looked at the door in front of her.

Through that door was a pedophile. A man who shouldn't be allowed anywhere near children. And yet he worked as a janitor at the elementary school. The thought of what he could have done, of all the children he'd had access to, made her sick.

He didn't deserve to leave the jail anytime soon, and Freya was going to make sure he didn't.

"Alright," Candy said, nudging Freya with her elbow. "Don't have too much fun in there."

"You're hysterical." Freya took another deep breath then pushed through the door into the interrogation room. John's head whipped around, his blank expression morphing into a frown for just a moment.

Then his mask was back on.

"Mr. Frank," she said, sitting down across from him. She dropped the Manila folder she held on the table. "So good to finally meet you. You're a hard man to track down, you know that? I had to call in the help of some friends."

He didn't respond.

"Let's get straight to the point. You and I both know you're deep in it now, right? You had a second chance at a good life and you threw it away to work at an elementary school. Not only that, but you coached the girls' soccer team. I'd argue those aren't the best ideas you've ever had."

Still no response. He stared at her, his expression dark. His hands rested in his lap, but his shoulders were hunched forward. Tight.

"Whose idea was it for you to work at the school?"

Nothing.

Fine. If he wasn't going to play ball with her, then Freya would do it her way. That's what John didn't realize—that there was a good way and a bad way to do this.

"I bet it was yours, wasn't it? You knew your brother could get you a job there and you thought... man, easy access to all those kids. What more does a pedophile like you want?"

He ground his jaw. Rage flickered across his face, then was gone. Interesting.

"Because that's all pedophiles think about, isn't it? How to get closer to kids. How to talk to them. How to look at them." She kept up her momentum and flipped open the folder in front of her. "Like these kids. Missing kids. Little girls who were on your soccer team and then suddenly... poof. They're gone."

John leaned forward, and she flipped the folder shut. She planted her hand on top of it. "Nuh-uh, John. You want to see them? You have to talk to me first."

When he finally spoke, his voice was so low, a rumble more than anything, and it surprised her. "I didn't want to hurt the kids. I just needed money."

"Mmm, and I guess with that pesky felony on your record, it was hard to get a job anywhere else, huh?"

"You don't get it."

"You're right. Because out of the two of us, John, one of us likes to hurt little kids; the other is trying to save them. Tell me what you did to the girls."

He jerked his head back like he'd been slapped and blinked at her. "I don't know what you're talking about."

"Sure you do. I really don't like it when people lie to me, John. It's time to come clean. You hurt these girls, ran, and got caught. Coaching soccer made it really easy to prey on them, didn't it? Let's talk about how we can make this better for you."

"I didn't hurt them! I love coaching them, love spending time with them, but I didn't do anything to hurt them. I wouldn't."

"That's what they all say. Tell me, John, was coaching soccer your idea or your brother's? Is he in on this with you?" She leaned across the table to get a better look at him. He was sweating, beads of it appearing on his hairline, but he didn't move to wipe them away. "Tell me. I want to know everything. If you work with me, I might be able to help you."

Lies. All lies. She'd never help scum like him.

No response.

"Why are so many of the girls on your soccer team missing? What did you do with them, John? Did you hurt them? Threaten their mothers? Talk to me."

He frowned. "What?"

"The missing girls on your team!" She slammed her hand down on the table. "Tell me what you did to them."

"I didn't—"

"Don't lie to me."

A pause, then: "I want my lawyer."

Freya's heart sank. Four words that would end this faster than anything else in the world. Hell, the entire department could be on fire and those words were scarier.

"John, don't do it like that. I can help you."

"Lawyer. Law-yer." He smirked.

She wanted to slap that grin off his face.

"Fine." She stood, making sure to take her folder with her. "That's how you want to do this? I can't help you now. You've said the magic word, sure, but any help I could have given you is gone."

"Lawyer."

Freya couldn't help herself from slamming the door behind her. Taking a deep breath, she crossed the hall and stepped into an observation room that allowed her to watch Candy's interview. From there, she looked in the room where Candy sat with Steven Frank. The man's body language couldn't have been more different than his brother's. He had his head in his hands, his elbows propped on the table. She watched as he scrubbed his hand down his cheeks before finally looking up at Candy.

He looked terrible. Dark circles under his eyes. Dry lips. Even his hair was messed up, and not in the purposeful bedhead way. While John Frank looked like he felt in complete control of the situation, Steven looked like he was falling to pieces.

She loved to see it.

"I can't tell you what a lawyer might offer you, Mr. Frank, but I do want you to know that the more willing you are to work with us, the better things will be for you. You've already admitted that you knew about John's conviction and hired him anyway, putting all of the children at the elementary school at risk. Then you let him coach the soccer team? Unbelievable. No jury will look kindly on you, but you can help yourself by being as honest as possible with me."

Steven nodded. He was crying and hiccupped, covering his mouth with the back of his hand.

Candy was unmoved. "Go ahead and write down everything that happened." She slid some paper and a pen across the table to him. "Don't leave out any detail, Mr. Frank. Trust me, you'd rather tell me the truth, no matter how insignificant it seems, than let me figure it out on my own. And I will figure it out." She leaned across the table, staring him down.

He looked up at her. Nodded. Reached for the pen.

"I know you keep saying you don't know anything about missing girls, but now's the time to come clean. Not later, not when we can tie you to your brother's crimes." Candy stood, pushing back from the table. "Write it all out, Mr. Frank. You have time."

She left the interview room, carefully closing the door behind her. When Freya met her in the hall, Candy's cheeks were flushed. "Any luck with John?"

"He lawyered up. Sounds like you got pretty far with Steven."

Candy nodded. "He's going to spill everything. The man is utterly terrified. Did John tell you about their mother?"

"Lawyer," Freya said, walking with Candy down the hall. They nodded at an officer stationed by the two doors.

"Right. One-note canary, huh? Well, their mom does have cancer, that much is true. And apparently they go and see her pretty regularly, especially when she's got chemo."

"The paradigm of goodness."

A laugh escaped Candy. "Pretty much. But that's not why they booked it the other day. Someone found out about John's proclivities. Sent him a blackmail note, and the two of them got scared."

"Ooh, interesting." Freya rubbed her hands together. "I wonder if it was a parent. Who would rather blackmail a pedophile than just turn them in?"

"Hard to say. Someone who thinks they have the upper hand, but that could be about anyone in this case." They reached the door to the second-floor lobby and Candy turned to talk to her. "But maybe this is it. This could be the end of it, you know. The soccer team, the missing girls, the pedophile..." Her voice trailed off as Freya reached for the door.

"It feels that way, doesn't it? We just need a confession."

"And to track down the girls' identities. And find the others who are missing."

Freya groaned in response, then opened the door and gestured for Candy to walk through.

"There you are." Kathy Foster, the desk sergeant, the officer who typically ran the front desk and handled walk-ins, stood in front of them, her hands on her hips, and shook her head. "You're a hard woman to hunt down, Captain."

"I've been in an interview room. What's going on?" Freya asked.

"There's a man downstairs." She consulted a piece of paper in her hand. "David Matthews. Said he talked to you before about his daughter Isa going missing?"

"He did. What's going on?"

"The wife is back. The daughter isn't."

THIRTY-EIGHT

"So she hasn't said a word since you brought her in?" Chief stood next to Freya, looking through the one-way glass into the small interrogation room where Tina Matthews sat by herself.

"Not a thing. First thing she said when I got her here? *Lawyer*. Of course."

"Let me guess, some two-bit guy in a cheap suit." Chief heaved a sign and leaned to the side, pressing his hands into his lower back.

"Worse than that. Jernigan."

Chief blew out a low whistle. "Oh, him." He closed his eyes for a moment and exhaled hard, giving his head a little shake.

Her eyebrows shot up. "He really gets under your skin, doesn't he? You mentioned before you don't like him, and I didn't have the best experience meeting him, but..." Her voice trailed off.

He gave her the side-eye. "Freya, you haven't been around in a long time, but the rest of us have, and we've all had to deal with that man. I'm surprised you haven't seen his face all over late-night TV commercials. *The lawyer of the people* indeed."

"I try not to watch TV. It's the last thing I want to do when

I'm exhausted. But don't stop now. Tell me more. I want to know everything you know about him professionally, because I've met him and I wasn't impressed."

"I've not ever spent a lot of time with him personally, but in the courtroom he's the epitome of every smarmy lawyer you've had the displeasure of meeting. He thinks he knows everything, and he's not afraid to sink as low as possible to win. You know why you don't play chess with pigeons, right?"

"Because they'll knock down all the pieces, crap all over the board, and then strut around like they won?" She had heard that saying a time or two before.

"Exactly. That's Jackson Jernigan to a tee. I feel for you when he gets in here all raring and ready to go."

"Well, maybe he'll be having an off-day. I'll give you one guess the strike I already have against him."

Chief shrugged. "He hit on you at the bar."

"I don't drink," she replied automatically. "So no. But his daughter hasn't shown up yet, and Veronica won't answer our calls."

Chief slowly turned and looked at her. "You don't say."

At that moment, Jackson Jernigan strolled down the hall in a cloud of expensive aftershave that made her eyes water.

"Chief," he said, acknowledging the man. "Captain. So good to see you both. I'm assuming my client has been taken care of but not bothered?"

"She's all yours." She stepped to the side and waited as he let himself in, then walked down the hall. Hopefully Jackson wouldn't be in there a long time before she got to chat with Tina.

Ten minutes later, Jackson opened the interrogation-room door and waved her in.

The room was small, with piped-in air and a blinking

camera set in the corner. Its black eye watched them, and Freya positioned the chair across from Tina and Jackson to ensure she wouldn't accidentally block its view of what was going to happen.

She sat down, putting her notebook in front of her on the desk, then clicked her pen once and set it beside the notebook. From her jacket pocket, she pulled out her tape recorder. This she set on the table as well.

Finally, she looked up. Jackson Jernigan was staring at her with pure hatred. How he felt about her was written all over his face, but Tina wouldn't look up. She stared at the tape recorder like it was a snake ready to bite her.

"Shall we begin?" Freya leaned back in her chair, grateful for the support on her lower back. "Mrs. Matthews, why don't you tell me exactly where Isa is?"

"My client told me she left her daughter with her husband, David." Jackson planted a meaty hand on the table, but Freya didn't look at him. She was too busy staring at Tina. "She went on vacation and when she returned, her daughter was gone."

Freya still didn't look at him. "Mrs. Matthews, you need to know where I stand right now." She paused until the woman looked up at her. "I'm worried about Isa. Right now, I have two adults pointing fingers at each other, saying the other person is responsible for their little girl going missing, but the only person who matters right now is your daughter."

Tina nodded. She swallowed hard but still didn't speak.

"You left Isa with David?" Freya asked. She fought to keep her voice steady and even. The last thing she needed to do was bring a lot of emotion into the room when everyone was already stressed.

"I did." Tina nodded, then pressed her lips together. "But I shouldn't have because now she's gone." Tears streamed down her face. "You have no idea what I'm going through! I thought I did the right thing, and now she's gone!"

"Mrs. Matthews, do you think anyone could have hurt Isa?" John Frank's face swam in her mind, and she pushed it away. She didn't want to mention his name outright and put the thought in Tina's mind if it wasn't already there.

"She's such a good girl," Tina said, pressing her fingers hard into her temples. "Everyone loves her." She dropped her hands to the table and began picking at her cuticles. "Nobody would hurt her."

"Mrs. Matthews," Freya said, keeping her voice low, "we need to find your daughter, and to do that, I need your help. Do you think David could have hurt Isa?"

The woman sitting across from her was close to falling apart. Freya glanced at Jackson, not surprised to see the man glaring at her. When Tina didn't answer, he reached out, lightly touching her arm.

"You can answer the question, Tina. You should, in fact. Help the police find Isa."

Tina closed her eyes and stilled her hands. After a moment, she finally looked up at Freya, her mouth pressed hard together. Fear flitted across her face, and she gave her head a tiny shake.

"Mrs. Matthews, if someone hurt Isa, you can't continue to protect them. I want to help your daughter, but I need your assistance to do that. I know this is scary, but please, help me help you."

John Frank. The soccer team. Freya needed her to mention one of those, to point her finger in that direction, and she'd be all over it. But she didn't. She just looked kowtowed, threatened, terrified of what would happen if she told the truth.

Freya needed her to move past that.

"Mrs. Matthews, I want to help you. Whatever happened, just tell me. My only goal is to find Isa and make sure she's okay."

The woman finally nodded, the movement stiff and tight.

Freya felt the change in her energy, and her lawyer must have as well.

"Okay. Yes. You need to know everything," she said.

Jackson stiffened in his seat. "Hold on now. Don't say a word to her, Tina. She's trying to trap you, and you better not let it happen." He pointed at Freya. "I'm the only one who talks to her. You need to direct all inquiries to me, Captain. Not my client." His face was red, his cheeks puffy.

Freya stared at him for a moment, trying to see if he would back down.

He didn't.

"I didn't hurt Isa." Tina cleared her throat, ready to continue, but Jackson cut her off.

"Tina, no." Jackson slammed his hand down on the table. It rattled, but Freya didn't blink. She wanted to turn and look at the mirror, but she wouldn't be able to tell if Chief was there. Even so, she had a pretty good feeling he'd be watching. There wasn't any way he'd want to miss this show.

"It was David. He hurt her," she said, raising her voice.

"He's the one who reported her missing," Freya said.

"Because he was scared." She rubbed her eyes, digging her knuckles into her skin. "You don't know how he gets. You don't know what he's like."

"I met him," Freya said. "And he was worried for Isa, but that's it. He wasn't unkind or out of control, so what are you getting at?"

"I need more time with my client." Jackson stood, planting his hand on the table.

Tina ignored him. "You think I wanted to move here? I didn't! And neither did Isa. But David made us. He told me I had to or he'd hurt me." Huge tears rolled down her cheeks. "I love Isa. I'd do anything for her. Anything to keep her safe."

Freya frowned. "If you love her so much, then why would you leave her with someone who scares you?"

Tina's mouth dropped open. "I didn't leave her. I loved her."

"Loved her? Past tense?" Her pulse kicked up a notch.

"Tina, you need to stop talking right now. As your counsel—"

"I had to save her." Faster than Freya could realize what was happening, Tina reached out and grabbed her hand, squeezing it so tight that her fingers started to cramp. "She was my baby."

"You keep using past tense, Mrs. Matthews." Freya breathed out the words, almost unable to speak. The hair on the back of her neck stood up. Even Jackson had slowed his bluster and was staring uselessly at his client. His tie was askance, his hair out of place.

It was all falling apart for him.

"It wasn't my fault." Tina's eyes were pleading. She stared at Freya like she was looking for forgiveness. "I didn't have a choice. You don't understand what it's like, do you? To not have a choice?"

"Why didn't you have a choice, Mrs. Matthews?"

The woman pressed her lips together and shook her head.

"Did someone threaten you?"

Nothing.

Freya felt like she was going to come out of her skin. "What happened? Who are you trying to protect?"

The woman shook her head. Her eyes were wide, her cheeks flushed.

If Freya didn't keep her talking, she'd clam up. That or Jackson would yank her from the interrogation room.

She had to change tactics. "It had to be scary, moving here when you didn't know anyone. And you were balancing a lot, weren't you? Work and getting Isa in school, helping her find friends. But you had friends too, didn't you?"

Tina nodded.

"Who was your friend?"

Tina opened her mouth. Glanced at Jackson. Snapped it shut and shook her head.

"Enough." Jackson picked his jaw up off the floor. "Enough. No more of this." He turned on his client. "Breathe one more word before you and I have a chance to talk in private and I'm walking out this door—do you understand me? Good luck finding anyone else to represent you if they know I turned you down."

"How did you come to represent her, Jackson?" Freya frowned at him. "She's new to town; did she throw a dart at the phonebook and hit your name?"

"She got lucky." He stood, grabbing Tina under the upper arm to help her up.

"Lucky because your kids are on the same soccer team?"

He glowered at her. "Unless you're arresting my client, Captain, we're leaving."

"You don't need to go anywhere," Freya said, turning to the woman at his side. "Mrs. Matthews, you're under arrest for child abuse. You have the right to remain silent. Anything you say can and will be used against you in a court of law. You have the right to an attorney," she continued, speaking quickly, watching as the light in Tina's eyes went out.

Jackson puffed up even bigger. Rage emanated from him. "You have no proof of that." He smacked the table with his open palm.

"Statute 14-318.2. She either created or allowed to be created a substantial risk of physical injury to Isa. Don't play this game with me, Jernigan." Freya wasn't about to let Tina Matthews walk out of the interview room. She knew what had happened to Isa—Freya was sure of it. No matter what statute she had to use, she'd keep the woman in jail.

If looks could kill, Freya would be dead. Jackson's mouth

was pressed into a firm line. Furrows appeared between his brows.

But she didn't care. Tina knew more than she was sharing. She was guilty, not only of hiding something from Freya but of hurting Isa. But more than that, she was scared.

It was entirely possible John Frank had hurt Isa, then threatened Tina. Even so, if the woman was protecting a murderer, she deserved to be behind bars. It wouldn't bring Isa back, but it could help save more girls.

This had to stop.

Something terrible was happening in Fawn Lake. She felt like she was right on the edge of it but couldn't figure out what it was.

But she would. She had to.

THIRTY-NINE

"And after that?" Brad sat on the corner of Freya's desk, munching on a donut from Esther. Freya had swung by earlier to grab something for her team to eat and also to check on the older woman. Not only was grabbing donuts a good opportunity for her to say hi to Esther, but it had been a hard day and nobody had gotten lunch. Donuts for lunch weren't the best option, but they were fast, and her team didn't have the time or luxury for a sit-down meal.

"He tried to drag her out of the interview room," she said, yanking her thoughts away from Esther, from how frail she'd looked, from how her hand had shaken a little as she'd boxed up the donuts. That was something she had to worry about, but not right now, not when she'd made strides on the case but still needed to make more. "She wasn't saying a thing."

"Just clammed up?" Brad raised his eyebrows. "Wised up, huh?"

"Exactly. Terrible timing for her to actually start listening to him. I'm pretty sure she would have dug herself a grave if he'd just kept his mouth shut for one more minute. But I arrested her. She's in jail, refusing to speak, refusing to eat. Told the jailer that she did everything she could for Isa."

"What a bunch of crap." Candy had been hovering in the office door but now entered, eyeballing the tank in the corner of Freya's office before grabbing a donut. "You said she started using past tense when talking about Isa?" When Freya nodded, Candy continued. "Yeah, she knows something. She's hiding the truth from you, and she may have been involved in what happened."

"I know. My problem is, since she won't talk, I don't have any more information about what's going on with the missing kids." Freya rubbed her temples. Her half-eaten chocolate-glazed donut sat on a paper napkin in front of her, but she didn't have much of an appetite.

"Well, I have a spot of good news for you," Candy said. "Steven Frank sang like a canary. He knows he messed up hiring his brother to work with kids, and he wrote out a magnificent confession."

"That is good news. I don't care what made him decide to sing, the fact that he wised up and turned on his brother is enough for me. You want to be the one to tell John that Steven rolled over on him?

"Gosh, yes. Do you mind if I do it? You can be the one to deliver the news if you want, but honestly, I'd love nothing more. I want to see the way his face drops. He should have come clean when he had the chance."

"Run with it. Nothing would make me happier."

"Yes!" Candy took a huge bite of a donut and spoke around it. "I'm on it. In, like, five more bites."

"After that would you go talk to David? You can tell him we arrested his wife and feel him out. Tina pointed her finger squarely at him, but I don't think he's the one who hurt Isa."

Candy nodded. "Consider it done."

Freya turned to Brad. "What have you got for me?"

"Well, I called the prep school to ask about Jessa, but they weren't helpful. And before you ask, yes, there's a warrant in process. Then I talked to Steffie's mom about the soccer team. From what she was saying, it sounds like a pretty cliquey group of moms. If you're in the group, you're in. If you're not, you're not. But the girls aren't like that. She sent me a bunch of pictures of the team."

Without waiting for Freya to ask, Brad pulled them up on his phone and handed it to her. She took it, knowing exactly what she was going to see.

And she was right. Young girls, all of them with huge grins. There were action shots of them running after the ball as well as ones of the girls celebrating, their arms around each other's shoulders, sheer joy on their faces.

They were so alive. So full of life. Little girls like that had their entire lives ahead of them. They should have been thinking about birthday parties and getting a dog, not about whether or not they were going to die.

"Interesting. I'm sure you're smarter than to ask outright, but did she express any concerns over John Frank coaching the team?"

Brad shook his head. "Not at all. And she said when he's not there, the other moms all step up to help coach. Mentioned Mindy coming once or twice but not being very good with the ball." He sighed. "Sorry I don't have much else for you."

"Not a problem. I'm glad you handled talking to them." Freya paused, thinking. "What's on your plate for the rest of the day?"

"Actually, I'm going to go see Jenny. Remember her—the girl who was in the bakery with her boyfriend when the glass was broken?" Brad grinned and tossed his napkin in the trash.

"Oh, I remember her. Tell me you got mom to let you talk to her."

"Oh yeah. She gave us a fake last name."

Freya closed her eyes. Goosebumps broke out on her arms. She'd known something was off with the girl when they met but hadn't pushed it because she had questioned herself. Now she felt stupid for not listening to her gut and figuring out what was going on with her at that moment.

"She said her name was Jenny Morgan, but that's her middle name. Her real last name is Corn."

"Corn?" She stared at Brad. "You can't be serious about that."

"Oh, I'm serious. You're more than welcome to go with me to interview her, but I have a pretty good feeling Chief is going to want you to stay away from this. You're way too close to it, as he would say."

"He'd hate me working this." Freya looked at her watch. From what she'd seen and what she remembered, Chief liked closing his office door around this time to catch up on reading reports. He operated with the belief that he'd put together a good team that should be able to handle problems without him, and they could call him if they ran into something unsurmountable. Chances were good he'd have no idea where she was going.

"Working it is not a good idea," Candy said. "Freya, you know I love and respect you, but Chief would be right. You're too close to this. To the Corns."

"I'm coming." Freya flipped the lid on the donut box closed and grabbed her phone and keys. "Do you want to drive, or shall I?"

Brad chewed his lower lip, then glanced at Candy. The younger detective stared at him, obviously trying to get him to stand up to Freya, but it wasn't happening. He sighed, his shoulders slumping forward. "I just want to go on record that I don't think this is a great idea."

"Wonderful. It's been noted. Now, do you have the address?" When Brad nodded, she began ushering the two of them out of her door. "Great. You're driving. As soon as we get this straightened out with the Corns, I'm going to talk to all of the mothers again. I want to see if any of the girls have come back to Fawn Lake. I'll also try to talk to John again if his lawyer will play ball."

"Why don't you do that and I'll go see Jenny Corn by myself?" Brad asked, but his face fell when Freya shook her head.

"Brad, you either drive me over there to see the Corns, or I'll remove you from the case, stick you in a broom closet, and have you filling out reports until you're old enough to retire." Freya locked her office.

"You wouldn't." He sounded wounded.

"She might," Candy said, then shrugged when Brad glared at her. "What? She's going to do what she wants. I'm not going to argue with her. Did you see what she keeps as a pet in there?"

Freya slung her arm around Brad's shoulders. "Let's go," she said, directing him to the stairs. "The sooner we get there, the sooner we can figure all of this out."

"If this was the Corn family, then you know what that means, right?" Brad sounded nervous.

"Oh, believe me. I know exactly what this all means. I also know that if that's the case, it's highly personal. The only way to get this to end is if I end it myself. I'm not going to sit back and wait for them to come to their senses."

"As long as you're sure." The two of them hurried down the stairs, their feet loud in the stairwell.

Freya stopped walking. She *wasn't* sure, that was the problem. Even though she wanted to handle this case, to know she'd done everything to protect Esther and make up for what she'd done when she lived here before...

She couldn't turn her back on the little girls.

"I can't go with you." She stopped walking, and Brad turned

around, surprised. "I'm sorry. I just can't right now. As much as I want to, Esther isn't in danger. But these girls are."

"I'll wait for you to handle it."

Freya shrugged. "Either way. It's seriously up to you."

Handling Esther's case would be the most satisfying thing. She needed to wrap it up with a nice little bow. Needed to be able to look Esther in the eyes and tell her it was over.

But not today.

"You know," Brad said, spinning his keys once before shoving them in his pocket, "they live right down the road from Madeleine Travis. You said you want to talk to the mothers, see if the girls are in town. You could start with her mom, Kelly."

"That's it." Freya's mouth was in a tight line when they stepped out into the sun. It was still hot outside, the air thick and muggy. "I'll swing by the Corn house with you, but then I'm going to Kelly's. These mothers know something—I'm more and more convinced they do."

Brad unlocked his car—a marked cruiser—and Freya hopped in. She angled the air vents to blow right on her face. "This ends today, Brad," she said, clearly continuing her thought from a moment ago. "And I'm going to be the one to end it."

FORTY

In all of her dealings with the Corn family a few years ago, Freya had never made it to this house. Jenny Corn and her family had been a smudge in her case notebook, people she knew about, but not the ones she was actively looking into. And then, when she'd made the arrest, when she'd arrested the wrong man for her parents' crimes, had they even come to the press conference?

Half of Fawn Lake had been there, so they'd probably been there too, pressed up against everyone else surging forward to see what Freya Sinclair had to say about the arrest. About stopping the reign of terror that had been inflicted on their small town.

Only it hadn't stopped with the arrest, had it? And that had been the base of the entire problem.

The man she'd arrested hadn't been the murderer. He'd been a Corn though, giving the family a good reason to hate her. She had done what she could to try to atone for her mistake. She'd paid for the caskets of her parents' last three victims.

She'd made a public apology to the wrongfully arrested.

But it wasn't enough, and she knew it.

Brad guided his car over a rut in the road, then turned onto a gravel driveway. "This is the address she gave me when I interviewed her at Parker's, and I looked into her. It's legit, although the rest of her story wasn't."

"You'd think criminals would lie about all the details that can trap them, not just some of them." Freya stared ahead, taking in the overgrown bushes on the side of the driveway, the thick grass in the front yard, the sagging tire swing hanging from an oak branch.

"She was nervous. She's pretty young, probably didn't even fully understand everything that happened when you were in Fawn Lake before. I'd wager someone else in her family put her up to it."

"It makes sense," she agreed. "Parker's was hit the day I returned."

"You think it's retaliation? Not a random crime?"

"Believe me, people can hold grudges a lot longer than you might think possible."

Brad parked the cruiser, and the two of them walked up to the front stoop. Unlike most of the houses in Fawn Lake, this one didn't have a wide porch. It had a small stoop, with just enough room for a dirty welcome mat and a half-dead pansy.

"Let me take the lead on this, okay? If you're the reason Parker's windows were broken, then I can only imagine the kind of reception you'll receive." Brad looked for a doorbell but ended up knocking instead.

Freya stood to his side and partly behind him. It wasn't in her nature to let someone else take the lead, especially when the case was so personal to her, but Brad was right. This case was personal to her because of Esther being involved but a lot more personal to the Corns.

The door swung open almost immediately, like the person on the other side had been waiting for the knock. The woman standing there looked exhausted, with limp brown hair, old blue jeans, and a stained apron.

"Mrs. Corn?" Brad tilted his head in greeting. "Are you Jenny's mother?"

"I am."

"I'm Officer Williams from the Fawn Lake Police Department. We're here to talk to you about some vandalism that we think your daughter might have been involved in."

The woman listened to Brad, but her eyes never left Freya's face. The lines around her mouth deepened as she pushed her lips into a scowl. "You're Freya Sinclair."

"I am." Freya nodded, then took a step around Brad so she and the woman were face-to-face. "I wanted to come here because we think Jenny is mixed up in something she shouldn't be."

"My girl didn't do anything wrong." Mrs. Corn crossed her arms and leaned against the doorframe. "She was just at the bakery. Is that a crime?"

"It is if she helped someone break out the windows."

The woman blinked, but her face didn't relax.

"Maybe a cousin of hers? I know how close your family is, how much everyone will stick together when something goes wrong."

"That why you put my brother-in-law in jail for a crime your folks committed? Were you sticking together with your family?" Every single one of the woman's words had a razor's edge to them. She leaned closer to Freya, so close the pores around her nose were visible. She smelled like grease and cigarettes, and Freya had to fight to keep from taking a step back.

"I did everything I could to fix it as soon as I realized the mistake." Freya's voice didn't shake, and she was grateful for that. It was a testament to how many times she'd stood in front of the mirror and practiced saying that exact thing. There wasn't any way she was going to move back to Fawn Lake and not be prepared to respond to what people were going to say.

"After you ruined my family's reputation." She scoffed. "Get off my porch. My Jenny did nothing wrong, and you can't harass her."

"We just want to know if she knows who broke the windows," Brad said, edging forward a little bit. "I know it doesn't seem like a big deal to you, but it is. And she's a suspect."

Both Mrs. Corn and Freya looked at him. Judging by the expression on Mrs. Corn's face, that thought had never crossed her mind.

"A suspect? She was just there. My girl didn't do anything wrong." Another scowl.

"I'm going to speak to your daughter. Unless you want her to get more wrapped up in this than she already is, I suggest you tell me what you know. Captain Sinclair and I are happy to go easy on her if she has information that will lead us to the vandal," Brad said.

There was a long pause. A wren nesting in the bushes by the front door chirped and fussed at them as she flitted around the branches. Freya felt sweat trickle down the back of her neck but didn't move to wipe it off.

Finally, Mrs. Corn broke. She shook her head and exhaled hard, dropping her hands against her thighs. "You promise me Jenny won't get in trouble? I think she has a shot at going to college and getting out of here."

"Officer Williams never goes back on a promise." Freya's voice was quiet so she didn't spook the woman.

"Okay." Mrs. Corn looked behind her into the house. "Jenny, get out here right now!"

There was silence, then the girl appeared, dressed in short shorts and a hoodie. She had the hood up over her head and glared out at Freya.

"Tell me who broke the window at the bakery." Her mother had turned completely away from Freya and Brad. "If you come clean, they're going to make sure you don't get in as much trouble."

Jenny dug her toe into the dirty welcome mat. "It was Brett," she finally admitted. She looked up, jutting her chin out at Freya. "Because of you."

Even though Freya knew the vandalism was connected to her, it still hurt to hear it. She nodded, keeping her mouth shut so she didn't say a word.

"I'm going to need more details from you," Brad said, his voice soft and encouraging. "Do you mind talking to me now, or do you want to come down to the station later?"

Jenny looked at her mother, then glanced at Freya. She hadn't said a word, but what she was thinking was clear. She'd talk to Brad now, but not with Freya anywhere around.

"I'm going for a walk," Freya murmured, touching him on the shoulder before she walked back down the driveway. The sun shone off the cruiser's windshield, distorting her reflection as she approached. Behind her, she could hear voices as Brad got all the information he needed to pin the vandalism on Brett.

She kept walking. Kelly Travis lived two houses down. Maybe, by not pulling up in her front yard, Freya could catch her off guard. If she didn't see her coming, she was more likely to answer the door.

Still, even though this was getting wrapped up, she felt sick. Coming home had been her way of fleeing to safety, of going to the one place she thought she'd be able to settle down and live out the rest of her life.

But people have long memories. And it was stupid of her to think anyone in town had forgotten what her parents had done.

What she'd done.

FORTY-ONE

Kelly hadn't been there. Neither had Madeleine, for that matter. Freya had circled the house four times, knocking on doors, peering through windows.

Nothing.

It was only after she went next door to talk to their neighbor that she'd seen a single person. The man had leaned on his rake, wiped the sweat from his brow, and told her he hadn't seen Kelly in a day or two, come to think of it.

Now nerves rushed through her as she dialed Esther's number. She hadn't been this nervous about calling the woman who'd raised her since she'd called to tell her she wanted to move back to Fawn Lake. Esther had been thrilled, telling her she'd been hoping for years she'd come home, and that it was a dream come true.

Now she had to tell her she was the reason Esther's window had been broken. Her feet slowed as she approached the library. It was an unassuming building but probably her favorite place in town. She'd hidden away in its walls as a kid, then as a teen, then as a young adult, looking for meaning and answers about who she was on the shelves.

Funny enough, most of the answers she received she'd gotten at Esther's table, not in the library stacks.

One ring. Two. Freya felt nerves eating at her, then Esther picked up.

"I was just thinking about you. How are you, darling?"

"I'm hanging in there. I wanted to let you know that Brad, one of our officers, figured out who broke your window."

"Oh, good. I knew you'd all figure it out."

Freya swallowed, her eyes closed hard. "Right. Well, it was one of the Corns. Retaliation for me putting their family member in jail."

The heavy silence that filled the line made Freya stop walking. She took a deep breath and was about to speak when Esther cut her off.

"What happened was unfortunate, Freya, but you have to move past it. You have to give yourself a break, then the rest of the town will too. Nobody could have done a better job than you did. Your parents... well, let's just say they knew what they were doing, and they were good at it. They fooled a lot of people, and it wasn't your fault that you were one of them."

"I just think—"

"I'm not finished, darling. This town needs you. The missing little girls? They need you. And the Corn family needs to come to grips with the fact that you made a mistake, but you also paid for it. Dearly. They need to move on like the rest of us have. Now, I want you to come for dinner."

Freya blinked in surprise at the change in subject. "Please tell me it's not another blind date."

"It won't be blind this time, will it? You both know what the other one looks like."

Freya smiled in spite of herself. "I can't tonight. This case... it's all-consuming and I can't walk away, not when everything's coming to a head." Silence from the other end of the line, and her gut twisted. "But I'll come by. Just to say hi, but you need to know I can't stay."

"I'll take what I can get, darling."

"Bye," Freya said, turning the phone to silent and slipping it into her pocket. She turned to walk past the library when something caught her eye. The community bulletin board had been installed, right here under the eaves, before she left Fawn Lake. It was the perfect place for teenagers to advertise babysitting services, for people to look for a dogwalker, for anyone downsizing to post items they wanted to get rid of.

Not that she needed any of those services, but it was almost impossible to walk past the bulletin board without looking to see what was offered. Freya slowed, walking along it as she drank in the information. It all seemed so small town—a missing cat, a request for someone to clean out gutters, information on the high school's upcoming graduation.

An open invite to join the elementary school soccer team.

She ripped that flyer down and crumped it up before shoving it in her pocket. She ran her finger along the rest of the cork board and was about to walk past the library when she stopped.

Something was there. Something that didn't fit in.

Her heart beat faster as she stepped back and turned to the board. There, right there.

"Moms of young girls—are you looking for community? Support? To make your girls as good as they can be?" She read the words out loud, goosebumps breaking out on her arms. "Join us for our next meeting and see how we can help you ensure your girls are good, they're clean, they're kind." She swallowed. "What is this?"

The only other information on the sheet was a time, date, and place of the next meeting.

Tonight.

Grabbing her phone, she snapped a picture, so she wouldn't

forget anything, then hesitated, carefully pulling the entire sheet down from the community board.

Clean. There was only one other person she'd ever heard use that word to describe a girl, and that woman's daughter was currently missing.

FORTY-TWO

After explaining her plan, Freya hung up with Candy and squared off against Esther's front door. Her detective was more than happy to put together what she needed for the evening, giving Freya ten minutes to see Esther.

Just ten minutes, then it was all about to hit the fan. She could feel it.

Paul opened the door for Freya and stepped out onto the porch next to her before she could squeeze through the door. "I hope it's okay I came for dinner. Esther was pretty emphatic about having me over, but I don't want to intrude if you'd rather have a quiet evening."

"Oh, I'm not staying. I know Esther wants me to, but I can't, not with work the way it is. But I wanted to swing by. Show my face."

"I'm glad. She worries about you." He paused. "She told me about who broke the glass at Parker's."

"Geez, did she tell you all of my embarrassing stories from when I was a little kid too?" Freya forced a smile to her face. "I'm sorry, that wasn't cool of me. I'm just... wow. Knowing that what I did is directly affecting her? I mean, it was bad enough when I fled town with my tail between my legs. But knowing that I brought the drama back when I returned?" She shook her head. It felt like the entire world was weighing down on her.

"Hey." Paul touched her shoulder. She stepped back, and he held up his hand in surrender. "Sorry, I won't touch you. But you didn't bring this on Esther. Trust me, she's been waiting for you to come back."

"Things got too dull around here, huh?"

"Something like that. I just wanted to make sure you're okay. She's moved on from it, and there's no reason to bring it up."

She eyeballed him. "Are you looking out for me?"

"Someone needs to." He laughed. "From what I've heard, you're having quite the time back home."

"Oh, geez." She felt herself soften. She wasn't great at letting new people into her life but had to remind herself that if Esther thought this guy was okay, that he probably was. Not only did Esther know most everyone in town, but after years of working with the public, she'd gotten pretty good at reading people and telling whether or not they were decent. If Paul was here for dinner—again—there had to be a reason he was welcome.

"Anyway, come on in. You don't have to talk about work if you don't want to. Heck, you don't even have to talk about your past or yourself. I'm more than happy to keep the conversation going, and, in case you didn't notice last time, Marla always has something to say."

Freya grabbed on to the change in topic. "She seems like a really good kid," she said as she followed Paul into the house. Before closing the door, she glanced over her shoulder. Nothing moved in the front yard, but she still wanted to make sure there wasn't anyone following her. Watching her.

It was one thing to have a target on your back. It was

another entirely to bring that target with you into the home of someone you loved.

"Oh, she is. I'd like to take all of the credit for the little person she's turning into, but I can't really do that, can I? So many people are involved in molding a child into who they become." Paul's voice trailed back to her as she followed him down the hall.

In the kitchen, Esther stood at the stove, dressed in a patchwork apron, Marla on a stool next to her. Freya paused in the door, watching as Esther consulted the little girl over something cooking on the stove. She held a spoon up to Marla's mouth, then the little girl tasted it and gave a thumbs up.

"Tastes good, huh?" Freya walked up to Esther and kissed her on the cheek. "I didn't know we were going to get the pleasure of you cooking for us, Marla."

The little girl giggled and shrugged. "Mrs. Esther said I could help if I wanted to. I love to cook, but I've never really learned."

Paul held up his hands in surrender. "I'll admit that my skills aren't really suited to the kitchen. I'd much rather be out hiking or swimming with my kiddo."

Freya saw the opportunity. Turning from the stove, she tried to appear casual and relaxed. "You ever have any weird experiences in the woods? By the lake maybe?"

"You know, it was just the most frustrating thing." He cleared his throat. "I'm sorry, I know I shouldn't let it bother me, but it does. I think I'm a great dad, and even though it would be easier for Marla to have a mom as well, that's just not how life worked out."

She frowned. She'd only recently met the guy but Paul seemed to be pretty even-keeled, so where was this frustration coming from?

"We were going to go swimming right there off the dock at Lake Everett. We'd hiked in with our towels and sunscreen and snacks. There was a group of women and girls there, but I didn't think anything of it. I really don't think I'm a scary-looking guy, but apparently I was wrong."

"What happened?" She hadn't moved since Paul started talking.

"They wouldn't let us in the water. Actually, they threw a fit when we tried to get in. Said it was some mother–daughter bonding time and men weren't allowed. The weirdest thing was that none of them had on bathing suits."

"What were they wearing?" Freya couldn't breathe. She stared at Paul, willing him to keep talking.

"Dresses. *White* ones, if you can believe that. Dressed like they were going to some fancy event instead of wading by the shore kicking up tons of mud." He shook his head and rolled his eyes at Marla, who laughed. "White dresses. Weirdest thing I've ever seen."

"So weird," Freya managed. For a moment, she wanted to tell him about the upcoming meeting she'd asked Candy to go to. It would feel so good to unload on someone, to trust that they were going to keep her secret, but she didn't let herself.

How well did she know this guy anyway?

No, better to keep her thoughts to herself. She trusted Candy. And Brad. Most of all, though, she trusted herself. Turning, she hugged Esther.

"Hey, I'm sorry, but I have to head off now." Guilt weighed her down but she managed a smile. "I'll see you soon though."

Esther cupped her cheek. "I know."

Paul was watching them. Even Marla had turned and was looking at Freya, her little mouth pursed.

"I have to go. I have a meeting." She kissed Esther's cheek and wiggled her fingers at Marla before turning to Paul. "Thanks for keeping an eye on her."

"Anytime." His voice was soft, and he reached for her like he was going to stop her but then dropped his hand by his side.

Freya nodded. Ducked her head, allowing curls to fall around her face. She'd love nothing more than to stay, to spend time with Esther, to feel like a normal person.

But she couldn't. Not when there was a meeting coming up. Not when she was closer than ever to figuring this all out.

Unfortunately, she couldn't show her face at the meeting, not after her press conference. It had given her information, sure, but it had also ensured that everyone in town knew who she was, even if they hadn't before. But most people didn't know Candy nearly as well. Candy was going to infiltrate that meeting, and if that didn't work? Freya was going door to door. Old school.

Knock and talks. Nothing else mattered.

FORTY-THREE

"Do I look like a mom?" Candy twirled slowly in front of Freya, obviously looking for approval. The khaki pants and matching sweater set were straight out of the 1990s, but together with the white sneakers and ponytail, she looked like a fresh-faced, but tired, mom.

"You look like the mom of every friend I had growing up." Freya nodded her approval. "Obviously, you should be wearing high-waisted acid-washed jeans to really fit the vision I have, but I'll forgive it."

"So generous of you." Candy sighed and smoothed down her sweater. "I'm going to melt in this thing."

"Maybe so, but it would be great if you could wait to melt until we get some information."

"Stop sweating until this sweater has proven it's useful. Got it." Candy grabbed an oversized purse and slung it onto her shoulder. "Does that complete the look?"

"Sure does. How does your earpiece work? Does it feel okay?"

"Feels fine." Candy touched the small piece of metal resting inside her ear. It would allow Freya to hear everything she said without her having to lift her wrist to speak into a microphone. As awesome as that looked in movies, it was a dead giveaway that someone was communicating with another person.

But the most important thing was Candy's sweater. One of its buttons had been replaced with a small camera. While sitting in her car, Freya would be able to see everything Candy saw. It was getting dark out and the chance anyone would recognize the button as a camera was too slim to worry about. Still, it felt strange sending her detective in to do her work, but she didn't have a choice.

"Alright. I'll be right down the road if you need me. Otherwise, best of luck." Freya got in her Jeep and Candy hopped in her unmarked Tahoe. Nerves raced up Freya's spine. She hated putting anyone on her team in a situation where she didn't know how it was going to play out.

She trusted Candy, of course she did. But she didn't want her to be in danger. It would be so much easier if she could infiltrate the meeting, but that would never work.

Candy was the only choice.

"Visuals good?" Candy asked, getting out of her Tahoe. She turned this way and that, and Freya nodded to herself before responding.

"Everything looks great. Try to mingle so I can lay eyes on everyone there. Remember, if it's not right in front of you, I can't see it."

"Ten-four." Candy cleared her throat and marched up the sidewalk to the house. Rather than getting to go inside, however, she was stopped in the front yard by a woman with long hair wearing a long white dress.

"Are you here for the meeting?" The woman's voice was airy and gentle.

Freya held her breath.

"Yes," she said. "I have a daughter and... well, I thought I could use some help."

"You came to the right place." The woman grabbed Candy's arm and gave her a squeeze. She was now standing so close it was impossible to see her face, just her torso. "I'm Hannah. I was like you before, just unsure of what to do because my daughter was so out of control. But it'll be okay."

"Your daughter." Candy cleared her throat. "How is she? Is she better?"

"So much better." When the woman pointed to the side, Candy turned to look. The setting sun flared in the camera for a moment, and Freya leaned closer to her screen, itching to get a better look.

If the woman was pointing for her to look at something, then surely the girl was alive. Surely she wasn't—

"Mama!" A blonde girl in a little white dress ran up and exploded into her mother's arms. The woman Candy was talking to took a step back, laughing.

"This is my Ariel," she explained, her eyes locked on Candy's face. "She was difficult, but we got her under control. I was worried she wouldn't be okay, that a full cleanse would be the only option, but I was wrong. Things are fine now." She kissed her daughter on the top of her head and then nodded to Candy. "Come on and sit. Where's your daughter? I'm sure she'll want to sit with you. Or maybe she'll go play with Ariel."

"I left her at home," Candy said, repeating the lie she and Freya had practiced. "With so many new people, and her behavior out of control, I just didn't know if bringing her was a good choice."

"I understand, but this is a safe place. She needs to come to the next meeting." There was a note of judgement in the woman's voice. Her eyes flicked past Candy, and she broke into a smile. "I'm going to go talk to someone, so I'll see you later. But remember, next time, bring your daughter."

"Right, my daughter," Candy muttered, turning to watch as

the woman walked past her. Hannah greeted a woman with a dark bob and pulled her into a hug.

"Ooh, I don't know for sure," Candy said to Freya, "but that looks a lot like Jennifer Peters. Surprise, surprise, her daughter isn't with her."

"Thank goodness she won't recognize you. Why don't you make your way to that circle of chairs I saw sitting out on the lawn?"

"On it." Candy walked slowly, taking her time. The women all around her chatted with each other. Some young girls flitted through, most of them dressed in white dresses. "And I'm going to keep my ears open for anything about the soccer team."

"You've got this."

After a few minutes, during which Candy sat still and watched as the other women found their seats and Freya mostly held her breath, a tall woman stood up. She didn't have to say a word for everyone else around the circle to stop talking. A hush fell, and the woman smiled, turning her gaze on everyone in turn.

"Good evening, ladies." Her voice was smooth. Honey. Melted chocolate. Candy sat up a little straighter, almost like electricity had shot through the group. "I'm so glad to see new faces here tonight. It seems like our little recruitment effort has worked." She waited until there was some polite applause, then raised her hands to stop it.

"As you all know, we're mothers supporting mothers. All we want is to help each other survive the stress and anxiety that comes with being the mothers of girls. Girls, as we all know, are very special, but they can be trouble. If they're not focused, not kind, not open to receiving what the world has to give them, then they will be a problem. If they're not taking care of themselves, they can be an issue. We know that girls can be better than society expects them to, and we provide the support mothers need to ensure they have wonderful daughters."

So far it didn't sound as creepy as Freya had figured it would be. A little unnerving, sure. And it definitely had some cult-like vibes that she didn't like. But didn't most crunchy mom groups?

The woman continued. "What I'd like to do tonight is welcome everyone who joined us. Coming tonight was a wonderful way for you to check out what we do, to make sure you understand how we can support you, and for you to reconsider your relationship with your own daughter. Is she happy? Kind? Thoughtful? Or does she push buttons and get into trouble? We want to know it all, then we want to offer you the support you need to deal with whatever you're facing. Remember: if a girl can't be good, can't shine that goodness in every moment of her life, then you have a responsibility to help her. To protect her from how the world will take advantage of her, how the world will dirty her and turn her against you. The world is a dangerous place, and your daughter won't survive it if you don't take care of her."

Freya hunched over her laptop. Her Jeep was hot, but she didn't want to roll down a window, didn't want to do anything that might accidentally attract attention. Still, she was about to come out of her skin with the desire to rush in there and see for herself what was going on.

"So I'd like us to all go around the table and introduce ourselves. Tell us about you and your daughter, what problems you're facing, and how we can help. We're all at various stages on our journey, but that doesn't mean we can't all offer each other support. Remember, the goal is lovely girls. Clean girls. Girls who can stand up to the pressure of this world."

There it was. What they were doing. Freya's blood froze.

The image on the computer shifted as Candy moved in her seat. She turned this way and that, taking in everyone around the circle. The women to the right and left of her didn't look fazed. They stared at the woman who'd been speaking with half-smiles, like they couldn't believe how lucky there were to be there tonight.

Freya drank them all in, trying to decide for herself if any of the women there could actually hurt their daughters. Was it possible they would be willing to kill them?

Candy exhaled hard as the woman next to her finished speaking. She turned to Candy, her eyes flicking down the sweater, her gaze on the camera button for a moment. Then she smiled and reached out, touching her on the shoulder. "It's your turn."

"Oh, hi." Candy cleared her through. "My name is Deborah. I'm here because my daughter, Sarah, is pushing my buttons." She forced a rueful laugh. "I'm sure you all know how that feels."

Freya sighed with relief when the women around the circle nodded at her. *Good. They were buying it.*

"Where's your daughter?" It was the woman Freya was thinking of as the leader, the one who had been talking and introduced herself so eloquently. "Most everyone else here brought their daughter with them, but you didn't." She sat across from Candy, her long legs crossed, her eyes locked on Freya's detective.

Candy swallowed. "Sarah is such a handful. I thought about bringing her, but she'd be causing a ruckus, trust me."

"All of the other girls who came have settled down." The woman was leaning forward now, resting her forearms on her knees. Her eyes never left Candy's face. "It's a shame that you didn't bring her so we could see how she acted around you, see what we can do to help her."

"I thought you said you can help everyone. Is it really a problem that she stayed home?" Candy sounded nervous, and Freya's foot began to bounce. "If I'd known it would be a problem—"

"Next time you'll bring her, or you won't be invited to join us. Now I'm only standing in for our leader because she couldn't be here tonight, but I know she'd say the same thing. This isn't a group for women who aren't willing to commit, do you understand me? It's for women who want to help each other, who want to support each other. How are we supposed to support someone if they won't even bring their daughter for us to meet? It just makes it feel like you don't really trust us, and that's not a great way to start out this relationship." The woman nodded like it was all taken care of, then sat back in her chair. "Let's continue with the introductions, shall we?"

Freya exhaled. For a moment there, she'd been convinced Candy was about to get kicked out of the meeting. She needed a daughter she could pass off as her own.

And more than that, Freya needed to find out who the leader of the group was.

FORTY-FOUR

FRIDAY

Freya and Candy sat next to each other in a booth at Over Easy. The red pleather seat squeaked a little when either of them moved, and the music piped through the overhead speakers meant that they had a little trouble hearing each other. Rather than leaning forward over the table to talk, they opted to sit on the same side. At least the loud music meant it would be more difficult for anyone else in the restaurant to eavesdrop on them.

Busy tables filled the room, and the smell of frying bacon permeated the air. It was the bacon that had brought the two of them to the diner, causing them both to agree to eschew baked goods at Parker's. Besides, Freya didn't want Esther thinking she could drop by the table and try to listen to what they were talking about.

Not that she was nosy. But this case had grown and grown to the point that even a nun who never gossiped would want a piece of it.

Their waitress appeared, clad in a small red skirt and matching apron. "Here you go, ladies," she said, producing two huge platters of food and nestling them on the table. "What else can I get for you right now?"

"More coffee would great, Penny," Freya said. "And thanks for this—it's just what we need."

"Fighting crime takes a lot of calories, huh?" Penny grinned. "I'll be right back with that coffee. Shall I just leave the pot for you two?"

"Seeing as you've already had to refill us twice, I'd say that's a good idea, if you don't mind." Freya pulled her plate closer to her to clear space. "There. That looks like a good spot for a pot."

"You got it."

Both Freya and Candy waited until their waitress had brought back a pot of coffee and left it before speaking.

"Okay," Freya said, putting down her fork. "I heard everything that went on last night, but I'm sure I missed some details. There had to be things you saw that I wouldn't have been able to pick up on just hearing conversation. First of all, did you recognize anyone there?"

"Jennifer Peters was there. I thought it was her just based off your description of her, but the picture you showed me confirmed it."

"She's hard to miss," she said, grabbing a piece of bacon and biting off the end. "How did she look in person?"

"Like a porcelain doll."

"Sounds about right. What else?"

"I didn't recognize anyone else there, but I really didn't think I would. Most of the people we deal with on a regular basis don't have the mental or emotional bandwidth to even think about *cleansing* their daughters. If their kids act up, they just backhand them and call it a day. Although you did hear the woman who spoke saying she was standing in for their leader, right? So the head honcho wasn't there."

Freya nodded. Their cups of coffee were starting to run low, and she filled them back up, waiting as Candy stirred a bit of sugar into hers before speaking again.

"It doesn't sound like you're going to get an invitation to return."

Candy laughed. "Oh, I'd say that's true. Trust me, the fact that I didn't bring my daughter with me was pretty shocking. You heard what the woman said to me, but you didn't see the looks of horror on the other mom's faces. It was like I'd run over someone's cat."

"Well, it was a good try. I don't know where we can rent you a daughter to take to the next meeting though."

Candy shivered. "I couldn't bear to bring someone with me. Seriously, Freya, these women are off their rockers." She sat back and looked at her plate. Half of the food was gone. "You'd think I hadn't eaten in days, wouldn't you?" Heaving a sigh, she stood up, pulling her wallet from her pocket.

"Let me—" Freya began, standing as well, but Candy cut her off.

"Nope. Just nope. You sit down and let me handle this. Anyway, I need to stretch my legs and pee. Drinking half a pot of coffee was okay in college, but my body doesn't love it now."

Freya sat back down to finish her toast, but she kept an eye on Candy as the detective made her way to the register. She had to thread her way through tables as she walked, causing some other diners to look up at her.

This was a great way to get a read on people. How they watched police, especially women, when they weren't acting in a position of power, could provide a lot of information and tell you how they'd act when you were acting in an official capacity. Candy stood at the register and handed Penny her card. Just as she was about to take it back and sign the little slip of paper in Penny's hand, a woman walked up to her.

Freya tensed. The woman's face was drawn and tight, and she stood a few feet away from Candy, gesturing at her as she spoke. Candy held her arms out a little then looked down at her waist, gently resting her hand on the butt of her gun.

Without realizing what she was doing, Freya started to rise out of her chair. Her own gun felt heavy on her hip, and she angled her body to slide out from the booth, but before she could, the woman stomped away from Candy.

She slammed into the front door, pushing it all the way open. The bell overhead jangled angrily, and Candy turned to look at Freya. It was silly to think that time could stop, or even feel like it might, but the air in the cafe seemed to grow thin. Candy took her card from Penny and signed the slip of paper, then threaded her way back to their table.

"She was at the meeting last night," Candy said, answering Freya's question before she even had a chance to ask it. "And yes, she recognized me. That's why her face turned that funny shade of red and she looked like she wanted to rip my head off."

"Let me guess—you didn't share with the group last night that you were a cop."

"You know as well as I do that I didn't. But now she knows, and she freaked out. They weren't too happy that I didn't have a daughter with me there last night, and this is going to be the nail in my coffin as far as going back to another meeting. I'm out. I'm burned."

She sighed, dropping into the booth across from Freya and resting her face in her hands.

Freya's heart raced. Candy infiltrating the group had been a wild idea but probably their best way to get information on the women and what they were really up to. Now that one of the women had made her for a cop, there wasn't any way she'd ever be able to get information from them.

"I have an idea," Freya said, reaching across the table to touch Candy's hand. "It's going to sound a little crazy, but I want you to bear with me and not judge me right off the bat."

"Okay. Hit me." Candy looked weary.

"I'm going back into the woods as soon as we leave here. Something's happening there, and I need to find out what it is,"

Freya announced, downing the last of her coffee. "John and Steven are wrapped up, and John isn't going anywhere. If he did hurt those girls, he can't anymore. The mothers aren't talking. I can't just sit around and wait for something to fall into my lap."

"Do you want company?"

Freya shook her head. "I want you at the PD handling any case that might walk in. I'll check in when I have service. Let's go."

FORTY-FIVE

Nothing moved in the forest except for a few birds high in the trees above Freya's head. She'd been out in the woods for hours, walking the trails, sticking close to the water. She was quiet when she moved, doing everything she could to blend in even though she was sure she stuck out like a sore thumb. When she passed groups of hikers, they always eyeballed her, taking in her lack of hiking boots, pack, and water bottle.

It was silly, to think that she'd have good luck right off the bat, but that was sometimes how these things went. Beginner's luck.

But there was nothing for hours.

She felt like she was going insane. Sweat dripped down the back of her neck, she was completely neglecting any other cases that were piling up on her desk, and even though she was sure this was a fool's errand, what was she supposed to do?

Just stop looking? Hope that another little girl died and this time they'd be able to pin the death on the mother? No, there were enough little girls missing already. She could barely handle the cloud of no-see-ums that swarmed her, hovering around her mouth and nose, the blisters rubbing on her heels, and the fact that every step in the woods began to feel like torture.

But she didn't know what else to do.

Until she found something. Not even a clue, just something to prove that she wasn't going insane. White and limp, the ribbon lay in the mud by the river.

Lunchtime came, and she rushed to her Jeep, peeling out of the mostly empty parking lot towards town. She pressed down harder on the gas as she sped towards town, the evidence bag on her passenger seat. Her first order of business was to call the bakery, just to check and make sure Esther was okay. Then she'd stop by her office and get something to eat, check in with Candy and then...

It had hit her, what she needed to do. Out in the woods, surrounded by nature, looking for signs of a terrible crime, her next step had come to her.

At a red light, she sighed, dipping her forehead down to the steering wheel. She had a headache. Her body hurt. Even though it felt good to keep moving, if only because it made her think she was being productive even when she wasn't, this wasn't sustainable.

She pulled into the police parking lot and called the bakery.

"Parker's, this is Esther." Esther answered on the first ring, something she tried her best to do.

"Esther, hi, it's Freya. I wanted to check in on you before I have some lunch. Do you need anything?"

She was out of her Jeep now, facing the bakery, watching from across the street. How was Esther? It would be easy to walk over there and check on her, but that was the last thing the woman wanted.

"I'm fine. I tell you that every single day and it feels like you don't believe me. Now, let a little old woman sit and eat a cookie in peace, okay? I'm going to be just fine, Layla."

"Freya," Freya corrected, her heart sinking.

"Oh gosh, Freya, I know who you are. I'm just tired, and I was thinking about your mother. Now, go." She blew kisses into the phone and hung up.

For a moment, Freya stood still on the sidewalk. The afternoon sun was hot on her head. A group of men in suits walked by, and she watched as they turned into the bakery for a little afternoon snack. Still, even though she knew she needed to get in gear and head up to her office, hearing Esther call her by her mother's name had thrown her for a loop.

Esther was getting old. Aging was normal, and everyone went through it if they were lucky enough, but Freya couldn't shake the feeling that she needed to do more for Esther. *But what?*

"Right now, you can go to your office and eat something. Figure out what's going on in the real world and not just in the woods," she chastised herself.

Finally tearing her eyes away from Parker's, she headed up to her office, stopping in the break room long enough to grab her lunch. At her desk, she ate mindlessly, clicking into the internet to look for any articles that might help her out.

But apparently Fawn Lake was the only town dealing with missing girls.

"Okay," she said, speaking around a bite of leftover pasta salad, "Candy can't infiltrate the meeting because she doesn't have a daughter. They'll never let you in without one, but maybe there's another way."

Facebook.

That's what had come to her in the woods. Groups of women needed someplace to connect, to plan out their meetings.

Facebook it was.

Freya grimaced but navigated to the site. For a moment, she debated reviving her old account, the one she deleted five years ago, but she changed her mind. Best to start fresh.

"My name is Carla Moore," she said, her fingers flying over the keyboard as she made a new email account and then used that to log into Facebook. "I'm thirty-four, single with one kid, and I need mom friends." With just a few clicks, she downloaded a picture of a lily from the internet, set it as her profile picture, then searched for mom groups in and around Fawn Lake.

She found eight.

"Oof, there are a lot of them. Okay, let me see. How about Local Moms Looking to Network and Crunchy Moms of Fawn Lake?" With a few more clicks, she'd asked to be admitted as a member. A moment later there was a ding, and a notification popped up. "Local Moms Looking to Network declined me?" She scrolled down the screen. "Oh, because they think I don't work. Jokes on them though. I do work, but I'm not a mom."

She pulled out her phone to check her email while leaving the Facebook page up on her screen. A moment later, while she was reading about a new procedure to handle evidence, there was a soft ding from her computer.

"I'm in." She put her phone down on her desk and clicked into the Crunchy Moms group. The first five posts were all about toxins in food and growing your own garden. She skimmed through a few posts on canning, one on grounding, which was apparently walking barefoot outside, and two posts on keeping backyard chickens.

But nothing about moms pulling their kids out of school for days at a time. "There has to be something here," she muttered as she clicked into the search bar. She paused for a moment then typed in *girls' trip*. Three results popped up, but nothing that seemed suspicious. The first post was made by someone looking to take their daughter to the coast and wanting restaurant recommendations, so that one was out. The second and third talked about planning picnics at the park.

Frustration ate at Freya. She just had to get some information from the women who knew what was going on, and to do that she had to make them trust her.

In under ten minutes, her personal Facebook page looked like she'd fit right in with the crunchy mom community. She gave it a once-over then popped back into the group page.

"Okay, it's time," she whispered, flexing her fingers before dropping them back to the keyboard. Behind her, she heard something shuffling, and she glanced back at Cinnamon. Tarantulas might not be everyone's preferred pets, but what was she supposed to do, leave it to die?

"Hi, mamas," she said, her fingers flying across the keyboard. "I just wanted to reach out and see if I could get some help. Being a mom is hard work, but having a daughter is almost enough to drive me to the edge! I can't seem to get her under control. She's loud and dirty and always thinks she knows better than me in regards to... everything. Does anyone have any words of wisdom? Or help? I just want to make sure she knows who she is and how to be good and true to herself in this world as she grows older. I feel so lost! Please help me."

She reread what she'd just written, her finger on the button to post. Finally, she pushed it, then opened a new tab to check her email. She'd only gotten ten junk emails deleted when there was a soft bing.

"You've got to be kidding," she whispered, clicking back into Facebook. "There's no way someone responded that quickly." The little red notification in the corner drew her attention, and she clicked it.

"What are you doing?" Chief knocked on her door.

Freya glanced up, surprised. How had she not heard him coming? She must have been too involved in what she was doing.

"Listen to this Facebook comment someone named Margot Monroe just wrote." Freya cleared her throat. *"Hey, mama! Keep your head up—you got this. Daughters are a special kind of hell, aren't they? But you just have to find the right group of people to support you while you deal with yours."* She finished and looked up at Chief.

"That sounds promising," he said. "I take it your little jaunts into the woods haven't yielded anything helpful?"

"Just that." Freya pointed at the evidence bag sitting on her desk. "Hang on—let me respond to this." She thought for a moment.

Tell me about it! I'd love any help you can give me. I swear, just when I think I have things under control with her, she changes the game. If I don't get her to calm down and stop being so insufferable, I don't know what I'll do. I thought six was supposed to be fun, not this much work.

"Okay. What can I do for you today?" She kept one eye on her computer, the other on the chief as she waited for both a comment and his response. He held the evidence bag, turning it over and over as he looked at the white hair ribbon inside. With a sigh, he dropped it back on her desk.

"You haven't checked the news today, have you?"

"What? No. I've been busy. Hang on." She opened yet another tab and typed in the site for Fawn Lake's news. It only took a moment to load, then the headline popped up, written in all caps, so big that it took up her entire screen. *"Elementary school principal and janitor brother arrested,"* she read. "Looks like our team did some good work then, huh? Got that scum off the streets and out of the school."

"The school board is in a tizzy. First missing girls, now this? They want an interview."

"With you? Have fun."

"Oh no." Chief laughed and shook his head. "With the woman who figured this all out, who ferreted out the news." He held out his hands, spreading them like a rainbow. "I can see the headline now: *local detective returns, locks up pedophile.*"

"But it wasn't all me. I definitely didn't get to the bottom of this by myself. It was my team." Freya felt her cheeks flame.

"Team." He scoffed. "You have one detective and a rookie cop. That's hardly a team. They'll be here in the next few minutes for an interview. Kathy will call you as soon as they arrive."

"You're kidding me." Her computer dinged, but she didn't look away from him. Chief had always been a hard one to read, with deep lines around his eyes and on his forehead and a mouth perpetually pressed into a straight line.

"I never kid. Nail your interview—make me proud. This is your chance to show anyone in Fawn Lake who doubted you that you're on their side. Don't let this one slip through your fingers, do you understand? You need to take credit for this. And you're welcome."

She nodded, but before she could respond, the phone rang. Chief saluted her and sauntered out.

Oh, she'd nail her interview alright.

She picked up the phone.

FORTY-SIX

"I can't claim this success as my own. Without the power of an incredible team behind me, I don't think John and Steven Frank would have been arrested this quickly, with this much evidence. My team consists of Detective Candy Ellinger and Officer Brad Williams. They were instrumental in the investigation and arrests of these two men."

Chief stabbed at his trackpad, cutting off the rest of the interview. "This is not what I meant when I told you that this was the perfect setup for you to not only claim the win as your own but get everyone in Fawn Lake on your side again." He glowered at Freya over the top of his computer. "Explain yourself."

"It wasn't my win to take on my own." She lifted her chin and stared at him before adjusting her gaze to the wall of awards behind him. The man could have had the large corner office with plenty of windows to look out over downtown, but he'd opted instead for a windowless office where he could hang all of his awards and diplomas.

"But you should have taken it!" He slammed his meaty

hand down on his desk to punctuate his words. "You have a target on your back—you know that, don't you?"

"I do."

"And yet you... what? Choose not to get rid of that target because you want to share some of the glory with *your team?*" He made air quotes around the words. "That's easily the dumbest decision I've ever been privy to, Freya."

"So glad I was the one in the position to make it then, and not you. I wonder how many fewer accolades you'd have if you shared credit where it was due." She stood ramrod straight in front of his desk, and the way he recoiled, like she'd punched him, told her that her words had hit the mark.

"Out," he hissed, thrusting his finger through the air at her. "Out of my sight, out of my office. I gave you this win on a platter, and you—"

"You did no such thing." She was pushing it. Ever fiber in her being told her to do what he said, to turn tail and leave, but instead she planted her hands on his desk, leaning closer to him. "You did *not* give me this win. My team did. I just refused to take it, to walk all over them, to ignore the hard work they put into it. Don't think for one second this was your win, Chief."

"I'm the one who hired you. You're supposed to make me look good. It was a comeback story, you know that? Most chiefs wouldn't have looked twice at you after what you did." He stood up, leaning forward, his nose only inches from hers. "Remember that the next time you think about biting the hand that feeds you, Freya."

"How could I forget it when half the people in town remind me of that every single day?" She turned on her heel and stomped out of his office. For a moment she was convinced he was going to call her back, not to apologize but to continue their argument.

He didn't.

She resisted the urge to slam his office door shut and walked past the second door in the hall without turning her head. Miriam Alvarez, his assistant, had had a front row seat to their argument, and Freya had no doubt she'd done her best to memorize everything they'd said.

There was nothing like working in a small building. Everyone knew everyone's business, and everyone in and out of a uniform who worked in the building would know what had happened before they went home that evening.

She managed to keep her head high until she made it into her office. Her hands trembled as she turned and closed her door, then she sagged against it, finally sliding down to the floor. Hot tears burned her eyes, threatening to stream down her face. She was exhausted, like she'd run a marathon. Her breath came in little gasps, and she leaned forward, grabbing her knees.

A soft knock at the door made her sit straight. Angry, she wiped the back of her hand across her eyes, rubbing tears and mascara on her skin.

"Freya?" It was Candy, her voice soft and full of concern. "Can I come in, or are you sitting right behind your door?"

"Hang on." Freya scrambled to her feet and turned before backing away from the door. "Yeah, come on in."

Candy pushed the door open and closed it halfway behind her. "Thank you." She held out a piece of wood.

"You're welcome." Freya took the wood, turning it over and over in her hands. "But what's this?"

"It's for Cinnamon. Brad and I wanted to get you something that you might like, but I thought you'd kill us if we got you flowers. Did you know that you can't just pick up wood from the ground for a critter like her? You have to buy special wood that's been cooked or heated or something so it won't have parasites." She shrugged. "Anyway, we heard the news report, and I knew how Chief was going to take it."

"Y'all are sweet. And he took it about how you'd imagine." Freya was grateful for a reason to turn away from Candy. She carefully lifted the lid on Cinnamon's cage and placed the wood inside, giving her tarantula another place to hide. "Seriously, I couldn't have done it without you two. I would have gone crazy trying to chase my tail with everything going on."

"Things have gotten weird in Fawn Lake." Candy crossed her arms. "How did it go in Clear Creek Forest by the way; did you find anything?"

"Just a white hair ribbon. But that's not the most exciting thing." Freya dropped into her office chair and swiveled to face her computer. "This is going to sound nutty, but with everything going on with that interview and Chief having a hissy fit, I forgot I got a message."

"Check it." Candy perched on the edge of Freya's desk. "I need to know."

Freya opened her laptop and typed in her password. It only took a minute to open the Facebook tag and check the notification.

"Okay, it's the same woman who was responding to me before. When I didn't find anything substantial in the woods, I figured I better change tactics, so I posted a little sob story about how hard it is to be the mom of a daughter and asked if anyone could talk me through it. She reached out, so this is good."

"Looks like she wasn't the only one who reached out." Candy pointed at the screen. "Look how many moms wanted to commiserate with you." She wrinkled her nose as she stared at the screen. "They all call you *mama*."

"It's a thing in this group. You wouldn't get it," Freya teased, then clicked on the message from the first woman. "Alright, let's see. She says that being a mom is the hardest job anyone will ever have and not to let anyone tell you different."

"Has she ever chased a naked crack addict through an alley?" When Freya snorted, Candy laughed. "Just saying."

"I rather doubt she has. Just a hunch. She also says that she's a member of a really supportive group who meets regularly to get help and advice so they can control their unruly girls and prepare them for the dangers of the world."

"Unruly. They're elementary school kids. What, do you want them to sit still all afternoon?"

"I think they'd like that, yeah. I'm going to ask her to invite me to the group." Freya typed quickly, then pressed the button to send. "Candy, this is a great start, but now what? I can't infiltrate the group to learn what they're doing." She sighed.

"Do you have any other ideas?"

"There has to be some way we can get accepted into the group. We're both burned, but maybe I could wear a disguise?" She rubbed her temples. "I don't know, I'll have to think about it."

Candy groaned. "I had the one chance, and I blew it. This could be so much easier right now."

Freya touched her on the arm. "It's not like you could have known they'd demand to see your daughter in person to let you in the group. Besides, they're nut jobs. They'll slip up, or we'll figure something out."

Her computer dinged.

"As I was saying," Freya said, clicking on the little red notification. "Ooh, she sent me a private message. It says: 'Hey, mama. I'm sorry you're struggling so hard, but let me tell you about who can help you. It might sound crazy, but she's really the best. If you can come to a cleansing ceremony, you'll see how we can help you!'"

She stopped talking.

"What? You know something I don't—I can tell. Who is it? Who's the person can help you and fix everything?"

Freya blinked up at Candy. She'd read the name correctly, she was sure of it. But it still took her by surprise.

She'd met her. They'd talked.

And now she had to find her again.

FORTY-SEVEN

The leader looked around at the group of women. All of them mothers, all of them willing to do whatever it took to make the world a better place, starting in their own homes. So many people weren't willing to commit to something like that.

But these women were.

Their daughters sat at a table in another room, all of them waiting quietly, all of them silently coloring while the adults talked. It was just better that way. At the beginning, the daughters had been welcome in the meeting, but they were too much of a distraction.

Some of them wanted to talk. Some of them had questions.

But the mothers didn't have questions. They were willing to do whatever it took to improve the world.

To improve their daughters.

The leader took a deep breath and raised one hand. There was some murmuring around the circle, but it stopped, all of the mothers looking up expectantly. That was the way it should be.

"You have all done an amazing job," the leader said. Their voice filled the tiny room, and it pleased them. "I want you to know how happy I am with each and every one of you. Some of your daughters have improved. They're kinder. Quieter. Willing to listen and be seen, willing to do whatever we ask. I appreciate that. They did the hard work and came out on the other side."

Some of the women nodded. One ran her hand through her hair and glanced around the circle.

"But some of you know not all of your daughters are progressing. Some aren't doing what we've asked. They're not making an effort to improve, to better themselves. If they can't be good now, how can they withstand what the world will throw at them? I know that's hard to hear, but it's why we're here."

A cough from the other room, then silence. Were the girls listening? Maybe.

"Soon," the leader said, and now they made eye contact with the nervous woman sitting across the circle. "It's time for a cleansing. Our last recruitment event went well, with multiple new mothers coming for help. We're going to invite them in, teach them our ways. It's the right thing to do. It's the only way to ensure our daughters can survive the world. Can stay good in the face of all the evil out there."

"It is," the woman next to the leader said. She lifted her chin; stared around the circle. "It's the right thing to do."

The leader touched her shoulder. "Tomorrow we meet at the river."

FORTY-EIGHT

Linda Brown. Mother of Zach and Liz Brown, homeschooler, daughter of the Earth, sister of humankind. The woman's Facebook profile "about me" section read like something out of a strange novel, and Freya frowned, then clicked to see additional pictures.

Her profile picture was a flower, just like Freya's. She was hiding in plain sight, making it almost impossible for anyone to find her.

It wasn't until Margot had sent Freya the link that she'd found the woman in charge.

It was her. Liz Brown's mother, the little girl who had gone missing, the girl whose neighbor had been the only one to notice that she was gone and to assume that something must be wrong. Liz smiled up from her screen, her arm around her mother, her other touching her brother on the shoulder.

Her hair was in pigtails, and she sat cross-legged on a picnic blanket. In front of her was a plate stacked high with slices of watermelon. Freya's stomach twisted at the thought that the little girl might be dead.

Zach wore the same wry smile he'd had on his face when Freya had met him in his backyard. He stared off into the distance, not looking at the camera, like he didn't really want to have his picture taken. They were in a field, with thick trees behind them. It was impossible to tell exactly where the photo had been taken, as the field could be any field in the world, but the location didn't matter.

What mattered was who this woman was.

The leader. The one who could talk to her about how to get her daughter under control, how to ensure that her daughter never acted out again. Freya had met her at the gas station and she'd seemed completely normal, but now it looked like she'd just been hiding her crazy.

"She's the best," she whispered, reaching out and touching the screen. "The best at what? Convincing you that you don't need your daughter any longer? Telling you that you can kill her and all of your problems will go away? There's no way this woman isn't a complete psycho."

She hesitated, leaning back in her chair. Linda already knew who she was, so she had to be careful about how she approached this. Freya needed to convince her to meet, needed to pick her brain about what was going on. But Candy's failure to get accepted into the group ate at her. If Linda had been there the night Candy had infiltrated the group, they could have figured this out so much faster.

But she hadn't been there. And now Freya needed to be very careful.

Finally, she came to a decision and grabbed her phone. It rang as she held it to her ear. She was about to give up when the ringing stopped and a now familiar voice answered.

"Freya, is everything alright?"

"Hey, Paul, I'm so sorry to call you in the middle of the day like this." She paused, imagining what the man must think about why she was calling. "Esther is okay—you don't have to worry about that. I just need to ask you a huge favor."

"I'm made of favors. Whatcha got?"

"This is a big one, and I completely understand if you say no. But I'm really close to cracking the case of these missing girls. I know who's behind it, and I'm going to reach out to her to meet with me and see if I can get some information out of her."

"Okay. I don't see what this has to do with me." There wasn't anger in his voice, only interest.

Freya latched on to that. "I had my detective try to infiltrate their meeting, but they caught on to her pretty quickly. They wanted to know about her daughter, wanted proof of her having one. Candy doesn't have a kid and neither do I. It's a huge ask, but can I take some pictures with Marla so she looks like she's my daughter and I can hopefully get the ringleader to talk to me?"

Silence. It stretched on for so long that Freya actually pulled the phone away from her ear to look at the screen. Had they been disconnected?

"You want to take pictures with Marla so you can pass her off as your daughter with a group of women who are hellbent on killing little girls? Doesn't everyone in town know who you are?"

"Honestly, I know it's insane, and I know I probably shouldn't even ask you this, but I don't know what else to do. I feel like I'm at the end of my rope and something has to give. I figured I could wear a ball cap or a dress or something completely out of the norm for me and turn away from the camera a little so she can't easily see my face. This woman and I only met in person once, and she's a little disconnected from reality. I'm at a loss. I don't know what else to do."

"That's a big ask."

"I know." She grabbed the pen on her desk and started

clicking it. "I know it is, and I also know I have no right asking you for this. You can turn me down and I promise you, I'll understand. I won't ever bring it back up. I just don't know what to do, and if I don't take care of this, it's only going to escalate."

A heavy sigh. "How many people will see these pictures?"

"Just her," she promised. "I want to send her a message and see if she'll meet. She'll want some proof of me having a daughter; I'm sure of it. I'll send her a picture of me with Marla and pass her off as my daughter and she'll never be the wiser."

She put the pen down on her desk and closed her eyes. She wasn't one for praying, but the thought crossed her mind.

"Okay. I'll do it."

"Really?" Freya sat straight up. "Paul, thank you. I can't thank you enough for trusting me. I promise you, Marla will never be in any danger. I wouldn't ask her to be. It's just a photo, and that should be enough to get me into this woman's graces."

"That's fine." He exhaled hard. "Um, I'm still working, and Marla's at 4-H club until five this evening. Chess club, can you believe that? She certainly didn't get her brains from me. Anyway, can you be at our house after that, and we can get you some pictures?"

"I'll be there. Thank you. I really don't know how to thank you enough for being willing to do this. For trusting me."

"I only trust you because of Esther," he said. "I want you to know that, Freya. You just have to make sure Marla is safe."

"She's safe," she assured him. "And after I get this photo and meet with this woman, I'll be one step closer to making sure that all the little girls in Fawn Lake are safe."

They hung up, and she stared at the clock. Her fingers itched to reach out to Linda immediately, but she had to wait. She had to meet with Paul; wait to get the photo with Marla.

She just had to hope that her waiting wouldn't put another girl in danger.

Her phone rang, and she picked it up. "This is Captain Sinclair."

"Freya, this is Kathy." A pause. "James Smith is here. He wants to speak with you."

FORTY-NINE

Freya eyeballed the man standing in the lobby of the police department. He was tall, with long red hair that brushed his shoulders. Clad in camouflage cargo pants and a tight black shirt, his ensemble was completed with a pair of black hiking boots. From what Linda had said about James, he was happiest outside, and he looked like it. When he heard her walking behind him, he turned, flipped his hair out of his face.

"James Smith? I'm Captain Sinclair." She held out her hand to shake his. She was running on caffeine and adrenaline but still felt exhaustion weighing her down.

"Nice to meet you." His hand was huge, his grip firmer than she'd expected.

She shook his hand, sizing him up at the same time. His cheeks were slightly sunburned. The backs of his hands were scarred. When he shook her hand, she could feel callouses on his fingertips.

He looked like a prepper, someone much more comfortable outdoors than indoors, like someone who could easily handle whatever came at them, no matter if it was an unexpected storm or a feral hog.

And, according to Linda, Liz was supposed to be with him. So what was the man doing standing in the police department looking for all the world like he was going to cry?

"I want to talk to you about my daughter, Liz." He swallowed hard. "Do you have a place where we can do that without everyone overhearing us?"

"Why don't we go upstairs to my office?" She led the way, her mind racing as they hurried upstairs. How much time had her team spent trying to track this man down, then he suddenly appeared out of nowhere? It was weird, and she couldn't wait to talk to him and figure out exactly what was going on.

Once they were settled in her office, she turned to him, a smile on her face. "Please tell me what's going on."

"It might not be anything." He scratched the back of his neck, then shook his head. "No, you know what? I told myself I wasn't going to do that."

"Do what?" Freya picked up a pen and pulled a notepad in front of her.

"Second-guess myself." A heavy sigh. "Liz is my daughter, but her mother and I aren't together. I'm not one for the white picket fence, but that's never been a problem before. Linda, that's her mom, she's always been fine with me having custody of Liz on and off. It works for us, and it works for my baby girl." He spread his hands wide on his knees, then looked up at her. "Only this time it didn't work out the way it's supposed to."

"What happened?"

"I'm supposed to have Liz, but when I came to pick her up, I can't find her or her mother. They're just... not here."

Freya sat forward. "Wait, what?"

"We don't have an official custody agreement. And before you get on me about that, I know it's stupid. But Linda and I haven't ever done anything with the courts, you know? It's not for the two of us. We're much happier just living our lives and making it up as we go along. So we had a baby together, but we're not the marrying type. It was okay for both of us to be separate and co-parent."

"But you said Liz is supposed to be with you right now? Have you tried calling Linda?"

He gave her a look. "Of course I have. I can't get in touch with her. I came into town yesterday and couldn't find Linda. She wasn't at the house, wasn't at the gas station. Her son—you know Zach?—yeah, he's something else, he told me Linda already brought Liz to me. But she didn't. I don't know where she is, and I don't know where my daughter is." His voice broke.

Keeping her cards close to her chest had always been something Freya was good at. It was a better option than spilling the beans and letting a suspect know that you were on to them. Her face was a mixture of concerned and interested. Best to keep hidden what she knew about Linda, or at least... what Linda had told her.

"Has Linda ever done anything like this before? Set a time for you to get Liz and then not shown up?"

He shook his head.

"When's the last time you saw Liz?" she asked.

"Oh, a month or so ago. She spent about five days with me camping and hiking."

"And when did you last speak to Linda?"

He frowned. "Oof, about a week ago. I called Linda, let her know I missed my daughter and wanted to see her. It's almost the season for blue ghost fireflies. We were gonna head into the woods, stake out a place to camp to try to get a good look at them."

Freya nodded but didn't respond.

James must have misread her silence for disbelief. "Get one thing straight, Captain: there aren't many things in this world that scare me, but something happening to my little girl? That's the stuff of nightmares. Keeps me up all night long."

"I can only imagine." Her voice sounded hollow. She swallowed and tried to focus.

James rubbed his temples. "I just don't know what to do. She told me to come by, that she'd have Liz packed up and ready to go. What do I do if I can't find my little girl? Where would Linda have taken her?"

His words washed over her. "I'll be honest with you," she said carefully, choosing each word to ensure she wouldn't upset him more than he already was, "I was looking for you, to verify that you had Liz with you."

A pause. She could almost see the man's brain working as he thought through what she'd just said. "Why did you feel like you needed to reach out to me to make sure I had Liz?"

"Because we wanted to check up on her. Make sure of her wellbeing. A neighbor called, reported her missing, and we offered to perform a health and welfare check." She dropped her pen to her desk.

"Do you think Linda hurt Liz?" James half-stood, then sat back down. He ran a hand through his hair and stared at her. By now, his cheeks were flushed. He was breathing quickly. "Do you think she hurt my baby?"

"I don't know." Freya held up her hands. "What I can tell you is that my team and I will do whatever it takes for us to find the two of them, but I'm going to need your help."

"I'll do anything."

"Here." She pushed the pad of paper and pen across the desk to him. "Write down all the places Linda likes to go. Not her home and work obviously. If you think she might be there, write it down. I'll send officers to each of them, have them run patrols. I'll also release a BOLO for Linda and Liz. Get their names and photos out there."

James wrote quickly, filling a few lines of the paper before pushing it back to her. "Do you think my baby is okay?"

She looked at him, weighing her words. There were few things worse than looking a grieving parent in the eye and lying to them. "All I know is I'm glad you're here. And I promise you, I'll do everything in my power to find your daughter."

FIFTY

"Alright, Linda," Freya said, opening a new DM with the woman, "I hope this works." She exhaled hard, trying to calm herself. Nerves ate at her as she worked.

There hadn't been any luck with the BOLO on Linda and Liz so far. Officers were combing Fawn Lake, looking into all of her favorite haunts. James had been more than happy to give her information on where Linda might be, but so far, nothing had panned out.

Waiting to take a photo with Marla had almost done Freya in. She'd been on the road looking for Linda until five. Then she'd sped over to Paul's, thanked him again for letting her get a picture with Marla, and hurried back to the office after their photoshoot.

Now her first action was to attach a photo of her and Marla to her message to Linda. The little girl had leaned into the act of being Freya's daughter, putting her arms around her and grinning as Paul had taken their photo.

It was strange, looking at her face grinning out from a picture next to the face of a little girl like that. The photo she was sending to Linda had Freya squinting away from the camera, wearing an oversized cardigan she'd borrowed from the lost and found box as well as a ball cap pulled down to shadow her face.

But the photo where Marla and Freya were happy, were both smiling like nothing in the world bothered them? That's the photo that made her choke up. She hadn't ever thought about having kids. Her parents hadn't been around much when she was younger, and she'd never imagined that she'd be very maternal. Then, when the truth of who they were had come out, she'd doubled down on that, swearing off of accidentally passing on any genes that should die with her.

But looking at her and Marla... she didn't know what it was, but there was something about seeing herself next to a child that made her smile. Maybe being a mother wouldn't be so bad.

"Yeah, right," she muttered, clicking away from the photo and into the message box. "Because you have so much free time, and I'm sure you'd do a wonderful job keeping anything more demanding than a tarantula alive."

Her brain raced as she thought about what to say to the woman. Linda Brown looked like every wishful homesteader. In her photos, she wore a lot of overalls and Muck Boots, standing out in her backyard by a little patch of dirt she called a garden. Sometimes Liz was in the picture with her, but most of the time it was Linda alone, looking for all the world like a woman in a survival movie.

"Hi, Linda," Freya said, her voice quiet in her office as she typed. Most everyone else on the fourth floor had gone home already, and it felt strange speaking as she wrote, but she wanted it to sound as natural as possible. "I'm Carla, and a mutual friend, Margot Monroe, told me to reach out to you. My daughter, Annie, is a handful. She's a nightmare, if I'm being honest. I don't know what it is about her, but I can't seem to get her under control, and I don't want her to be like this the rest of her life. I want her to be better. I owe it to her to ensure she's better, that she can survive what the world will throw at her."

She sat back in her chair. "This is gross," she announced.

Her cursor blinked back at her like an accusation. As disgusting as she felt writing these words, she knew she needed to finish the message.

A heavy sigh, then she started typing again, speaking as she did. "Will you please help me? I don't know what to do with her, but you're the expert. At this point, I'm willing to do whatever. Annie is completely out of control. She doesn't seem to understand that being good is the only way to survive this world."

That was good, right? Not too much? Maybe a little desperate, but what other tone was she supposed to have in her message? She *was* desperate, if she was being honest. Not because of some child that was ruining her life, but because of what would continue to happen in town if she didn't nail this woman.

She scrolled back up to the top of Linda's Facebook profile and read her "about me" again.

Linda Brown. Mother of Zach and Liz Brown, homeschooler, daughter of the Earth, sister of humankind.

"Candy!" Freya leaned to the side of her desk and called to her detective before looking back at her screen. She needed to reach out to Linda, but that wasn't the only thing they needed to do. They had to get information about the homeschoolers. Sure, they'd tried, but just trying wasn't enough any longer. "Candy! Get in here!"

A chill raced down her spine.

Candy appeared a moment later, two cups of coffee in her hands. "Hey, where's the fire? I realized you and I were the only ones here besides dispatch and patrol, and I thought we could use something to get us through the rest of the evening." After offering Freya a cup and taking a sip, she raised her eyebrows and waited.

"The two dead girls nobody has come forth to claim? They have to be homeschoolers. It's the only thing that makes sense."

Candy nodded. "We've tried to get information about homeschoolers in the area from the North Carolina Department of Non-Public Education, but they're a nightmare."

Freya nodded. "I know. When I talked to Lance and he told me how little oversight there is in North Carolina, I knew we had to look into this, but they're not playing nicely. If nobody's monitoring where the homeschool kids are, then they'd never know when one went missing, and they're the only ones with information on these kids. When Brad reached out to them, they didn't want to help us at all. Not without a warrant anyway, and even then they sent it to their lawyers. Their very slow, very meticulous lawyers."

Candy shook her head. "They can't keep dragging their feet. When did he send them the warrant?"

"Yesterday."

"That's ridiculous. Do they not realize these kids are in danger?"

"I have no idea." Freya stretched her arms over her head. "This is what's going to happen. I want you to read this and then reach out to the North Carolina Department of Non-Public Education again. Tell them to get in gear, that we're not waiting around any longer. That we have lawyers too, and that I'm more than happy to get them involved if they keep dragging their feet helping us. See if they'll give you any information on girls in the area. I'd rather go that route than plaster their photos all over the news and wait for someone who knows them to come forward."

"You got it, although I don't think they'll be open again until Monday since it's after five." She took another sip of coffee. "But you know what? That won't stop me from hunting down some personal phone numbers and making this happen. Now, what was it you wanted me to read?" She leaned forward to look at the computer screen.

"It's a message to Linda. I just need to know: is it too much? I need to sound desperate enough for her to take pity on me. The last thing I want is for her to ignore me."

"It's pretty desperate," Candy said, "but I think that's good. I mean, honestly, you have to be at the end of your rope to be willing to kill your own child, right? I can't imagine that women make that decision lightly."

"I don't think they realize they're going to kill their daughters," Freya said. "These women aren't stupid. They're not uneducated. They're desperate for a break, for some help. So Linda talks them into cleansing their daughters, into making them better, and sometimes the girls don't make it."

"You mean 'if they're bad' they don't make it." Candy made air quotes around the words. "That tracks with what I was hearing at the meeting I went to. If they're good and can change, be saved and clean, the girls will walk out of it in one piece."

"Exactly."

"Like the Salem witch trials. If they floated, they were a witch. If they drowned... whoops. Guess they weren't."

Freya clicked the send button and then took a long drink of her coffee. "I met with Paul, and he let me take some pictures with Marla so she looks like she's my daughter. The last thing I wanted was for this woman to sniff me out the way you were sniffed out at that meeting."

"Smart. So what are you thinking? You meet with this Linda Brown, then what? Do you think she's just going to confess to you that she killed her daughter?"

"Ha! I wish. My first hope is that she doesn't recognize me in this photo. I don't think she will, since she seems to be a little bit out there. I thought at first that it was surprising she had a Facebook since she's so into nature and homesteading, but then

I realized that she has to have some way to brag to people about what she's done in her garden. Chances are... maybe not *great*, exactly, but good that she has no idea who I am."

"So she reads this and takes pity on you? Her agreeing to help you isn't enough. We need her to actually meet up with us, especially since she's in the wind."

"I know. If she won't agree to meet up, I'm going to have to hunt her down another way, and we're already having trouble finding her. James gave me information on where she likes to spend time, but officers keep coming up empty, so we really need this to work. I'm planning on getting an invite to this little cleansing ceremony everyone keeps talking about. I can't show my face there, though, because she would recognize me immediately. So no showing up to the party through the front door."

"But there's always a back door," Candy said, and Freya nodded.

"Yep. All I need are the details of the next ceremony and we can get together a team to stop them. I want to catch these women in the act, so there's absolutely no way they can wriggle out of it. They're horrible people, and I plan on putting them all where they belong. I just have to wait on their ringleader to message me back." She glanced at her screen.

The little circle next to her message had changed from a checkmark to Linda's profile picture. Candy saw where Freya was looking and leaned over to point.

"See that? She's read what you wrote. Right now she's probably checking out your Facebook profile and deciding whether or not she should respond."

"No pressure." Freya drummed her fingers on her desk. Little bubbles appeared in the text box and then disappeared. "Oh, she's typing. It's happening."

Candy stood and walked around the office. "I don't think I've been this nervous since waiting on a boy I liked in high

THREE DROWNED GIRLS   277

school to get his act together and invite me to prom. Did you have a cute date for prom?"

"You're trying to distract me," Freya said, glancing up from her screen. "But no, I didn't. I didn't even go to prom after braving homecoming one time. Esther and I stayed home in our pajamas and ate Chinese takeout while watching *Sixteen Candles*. It was everything I wanted at that moment, and I'd do it again."

"No prom." Candy frowned. "So no fancy dress, corsage, or limo ride with your friends?"

"Exactly. Also no sweaty boy trying to pull me closer to dance, nobody drinking too much in the bathroom and throwing up on me, no hair sprayed to the heavens to the point it was more like a helmet than my actual hair. Oh, she responded. Check it out." She read it to herself before reading it out loud to Candy. "*Hi, Carla! I'm so sorry to hear you're struggling with Annie. Everyone says that having a daughter is such a blessing, but it can be a trial. I'd love to talk to you more and see if I can help you.*"

"Great, that's great. No invite, but we can work with this. She needs her ego stroked, so work that angle."

"Good call. I want to end this. End her." Her fingers flew. She wasn't entirely sure what to write, but that wasn't going to stop her. "*Thank you so much,*" she said as she typed. "*I've literally been at my wit's end, but you can help me, I know you can. The thought that this nightmare with Annie could be over is a relief. I need it to end. I need her to be better. I need her to be strong and pure enough to survive this world.*"

"That sounds really desperate," Candy said. "Good. She's going to think you two are on the same page from the beginning."

"That's my hope..."

The bubbles were back. "*You sound like a woman after my own heart! I can tell you, as soon as I took care of things with my daughter, Liz, my life got better. If little girls can't be clean, can't be good, they can't handle this world. I needed to help her, clean her, and I did,"* Freya read. "That's enough for me to get a warrant by the way. It's almost a confession."

"Try to get an invite," Candy urged. "Tell you heard about the cleansing ceremony and you think it's your only option."

"Right. Okay." Freya exhaled. *"I heard you were the best for fixing problems like this. I just need my daughter to be better. Margot mentioned a cleansing ceremony, and if that will give me the fresh start I need, then I'm willing to do it. Please help me—you're my only hope."*

"'Help me, Obi-Wan Kenobi,'" Candy said, laughing. "Let's hope she's not a *Star Wars* fan, although I don't really think that's a concern."

They waited while Linda typed.

"You poor thing," Freya read. *"I'm sorry you're struggling so much. I don't usually invite new mothers to our ceremonies without having them come to meetings first. It's just best that way. Helps us make sure everyone is a good fit."* She sighed.

"I've got it," Candy said. "Tell her: *I'm happy to do whatever you need me to do, but please don't make me wait. I'm desperate. I'll do whatever you say.*"

"Ooh, I like that. People like this are so delusional. They think they're the only ones who can help a person—that they're the only ones who know how to get out of a bad situation. I'll be shocked if that doesn't work." Her fingers flew on her keyboard.

Candy sat down on Freya's desk. "It has to work."

"It'll work," she agreed.

The bubbles popped up.

They disappeared.

She felt like she was going to throw up.

Candy stood. "I'm going to start finding those phone numbers," she said, but Freya held her hand up to stop her leaving.

The bubbles reappeared. They bounced on the bottom of Freya's screen for a long time before disappearing when words popped up.

"What is it?" Candy leaned over to see the computer screen. "Please tell me she bit."

"She bit. Hook, line, and sinker." Her fingers flew over the keyboard. "*I'll do my best to get off work,*" she said as she typed. "*Thank you so much for helping me! You're the best. I can't thank you enough.*" She pressed send and turned to Candy. "Linda sent me the information on the next cleansing ceremony. It's tomorrow afternoon."

FIFTY-ONE

It wasn't their fault, the little girls. No, she couldn't think of a single little girl who was made dirty and wrong because of their own fault. It was just how the world was.

She'd known for a long time that her job was to fix them. To take those little girls who were so broken and so dirty and make them better, make them whole, *cleanse* them.

But she didn't blame the girls. No, not *blame*, never blame, because how they were wasn't their fault. It was just that the world was terrible and hard and would grind you up and spit you out. And that wasn't fair to the girls.

Not if they could do more than just survive the world—if they could be good and kind and make it a better place.

And that's why she started to cleanse them. Fix them. Make them better, and clean, and ensure that they wouldn't be tainted by the world. And yes, that meant that some of them didn't survive. Sometimes, the water got in them, and instead of cleansing them, it took them away.

And that just meant they were too dirty to survive. It just meant they weren't good enough for this Earth. The mothers understood that.

Growing up, all they had heard was to be good. Be clean. Be strong, but not too strong. Don't embarrass anyone. Don't cause a scene. Make sure everyone knows how perfect you are, how wonderful, how in control and careful, and untouchable.

It was a gift. The cleansing was a gift, a chance at a better life, a promise to the future and to the world that the little girls from Fawn Lake would be the best in the world, would be kind and clean and perfect.

And if some people didn't see it that way? That was on them. Only the strong mothers, the ones who really loved their children and wanted a good world for them, would understand.

Society might say those mothers were weak. That they were too willing to give up their children, but the leader knew better.

Those mothers were the strong ones. And those little girls? The ones who went into the cleansing but didn't survive? The ones taken out of the harsh, cruel world, before anything bad happened to them?

They were the lucky ones.

FIFTY-TWO

SATURDAY

Gnats clouded around Freya's head, but she didn't move to brush them away. Sun filtered down through the leaves above them, and a bird scuffed around in the brush, but still she didn't move. She couldn't see anyone else on her team, but they were there, as silent as her, everyone waiting for the signal to go.

When the bird stopped scratching in the dry leaves, a thick silence fell in the woods. It was oppressive and broken only by the whine of a mosquito. She waited until it landed on her cheek then slowly lifted her hand to kill it. She didn't slap it, not wanting to make the sudden noise, but instead pressed her thumb down on it until it crushed against her skin.

The earpiece she wore was silent. It had been comfortable when she'd pressed it in place an hour ago but now felt awkward. Rather than reaching up to shift it around though, she stared harder into the woods; forced herself to listen for any sign of water.

They were close. On the map they'd seen this morning before heading out, it had looked like it was going to be a straight shot from where Freya stood to the river. They were meeting there this time, although apparently the cleansing had happened in the lake last time. Linda said she liked to rotate between the two so nobody would ever be able to guess where they would be each time.

She'd told Freya about how a man and his daughter had interrupted them once. That she'd almost lost it telling them to leave, that she had to be careful.

It was the rambling of a person pushed so close to the void that they'd decided falling into the void would be a better option than trying to remain a good person.

"Team, move forward. They're in the water." Freya stiffened as the voice in her ear crackled to life. Grateful, she took a step forward, then another, still moving slowly. Her steps were measured and careful to keep anyone from hearing her.

More steps. Dead branches and a fallen tree were in her path, and she scrambled over them, ignoring the pounding in her head. She clambered over a huge fallen tree, the bark scraping her palms, then ducked under a low branch.

"Slower now," the voice commanded, and she paused. She was coming in from a ridge and would have to slide down it to reach the river. When the assignments had been handed out last night, she'd thought about taking an easier one, but there wasn't any way she was letting anyone else get there first. From the ridge, she'd have the perfect vantage point and would be able to see everything before it hit the fan.

"They're in the river. One girl is in the water, dressed in a white dress."

Her heart beat faster. She had a very good feeling what that white dress meant. "The girl in the river is in danger," she whispered. Her voice would reach everyone's ears, hopefully making them more aware of what was going on. It didn't matter how much she'd explained to the team what was at stake, what they needed to do, how they needed to act, part of Freya was terrified this was going to go wrong. And if it did, it would all be on her.

"Copy. Watch for the girl in the river. You all know your targets."

Well, that wasn't entirely true. They knew what they were supposed to do, but besides the limited women Freya and Candy could name as part of this group, there wasn't any way to know for sure who would be in there. Undercover officers stationed in the parking lots had kept an eye out for hikers fitting the description of the women, but the warmer weather had drawn crowds.

The water was cool and tempting, and it was the time of year where many students and adults alike called in sick to take advantage of the nice weather and go swimming. It was the weekend, which meant the water was even more tempting. The parking lots were full of local and tourist vehicles. Knowing exactly who was there for nefarious reasons was impossible.

They just had to do their best.

She pulled her weapon. Checked the safety. The grip bit into her skin, and she squeezed it tighter, enjoying the slight discomfort. You should never pull your weapon without reason, and the pain of the grip cutting into her skin reminded her of that.

Sweat trickled down her back. If she strained her ears, she thought she could hear the sound of water. The river was so close, but her heart pounded, making it difficult for her to focus on any other sound.

"Ten seconds."

She tensed. Under her foot, a stick cracked, but the sound wasn't nearly loud enough to worry about. Nobody would have heard it, especially if they were close to the river. That rushing water was sure to drown out any other sound.

"Five."

She closed her eyes. Breathed through her nose.

"Four."

Another deep breath.

"Three."

Now Freya opened her eyes. She leaned forward, her legs tense, ready to burst through the underbrush. Time was of the essence. Not only did they need to keep anyone from escaping, but they had to make sure nobody got hurt.

"Two."

So close.

"One."

She took off like a shot, ignoring the pain in her hip, ignoring how her toe caught on a branch and she tipped forward for just a moment, just enough to worry her, but then she caught herself and she was back, pushing past a thick pine with low branches, coming out on top of the ridge, skidding to a stop just long enough to take in the scene below her.

There.

In the water.

A little girl in a white dress. Her hair was done in braids down her back, her eyes wide. They made eye contact for just a moment, then the woman standing next to the girl planted her hand on her head and pushed her down under the surface of the water.

FIFTY-THREE

"No!" The sound burst from Freya, and she hurtled down the ridge, catching her ankle on the sharp edge of a broken stick, ignoring the pain that seared across her face when a branch hit her on the cheek. She blinked to protect her eyes, then kept running.

She was a good shot. You didn't spend hours at the range getting better and better to not feel confident carrying a gun, but a shot like that? When Linda was right next to the girl, the girl herself fighting back, the woman's body twisting and straining as she tried to keep the girl underwater?

No. That shot was too much, even for her.

She wouldn't risk it.

Instead, she ran, falling once when the toe of her boot got caught on a root but getting right back up. Other officers streamed out of the forest. The small knot of women at the riverbank scattered, but she didn't slow down to make sure they got caught.

They'd get caught. Everyone knew their role, and hers was to get to the little girl in the water. The women wouldn't be able to get away, not with that much panic coursing through their veins. They were scared, and scared people were stupid people.

Frigid water splashed up on her, soaking through her clothes. Freya ignored it, never taking her eyes off the little girl in the middle of the river. The woman holding her down twisted around to look at Freya. Her mouth was open, her eyes dark slits as she glared.

"You can't have her!" Linda screamed, twisting her fingers through the girl's hair. She stepped back, yanking the girl with her. The girl breached the water, her mouth open to suck in air. Before she could make a sound though, the woman slammed her back under the water, locking her elbows to hold her down.

Freya slipped on a flat rock but caught herself, pinwheeling her arms to keep from falling. Bracing herself against the current, she leveled the gun at the woman.

"Let her up now!" Her finger tightened on the trigger. Behind her, officers were yelling. Women cried. But Freya never looked away.

"You can't have her!" Linda's voice was terrible, high and tight, rippling with anger. Rage had made her face splotchy. Foam from the girl fighting back bubbled up between them. "I have to clean her!"

The girl didn't have much longer.

"Last chance!" Freya's finger tightened more. Just a tiny twitch, one little bit more pressure, and the woman would drop like a stone. But the girl would survive.

"You go to—"

Freya pulled the trigger. The sound echoed off the surface of the water, punctuated by the splash of Linda screaming. Turning. Fleeing. Ignoring her, Freya hurried to the frothing water, holstering her gun as she moved.

She plunged her hands into the river. Water lapped at her thigh, which meant it was deep enough to swim, but the girl should still be able to stand. Her hand hit something soft—*the girl's shoulder?*—and tried to grasp it but couldn't get a grip. Rage ripped through her and she screamed, dropping to her knees in the water.

Her face went under, and she opened her eyes. Bubbles made it difficult to see, but she blinked hard, thrusting her arms out in front of her. Finally, her fingers brushed cloth and she grabbed it, yanking it up as she stood. Water streamed from her body as she pulled the girl out of the water.

The girl's head lolled back, her mouth open. Water pooled in the depression in her neck, and her arms hung loosely by the side of her body. "She's not breathing!" Freya screamed the words, turning back to the riverbank. It hadn't seemed like a far way to go when she'd rushed into the water, but now the distance stretched out in front of her, seeming to grow as she took step after step.

The girl weighed close to nothing, even soaking. Her body jostled up against Freya's chest as the detective found her footing to the bank. There, she dropped to her knees, putting the little girl down in the mud.

Fingers under the chin, fingers pressing her forehead back. The girl's face tipped up to the sky, a smattering of freckles resting like dirt against her cheeks. Freya pressed her lips against the girl's and blew two hard breaths, then sat back, linking her fingers together and pressing down on the girl's chest.

Her elbows locked, she pumped. The Bee Gees' "Stayin' Alive" ran through her head as she kept rhythm. Somewhere, off to her side, someone was screaming. A woman, calling for her baby.

Freya ignored her. She ignored the officers standing around her, even ignored Candy when the younger detective tried to push her out of the way to help.

"Let me," Candy began, but Freya had stopped compressions and was breathing into the girl's mouth.

"Come on—breathe!" Water dripped down her cheeks and onto the girl's face. "Take a breath!" She choked out a sob, linking her fingers back together to resume compressions. The girl's chest bounced under Freya's strength. There was a loud pop as a rib snapped.

"Freya," Candy began, but Freya shook her head.

"Let me make her breathe!" Freya yelled then shifted her weight to the side, gently tucking her fingers under the girl's chin. Candy grabbed Freya's shoulder and she shook, trying to slip free.

"Freya, she's breathing! You have to stop! She's okay!" Candy screamed the words in her face then kneeled next to her captain and grabbed her hands, squeezing them hard as she shook. "She's alive, she's breathing. Look." Carefully, Candy pressed Freya's hand to the girl's neck.

There. Soft and fluttery, like a butterfly, but there—her pulse so light it was hard to feel. Freya pressed her fingers harder into the soft neck.

It didn't stop. Her heart kept beating. She kept her fingers on her pulse until an EMT took her by the shoulder. Then she stood, watching as the little girl was loaded onto a stretcher.

People were still yelling. Someone was still crying.

Linda.

Freya turned back to the river. She wasn't getting away with this.

That was all that mattered.

FIFTY-FOUR

Freya bolted into the woods. Linda had a head start on her, but Freya wasn't going to let that stop her. She couldn't shoot Linda, not when the woman was fleeing. When she was trying to drown the little girl, that was one thing. But she couldn't shoot her now.

She had to catch her.

Her pants clung to her legs, her boots squished with each step, but she ran faster, pumping her arms to drive herself forward. Behind her was pandemonium. The little girl was screaming now. Even though the sound was out of place in the woods, it meant she was alive.

But no matter what she heard, Freya couldn't stop. Not now. Not when Candy was with the little girl, who was fine; not when Linda was going to try to get away from her.

Linda. This entire thing came back to her. And there wasn't any way Freya was going to let her get away. Linda was going to pay for what she'd done. She was going to be right there the entire time, making sure of it.

A low branch in front of her made her slow down. She

ducked, scooting under it, thick pine needles brushing her hair. She straightened back up and paused, just for a moment, only long enough to catch her breath. Then she looked down at the ground.

She wasn't a prepper, and she certainly wasn't a hunter. But she knew enough about tracking from growing up in a small town and spending most of her childhood outside. Disturbed leaves and pine needles told her she was headed in the right direction.

Freya hurried around a thick tree, ignoring briars as they ripped into her pants. She stepped carefully over a rotten log, then ducked once more under a thick, low branch.

She never saw it coming.

Linda stepped out from behind the tree, a thick piece of wood in her hands. A guttural scream ripped from her throat as she swung it straight into Freya's face.

Her nose crunched.

Blood poured from it, dripping down her chin, soaking into her shirt; at the same time, her eyes flooded with tears. Bright pain shot through her, and she screamed, bending over and covering her face with both hands.

"You can't have them!" Linda dropped the wood and launched herself at Freya. Her arms wrapped around Freya's waist as she slammed into her. Freya stepped back, desperate to find her footing, but the ground was soft, and pine needles shifted under her.

She fell, Linda on her. The impact knocked the air from her lungs, and she tried to gasp for breath. But no matter how desperate she was to fill her lungs with air, her diaphragm remained temporarily paralyzed.

Fear ate at her, and she reached up, bracing her hands against Linda's shoulders. The woman twisted out of her grasp, leaning closer to Freya as she screamed.

"They're mine! I'm saving them!" Spit flew from her mouth

and landed on Freya's cheek. Her eyes were wide, her lips pulled tight into a grimace.

Freya inhaled, a wave of dizziness washing over her before she could speak. "You're crazy! You know that? You're not saving them; you're killing them!" She brought her knee up, shifting it under Linda's hip. Linda grabbed her by the throat, her fingers tight around her neck.

Black spots appeared in Freya's vision. She responded by digging her nails into Linda's wrist. The woman screamed, then released her, raising her hand to hit her again.

It was Freya's chance, and she took it, shoving her knee up and to the side, throwing Linda onto her back.

"No!" Linda started pushing up, but before she had a chance to recover, Freya was on her, pinning her down to the ground. Her fingers pressed hard into Linda's wrists; her knees pinned her hips in place. Blood dripped from her face onto Linda's, but neither of them moved.

Their noses were an inch apart. Their eyes locked on each other.

"You didn't think you were going to get away with it, did you?" Freya asked, her voice quieter now. The birds had all fallen silent, and, for a moment, it felt like they were the only two left on Earth.

"They need me," Linda said. She tried to move her hand, but Freya squeezed her wrist tighter, keeping her in place. "Don't you see? They need me. You have to see it. They did! The mothers did! They saw what I needed to do to help them, to help their little girls."

"I see that you're crazy," Freya told her, slowly rocking back. "That you need psychological help." What she needed to do was get off the woman, turn her over, cuff her. Once she was in handcuffs, she wouldn't be nearly as much of a threat. But until then...

"I'm going to let you up," Freya told her. "Do something

stupid and I promise you I'll make you regret it. Just move slowly. No rush."

Linda nodded. Her jaw was tight, her teeth locked together. Freya kept her eyes on her as she carefully sat back, reaching for her taser. Just in case. She'd hold it on her just long enough to get the woman on her stomach. Then she'd cuff her and get her out of there.

"Roll over," Freya said. "Slowly. Take your time—we're not in a rush."

Linda did as she was asked. She glared at Freya as she slowly turned, rolling her hips to the side.

Freya breathed a sigh of relief. "All the way over." Blood from her nose still poured freely, but she didn't want to touch it. Every breath hurt. She took tiny sips of air through her lips, terrified to try to breathe through her nose.

Linda lay on her stomach.

"Put your hands behind your back." She kept the taser trained on her but reached back, carefully unhooking her handcuffs from her duty belt. She flipped her wrist, then slid the single strand of one side through the double to open it.

Linda sighed. "You can't arrest me," she began, but Freya cut her off.

"Watch me." The handcuffs' teeth clicked loudly as she Mirandized the woman at her feet. When she was finished, she grabbed Linda under the arm. "Up. Walk. You can't hide any longer, Linda. You're going to pay for what you've done to these girls, their families, and the people of Fawn Lake."

They picked their way through the woods, Freya pinching the bridge of her nose. By the time they reached the river, the bleeding had stopped.

She ignored the stares as she helped Linda cross the river. It was only when Brad took the woman from her that she felt like she could breathe.

It was over. It had to be.

FIFTY-FIVE

It was the same interrogation room where Freya had met with Tina, only now Linda Brown sat inside. Her long hair was tangled and pushed back from her face. She'd had to change out of her flowy white dress and into a prison jumpsuit. Those tended to be itchy and uncomfortable as a rule, so it wasn't surprising that she kept pulling the fabric away from her chest. She shifted, trying to find a comfortable position, but the chairs were hard, the lights were bright so interviewing detectives didn't miss anything, and the entire room was hot.

Freya stood at the one-way glass with Chief. He had his hands shoved deep in his pockets, a tired expression on his face. From time to time, he glanced at Linda, then turned to look at her. She kept her eyes fixed on the woman in the interview room. That was who really mattered, not the man next to her, not the people in the lobby looking for answers, not the other women currently being interviewed and booked.

Linda Brown. Homeschooling mother of two, homesteader, murderer. How she managed to be charismatic enough to convince multiple women to kill their children... who knew?

But she was determined to find out.

"She's crazy." Chief cleared his throat. "That's the defense they're going to use—you know that, right? That she's lost her mind, that she didn't know what she was doing, that she needs psychiatric help and that the state should foot the bill."

She didn't respond. She inhaled. Held it. Exhaled. Finally, she turned to him. "I want you to admit that I was right. You can do it here, with just me, or you can do it in front of everyone. I'll give you that option, Chief, but I need to hear it. Otherwise, I don't know how I'm going to work with you when I know you're willing to throw me under the bus when you think I'm wrong."

His eyes snapped to hers. "What?"

"Apologize. You were wrong. I'm not the same detective who used to work here. I'm better. Smarter. You need to respect that, and you need to trust that I know what I'm doing."

"Freya," he said, then he snapped his mouth shut. Shook his head. "I thought you were wrong."

"Right. But I wasn't. I was right, and you should have listened to me."

"But before—"

"I made a mistake." *How long was she going to have to apologize for that?* "Like everyone else in the world does from time to time, but that doesn't mean you get to hold it over my head for the rest of my life. You think I haven't suffered enough for my mistake? You think I don't see the faces of the victims I failed every single time I close my eyes?" She was breathing hard now, worked up and angry. His calm demeanor only upset her more.

"My mistake didn't result in someone dying."

"Your mistake almost did. It would have if I hadn't ignored what you told me to do and figured it all out on my own. Apologize." She fingered the badge on her hip. "You need me."

Chief closed his eyes. He rolled his head from side to side, loosening up his neck. Finally he looked at her. "I'm sorry I didn't trust you, but I couldn't."

"That's a terrible apology."

"You made it impossible when you made that mistake."

"Yeah, and how long do I have to pay for that?" She pressed her hand against the glass. Inside the room, Linda sat still. She stared at the wall ahead of her like she was watching a movie. "How many years do I have to find killers and lock them up for you to finally let go of the past, for you to finally get over yourself and give me the grace I deserve?"

"I don't know."

"Well, figure it out. My team supports me. It sure would be nice if my chief did too." Without giving him a chance to respond, she opened the door and walked into the interrogation room. The door had the tendency to swing back open if not firmly shut, so she closed it hard, nodding when she heard the latch click.

Linda Brown looked up. "How long are you going to keep me here? My son needs me. Zach needs his mother."

"An officer is looking for your son right now. Trust me, his safety is important to us." She pulled out the chair across from the woman and sat down. "You and I have a lot to talk about, Linda. You're a difficult woman to track down."

Linda leveled her gaze at Freya. Her eyes were dark, but the expression there was blank. It almost looked like there was nothing going on behind her eyes. "What do we have to talk about?"

"Why did you kill Liz?" Freya didn't have proof the little girl was dead yet, but she was sure it had happened. And that Linda had something to do with it. "And why did you convince so many other mothers to kill their daughters too?"

"I didn't *kill* Liz. I cleansed her." She leaned back, the corners of her mouth lifting up in a smile.

"Oh, I'm sorry, my mistake. I thought that when you gave a child a bath to clean them up, then they'd stay alive. I didn't realize it involved killing them."

A full minute passed. "You don't understand."

"You're right, I don't, but I'm a fast learner. Why don't you spell it out for me?"

Linda looked away. Her mouth was now pressed into a firm line, and she shook her head.

"You don't want to explain it to me? Fine. That's fine. Why don't you go ahead and tell me where you buried the bodies?"

Still nothing. Finally, a deep breath.

"This world is terrible," she said, and Freya froze, waiting. "It's dirty and it's dark and it's... painful." She spat that last word like it tasted bad. "If they can't be good, can't be *clean*, then they'll just be part of the problem as they grow up. That's what my father always told me. To be *good*. To be *clean*. And you know what? I wasn't. And I suffered."

"I'm sorry for what you went through."

Linda scoffed. "You wouldn't ever understand what it was like. I wasn't good, or clean, or anything he wanted me to be, so he punished me for that. He gave me to his friends, told me that only happens to girls who are dirty. I'm not letting that happen to any more girls."

"So you kill them?"

"No! We do everything we can to help them be better, to make them clean. We do what we can to prepare them for the world, to make sure they're ready for it. You know how dark and dangerous the world is. How dirty. How it will hurt them. I want to keep that from happening. And if they can't handle it, if they can't listen and be good and clean..."

She stopped talking.

"What happens if they can't be good and clean, Linda?"

"We *wash* them. We cleanse them. Inside and out. The end goal isn't death, Captain. It's goodness. It's cleanliness."

"And the mothers all agree to this? They know about the risk of killing their daughters and they're okay with it?"

"They want what's best for the future. If their daughters aren't going to improve the world, aren't going to be able to stand up to what's going to happen to them, then we have no other choice. We have to protect them. The dangers start now, when they're so young. If we don't make sure they can withstand what the world will throw at them, who will?"

"Tell me about the two girls we found in the river. They weren't buried with the others. Why?"

Linda took a deep breath and closed her eyes before speaking. "It wasn't working. Cleaning the girls. They needed to stay in the water longer, to ensure they were as clean as possible. Those girls were from our newer families."

"Homeschool families."

Linda nodded.

Freya tapped her fingers against her leg, unable to respond. She'd guessed the women involved had issues, but this? It was unfathomable.

Then something hit her. "Linda, how well do you know John Frank?"

"John." Linda turned; spat on the floor. "The pedophile."

"Ahh, so you did know. How long ago did you find out?"

"Not very." Linda crossed her arms and leaned back in her chair. "Long enough."

"Long enough to blackmail him." Freya tried to see things from Linda's point of view. A pedophile working at the school, coaching soccer... that was enough to help confirm what she believed—that everyone was out to get her daughter. "So you sent him a letter, let him know you were on to him. What was the end goal there?"

"Getting him away from the girls. But by then, they'd already been exposed to evil. We'd been cleaning our girls, but we had to move faster. See who could withstand it. Who couldn't. That entire soccer team had been exposed, but not all of the mothers saw it that way. I wanted to help them all, help every girl on the team, but some of the mothers wouldn't let me."

What Amber's mom had said about the soccer team, about some of the moms demanding perfection, came back to her. A chill raced up her spine. "Where are the rest of the bodies, Linda?" There would be time for a psych eval later. More interviews would come, but right now she just wanted to find the little girls.

Linda shook her head. Her lips pressed firmly together as she turned away.

Freya stared at her. She'd want to keep the girls close. After all this work, she'd need to know they were safe. Closing her eyes, she pictured Linda's home and property.

That was it.

"If you don't know where the bodies are buried, then I guess you won't mind if we dig up your garden?" Freya started to rise, but the response to her words was immediate.

Linda flew forward in her chair. She slammed her hands on the table, heat rising in her cheeks. It was the first time she'd shown any sort of emotion since getting arrested, and Freya paused.

"Yes? Do you have something you want to tell me before I go to your house to see how the digging's going? I'm more than happy to leave you in here, or we can start the booking process, if you'd like. Just trust me, you're not getting out of that jumpsuit anytime soon."

"You can't dig up my garden."

"Oh, a search warrant signed by a magistrate will say differently. It's amazing how easily you can do whatever you want when there are missing girls at play. Everyone in town wants to find them as badly as I do. You'd be surprised how many shovels we have handy."

"It's my garden. I love it there. It's where everything is good and perfect and—"

"Where you buried the bodies of the little girls you *cleansed*?" Freya rolled her eyes. "I had a pretty good feeling that might be the case. Do you really think you're helping the girls? Or are you just crazy?"

"Don't touch my garden!" Linda screamed. Even though one of her wrists was handcuffed to the table, she lunged, reaching for Freya. Her outstretched hand swiped the air in front of Freya's bandaged nose.

She took a step back. "Not cool, Linda," she said, then turned and waved at the glass. "I thought you and I could sit down and talk things out, but now you're going to your cell. And I'm going to your garden."

The door opened, and a uniformed officer entered. He nodded at her then approached Linda. "Linda Brown, I'm going to put your handcuffs on and take you to your cell. Turn around and make it easy on me."

"You can't go there!" Linda ignored him. She strained against the cuff fixing her to the table, her eyes bulging, her hand clawing through the air towards her. "You leave them be!"

Freya let the door slam closed behind her. Even so, the woman's voice carried into the observation room, but she didn't turn around to see what was going to happen.

She knew.

The officer would handcuff her, take her to her cell. She'd fight him, and while he wouldn't be rough, he wasn't going to wear kid gloves either. Nobody really worried about the feelings of someone who would hurt a child.

She had seen that firsthand when she was a younger officer.

"I'm getting a warrant to dig up her garden," she said, waving over her head at Chief. He still stood by the glass, staring in, watching as Linda Brown fought her handcuffs, but that didn't matter to her.

Nothing mattered but wrapping up this case. Finding those little girls.

Getting them justice.

FIFTY-SIX

Linda Brown's house was lit up like it was the middle of the day. When Freya had worked in Fawn Lake before, the town hadn't had oversized spotlights to bring to crime scenes, but now they surrounded the property, their huge bulbs all turned on. Moths battered themselves against the bulbs, but she barely looked up as she walked past them to the police tape.

"Freya Sinclair," she said, holding out her badge for the officer to see before ducking under the tape. Even though most people in town knew who she was, the last thing she wanted was to assume someone would recognize her. There must have been a lot of employee turnover recently, if the young officers standing around were any indication.

Her face ached. Even bandaged, even with Tylenol, the pain was constant. She needed to get home and ice it, to try to dull the pain, but bed was a long way away. Around the side of the house she went, following the noise of the crime scene.

Most crime scenes felt alive, with some sort of energy, and this one was no different. There was a buzz in the air as she approached what had once been Linda's garden. Someone had brought a backhoe to make digging easier.

Large mounds of dirt were piled on the ground, the smell of their freshly turned soil scenting the air. A cadaver dog strained at the end of its leash; its nose pressed to the ground. As she watched, it lifted its head and bayed once, digging its paws into the ground as its handler pulled it back.

Immediately, three men took the dog's place. They all had shovels and wore thick work gloves. Each of them had a fine sheen of sweat on their foreheads, and they all began digging without speaking to each other.

"It's going to be a long night, but the officers are fueled by adrenaline. Makes digging easier, if nothing else."

Surprised that someone was talking to her, Freya turned. "Lance," she breathed, relief at seeing the medical examiner standing next to her almost palpable. "Who called you and got you out here?"

"That would be your detective," he said, nodding towards where Candy stood closer to where the men were digging. "She called me in a tizzy, said that I needed to get over here as quickly as possible and that I needed to be prepared for a long night." He held up a travel cup. "I only paused long enough to make some coffee, then I headed over."

"Candy's good at this," she said. "I didn't even see her over there. I'm glad to know she's running the show."

When Lance spoke again, his voice was lower. Any excitement in it had faded. "How many bodies are we hoping to find tonight, Freya?"

"At least five." Her stomach flipped as she thought about each of the girls she was trying to find. Madeleine, Isa, Sophia, Liz, Lena. And what about Jessa? They still hadn't heard back from the prep school. She swallowed hard. "All young girls."

"Do you think this is related to the girl you found in the river?"

"She's one of them," she said. "Both of the river girls are actually. Linda told me the girls weren't getting clean enough, so she was leaving them in the water for longer. If we hadn't stopped them today, we would have three drowned girls. Three bodies to try to identify."

"That... makes sense in a twisted way, but I don't like it."

"Me either." She heaved a sigh. "To really get into her head, to understand her, I needed to know how the girls died, what happened to them."

Lance reached out and rested his hand on her arm. "Hey, you leave that to me, okay? I shouldn't have brought it up. You and I work best when we keep our eyes on our own jobs. I'll tell you what happened to your girls." He paused, and she shifted position, reaching down to massage her hip.

"You're right," she said finally. "As always."

He chuckled. "I could sit," Lance said, pointing past her to a low brick wall. "Right over there. If we claim spots on that wall, then we can keep an eye on the action and rest a little. It's going to be a long night."

She eyeballed him. "You're only offering that because you feel bad for me and worry about my hip."

"Oh, Freya. You're one person I could never feel bad for. You don't deserve that. Come on—even if you don't want to sit out of the principle of the thing, I do. You think I'm used to standing around at a crime scene like this all night? Nope, I am not. I much prefer working in my dungeon. There's air conditioning."

The two of them made their way over to the brick wall and sat, still watching the officers digging.

"How long have you been out here?" She pulled her phone from her pocket to check for messages. Nothing. The murdering mothers were all booked at the jail. Ray Barnes, the magistrate on duty, didn't like staying late or coming back in once he'd left for the night, so she was sure he was going to be in a mood.

Whatever. When tragedy like this struck, it was up to everyone in town to band together and take care of it.

"Just an hour. I told my wife not to wait up for me, that I'd be home well after she finished having her beauty sleep."

She looked at him in surprise. "You have a wife?"

"Shocking, right? You missed a lot while you were gone, Freya. But we're glad you're back."

She sat in silence, her eyes locked on the digging. After a while, it felt like the two of them went into a fugue state. She could be dreaming, or watching a movie, or even reading a really good book, but she knew none of those things were true. Time passed slowly, a strong breeze blew, and finally one of the men digging called out.

"That's my cue," she said, standing up. She was stiff, and she stretched her leg out in front of her, hinging at the hip to wake up the joint. "I'll see you over there in a minute, Lance."

He responded, but she was barely listening. Pushing past a group of officers who were crowding forward, she stepped up to the hole.

Even though she knew what she was going to see inside, what she found was worse than she'd expected.

FIFTY-SEVEN

The sheet covering the girl had been pulled back, and although it had managed to keep most of the clumps of mud off her face, small bits had fallen through the weave. Her cheeks were sunken, her eyes closed, and her skin covered in a fine layer of dirt.

Her lips, which were once probably rosy and plump, had started to collapse in on themselves. They'd taken on a gray color and began to pull tight on her face. Even though she had hollow cheeks, her skin across her chin, brow, and cheekbones was taut. Pushed back from her face, her hair was dark with dirt, making it impossible to tell its natural color.

Still, Freya recognized her.

She rested on her back, her hands on her chest. Dead flowers were tucked there, like she'd been holding a bouquet and simply lain down for a nap. Twisted and thin, her fingers looked like that of an older lady. Her feet were bare, and her white dress was stained the color of mud.

Freya didn't move. She took in all the details—the flowers, the braids, the white dress—and locked them away in her brain for her to examine later. Candy stood next to her, a camera pressed up to her face. She snapped photo after photo, making sure to get all the details.

Liz wore a ring that looked like it had come from a gumball machine.

"Lance," Freya called, and then the ME was right beside her. "Like I said before, I'm not an expert, but she's been in the ground a while."

"Yes." Lance kneeled down by the shallow grave. Liz's face was barely three feet below the surface of the ground. The men digging must have found her relatively quickly but then taken their time clearing out as much dirt as possible before announcing what they'd uncovered.

"Without a thorough examination in my lab, I can't tell you exactly how long she's been dead or buried, but I can tell you it's been more than a few days." He stood back up. "As soon as you've taken your pictures, I want her sent to my lab. Unless you need me here to oversee the handling of the other bodies, if you find any, I'd rather get to work."

"That's fine. We'll have them brought to you. I'm assuming there are going to be more. Unless each child is buried at her own house, but that doesn't feel right. Linda... She was terrified when I mentioned her garden. I think they're here. She'd want them close."

"The ground has been disturbed recently," Candy said, "but it is a garden. It's hard to tell how much is because she's out here planting and moving things around and how much is because she buried bodies out here."

"Dig up the whole thing," Freya said. "But I want Liz sent to the morgue now. The sooner Lance can get started, the sooner we'll have answers."

Candy nodded and walked across the yard, moving with purpose, then stopped to talk to a few men standing with a stretcher. She gestured as she spoke until they nodded, then when she kept walking, they headed towards the grave.

"That's my cue to leave," Lance told Freya. "Is it okay if I call you as soon as I start to find anything?"

"You can call me every five minutes if you need to. Don't you dare leave anything out." She exhaled and checked her watch. The night was going to drag on for hours yet. Everyone on the team needed to get home and sleep, but that wasn't going to happen anytime soon, not when so much was at stake.

"Alright. I'll be in touch. Just keep your phone on."

"Of course." She gave him a mock salute and headed back to her Jeep to grab some water. She ducked under the police tape and exhaled hard, then breathed in the cool night air. Across the road, the neighbor's house was all lit up. That always happened in cases like this—people struggled not to be nosy when the worst was happening. It didn't matter how terrible someone's day was, there was always someone wanting to watch.

"Hey, I remember you," came a voice from nearby.

She turned, doing her best to place the voice. How many people had she talked to recently? Too many to count, and the voice didn't stand out.

"You came by looking for my mom and sister." He ran a hand through his hair and stood next to her. "I'm Zach. We met when you were looking for them."

"I remember. How are you holding up with all of this? Please tell me you haven't been around this entire time, watching everything."

He grimaced. "I just got here." He gestured to the house. "I was with a friend and left their house. I can't believe it, you know? My mom... I mean, I knew for the longest time that she was kinda weird. Everyone called us weird, even some of the other homeschool families." He laughed, the sound rueful. "But I had no idea she could do something like this. Do you think she hurt Liz?" His voice broke, and he scrubbed a hand down his face.

He didn't need to know the truth. Not yet. "I don't have an answer for you yet. All I know is that we're going to look at this from every angle and figure out what happened to your sister."

Zach shook his head before she finished speaking. "That's her in the garden, isn't it?" Tears shone in his eyes. "I should have known something was going on, but I wanted out of here. And Liz... she's annoying. A little sister who only wants to hang out with me. I hate it. *Hated* it."

Her chest hurt. "Relationships are hard," she said. "You not wanting to hang out with your little sister didn't do this, Zach. You had nothing to do with this—do you understand me?" As she spoke, an officer approached. Her time was limited, since they'd want to get the boy somewhere safe, somewhere they could keep an eye on him.

"Yeah, sure. She drives me nuts, but she's still my kid sister." He fumbled his phone from his pocket and dragged his thumb across the screen. "You want to see a picture of the two of us? I actually took this about a month ago when I took her to the river to swim. She'd been dying to go after Mom took her, but then I got in trouble."

"Why did you get in trouble?" She took the phone from Zach and stared at the picture on the screen. In it, Liz was alive and happy, standing in knee-deep water, cheesing hard for the camera, Zach's arm draped around her shoulder. It was almost impossible to reconcile her with the dead body in the garden.

"Oh, because Mom said that the water was for her and Liz." His voice grew hard, and he took the phone back. "Like I wasn't good enough to take her, I don't know."

"It sounds really hard." She paused, searching for what to say next. "I'm sure we'll be talking soon, but right now, I want you to take care of yourself, okay? Get something to eat, get some sleep. This is terrible, but I promise you, it will get better." She turned to leave him, but he reached out, grabbing her arm before she could walk away.

"When?" he pleaded with her, his voice breaking on the word. "When in the world will it get better, and how can you be so sure? My mom... She was horrible. If she really did this, really killed Liz, then how am I to live with that?"

She shook her head. "You just do. Trust me, it's hard, probably the hardest thing I've ever done. But you have to remember that you're not your mother, just like I'm not my parents. They all made their own decisions, and you and I get to make our own. We can choose to leave our mark on the world in a better way."

He took a shuddering breath, then nodded. "Okay. I can do that. I can be better than her."

"You are better than her," she assured him. "Also, get some therapy. It helps."

"Yeah? You know that from personal experience?" A small smile played on his lips.

"Boy howdy, do I. And find someone who can love you the way you deserve. You'll get through this, Zach." She gave him an encouraging smile and disentangled herself, walking quickly to her Jeep.

The noise from the evening was getting to her. The sound of shovels slipping into the dirt, people chattering, the bang of car doors opening and slamming shut. She passed a news van, the anchor just putting in her earpiece.

"Captain Sinclair!" The woman sounded way too happy to be at this terrible crime scene. "I had a feeling you'd be involved in this! Do you have anything you want to share with our viewers? Do you feel for the boy of the woman who killed so many children? Does it make you think about your own parents?"

Freya squared off on the woman. She took a deep breath, then, without saying a word, she turned and stalked to her car. Grabbed a bottle of water.

Slammed the door as hard as she could.

It was going to be one of the longest nights of her life.

FIFTY-EIGHT

SUNDAY

Instead of continually getting up and walking into the break room to refill her coffee, Freya eventually moved the pot to the credenza behind her. It sat next to Cinnamon's tank, constantly brewing. Candy moved into the same office, placing her laptop across the desk from Freya's. The two of them worked in silence, the quiet of the office only broken by the sound of the coffee pot gurgling or someone leaning in the door to ask a question.

Outside, fingers of light played against the front of the building. When Candy finally noticed the light seeping in through the blinds, she got up and opened them but then sat right back down. They had a lot of work to do.

At 7 a.m., Chief leaned in the door. Dark circles under his eyes made it clear that the man hadn't slept much, if at all. He needed to shave; his uniform was wrinkled. The three of them made quite a team running on adrenaline and coffee.

"I've got all the mothers in interrogation rooms for you," he said. His voice was croaky. "They're all nervous wrecks, and half of them have called for lawyers. Well, one lawyer. Jernigan."

"But that means half of them haven't," Freya said, closing her laptop with a satisfying click. "Let me guess—you're giving me the gift of interviewing these moms because later I'm going to have to knock out a press conference and try to put some rumors to bed before they really start circulating."

"Bingo." He pointed at her, snapping as he did. "You see? This is why I hired you, Sinclair. Always on top of it."

Freya nodded and turned to Candy. "Shall we divide and conquer?"

Candy nodded, closing her laptop and stretching. "I thought you'd never ask."

Five minutes later, Freya opened the door to the first interview room. Candy was already walking into another room to speak to the mother waiting in there.

"Good morning, Mrs. Peters," Freya said, closing the door behind her and sitting across from the woman.

Jennifer straightened her back, sitting up and staring at Freya. She looked just as tired as Freya did, with dark circles under her eyes and her hair a mess. As if she could tell what Freya was thinking, she reached up and ran her fingers through it, trying to smooth it out.

It didn't help.

She was a far cry from the woman Freya and Brad had met at her photography studio. While then she'd looked like she'd just left a catwalk, now she looked terrible. Very little sleep and no time for makeup would do that to you.

"Do you remember me? I'm Captain Sinclair," Freya said, sliding into the seat across from her. She held a folder with a photo of Jessa in the morgue. Even without having Jennifer or Winston ID the body, she recognized Jessa from the photos Jennifer had shown her. The little girl was dead. "Before we get started, is there anything you want to tell me first?"

Jennifer lifted her chin. It wobbled a little, but she shook her head.

"Great, then we can get started." Freya exhaled hard, fingering the edge of the folder. "As you know by now, we recently exhumed your daughter's body from the property of your friend, Linda Brown. Now we've found out there was a bit of a cult with mothers—"

"It wasn't a cult."

Freya arched a brow. "Go on. Tell me what it was then."

Jennifer paused, then started speaking quickly, her words rapid-fire. "It was a way for us to get the help we needed with our daughters. This world is so hard, you know?" Her eyes were bright as she looked at Freya. "And Linda, she told us she could help us. That she could tell if our girls were going to struggle in the world or if they'd be successful. Jessa was so difficult, and I needed time to myself to work. I couldn't do that with her always causing problems."

Freya didn't dare breathe.

"She told us some girls could handle the stress and anxiety of the world, but others couldn't. That some could be clean and make their way through the world without getting dirty, without being damaged. Those girls were stronger, better. But some girls were weak. They had to be clean, you see."

"So you let her drown Jessa?" Freya fought to keep the horror she felt out of her voice.

"No!" The word burst from Jennifer. She looked surprised at how loud it was and shook her head. "No, of course not."

"But Jessa died."

Jennifer shook her head. "No, don't you see? We made her clean. She wasn't strong enough to handle the world. She wasn't good enough. She was always underfoot, always causing problems. It's not my fault she wasn't strong enough to handle it."

Freya flipped open the folder and spun it around. She

pushed it in front of Jennifer and tapped her finger on the photo. "You killed her."

Jennifer looked away.

"No, you don't get to ignore the consequences of your actions," Freya said, tapping the photo of Jessa on an autopsy table even harder. "Look here. Look at it! This is your daughter. She's dead. You killed her!"

"No," Jennifer said, shaking her head. Tears streamed down her face. "No, you're wrong. It's not my fault. Jessa was headstrong. She was difficult. The doctors said she was fine, that she was testing boundaries, but you don't understand. It's been like this since she was two. We had to get a nanny, but even then, I knew she needed to be better."

"So, what? How did you find Linda and her group?"

Jennifer exhaled. "The soccer team, but we really connected online. I was desperate, and she could tell. Lara kept telling me Jessa was good, that she wasn't the problem I said she was, but she was wrong. She suggested I put her in sports to help burn off some energy and even found a soccer team for her to join. Homeschoolers, public school kids, even kids like Jessa, who were always in trouble, were all welcome. I hated it, hated taking her to practice when I had better things to do. But I met Linda there. She helped me see I wasn't insane. This group... what Linda was doing? She's been doing it for years. They all agreed to give it a few years to see if their daughters would be better. To see if they could stand up to the pain and horror of this world. And they couldn't."

It was too much. Freya closed the folder over Jessa's face and pulled it closer to her again. "Did you know there was a possibility that Jessa might die?" Even she didn't recognize her voice, it was so quiet.

Jennifer closed her eyes. "There was always a possibility—that's what Linda told us. But I didn't think it would actually happen to Jessa."

"But it did. And you went on with your life like nothing happened."

Jennifer closed her eyes. For the first time since Freya had met her, the façade she'd so carefully constructed crumbled. She let out a sob. "My life is over! My girl is gone. And Linda... she told us what would happen if we went to the police. That she'd turn on us, tell you that we wanted this, that we killed our girls." Tears streamed down her face, and she angrily wiped them away. "Don't you see? I just wanted her to be good! I wanted it to be easier! But I didn't want her to die. I couldn't tell Winston what I did. I had to lie to him so he didn't leave me too, so I said I sent her to boarding school. He had no idea. Linda took everything from me. It's over."

It *was* over.

Freya stood. When Jennifer also moved to stand, Freya shook her head. "You're not going anywhere for a long time. Might as well make yourself comfortable."

In the hall, she met Candy. The younger detective's face was pale, her jaw set.

"Did she give you anything?" Candy asked, jerking her thumb at the door Freya had just exited.

"A cock and bull story. She's placing all the blame she can on not only Linda but on Jessa for being difficult and a troublemaker. You?"

"Same." Candy sighed and yawned. "I was in there with Madeleine Travis's mom, Kelly. She's delusional."

"They all are. Completely off their rockers, but in the end, that won't matter. We're going to nail them all to the wall. None of them are walking away from this, not after what they did."

"Even with God's gift to the courtroom, Jackson Jernigan himself, representing half of the mothers?"

Freya grimaced. "How he can help any of them when his wife murdered his daughter, I don't know. But yes, even with him in charge of this farce. I don't care what he does or how he tries to spin this, I don't see a way he's going to get these women out of here."

"I'd bet you anything that—" But whatever Candy was going to say was cut off with the slam of a door.

Jackson stomped down the hall. His cheeks were bright red, his hands clenched into fists. He wore a suit, as always, but hadn't shaved yet. When he approached Candy and Freya, his eyes narrowed.

"Jackson. How are you doing?" Freya asked. She studied his face. He closed his eyes and exhaled hard before looking at her again. The man was a nightmare to deal with, but he'd just lost his daughter. Nobody deserved to go through that.

He shook his head. "I'm dropping them all. All of them," he repeated. "As for who's representing my wife, that's their decision. What they did..." He paused. Swallowed hard and ran his hand through his hair.

Freya nodded. "I'm so sorry," she said, reaching for his arm. He let her touch his shoulder, then jerked away, hurrying down the hall.

"That just got interesting," Candy said.

Interesting was one word for it, sure.

FIFTY-NINE

"I think we're done here," Chief said. His words came out in a croak, proof of his exhaustion. He rubbed a hand into his eyes and groaned. "Sinclair and Ellinger, you two did a good job talking to the mothers. The fathers have been interviewed and— get this—let go. Brad Williams did a good job handling that mess and interviewing Mindy Stevens. Whatever this was, it was only the mothers.

"You," he continued, pointing at Candy. "Good work collaborating with the people at the Department of Non-Public Education. I know Brad served them with a warrant, but you rode them long and hard to get us what we needed. They finally gave us enough information to ID the two girls found in the water so we could arrest their mothers. I'm just glad we didn't have to share their photos with the entire town."

"Thanks." Candy inclined her head. "Freya figured out the link. I was just the gopher."

Chief stared at her then turned to look at Freya. "Go home. Rest. You look terrible."

"Gee, thanks. But are you sure we're done? You said before you wanted me to do a press conference. And what about an interview with the papers? Everyone in town knows something was going on last night, but nobody really knows what it was. We should put the rumors to bed now before we leave."

"Rumors. They're always around. No matter what we do, people are going to talk." He glanced at Candy, then looked back at Freya. "I can't have either of you appearing on TV right now looking like you got in a fight with a family of raccoons." He paused. "And lost."

"You don't look much better," Freya said. "You going to head home to get some rest too? Sounds like it's what the doctor ordered."

"I'm going to take a nap in my office in case anything else hits the fan. Then, when you two get back, I'm going to trade out. Help me out here, Freya. Do what I say, for the first time in your career." He paused. "And I owe your team dinner, so order whatever you want from Marino's Pizza when you all get back. On me."

"Fine." She shut her laptop with a satisfying click. Candy did that same. "Five hours once my head hits the pillow. Deal? But first, take this." She held a piece of paper out to Chief.

"Deal. What is it?"

"The names of the dead girls. Sophia Jernigan. Isa Matthews. Liz Brown. Madeleine Travis. Jessa Peters. Georgina Taylor. Lena Reid. The news will want information, and you need to make sure they print their names. These girls don't deserve to be forgotten."

Chief was silent for a moment. "Thank you. I'll make sure they're not." A slight pause. "And I'm sorry for not trusting you." Chief rapped his knuckles against her doorframe in goodbye and then shuffled down the hall.

Unexpected. But she'd take it.

Candy eyeballed Freya. "Are you really going to go straight home and go to bed?"

"Of course I am. But there's a new route to my house I wanted to try out."

"Oh yeah? Does it run by Parker's?"

Freya shook her head. "Nope, that's a phone call I can make later. The route does run by the hospital though, strangely enough."

"So weird." Candy chuckled. "If they would stop working on the roads around here, then maybe you could just take a straight shot home. But if you need to swing past the hospital first, what other option is there?" She yawned and stretched. "Do you need company on that drive?"

"Nope, I'm fine." Freya grabbed her bag and gestured to the door. Outside, she locked it up. "Get some rest, Candy. You're the best."

Ten minutes later, she was parked at the hospital and headed in to see Lance. The sheer exhaustion she felt had given way to elation. This was normal, if not concerning. She honestly felt like she could take on the world but knew as soon as she went to bed, she'd crash.

"I wondered when I'd see you," Lance called out. He stood in the middle of his room, a king surveying his domain. His white lab coat was pristine as it always was. Cool air pumped through the vents in the ceiling made goosebumps break out on Freya's arms. She rubbed her hands up and down them as she approached Lance.

"How's it going?" she asked, reaching out to lightly touch an autopsy table for support.

He raised his eyebrows. "I should be asking you the same thing. Freya, why are you on your feet right now? You need rest, not to be running around like you think you're a superhero. You look like a zombie."

"Thanks for that. I'm actually on my way home to go to bed.

Chief's orders. But I wanted to stop by here first and make sure things were going smoothly. See if there were any surprises."

"You need to take better care of yourself," he said, turning to pick up his clipboard. "I worry about you running yourself ragged. Who do you have looking out for you?"

"Lance..." She sighed. "Just give me the facts. I'm not going to be able to sleep until I know for sure that everything is as expected."

"All of them were drowned," he confirmed. "Five bodies were dug up last night and into the early hours this morning. The last three of them brought in I haven't had a lot of time with, but I did a preliminary investigation because I had a feeling you might come by to harass me about it."

She didn't say a word. She couldn't.

"I can safely tell you they drowned, but don't tell the news. Not until I'm finished."

"Anything else? Is that all?"

He frowned at her. "Are you looking for something in particular? Do you have information I don't?"

"No, I just wanted to know. Drowning someone? That's not a quiet, easy way for them to go. It's loud. Violent. Traumatizing. The girls probably tried to fight back, but they were young. Little. Depending on how big the person holding them down was, how strong they were, there really wasn't a chance for them to survive it." She swallowed hard.

Lance didn't argue with her.

"So that's it?" She slammed her fist on the metal table. The sound rang out in the stillness of the morgue. "There was a group of mothers who thought their daughters couldn't handle the world, couldn't be good in it, so they drowned them? That's sick."

"I know." Lance sighed and put the clipboard down. "I'll have more for you later, okay? You can swing by, or I can call you, but right now, you need to sleep. Nobody has good judgement when they're exhausted."

Freya eyeballed him. "Did you sleep?"

"Catnaps. Three of them so far. I'm trying to pace myself so I don't pass out for an entire day. I wanted to get this all finished as quickly as possible, but they're dead. They can wait a little while." He sighed. "Go home, Freya. You and I know there isn't anything for you to do right now. You can't undo what happened, but I know you, and I know you're going to keep it from happening again."

She nodded. She walked slowly across the morgue then up the stairs, and soon she was in her Jeep, driving on autopilot. The sun rose rapidly behind her, filling her car with a rosy glow.

But she ignored all of it. She ignored how the tops of the trees glowed gold in the sunrise, how steam rose off the lake she passed, how there were already young moms walking, pushing strollers, trying to enjoy the outdoors as much as possible before the heat became overwhelming as the day went on.

All she could think about was those girls. Why parents sometimes failed their children.

When she got home, she checked the mail that had piled up over the last few days, not really expecting anything but still wanting to make sure she didn't miss anything.

Bills, a notice that the road-widening project that had threatened to consume part of her front yard had been delayed, and finally a letter from Smithfield Correctional.

She scoffed. In her kitchen, she opened the bottom drawer by the refrigerator and tossed the letter inside, where it landed on a pile of others just like it.

She slammed the drawer shut.

SIXTY

The only sound in Parker's was from Esther cleaning up a few baking sheets in the kitchen. The air was thick with the scent of chocolate and almonds. Since the floor had recently been mopped, it shone, and the smell of vinegar mingled with the sweet smell of baking. Outside, the people of Fawn Lake walked to and fro, most of them either on their way home from work or headed to dinner.

Freya's feet ached. Her entire body was sore, to be honest. She sighed and wriggled her toes inside her boots to try to stretch them out. One of the perks of being a detective and not a patrol officer was that she could choose her own boots to wear and didn't have to stuff her feet into the cement blocks that street cops wore. Even still, the aches continued up her body to her knees and hips. Not even her head was spared—she could feel a bit of a headache coming on.

Getting a few hours of sleep had been necessary, but her brain wasn't firing on all cylinders yet. Chief had been thrilled to be relieved to go home and nap. She had locked herself away in her office with Candy, the two of them filling out report after report before Brad joined them and they ordered pizza.

Now she finally felt like she could catch her breath.

"To a job well done," Freya said, raising her cup of coffee in a cheers to Candy and Brad. The two of them sat across from her in a booth, each of them with a cup of coffee in front of them. Even though officially closed for the evening, Esther hadn't minded one bit when Freya called her asking for a place to sit and drink some coffee. She'd been thrilled to unlock the front door, had admonished them not to make a mess, then delivered three cups of coffee and made herself scarce for a bit.

"To a job that kicked my butt," Candy responded, lifting her coffee.

"To bed tonight," Brad said, laughing.

They all touched cups and took sips. Once they'd put them back down on the table, Freya was the first to speak.

"Y'all made my move home a lot easier than it had to be," she said, looking each of them in the eye. "I'm serious; I don't know that I could have handled everything happening all at once without you. It was pretty much the perfect storm around here, and that's exhausting."

"The break-in," Candy added with a nod. "That's quite a welcome home, Freya."

"It was a big middle finger," Brad added.

"Oh, I get it. I'd rather take the heat for people I care about any day. And then the pedophile janitor and the enabling principal." She pointed at Candy. "You ran with that once we got everything in order. Thank you for taking care of it."

"Believe me, I was thrilled to put them in jail. Of course, now the school has some positions to fill, but the school board is going to be on top of it. The assistant principal from the middle school is stepping up to finish out the school year, and a janitor who used to work at the middle school came out of retirement to help. It's working out."

"And Mindy?" Candy angled her body to get a better look

at Brad. "While we were cleaning up the mess with the mothers after our naps today, you were dealing with her."

"You said she knew about John, but I couldn't prove it. I tried though. I had her in to interview her, but she wouldn't break. Asked me out at the end though. I told her I don't date people who associate with pedophiles." His cheeks were pink. He glanced at Freya, then looked back at his cup like it was suddenly the most interesting thing in the world.

"It seemed personal for you." Freya's voice was soft. She didn't fully expect a response, but it was something she'd been thinking about for a while. "Nobody wants little kids to get hurt, don't get me wrong. But this seemed more than that. You took ownership of it... with Mindy, with the soccer team."

For a moment, Brad didn't answer. He stared over Freya's head, his fingers tight around his cup. Finally, he gave one short nod. "It was personal, but that's really all I think I can say about that right now."

Candy reached out and rested her hand on his arm, giving him a gentle squeeze. He glanced at her and smiled, then took a long sip of his coffee.

"And the baby killers are all locked up." Candy cleared her throat. "I have to tell you I had no small amount of satisfaction seeing them behind bars. Of course, trials will come up in the next few months, and they're all going to plead not guilty, but Linda Brown, she's raving. She tells anyone who listens how she's not only proud of what she did but that she'd do it again."

Freya shivered. Fingers of fear danced down her spine. "Parents who don't protect their children deserve to have the book thrown at them," she said. "I don't think I'd worry about any of them getting off easy, Candy. I saw we made the front page of CNN.com this morning. All of that national attention will ensure they pay for their crimes."

"That's the last thing our town needs to deal with," Candy mused. "Do you think more reporters will come by?"

"They're already here." Freya nodded at the huge front windows where an out-of-town news van had just pulled up to the police station. "Just remember, keep your head down, you don't have anything to say, and keep walking. That's the best way to deal with vultures like this."

Esther walked over and placed her hand on Freya's shoulder. "I'm so glad you're home, darling. And safe. I know this has to be bringing back bad memories."

Freya paused. Both Candy and Brad were looking at her, waiting for her to speak. She swallowed hard, then reached up and touched Esther on the hand. "I needed to come home. But I also had to leave." She turned in her chair to look at Esther. "Does that make sense?"

Esther smiled. "It does."

Candy cleared her throat. "Freya, I know you're not really keen on talking about what happened, but you know we're here for you if you ever want to. It's good to talk things through, and I don't want you to pretend like it never happened, or like we don't know what happened."

Freya nodded. "I know. I ran to Texas to get out of here after my parents went to prison. Arresting them... I had to do it so I could sleep again at night. I just wish I hadn't arrested the wrong person to begin with. Three people would still be alive."

"Hey." It was Brad, and he leaned forward, looking her in the eyes. "You carry a lot of guilt over what happened. Remember that you were the one who put all the pieces together. If not for you, your parents would have kept killing. And I want you to know how glad we are that you're back."

She nodded. There was a thick lump in her throat, and she swallowed hard, forcing it down. "Texas was terrible," she admitted. "I hated it there. It's so hot and dry and... brown. But I was able to get a job at a small police department and let things blow over here, so I guess it was what I needed at the time."

Esther squeezed her shoulder. Freya didn't look up but heard the woman walk back to the kitchen, giving her space. "I never thought I'd be the type of person to turn tail and run, but that's what I did. It was horrible leaving Esther behind, but I didn't feel like I had a choice. Not at the time."

The three fell silent for a moment. A loud bang from the kitchen made Freya wince, but when she heard Esther bustling about afterwards, she relaxed. Now that she had time to actually breathe, she had to see about what care Esther needed. The woman was going to fight having help, but that didn't matter. She wasn't going to be able to sleep or work without worrying about her.

Brad cleared his throat and took a sip of his coffee. "Esther brews a mean cup of joe," he said, clearly changing the subject.

Freya was grateful. Embarrassment and frustration coursed through her, and she welcomed the chance to talk about anything different.

"Any word from the cutie neighbor down the street?" Candy grinned at Freya.

"Cutie neighbor?" Brad took a sip of his coffee. "Spill."

"Paul," Freya said, nodding. "After I convinced him to let us take pictures with his daughter so I could send them to Linda and get her to meet with me, it's been pretty quiet. I don't want him to think I just used him, but I kinda did."

"Kinda," Candy agreed. "You can make it up to him though."

"Yeah? How? I don't think there's a card designed specifically to apologize-slash-thank someone for letting you use their daughter as bait with a cult leader-slash-serial killer." She gestured with her hands. "He's a really nice guy, but everyone has limits."

"You should take him dinner," Brad offered. "Men love food, don't forget that."

"Women love it too," Candy said, elbowing him. "Don't be sexist."

"I'll take him dinner," Freya said, nodding. "That's a good idea. Besides, I like spending time with him and his daughter, Marla. Now that I'm not worrying about someone killing all the little girls in town, I feel like I might be more fun to have dinner with."

"I can smell the love in the air." Candy looked like she was holding back a laugh.

"And I can smell the demotion," Freya said dryly. "Do you still have your patrol boots stashed in your closet?"

Candy sobered immediately. "Please no. I'll be good, and I won't mention it again. Just don't make me go back to the road."

"Hey, the road isn't so bad." Brad stretched. "I'm having a pretty good time."

Freya rolled her eyes. "You're *having a pretty good time* because you've been hanging out with the detectives. I know what you're trying to do, Brad. You're trying to make yourself indispensable, trying to wheedle your way in."

"Yep. Is it working?"

"It's not *not* working," Freya admitted. "But imagine for a moment if I stole you away from Lieutenant Dalton. We love having you as an unofficial part of the team, but that's as far as it can go right now. You understand that, don't you?"

"Ten-four I understand. And I'm here to serve." He grinned, although his mouth was tighter than it had been a moment ago. After just a second, however, he grinned and looked more relaxed. "One day though. Maybe there will be a desk for me upstairs."

"I can't promise anything, and you know that," Freya told him, "but do know how much I've appreciated having you on the team. We couldn't have handled this all without you."

"Well, maybe we could have," Candy teased, winking at

Brad, "but you did make everything easier. And if you do ever get moved upstairs, I'll be glad to have you on my side."

"Fair enough." Brad checked his watch. "Now, if you don't mind, I do have other things to do. You two be good."

"We're nothing but good," Freya said. "Thanks again. Hopefully we can work together again, but maybe not on such a big case."

"I'll look forward to it," Candy remarked, calling out the words as Brad waved and let himself out of the bakery.

For a moment, the two women sat in silence at the table. Finally, Candy spoke. "Looks like you're not the only one with some trauma in your past informing how you work, huh?"

Freya nodded. "I have no idea what happened to Brad to make him take the case with Mindy and the soccer team so personally, but I can imagine. Still, I'm not going to speculate."

Candy twirled her cup on the table. "How are you doing really, Freya? I know you're worried about Esther, but what else? When everything fell apart, you left before we could talk." A pause. "Do you hear from your parents?"

"They reach out. Well, they send letters, but I'm not reading them, and I'm certainly not interested in being in contact with them." Freya chuckled, the sound painful. "What would I say? 'Thanks for trying to kill me, Mom? Luckily you only shot me in the hip, but it hurts every time I walk?' Or how about this: 'Maybe if you two hadn't done what you did, we could all be a happy family? Why did you two have to be serial killers?' At least I ended up with Esther out of the deal."

"Most people couldn't have gone through what you did and come out on the other side."

Freya nodded. "Thanks, but I didn't have a choice. It was play the hand they dealt me and make sure they went to prison or just fall apart. You know, when they abandoned me as a teenager and left Fawn Lake, Esther took me in. I thought my life was over. Then I grew up, went through BLET, became a cop, and they came back to kill again. It was... horrible... when I realized my parents were serial killers. Worse, still, when I realized they'd been doing it in the same house I grew up in and I had no idea. Figuring out it was them and then catching them? It had to happen for me to heal."

"And you think you're fully healed?" Candy locked eyes with Freya, who gave a small shrug.

"As healed as I'm going to be. I was in therapy the entire time I was in Texas. Now that I'm back, I really just want to put everything behind me."

"I'm here for you if you need me. That's all. I'd never try to push you to talk about it before you're ready." Candy gave her a small smile. "Oh, but before I forget, you promised me you'd tell me why you have a giant spider in your office."

"Oh, Cinnamon." Freya shook her head. "It's not some big secret. I arrested this guy in Texas, and he was going away for a long time. No family, no friends. All he was worried about was that stupid spider and who would take care of it. So I took it. I didn't want to just leave it to die."

Candy stared at her. "You're too good, you know that? Seriously, Freya." She grinned, then slipped from the booth. "Now, if I don't get home with my leftover pizza soon, I think I'm going to come out of my skin. You need anything, boss?"

"Nope, nothing. I want to go home. Shower. Put on pajamas. I want to watch some really terrible TV that will make me forget about everything that just happened. And then, tomorrow, I want to come into the office. Eat a donut from here. Laugh with you about all the tourists getting lost on their way to a hike. I want it to be home, without the drama."

"Ooh, I can't promise that. But we'll get through it. I'd follow you into battle anywhere." Candy jerked her chin towards the kitchen. "Need any help with Esther?"

"I'm going to need all the help I can get, but not right now. She and I have a lot to talk about, and I can promise you, she's not going to like it." Back at home were some brochures Freya had picked up from some home health nurses. Nothing major, nothing that would completely strip Esther of her independence. Just someone to putter around while Esther puttered around, to make sure she didn't fall, to ensure Freya knew if anything bad happened.

"Alright then. My sofa calls. Heck, I might even crack open the ice cream I hid from myself in the back of my freezer. Just go all out. See you tomorrow."

Freya waved, then got up and locked the front door after Candy left. She could still hear Esther cleaning in the kitchen and decided to go help her. Esther needed help, that much was clear. But how much she needed, she wasn't sure. Tonight, though, she wasn't up to the battle of bringing up her plans for Esther's future.

Tonight, she'd spend time with the one person in town she loved more than anything, then go home to relax.

SIXTY-ONE

Chili bubbled away on the stove, the delicious smell filling Esther's kitchen. Freya sat across from Esther at the dining table, two glasses of water between them, a little container with Esther's pills off to the side. Freya was hungry and ready to serve the chili, cut pieces of cornbread, and bring molasses to the table.

But first she wanted to talk to Esther.

It had taken them an hour to clean up after closing down the bakery, but Freya had been more than happy to sweep and wipe down counters. It felt like she was a teenager again, working there after school. Esther never came down hard on her when she made a mistake at the bakery; she was just always there, a constant presence, helping to guide her.

"Thank you," Freya began, but Esther shushed her, holding up a hand to prevent her from saying anything else.

"No need to thank me, darling. You know that."

Freya nodded. Took a sip of her water. "I'm not talking about what you did today, opening up your bakery to the three of us. I'm talking about what you've done for me my entire life."

When Esther didn't respond, didn't try to stop her from

continuing, she kept speaking. "I know inviting a teenager into your home when you'd never raised any couldn't have been an easy decision."

"You were surly," Esther said with a wink, and Freya laughed. "But opening my home to you was the best thing I've ever done. Don't you think for one moment it wasn't worth it."

Freya shifted in her seat. It was almost impossible for her to not think about the letters from her parents, how they'd reached out to her, how she'd never responded. "I think what blew my mind then—and still does now, if I'm honest—is that you didn't know me. You didn't know my parents. All you knew was that there was a teenager who needed help, and you were willing to reach out to help me. Why?"

She'd never asked the question. Not in such a straightforward way at least. Sure, the two women had danced around their relationship in the past, touching on how it came to be, but never this directly.

Esther sighed, the sound soft. She smiled at Freya, the corners of her eyes crinkling. "Do you remember Mrs. Harris?"

"Mrs. Harris." Freya closed her eyes and focused on the woman's name. She was excellent with names; always had been. "I think so. She had curly white hair and lived down the street from my parents. Whatever happened to her?"

"She died," Esther said. "Years ago, but that's not the point. The point is, she was one of my regular customers. Used to come in every single morning for a cup of decaf coffee and a donut. At first we had a work relationship. I'd ask her how she was, she'd tell me some version of the truth, and we were both happy about that. Then she kept coming in, and I made an effort to get to know her. Imagine my surprise when one morning she comes in beside herself about this teenager who needed a place to stay."

Freya sat incredibly still. She'd never heard this part of the story before.

"Lois—that was Mrs. Harris's first name—had raised a pack of girls and wasn't interested in doing it again. Said she'd done her time." Esther laughed. "But she was so upset about this teenager who'd been abandoned by her family, who needed help, who needed love. And that teenager, my darling, was you."

"I remember her telling me to come talk to you," Freya said slowly. "I knew who you were because everyone knew you. My parents would bring me here from time to time when I was younger to get donuts, but you and I never talked much then. I mean not to the point where I thought you'd ask me to live with you."

"Well, it was the right thing to do," Esther said with a nod. "Lois was pleased because she knew you were taken care of. I was thrilled to have you in my house. It was so nice having another person in here; that guest room had sat empty for way too long." She pointed up at the ceiling, and Freya glanced up as if she were going to be able to see her old bedroom.

Blue walls because Freya had hated the pink ones that were originally there and Esther hadn't minded repainting them. An old iron bed they'd spray-painted white. It was the first time she'd felt like she'd had any agency over her life, and painting the bed had felt like she was finally able to come into her own.

"You didn't have to do that," she said, finally getting up to spoon the chili into bowls. After cutting two huge slabs of cornbread, she carried everything to the table. "I'm sure people thought you were nuts."

"When have I ever cared what people thought about me?" Esther asked with a grin. She moved her water out of the way as Freya put their food on the table. "Thank you, darling; I was just getting hungry."

"Well, thank you." Freya felt a lump in her throat and poured molasses on her cornbread as she tried to ignore it. "For taking me in, for raising me. For all of it."

"Freya." Esther reached out and took Freya's hand.

Freya looked down at her food, but after a moment, she forced herself to look at Esther.

"Being a part of your life has been my greatest pleasure. Having you back home in Fawn Lake? Nothing could make me happier. I know your road to get here was long and hard and not one you'd ever want to walk again. I wouldn't want you to, darling. It was hard and painful, and I wish I could have been there for you more than I was when you were in Texas. But you're home now, and even though you no longer live upstairs, you're still my girl."

Freya flushed. She squeezed Esther's fingers then nodded. Ever since she'd returned to Fawn Lake, this was what she'd wanted. Time with Esther, without any worry of what people thought about her weighing her down. She'd sleep tonight; she knew she would.

"Thank you." She took a bite of chili as she thought about what to say next. How did you thank someone for not only changing the entire trajectory of your life but later being there when you needed help picking up all the pieces? It was crazy to consider even trying to do it, and she hadn't ever been great with words. Actions were more her style, but again, what could she possibly do to show Esther how much the woman meant to her?

"Thank you for everything," she said. Her spoon clattered as she dropped it into the bowl. "For taking me in, surly as I was. For loving me even though I didn't think I was worthy of it. For being here for me now, as an adult, when I still need your love. You've done more for me than anyone else ever has, Esther."

"You're easy to love, Freya." Esther took a bite of cornbread, grinning as she did. "Don't you dare forget that, okay? I think you have in the past, but you're so, so easy to love. Everything about you, from how passionate you are about your job to how

fiercely loyal you are to your friends. You're a good woman."
She winked.

There was nothing to say to that. So Freya nodded. "Good chili," she said.

"The best," Esther agreed. "Maybe I'll close the bakery."

Freya looked up. "What?"

"And open a restaurant." Esther grinned at her over a bite of chili. "What do you think, darling?"

"I think you'd be trading one bad habit for another. And you need to stop trying to give me a heart attack—I only just got home."

Esther laughed. "You know, my mother would have loved you. She always said that when you were in trouble, all you needed to do was come home and put your feet under the dining table. That's when you knew you were going to be okay. When you were going to get the support you needed. You're home, Freya, and I'm so glad you are."

They ate in silence. She was home. Tonight she'd sleep deeper than she had in a while. Even though her involvement with the case was finished for now, the town still had to heal. There were funerals to plan, trials she'd be subpoenaed for. The town had a lot of healing to do.

Freya knew all about that.

EPILOGUE

TWO WEEKS LATER

The girls had all been buried a week ago. Then, the cemetery had been a bustle of activity, feeling more like a county fair than anything else. Since none of their plots were close together, the back-to-back funeral services had stretched from one end of the Fawn Lake Cemetery to the other. Mourners and gawkers alike had rubbed elbows, trampled grass, and tried to imagine how something so terrible could ever happen in their small town.

Again.

Now, though, the cemetery was mostly empty. In the far corner, where the oldest graves were, a groundskeeper removed dead flowers from a vase. His wheelbarrow was piled high with browning carnations and daisies. For such a big event, the city had decided to fill the vases on all the headstones with flowers, but now everything was old, and abandoned, and dying.

Freya stopped to pick up a damp teddy bear and place it back at the grave of Liz Brown. The bear was purple, its fur matted, its crooked smile more creepy than comforting at this point. The bear stared at her with blank eyes that had been scratched from being played with. She shuddered and turned, shielding her eyes with her hand as she looked across the cemetery.

Even though the graves were filled and sod had been placed over the freshly turned dirt, the grass growing on each of the new graves was a slightly lighter green than the more established grass. It was easy, from her vantage point on the hill in the middle of the cemetery, to pick out where the little girls had been laid to rest.

In time, the grass would age, the color would change. It would be more and more difficult for anyone who wasn't intimately familiar with the cemetery to guess where the new graves were.

She shivered. Wrapped her arms around herself. If someone asked her why she was there, she wasn't sure she'd be able to answer. Her visit wasn't required by the police department.

No, she was there for herself.

Along the side and back of the cemetery was a thick grove of trees. For years, the city had talked about putting in walking trails there so visitors could enjoy the cool air of the forest while still being near their deceased loved ones. After nobody stepped up to foot the bill, however, the plan had been scrapped.

The woods remained though, acres and acres of them, silent sentries standing watch over the dead.

Freya rolled her shoulders back. Since the murders had been solved, she'd picked up yoga. Just ten minutes of stretching in the morning helped her feel a little less crazy, helped her focus more at work. The instructor she followed online, a thin twenty-something with perky breasts and a plastic smile, assured her through the computer screen that, with time, all of her aches and pains would disappear.

That remained to be seen.

The clouds moved overhead, the sun finally breaking through. In just a few minutes, the air would heat up, and the day would become so hot she would be grateful for the opportunity to head back to her office. There was always work to be done, and hopefully some time for her to work on the cold case in her bottom drawer.

She turned to walk back to her Jeep, but the skin on the back of her neck prickled. Slowly, so she could look as natural as possible, she turned and looked behind her at the woods. Sunlight hadn't broken through the thick branches yet, and the dark between the trees was unnerving.

Nothing moved.

"Who's watching me?" she asked, taking her time as she looked along the tree line. "I know you're there, but I don't see you." Her voice was quiet.

Still, nothing moved. No flash of color, no sound, nothing that would clue her in to where something was standing, watching her. Or *someone*.

She shivered, the feeling of someone dripping ice water down her spine making her stomach clench. She could investigate and, for a moment, she reached for her gun, brushing the tips of her fingers against the textured grip, but then she stopped herself.

The feeling of someone watching her wasn't reason enough to run, half-cocked, into the woods. But what if it had to do with the only case she'd fail to solve when she'd lived here before?

Taking a deep breath, she forced herself to relax. What were the chances that the killer would wait until now, when she finally had a clear plate, to come back into her life?

Slim to none. They'd been inactive for so long, it didn't make sense for them to pop up now. The Fawn Lake Killer wasn't in the woods watching her. That was the fear of someone who couldn't get their stuff together. Besides, if someone wanted something to do with her, she'd find out soon enough.

Turning, she strolled back to her Jeep, making sure her steps were measured, slow, unhurried.

Freya had learned a long time ago not to go looking for trouble. It seemed like enough of it found her as it was.

A LETTER FROM EMILY

Dear reader,

Thanks so much for reading *Three Drowned Girls*! I've loved getting to spend so much time in Fawn Lake with this amazing cast of characters, and I hope you've enjoyed it just as much as I have! If you did, and would like to keep up to date with all my latest releases, just sign up at the following link. Your email address will never be shared and you can unsubscribe at any time.

www.bookouture.com/emily-shiner

I loved writing *Three Drowned Girls* and getting to meet the entire Fawn Lake team. I knew Freya would be a force to be reckoned with, and she turned out to be just as driven, passionate, and kind as I hoped she would. I can't begin to count the early hours I spent discovering the stories Fawn Lake holds, and I hope to spend many more! Learning about police procedure and forensics was fascinating, and I can honestly say I loved all of the research I did for this book.

If you loved Fawn Lake, Freya, and the rest of her friends as much as I did, I'd be very grateful if you would write a review. Not only do I enjoy hearing what my readers think about the worlds I've created, but reviews make a huge difference by helping new readers discover one of my books for the first time.

I truly love hearing from my readers and personally respond

to every message I get. Please feel free to reach out to me via my email at emily@authoremilyshiner.com, or you can get in touch through social media or my website.

Thanks,

Emily Shiner

www.authoremilyshiner.com

 facebook.com/authoremilyshiner

x.com/authoreshiner

 instagram.com/authoremilyshiner

ACKNOWLEDGMENTS

I can't think of a better team to bring Fawn Lake to life than the amazing staff at Bookouture! Many, many thanks to everyone who touched this book, especially Kelsie Marsden, who was beyond helpful in bringing Freya to life.

Thank you to my family, for the many cups of tea, warm blankets, and alone time so I could write and edit and moodily stare off into space. Thank you to Claire for reading this book as many times as I have, for thoughtful suggestions, and for humorous notes that made me laugh.

To my husband, who explained crime scenes and police procedure in minute detail over and over so I could ensure as accurate a representation as possible in the book.

And, most importantly, to my readers! For your DMs, your tags, and your wonderful comments. I can't thank you enough for allowing me to live my dream and for celebrating with me as I create another world I love so much.

PUBLISHING TEAM

Turning a manuscript into a book requires the efforts of many people. The publishing team at Bookouture would like to acknowledge everyone who contributed to this publication.

Audio
Alba Proko
Sinead O'Connor
Melissa Tran

Commercial
Lauren Morrissette
Jil Thielen
Imogen Allport

Cover design
Mary Luna

Data and analysis
Mark Alder
Mohamed Bussuri

Editorial
Kelsie Marsden
Sinead O'Connor

Made in the USA
Monee, IL
12 November 2024